THE PROMISED LAND

POETRY BY RUHAMA VELTFORT

Whispers of a Dreamer

Miles on the Bridge

Ruhama Veltfort

THE
PROMISED
LAND

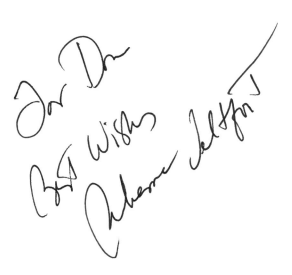

MILKWEED EDITIONS

With the exception of historical persons, the characters and events in this book are fictitious. Any similarity to real persons, living or dead, is coincidental and not intended by the author.

Published 1998 by Milkweed Editions
Printed in the United States of America
Jacket design by Adrian Morgan, Red Letter Design
Jacket painting by David Lefkowitz
Interior design by Will Powers
The text of this book is set in URW Antiqua.
98 99 00 01 02   5 4 3 2 1
First Edition

Milkweed Editions is a not-for-profit publisher. We gratefully acknowledge support from the Elmer L. and Eleanor J. Andersen Foundation; James Ford Bell Foundation; Bush Foundation; Dayton's, Mervyn's, and Target Stores by the Dayton Hudson Foundation; Doherty, Rumble and Butler Foundation; Dorsey and Whitney Foundation; General Mills Foundation; Honeywell Foundation; Jerome Foundation; McKnight Foundation; Minnesota State Arts Board through an appropriation by the Minnesota State Legislature; Creation and Presentation Programs of the National Endowment for the Arts; Norwest Foundation on behalf of Norwest Bank Minnesota, Norwest Investment Management and Trust, Lowry Hill Norwest Investment Services, Inc.; Lawrence and Elizabeth Ann O'Shaughnessy Charitable Income Trust in honor of Lawrence M. O'Shaughnessy; Oswald Family Foundation; Piper Jaffray Companies, Inc.; Ritz Foundation on behalf of Mr. and Mrs. E. J. Phelps, Jr.; John and Beverly Rollwagen Fund of the Minneapolis Foundation; St. Paul Companies, Inc.; Star Tribune Foundation; James R. Thorpe Foundation; and generous individuals.

Library of Congress Cataloging-in-Publication Data

Veltfort, Ruhama, 1944–
    The promised land / Ruhama Veltfort. — 1st ed.
      p.   cm.
    ISBN 1-57131-022-3 (acid-free paper)
    1. Overland journeys to the Pacific—Fiction.   2. Hasidim—West (U.S.)—History—Fiction.   3. Jews—West (U.S.)—History—Fiction.   4. Oregon Trail—Fiction.   I. Title.
PS3572.E42P76   1998
813´.54—dc21   98-21805
                                                                    CIP

This book is printed on acid-free paper.

For Ben and Zena

Sail forth—steer for the deep waters only,
Reckless O soul, exploring, I with thee and thou with me,
For we are bound where mariner has not yet dared to go,
And we will risk the ship, ourselves and all.

Walt Whitman, "Passage to India"

THE PROMISED LAND

POLAND, 1824

1

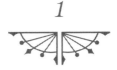

CHANA

M Y H U S B A N D , may his soul rest in peace, used to curse his enemies with the saying, "May you get everything you want." Such was to be my fate, though I was never his enemy. As a small child, I wanted nothing more than to escape from our bleak, tiny village. And escape I did, all these thousands of miles, to this strange country whose very existence was beyond anything I could even dream.

My brother became an idiot after the fever. I had a baby sister, too, who died in the same epidemic, but that was never spoken of; her little life and death were wiped away in one stroke: the tragedy of my brother. I myself was never even sick, though many in our village died, Jews and goyim, but what happened to my brother was worse than death.

God was cruel. My mother and father had prayed with all their poor hearts that their only son might live. Live he did, but he never spoke again. He remained lethargic and simple except for sudden and unpredictable outbursts of rage, when my father needed the help of one or two neighbors to tie him to a tree with wide leather straps. There he would thrash and howl until he collapsed into an exhausted sleep.

My brother was nine years old at the time of the epidemic; I was five. My mother was still young, but she had been close to death herself, and she was never again the same. I had already begun to help with the washing, the firewood, our poor meals. My mother was angry at me for having survived unscathed, and she beat me with a sharp wooden switch, cursing my slowness and my mistakes. She gave birth three more times, but two of the babies were still-born, and the last lived only a week. They were all sons, too—salt for her wounds.

When I was nine, things changed again, for the worse. My desperate father began to visit a famous holy man, a tzaddik, who lived many miles away in Przemysl. This rebbe was said to be a wondrous miracle worker, the great-grandson of a direct disciple of the Baal Shem Tov himself, and my father believed he could cure my brother.

At first my father went to Przemysl only at the High Holy Days and Passover, but he began to go more and more fre-quently, and eventually we realized he was not coming back. At the same time, my brother's rages became fewer, though they still struck erratically with the violent force of a thunderstorm.

One year in the late spring, around the time of Lag b'Omer, I heard my brother's maniacal bellow as I returned from the edge of the forest where I had gone to gather kin-dling. I heard his roars and my mother's cries, and Yaacov the woodcutter's son heard, too. Yaacov called out for his friend Shlomo, and I watched them, two big, strong young men, running to our house, coming to help. It was after-noon, and the sun was sitting on its bright spot halfway be-tween the horizon and meridian, where it would seem to hang for several hours. The days were getting long and warm, and the tall grass scratched at my bare legs as I walked slowly across the meadow with my little bundle of kindling.

I was in no hurry to see my brother struggling like a wild bull calf between Yaacov and Shlomo. My mother lay on the ground where my brother had struck her. I was afraid to go to her to help her up, but I came close enough to see my lunatic brother twist his head and sink his teeth into Shlomo's hand. Shlomo screamed, and in one long, smooth motion Yaacov bent to the ground, seized a piece of wood, and struck my brother on the head.

He fell so heavily and silently that I knew immediately that he was dead. *Blessed be the True Judge, who causes death and makes alive.*

My mother sat up and wailed. If she didn't tear her dress, it was because it was the only one she had. Yaacov began to sob; Shlomo sucked at his wounded hand and stamped the ground in pain. Other people of the village were coming near, drawn by the sounds of drama. I ran back toward the woods.

I didn't stay there long. The nights were cool and there were wolves. I only meant to give my mother a chance to calm down. One might have thought she would be happy to be relieved of such a burden. But who knows how someone will receive a gift from God? She stopped speaking to everyone but herself, and then she was not always intelligible. We often had nothing to eat; between this and my mother's beatings, I came to avoid our house as much as possible.

Sometimes I helped the village women with chores in exchange for food. Probably they would have fed me anyway, because times were not so hard just then, and most of them were kind and pious people. They were willing to believe my mother's hardships were the Lord's judgment, but I was still a child and might yet be redeemed. It satisfied them to care for me, because it proved my mother's iniquity.

I slept at home, but when the first light woke me, I ran outside as fast as I could, so as to be gone before my mother rose. She always woke groaning now and would begin reciting, as if it were a prayer, the pains and complaints of her miserable life. If I crossed her line of sight, she would run after me; if she caught me, she would pull my hair or kick at my legs.

A few people in our village kept chickens, and sometimes I would sneak an egg for my breakfast, piercing the shell with a needle and sucking the egg out raw. I knew where the cresses and lettuces grew by the river, too, and there was a sweet root I dug that was good to suck on and chew.

A light haze hung over the river early in the morning. I knelt down and splashed my face with the cold water, letting a little of it run into my mouth. I was careful not to really drink any, even though it was hard to believe what our rabbi said, that this was where the cholera came from. I wondered how I could catch a fish. I watched the berry bushes to snatch the ripe berries before the birds did. I imagined living here outside forever and beat down a clump of tall grass and rushes to make myself a little house.

People in the village fed me, but they also talked. It isn't right for a girl to beg. They said that if the wolves didn't eat me first, the nuns would kidnap me, and they made it sound as if it would be better for me if it was the wolves.

The *shochet*'s wife and the rabbi's wife put their heads together. Together, they went to my mother, who tried to drive them off with a broom. But the rabbi's wife was clever enough to give my mother a few gold coins: my pay in advance. The *shochet*'s wife was expecting a baby in a few months. Because she was already over twenty and had had no living children, only a miscarriage, the women thought that she should not do any housework or, especially, dress the chickens that the *shochet* killed. I was to live in their house and be her servant.

The *shochet*'s wife was named Rivka. She did not beat me, but I didn't like her. Their house was much bigger than my family's; it had four rooms and a wood floor instead of packed dirt, but all the rooms smelled of blood. At night, when I tried to sleep, I thought I could hear the cries of all

8

the chickens and animals that had been slaughtered in the yard.

I rose early every day to poke up the fire. They had tea in the morning, and I brought Rivka her glass while she still lay in bed. She would smile at me from her thin, sallow face and then begin to whine softly about what was to be done that day. As it turned out, the *shochet* himself had to dress the chickens if Rivka was not to do it; I was not able even to look at those corpses, much less touch them. And in fact, hungry as I was, I could not force myself to swallow even a bite of meat.

There was plenty of other work to keep me occupied— washing clothes, trying to clean the chicken smell from the wooden floors, picking wild berries for Rivka to make a kind of sour preserve. Whatever I did, Rivka's soft whine followed me everywhere, and while it was nice to be free from my mother's stick, I always longed to be free again to walk in the woods, to find where the mother rabbit had hidden her babies, to see a deer flash by through the trees, to watch the lazy, silvery fish.

In the afternoons I walked with Rivka to the cemetery, where she stood beside her parents' graves and prayed for a healthy child. My brother's grave was nearby, but I never even looked at it. I only liked to stand very still with my face to the sky, feeling the movement of the air on my skin, letting the breeze play in my hair. When Rivka was through praying, we returned home so that she could make supper.

Everything in that house was directed toward the evening meal, when Ephraim came in from the shul where he prayed every day after his work. He was a small, thin, melancholy man with enormous folds of skin under his eyes. But even during the week, not to mention Shabbos, you would think Rivka was serving supper to the Messiah himself. Whether it was a meat meal or a dairy meal, a dozen little dishes were carried to him—always served by Rivka's own hands—as if they were offerings placed on an altar. He tasted everything but never ate much. When he pushed a dish away unfinished, Rivka frowned first, then looked accusingly at me from her small black eyes. At least there was always plenty of food left over.

On a fall morning just before the New Year, the sun rose as warm and golden as if it would be summer again. Ephraim had a little sister, Malkuh, the child of his parents' old age, who was to be married that day to a man from Zamosc. Rivka had loaned me to the old parents for the whole week, to help with the preparations.

Malkuh was a beautiful girl, plump and rosy, with golden hair. There were no other children left at home, so she had always been spoiled and petted. She had never had a trouble in her life; no wonder her face was so smooth and perfect.

She cried all day the day they cut her beautiful hair off. Secretly I was happy and also ashamed for feeling so. Malkuh whined and ordered everyone around. She asked me to bring her tea with raspberry syrup, then threw it down because it was too sweet. I was angry, but I felt sorry for her, too. She looked so funny. Her mother had bought her a beautiful curled wig from Russia, but nothing would ever be as beautiful as that lost golden hair, fine as silk, which lay now in heaps on the floor. As I watched her mother and aunt gather it up to burn it, I wanted to steal a lock for myself. God only knows what I would have done with it.

On the day of the wedding, they sent me out to get fresh straw for the kitchen floor. I nearly danced across the road to the edge of the peasant fields where they did the threshing, to pick up some leftover straw. In the shivery haze I breathed deeply and swung my skinny arms. I longed to walk all the way to the river, but I was afraid I would be missed. Already they would be sweeping out the dirty straw and complaining that I was taking too long.

A little flock of geese flew high over my head. I wondered

what it would be like to fly away with them, but I couldn't imagine where else in the world to go. I knew there were other villages, even cities. There were places that people who passed through our village had come from, or were going to—Lvov and Cracow; there was Przemysl, where my father had gone away to his rebbe. People in our village talked about an emperor who had marched from France with his army to conquer Russia. But these were all just names to me, like Mount Sinai or Gan Eden.

I piled the straw in an old tablecloth I had brought, tied the corners together, and slung it over my back. It was a big pack, but the straw was light, and as I walked back I pretended I was a peddler, carrying goods to trade in another, faraway town.

I stopped outside the inn, where the musicians were practicing for the wedding. Malkuh's parents-in-law had brought the klezmer from Zamosc, and Chaim Loeb, our village fiddler, was playing with them. It was a sad, eerie song, Mother Rachel crying for her children. I wiped my eyes, full of dust from the straw.

Malkuh sobbed all the way to the *chuppah,* her old parents on either side of her, the other relatives crowded around. Her veil covered her face, but I could see her shoulders shaking. Her bridegroom came in with his parents and brothers, very solemn, with a long, thin face pale as candle wax, and great, dark eyes. I would have cried to marry him, too. But when he smashed the wine glass with his heel, I clapped and cheered *mazel tov!* with everyone else.

The long tables were heavy with the food we had been cooking all week and the dishes the guests had brought. Everyone was there, even my mother, pale and thin as a shadow. I saw her shoving a piece of pastry into her mouth, eating like an animal. I didn't approach her; I hoped she had forgotten me.

The musicians played so beautifully that even I danced like other girls. Everyone was so warm and happy from the wine and the music that they forgot to laugh at me, the meshuggenah's daughter, the orphan.

When I noticed Rivka looking at me, I knew what she was thinking. Someday I would have to be married off. The town would have to collect my dowry, and Rivka and Ephraim would have to find a bridegroom. I was as thin as a stick, and my skin was scabby and rough from when I had lived outside. What was worse, I did not know how to speak to people. Even the other girls of my age in the village terrified me. They laughed at me openly, and behind my back they called me Wolf-Girl and Savage.

Secretly I hoped that no matchmaker would ever find me a husband. The idea of marriage terrified me. I yearned to live in my reed-and-grass house by the river with the animals. They were silent and trusting, and I imagined that even the wolves were kind.

Just before Chanukah, after the snow had come, Rivka's groans woke me in the middle of the night. Ephraim, disheveled and frantic, burst into my room and told me to stay with her while he went for the midwife. Rivka lay crying and moaning, her huge belly in her white nightdress shining like a mountain in the moonlight.

I kneeled beside her bed. My hand trembled as I touched her forehead. My touch made her scream and toss her head. I jumped back.

"Rivka, it's all right," I said feebly. "It's all right, the midwife will be here soon. Do you want water?"

"God help me!" she screamed. "I can't bear it!"

The night was so cold I was shivering. I wanted to go and poke up the fire, but I was afraid to leave Rivka's side.

"Help!" she cried. "God, help! Someone, help!"

I was terrified. I had not the slightest idea of childbirth; surely the baby would burst out of that mountain any minute. But blessed be the Holy One, *Ribono shel Olom*, in only a few minutes more the midwife burst into the room. And then came Malkuh, the new bride, and Rivka's sister, and the Rabbi's wife, and I breathed easier.

"Chana!" scolded the Rabbi's wife. "Why are you sitting there like a dummy? Go make tea!"

The midwife took a piece of tailor's chalk and drew a circle around Rivka's bed to keep the witches away. She pressed her hand on Rivka's belly, murmuring while Rivka screamed.

"That's right," she soothed. "Scream, cry, get it out."

Even as I ran to the kitchen I could hear Rivka yelling. Ephraim had fled to the study house to pray. I tried to hurry with the tea, but my hands shook terribly. I was so nervous, not only from Rivka's groans and screams, but because there were so many people in the house.

"*Oy!* God in heaven, save me! I'm breaking in half!"

"Yes, dear, work a little harder. That's right, just a little harder. . . ."

It went on all night and far into the morning. When the sun was high, I went back into the kitchen to see about making some food for all the people.

"Look!" I heard Malkuh cry out. "Look! Here it comes!"

Rivka gave a tremendous, drawn-out groan and then whimpered. I heard a sweet, tiny, thin cry, and the women clapped and shouted, "*mazel tov! A boy! Mazel tov!*" Tears sprang to my eyes, and I rushed back to see.

The midwife wrapped the tiny creature tightly in a cloth until only his little red face peeked out. Rivka held him close and gave him her breast; as he began to suck, the women cheered and clapped again. *Blessed art Thou, Lord our God, King of the Universe, Who is good and does good.*

They named him Moshe-Yoel. I loved that little baby and never minded when Rivka asked me to carry or rock him for awhile. She liked to do everything for him herself, but before he was a year old, she was pregnant again. The midwife told her to wean Moshe-Yoel immediately, so I began to take care of him most of the time.

By the time Rivka's little daughter, Sorah, was born, Malkuh and her husband had moved to the house next to us and had a baby of their own, Shimon. Yossel was an important scholar; he spent all his time in the study house when he wasn't traveling to some other town to meet with famous rabbis and learned men. Malkuh kept a little dry goods store, and it was easier for her if I took care of her baby along with Rivka's two little ones.

Taking care of the children was my great joy. When the day was warm enough that Rivka and Malkuh didn't fear the babies taking a chill, I would walk up and down our little street with them, just to be outside. Moshe-Yoel ran ahead and little Sorah toddled behind on her chubby little legs, while Malkuh's Shimon struggled to keep up with her. Soon Rivka had another son, and I carried baby Zvi in a sling on my back as the peasant women did. I felt happy in a way I never had in my life when Sorah reached up to take my hand in her little fingers, or when Moshe-Yoel shouted at me to look at a bird's nest in a tree or watch a leaf race on a swirling current in the gutter.

I was still afraid that I might meet my mother in the street. Mostly she stayed in our old hut, but occasionally she came out and wandered through the village like someone's dream of a witch, her old wig tangled, her clothes in rags, her eyes wild as whirlpools, her hoarse voice raised to heaven in eternal curses and complaints.

Around the house the children and I played together. I pretended that I was a great bird, swooping down to rescue them from some unnamed danger. I would put on one of Rivka's old shawls, letting it flap over my shoulders to make wings, and fly around the room while the children shrieked and laughed in a corner. "Look out!" I made my voice deep, like a growl, "The wolf is coming behind you!" while they

14

screamed, pretending terror. Moshe-Yoel would stand and wave his arms to fight, while little Sorah tried to protect the baby. Then I'd cover them with the shawl, wrapping them in my arms as we collapsed in a heap of laughter.

When my blood started, I was scared out of my wits. I lay down, weeping in fright, while the children huddled around me. I was sure I was going to die. I wished I had learned more prayers.

When Rivka came from the market, I stammered out what was wrong. She pulled me to my feet and slapped my face. Then she laughed.

"Don't worry," she said. "A slap—that's what my mother gave me. At least now I know you're all right. I was worried for you; it should have happened two years ago. It's woman's fate, the curse of Mother Eve." She looked at me like I was a cabbage in the market. "But how will I ever find a husband for you?"

I sniffled and hugged little Sorah, who was pulling at my apron. A husband, I thought, I need like a hole in the head.

2

YITZHAK

YITZHAK BREATHED DEEP in the summer twilight; the air was so soft. He lay on his back so he could see the little leaves above him dance with the river breeze. He was a lanky, skinny boy whose red hair curled in long side-locks from under his skullcap. Once again he had gotten away early from the Talmud teacher. It was only because the old fart wanted his nap so badly, the boy thought, that he even pretended to believe my story about a stomachache.

His father, Rebbe Mendel of Przemysl, was the great-grandson of a direct disciple of the Baal Shem Tov himself. Three dozen disciples lived at his grand court, and hundreds more came to him, begging him for a remedy or a miracle. Rich and poor, they had made him wealthy with their donations.

The boy sighed with the sweet feeling of lying outside in the summer grass. He was almost truly happy now. He knew they were missing him already at home; he could imagine Mamma's frantic whine, the cluck-cluck of his two older sisters trying to soothe her, his twin sister, Feigl, offering some weird distraction. There was Bubbe, his grandmother, sitting smugly by the fire, defending him. He thought: If I murdered them all and torched the entire town, Bubbe would speak out from the world-to-come to make excuses for me, explaining to the Almighty Lord of Hosts and all the angels that I was innocent of any wrongdoing, that my parents didn't understand me. And how could they understand why he preferred the company of trees to the society of Hasidim, why he would rather press his face into the scratchy grass than into the hot bosom of his family?

He watched the sun fall behind the trees; he knew that by now his father's disciples were gathering for the prayers and singing before the evening meal. And now that he was a man, a son of the covenant, bar mitzvah, his father's only son and heir, he must be there in his silk caftan, at the rebbe's right side.

But it was exquisite to lie under this tree; it was worth the mosquitoes. From across the meadow came the sound of spectral voices, singing in harmony. They sang in a strange language, not even Polish, an alien, forbidden sound. Each note seemed to hold the light of the entire creation, *ha'Olom*. Yitzhak shuddered with delight and fear. He rolled onto his stomach, pressing himself against the warm ground, feeling himself melt into the center of the world, as the voices of those goyische angels floated around him.

He was not supposed to hear them. They were Christian monks, those angels, but he had been running away from home, from cheder, from the study house to listen to them sing for as long as he could remember. As a little boy, he had believed what his mother told him about them: They would steal him, they would cut off his circumcised *putz* and make him a Christian. But even that dread was not as strong as the enchantment of their music. Now he knew better; the monks were just men who believed in Jesus Christ instead of in the Holy One, blessed be He, men who had given up women forever to work and sing for their God who hung on their walls on a piece of wood.

The breeze from the river turned chilly as the sun lowered. Soon it would be time for Rebbe Mendel and his disciples to pray and sing. Yitzhak might not be afraid of the monks anymore, but he knew his father's cold rage. With an enormous struggle he pulled himself up, shook the mist from his head, and turned toward home.

He entered at the rear of the house, edging past the group of beggars at the kitchen door. His twin sister, Feigl, was ladling out plates of soup for them. The moment he stepped over the doorway, the screeching began, an awful mockery of the angelic choir. His mother didn't even come up to his shoulder, though he was only fifteen, but what she lacked in height she made up in voice.

"Have you no shame? Where have you been all afternoon, with your foolishness? Don't you know they are all waiting? What will they think of you?" Her slaps fell around his head.

He cowered, covering his ears with his hands. "Mamma, please!"

His sisters, embarrassed, pretended nothing was happening, but Anya and Batya, the two servant girls, couldn't help snickering.

"Leave him alone," Bubbe spoke from her seat by the fireplace. "He's young, it's a beautiful summer day. He's so thin and pale, he studies too much as it is. It's not healthy."

Another of Bubbe's lies, he thought gratefully. He hardly studied at all, to his father's shame. But if his mother held an onion in her hand, his grandmother would say it was a potato. He hunched down to give his Bubbe a kiss; he tried to make it quick, but she pinched his cheek anyway, so hard it brought tears to his eyes.

"*Oy, mushki,* so thin!" For once, Bubbe was telling the truth. "If you turned sideways, you'd disappear."

He straightened his cap and slipped through the doorway into the front room. The rebbe glowered over his beard. Standing next to him was Mordecai, his fawning secretary. Apologizing would be worse than useless. It was time to pray, and they would pray whether he was there or not. He

18

sidled into place beside his father and mumbled the words of the prayer automatically.

Feigl had just become engaged, and with sick terror Yitzhak suspected that his father had already chosen a wife for him, Roitzl, the daughter of Reb Moshe. Yitzhak had grown up with the girl, and he would rather have had cholera than Roitzl for a wife. May the Lord forgive me, he thought, but I would even rather be like those goyische monks and live without any wife. Roitzl was only thirteen years old, but already she outweighed him by thirty pounds.

Roitzl always had something in her mouth, a sweet bun or a knish. Others considered her beautiful, but Yitzhak was disgusted by her plump shape. She was a butterball, a fried dumpling, and the thought of being married to her was a bad dream of smothering under rolls of oily flesh.

The Hasidim began to sing; Reb Moshe grinned wildly from the opposite side of the table, spittle shining on his long, thin beard. The men swayed as the singing grew louder and faster. Yitzhak winced as his father's elbow gouged into his ribs; he sang louder, more passionately. On his right swayed a fat man he didn't recognize—from Turkey, by the look of his dress. Squashed between the Turk and his father, who was also very stout, Yitzhak felt icy sweat on his forehead, a dead taste in his mouth. Only the close pressure of bodies on either side of him kept him upright. It was said that in Rebbe Mendel's court the atmosphere was so holy that every day was like a Shabbos. With all his heart he prayed that his bowels would hold their contents tight. Desperately, he tried to remember the smell of those twilight trees.

Yitzhak's prayer was answered. The song passed, the moment passed, but thanks be to the Holy One, the Highest of the High, nothing inappropriate passed from his body. His father made the blessing for wine; the Hasidim shouted and raised their glasses: "*L'Chaim! L'Chaim!* To life!" Reb Moshe nearly spilled his glass as he lifted it across the table toward Yitzhak. The gold candlesticks gleamed on the white satin cloth. Yitzhak's father glowed.

Yitzhak's mother and sisters and the servant girls brought dishes of food. The rebbe took a healthy portion from each one and then waved the dish away to the others, who pushed and shoved to grab the pieces he had touched, his *shrayim*, leftovers. The din and confusion and smell of food were overpowering; Yitzhak's stomach churned again.

He could not eat. The secretary, Mordecai, looked at him down the side of his nose and raised his eyebrows.

The rebbe looked at his son. Rebbe Mendel's more ignorant disciples believed he could see for hundreds of miles, even into the future. Yitzhak's grandfather, may he rest in peace, was known to have had such a look. Yitzhak didn't believe this of his father, but this look still made him cringe. Rebbe Mendel looked at him as if he could not bear what he saw.

"Quiet!" Mordecai struck the table with his hand. "Quiet! The rebbe has an important announcement!"

Some forty faces framed with beards and sidecurls looked at Rebbe Mendel from around the table. Yitzhak began to shake.

"Yitzhak, stand!" his father commanded.

Yitzhak's teeth chattered as he got to his feet, leaning forward against the table to support himself.

"Yitzhak, my son and heir, is to be a bridegroom! Reb Moshe, stand!" Rebbe Mendel raised his glass. *"L'Chaim!"*

Reb Moshe burst into tears of joy. Yitzhak closed his eyes. The room spun around him; he could no longer hear his father's voice. He heard the angel choir of the afternoon; he heard a whirlpool in his head as if everyone in the world was talking at once, and then he fainted.

Feigl sat beside his bed holding out a glass of tea. Feigl, little bird. She was thin as Yitzhak, tiny and dark. She spoke in a kind of song, the way they had once talked together in their own secret language.

"Roitzl, Roitzl, what a poitzl! What a fat-zl, fat-zl Roitzl!" Yitzhak smiled weakly at her.

"Poor Yitzy," she crooned. "Poor, poor Yitzy. What will you do? You'll be crushed! The morning after the wedding, when they bring out the sheets, there you'll be, just a little puddle!"

"Feigl, stop!" The tea was sweet and heavy with raspberry syrup, Bubbe's favorite remedy.

Feigl danced around the room. She was marrying someone she liked, at least. Asher was a twenty-five-year-old widower with two little boys. A kind man, just a "little one" of Rebbe Mendel's Hasidim, who came only on Shabbos and holidays. In spite of being the rebbe's daughter, Feigl hadn't been easy to match. She was a little strange, and her parents were relieved to have found her a decent husband at all.

She stopped her dance in the middle of a step and looked at her brother. "Yitzy-pitzy, you had your dream-aleem-aleem again last night, didn't you?"

Yitzhak didn't remember telling her about his awful dream, though he remembered well enough when it had begun, back when he first realized how his father hated him. He had been about six, and he had asked a stupid question: Why did they only pray at special times, instead of all the time, with every breath? Rebbe Mendel had slapped him, hard.

"The King of Kings, the Holy One, blessed be He, gave us the Law," he had said. "We pray at those times it is given us to pray. Heretics like the Cracower, Shmuel Salomon, pray whenever they like. Perhaps you are his son and not mine." His voice had been bitter as acid. That had been the first time he had heard the name of his father's enemy, too.

It didn't bother him so much that Feigl knew when he dreamed; she often knew his thoughts. But he resented her assuming that it was her dream as much as his. He didn't answer her right away.

Feigl sat on the bed and poked him, nearly spilling the tea. "Come on, Yitzy. You had it last night. I can still see its shadow on your ceiling." She pointed up.

"Silly Feigele," he said. "Dreams don't have shadows. It's my dream, anyway. It comes from my own mind."

Her eyes widened. "Then where does it go? How does it know to come back? We had the same mind before we were born, don't you remember? You're the silly one, Yitzy-glitzy-kabitzy."

He sighed. He didn't know why she wanted to share his hellish dream, but he would talk about anything now, to keep from thinking about Roitzl.

"All right," he began, "so it's nighttime. It looks sort of like our town, like Przemysl, only it's different. I come out of our house to see why it's so different. There's a wind, and the wind blows harder and harder, it makes a sound, like people crying . . . like many people crying. I'm frightened, but I can't go back inside. Then there is a roaring monster in the sky, and our house catches fire. The whole town is on fire, and we all run out. Our family, the Hasidim in the court, the servants, then the others in the town, the *Misnaged* rabbi, the dairywoman, the tailor, all their families—we run, but the bad people catch us and push us inside a box, like a wagon."

"The goyim, too?" Feigl asked, even though she knew the answer.

"No. Just us, just the Jews."

His mother burst into the room, and Feigl, delinquent in some task, flew out.

Mamma bustled to the bed with a damp white napkin for Yitzhak's forehead. Her elegant new wig was crooked, a sure sign of distress.

"Yitzhak, what is it, baby mine? If only you'd eat, you wouldn't faint. So much excitement, a bridegroom, is that it? Or did you catch a chill somewhere?" She shrieked back at the doorway: "Anya! Bring food!"

"Please, Mamma," he nearly gagged. "Please. I can't eat. Please." He was afraid he would start to cry. Worse, if he saw the food, smelled it, he'd throw up.

"What's wrong with you? Think of the poor children who go to bed hungry at night. Look what you're doing to me. You'll make me sick, too."

Anya approached with a huge tray. His stomach tightened; the dead taste was in his mouth again.

"Mamma!" he gasped. "Just a little soup, all right? Please? Some of your wonderful soup?"

"Anya!" Mamma scolded. "Idiot! What are you doing with all that? Don't you hear him? Soup he wants! Never mind, I'll do it myself." She shook her head and addressed the ceiling as she followed on Anya's heels.

Yitzhak lay back, gathering strength for the soup. Maybe he really did have some disease. He couldn't tell whether this sick feeling came from his heart or his body.

He hardly knew which was worse, the dank, stuffy study house where the old Talmud teacher whined and berated him, or home, where his mother and sisters smothered him with endless plates of food. A bowl of potatoes in melted butter, a dish he used to like, made him imagine Roitzl's greasy, swollen body. The more they brought, the less he could eat; these refusals sent his mother into a frenzy of shouting at the ceiling, which his older sisters dutifully mimicked. Who ever heard of a boy who wouldn't eat? Bubbe made Mamma cry harder, with a nasty remark about her cooking.

Roitzl's mother heard that Yitzhak was sick, and had the chutzpah to demand that he be seen by a doctor. Yitzhak's mother muttered that if Yitzhak had two heads and a donkey's ears, the family would still be lucky to marry their daughter to the son of the great Rebbe Mendel. She would show those parvenus; she sent for a real doctor, all the way from Cracow in a fine carriage.

But the doctor found nothing wrong. The boy, perhaps,

had a sensitive temperament, not unexpected for the son of such a holy man. He prescribed a tea of chamomile and peppermint; Yitzhak's mother paid the bill with pride and relief. She turned her attention to truly important matters: Feigl's wedding, only two weeks away. Rebbe Mendel, who did not trouble himself with worldly concerns, gave thanks to the Holy One, the Healer of All, and directed Yitzhak back to his studies.

"*Pan* Yitzhak!" The teacher sarcastically addressed him with the title of a Polish gentleman. "*Pan* Yitzhak, will you honor us with your attention, please, and explain this passage regarding fences?"

In the thick air of the study house, Yitzhak heard the wheezy cough of the old tailor in the corner, swaying over his book.

"The, the, the one who builds a fence . . . he has the, the . . . if he has not, uh, uh, not, . . ." Yitzhak stared dully at the page before him.

The Talmud teacher brought his pointer down, *crack!* on the table, not an inch from Yitzhak's fingers.

"I'm sorry," Yitzhak stammered. "I'm sorry, Reb, my head . . ."

"I'll give you something for your head!" the teacher shouted, raising the pointer again.

Yitzhak ducked.

"Out! Out! Out!" The teacher's eyes glittered red. "May the Holy One, blessed be He, have pity on your poor father! The Lord alone knows what your parents have done to deserve such a son!"

Leaving his coat behind on the bench, Yitzhak fled out into the street and the crisp fall air, throwing back his head to the sky, running out beyond the town, out into the fields. He threw himself on the ground, sobbing out his rage and shame that he was no true son to his father.

He turned his face, wet with tears, to the sky and listened

for the song of the monastery choir, but he heard only the autumn-tall grass rustling in the river breeze. There was a voice in there, a whispering voice. He strained to hear past the pounding of his heart.

At first it was just a hiss, a swishing. And then he sat straight up. *"Shmuel Salomon,"* said the grass. *"Shmuel Salomon. Shmuel Salomon. ShmuelSalomon . . . Shmuelsalomon-shmuelsalomonshmuelsalomon."*

The voices of the monks came dimly over the rustling grass. Yitzhak felt as if a great hand rested gently on his forehead, steadying him. Peace enveloped him, and certainty. His father's enemy. He was going to Shmuel Salomon of Cracow, and he would never return to Przemysl. If he did what he had been always expected to do—succeed his father, marry Roitzl—he would die. Clouds passed in the sky above him. He watched them, aware of the endless blueness they moved in. He could not stop to think now; what he thought was unthinkable, impossible, preposterous. But it was sure.

The eve of Feigl's wedding, Yitzhak dreamed more vividly than ever. The screams and flames spread beyond the town to all of Poland, to the entire world; unable to scream, he woke, soaked in sweat.

Feigl sat in her nightdress by his bed.

"It's horrible, Yitzy!" she whispered, but her eyes shone.

"Can you see it, too?" he whispered back.

She nodded. Yitzhak took her hand.

"That was the worst one ever," he said softly. "Bad luck for the wedding."

Feigl shrugged. "For *your* wedding, maybe. If that's a dream, what is this?"

"Feigl, make sense!"

"Are you going to marry Roitzl?"

"Only when the Messiah comes."

"I know. I already knew."

"You scare me, Feigl."

"Why? Because I see what you're afraid to know? We had the same mind before we were born, the same mind that knows the what-is-to-be."

He sulked. "I bet you'll look funny without your hair," he said meanly.

"All right, then. Keep your silly dream-oleem-oleem. Tomorrow I'm the *kalla*, the bride, the queen." She sang:

> *Yitzy-bitzy, went to pray,*
> *Yitzy-witzy, far away,*
> *All one night and all one day.*

Yitzhak thought of the message in the grass. *Shmuel Salomon.*

"Listen, Yitzy. Tomorrow I am marrying Asher. We won't be in the same dream anymore. Take this."

In the knotted handkerchief she handed him were a string of pearls and a pair of gold earrings.

"Tomorrow," she whispered. "It's the best time for you. So much excitement—a feast, musicians, comedians. Everyone is dancing, and you dance away, far away, all one night and all one day. Keep those, you can sell them."

She was like the dragonflies in the field, never lighting on anything for more than a moment. He would miss her, his crazy witchy sister. A curtain was parting, tearing in half, opening on to . . . to what? Yitzhak didn't know.

After she left, he stared at the ceiling, trying to see the shadow of his dream there, until he heard the sounds of the household waking to prepare for the wedding, even before first light. *Sh'ma Yisroel, Adonoi Elohaynu, Adonoi Echod,* he prayed in a whisper.

3

YITZHAK

NEVER HAD HE SEEN such large buildings so close together, so many wagons, nor such wide, cobblestoned streets. It worried him; only goyim could live in such a place. He wandered all day, staring at everything: crowds of people, swift carriages, the huge cathedral, the iron gates of the university. Little by little he began to notice Jews, and followed one until he was safely in the Jewish Quarter. The first person he asked directions from sneered at the mention of Shmuel Salomon's name, but an old peddler with a kind face and pale eyes pointed out the way.

Tired and dirty, Yitzhak entered the shabby court. In the dark front room, his eyes gradually made out the figures of Hasidim sitting on benches or on rugs on the floor. Shmuel Salomon, the Tzaddik of Cracow, sat behind a little table. He was small—Feigl's size, Yitzhak thought madly—yet a magnetic nimbus hung about him like an extra cloak. He looked up.

"Don't stand in the door!" he shouted roughly. "Come in or stay out!"

Yitzhak was dizzy with panic and hunger. The rebbe's rough voice reminded him of his father. Road dust or awe scratched his throat until he coughed violently.

"Excuse me, Rebbe," he whispered, when he could speak.

The rebbe made a little wave of forgiveness. Watching that subtle movement, Yitzhak breathed deeply and staggered forward. He was home, he had found his place.

"I have come . . ." he stammered.

"So I see." Shmuel Salomon's eyes were black pools; Yitzhak felt himself fall in.

"I mean, I would like to study with you."

"*Nu,* who is this 'I' who wants to study?"

Dully, Yitzhak considered what the rebbe meant. If he gave his real name and town, he might be sent away; the rebbe might demand that he obtain his father's permission. He did a foolish, terrible thing then; he lied, inventing a small town near Warsaw and a wife just lost in childbirth, the baby, too. Now he had no responsibilities in the world.

Shmuel Salomon looked at him gravely. Yitzhak blushed.

"We don't do much studying here," the rebbe said. "If you want scholarship, you should go to Vilna, to. . . ." He named a *Misnaged* rabbi famous for his diatribes against Hasidim.

Loud laughter filled the room, and Yitzhak realized that everyone was listening.

Tears of humiliation came to his eyes. "Please," he implored, falling forward onto his knees.

The room was silent but for someone muttering in the back. Yitzhak heard a sound like insects humming in the field. He had never felt such fear—or such love. The little rebbe stood and pulled Yitzhak up in front of him. The strength in his tiny arm was astonishing.

"A Jew should stand on his feet," he said. "But if you would like me to help you, hold on to me."

Yitzhak looked into his eyes, saw a flicker in the pool like a fish jumping. The rebbe was laughing very softly. Yitzhak bent to kiss his hand.

Yitzhak was so disoriented that he hardly realized it was the afternoon before Shabbos. He felt wrapped in fog, unobservant of his surroundings, too shy to speak to anyone. On the way to the evening prayers, a thin, pink-cheeked young man introduced himself as Eisik and seemed to take an interest in him.

"You will see," he said. "Shabbos with our rebbe is like no other."

Unsure of what response to make, Yitzhak only looked at the man questioningly.

"People call our rebbe a heretic," Eisik explained, "but he is a very devout man. He has even traveled to Jerusalem, to the holiest place of all, where Solomon built the temple. And he has studied there, with Jews of the East."

Yitzhak wanted to ask more, but they were already in the hall, pushing together and straining to see the rebbe seated in an armchair at the front of the room.

His companion put a finger to his lips. "Sometimes he talks first, sometimes later, after the songs—"

The hum of voices in the room hushed immediately when the rebbe stood. The melody he began was not familiar to Yitzhak; he strained to make out the words: *L'shem yichud kudsha brichu, Ush'chintay....* The Hasidim crowded shoulder to shoulder, singing and swaying back and forth. Yitzhak started at the sound that now began to fill the hall, a sound he could not at first identify. He felt confused, not sure he could trust his ears. But no! The melodious chanting had indeed been joined by the music of a long horn, made of wood ... on the Sabbath! Yet the sublime sound reached into Yitzhak's heart and vibrated there with the song. *L'shem yichud kudsha brichu....* His eyes closed as he began to sway, to move his lips.

But Eisik nudged him again and nodded toward the musician. He leaned over to speak into Yitzhak's ear. "In Jerusalem, too, our rebbe has had a vision, as if he remembered himself the music that was played when we still worshipped in the temple, in ancient times."

Yitzhak heard with only a part of his mind. The rebbe and the Hasidim were singing louder, faster. The song of the

29

horn curled in the air. He felt himself swept up, and gave himself over.

He slept on the floor in a room with two other young Hasids. They seemed not to like him; they spoke to him only to whine that he was in their way, that he had hung his shirt on the wrong nail. Yitzhak moved his pallet to the back corner. That first glance of Shmuel Salomon's held his heart in an iron vise, but in his miserable, agitated mind, he wanted to disappear.

It was the week before the New Year, and from all over Poland Hasidim were already crowding into the rebbe's court. Though the rooms were packed to the rafters, Yitzhak noticed that not so many came here as to his father every year, and these men were not so well dressed. Yitzhak knew how to lose himself in the throng, to hide like an anonymous, invisible bug. Scurrying to prayers on the evening before the holiday, he miraculously found himself crushed into a place in the circle near the rebbe, instead of at the back of the room with the other nobodies. Thrilled at his luck, he wondered if this was a sign from God.

Yitzhak swayed and chanted: *"Ain Kelohaynu, ain Kadonaynu. . . ."* Pressed shoulder to shoulder against the other men, hip to hip as more crowded into the circle, he breathed their sweat, their breath, their gas. The chant rose: *"Ain K'Malkaynu, ain K'Moshi'aynu. . . ."* Yitzhak closed his eyes, faint with odor and devotion. He felt the circle turn like a great wheel, whirling upward into space as though his feet no longer rested on the ground. He didn't know any longer if his eyes were open or closed. Golden light, the color of sunset, permeated the space around him.

In a moment Yitzhak felt his eyes were open; chanting, swaying, he blinked to be sure. When he closed them again, the rose-gold light remained behind his eyelids, filling his head, filling the room. He had never seen anything so beautiful. He trembled all over, held within his skin only by the pressure of bodies on either side. The chant rose to a cry: *"L'shem yichud kudsha brichu, Ush'chintay! Sh'ma Yisroel, Adonoi Elohaynu, Adonoi Echod!"* Yitzhak dropped deep into the silence that followed, for just an instant, before the circle exploded into a shouting, moving crowd pressing into the other room, where the New Year meal waited on the table. It was nearly midnight.

Yitzhak stayed behind with the light, his beloved light, as the men rushed past him. When he finally shook himself back to earth and followed, the rebbe was seated at the head of the table. His disciples elbowed each other for a chance at the scraps of food the rebbe passed out from his plate, specially blessed. Yitzhak sat shyly and ate slowly.

At the end of the High Holy Days, the visitors returned home and the rebbe's court settled into a lonely, austere stillness. Yitzhak felt he must be the loneliest of all. At his father's court, people had been jealous of him, the rebbe's heir, but at least they had paid him attention. He didn't understand why everyone here was so cold; perhaps it was just that no one had any reason to flatter him. There was such a presence of power around Shmuel Salomon that each Hasid seemed to be trying to grasp it for himself, like the scraps from the rebbe's plate. As if there was not enough to go around, as if it was not the same infinite, abundant life that had set the universe whirling!

At night, as Yitzhak waited for sleep, he lay fearful of a knock on the door, his father's messenger come to fetch him. Slowly he realized that he had been given up, and then he raged to think of that pompous fool, Mordecai, standing in his place. His father was happy that he was gone! He consoled himself, imagining his mother and grandmother grieving. He imagined the goyische monks, still singing sweetly across the fields of Przemysl. Eating kreplach one evening, he had a sudden memory of Roitzl, and with unreasonable jealousy wondered who she would marry instead of him.

Only the prayers made up for his anguish and isolation. Shmuel Salomon liked to say that prayer made life itself worthwhile, and Yitzhak had never before prayed so intensely. The faces that in daily life seemed dull or contemptuous were suffused with a warm brilliance during the rebbe's prayers; they became the faces of the brothers and comrades he had never before known. One Shabbos Eve in that spinning circle, Yitzhak felt himself flying above a vast golden desert under a deep, turquoise sky splattered with stars. He carried this image in his heart, like Ezekiel's wheels, spending each day longing for evening, to meet his beloved vision again.

Here, certainly, were observed the regular times for prayers, as they had been commanded and followed from generation to generation. But it was true, what his father had told him long ago, that the Cracower Rebbe led prayers whenever he liked; he had abolished the service. At any time of day, even the middle of the night, Shmuel Salomon might run through the court singing at the top of his lungs, rousing the Hasidim from their chores, their books, their beds.

"*Sh'ma Yisroel! Sh'ma Yisroel!*" he shouted. "Wake up and listen, Jews! The Messiah will come when he comes, he is not watching the sun or the moon! Are you ready? Will you be asleep? Will you be stuck like a stone with your nose in a book?"

And like shamed children, the Hasidim clustered together to pray. Yitzhak copied their manner of wearing tefillin and tallis, phylacteries and prayer shawls, day and night, yes, even sleeping in them—the rankest heresy to his father! Shmuel Salomon's Hasids were ready at any moment to pray; in those predawn routs, the rebbe's enthusiasm whipped the cobwebs of worldly thoughts from their heads as they chanted: "*El Shaddai! El Chai v'Kayam!* O Almighty, Ever-Living God!"

In Przemysl, Rebbe Mendel's Hasidim had done no work

but study, waited on by servants, but here, everyone had to do some chore. Yitzhak's was to clean the crude board floors of the compound with broom and water every day.

One morning, as he was sweeping the front room, one of the Hasidim, Yoel, huge as a bear, stuck his legs out from the bench where he sat reading, propping his heavy boots directly in Yitzhak's path.

"Hey, excuse me, move your legs," Yitzhak complained.

"Go around," Yoel growled. "I'm stretching."

Yitzhak was indignant. For all his failings, he was still the son of the great Rebbe Mendel of Przemysl! This man looked like a peasant with his huge hairiness, his great boots.

He stared at Yoel's legs. They were like tree trunks.

Yoel laughed. "Serve the Lord with joy," he sneered, drawing in his feet.

Yitzhak, seething, pushed his broom.

That night, he dreamed his red, horrifying dream. In the fires, the screaming, and the confusion, a demon with Yoel's face shoveled live children into a huge fire. There were explosions, more fire; the heavy, sick stench of . . . what? Yitzhak woke in a cold sweat.

He had thought his nightmare wouldn't dare to come into the holiness of Shmuel Salomon's atmosphere. He lay awake in despair; thoughts of the tedium and discontents of his days here pecked at him like long-beaked birds. He tried repeating prayers, but they didn't ease him. What was he doing here? The memory of lying in the summer field tore at him with excruciating clarity. He felt as unworthy and miserable here as he ever had at home.

Yoel had a small clique of followers, all as large and coarse as he was. They came into prayers and meals together, forcing the others to make way. They were solicitous of the rebbe, staying close to him like a bodyguard. While Eisik was the rebbe's official secretary, it was Yoel who was always physically nearest to him. No one prayed more loudly or sang more fervently than Yoel.

Some things here were the same as at his father's court. Yitzhak saw the way that Eisik and Yoel eyed each other, the attentiveness of their respective cliques. He had seen the same thing at his father's, the jockeying for favor, the rise and fall of dukes and ministers. Yitzhak had been wise as any young crown prince to the ways of court life, but now he wished he was as innocent as a dairyman's son of the intrigue around him. At least here he did not have to be a part of it.

One afternoon, Eisik beckoned to him, smiling.

"He wants you to come to him, to his study," he whispered.

Yitzhak didn't have to ask who "he" was. He shuddered, wondering if he had been found lacking in some way. His stomach seethed with the worry that he might be summarily dismissed. He was assailed by the same mixture of fear and love that had overpowered him at his first sight of the rebbe. Eisik urged him along; Yitzhak hurried.

The small, spotless room held only a few narrow shelves of books, a table, and two chairs. Eisik showed Yitzhak in and closed the door. Yitzhak clutched his hands together to keep them from shaking; his stomach gurgled wildly. Shmuel Salomon was seated in his armchair, holding a glass of tea. He gave Yitzhak a piercing look and gestured to the other chair. Yitzhak inclined his head and sat down gingerly.

The rebbe was such a tiny man, with yellowish skin and sparse white hair. His thin beard, also white, moved up and down as he spoke in his sing-song, storytelling voice.

"There is a story the Rizhyner rebbe used to tell. A young disciple of the great Dov Baer of Metzerich was married. His father-in-law was an enemy of the Hasidim and demanded he make a choice between his rebbe and his wife. Of course, the young man promised he would never again return to Metzerich. But in time, he couldn't bear the separation from his rebbe and fellow Hasidim any longer, and went back for a visit. When he returned, his father-in-law was furious and dragged him off to the rabbi to be judged. The rabbi consulted the law books and declared that the young man's broken promise was grounds for divorce, and so his father-in-law threw him out on the street. With no one to take care of him, the young man soon fell ill and died.

"And now," said Shmuel Salomon, "what do you think? When the Messiah comes, the young man will bring his father-in-law and the rabbi to him for justice, for causing his death. The father-in-law will say, 'But I consulted the rabbi! What else could I do? I did as the rabbi said.' And the rabbi will say, 'What could I do? I consulted the Law, the *Shulchan Arukh,* and I did as the Law said.' And what does the Messiah say?"

Shmuel Salomon leaned forward. "He will say: 'Yes, the father-in-law is right to do as the rabbi said. The rabbi is right to do as the *Shulchan Arukh* said. And the Law, the *Shulchan Arukh*—of course that is right.' And what then? Then the Messiah will take the young man into his arms and embrace him and say, 'But I have come for those who are not right.'" The rebbe looked into Yitzhak's eyes.

"*Nu,* Yitzhak—son of Rebbe Mendel of Przemysl," he said quietly.

Yitzhak jumped in his seat. How had he been found out? It was agonizing to think he would be banished, sent home. He had been miserable sometimes here, true, but now, in the rebbe's presence, he didn't want to trade his misery for anything. It was his coin to pay for the nightly ecstasy of the rebbe's circle.

"What is it to me?" whispered the rebbe. "All of the holy sparks must be gathered in from where they lie hidden in the shells of darkness. All. If you are here instead of there, it is because this is where you are to be." He drained his tea.

Yitzhak waited. He was not sure he understood, but he was afraid to show his stupidity with a foolish question.

It seemed a long time, sitting in silence. His head became extremely heavy. He struggled hard; how could he be falling asleep in an audience with the rebbe? He tried to shake himself, but his body wouldn't move; he was paralyzed like a frightened animal. Yet he felt no fear now, only a deep quiet, as if he were already in a sound, dreamless sleep.

Suddenly the red light of his dream flared; its terrifying images sped before his eyes. So his eyes were closed! He blinked, unnerved. A sound from Shmuel Salomon's throat startled him.

"This dream of yours is true," the rebbe said. "If, in fact, it is a dream at all. It comes from the Other Side, the Side of Darkness. It's what brought you to me, because I have also seen such things. I think it is meant to show us the power of the Other Side, the shells of darkness and evil that hide the holy sparks. And it may triumph! And what can we do, we who are in exile? We must do everything we can to hold it back, we must do every small thing we do in the name of the unification of the Holy One and the Shekhinah. . . . *L'shem yichud kudsha brichu, Ush'chintay. . . .*" He smiled. "The Torah, the Law, is more than regulations; it is Life itself. If we have that *kavannah,* that intention, in everything, then everything we do succeeds in the eye of the Holy One."

Yitzhak saw light shimmer around Shmuel Salomon's head. He couldn't take his eyes from the rebbe's lips as he spoke.

"Everything we do," he said softly. "Drinking tea. Praying, dancing, sweeping. Even dreaming."

Yitzhak was wide awake.

Shmuel Salomon stared back at him. When he spoke again, his voice was hard. "What do you think life in this world is? A man is condemned to death, and he sits in a cart drawn by two horses who know the way to the gallows. The two horses are called Day and Night, and how they run, how they gallop! Hell exists not in the other world, but here. Only everyone is afraid to admit it."

Yitzhak felt very cold. He whispered, "Then . . . where is God's mercy?"

Shmuel Salomon began to laugh. He laughed harder and harder, coughing and howling as tears streamed down his cheeks, and Yitzhak, wondering if his rebbe was truly mad, laughed with him.

4

YITZHAK

Now THE BOOKS that had been opaque and incomprehensible to him in the study house of Przemysl began to reveal their secrets. The letters no longer frustrated and mocked him but shone like windows into another world. He heard in them the sounds from which the Holy One, blessed be He, had created the universe. The three great mother letters spread their colors before him: the golden goodness of *alef,* the dark waters of *mem,* the bright fire of *shin.*

Every night, for hours, those amazing prayers raised Yitzhak to a swelling rapture until he forgot that there could ever have been such a place as Przemysl. He forgot his father, his mother. He forgot, even, his dream. Yet sometimes when he first awakened, chilly and stiff, to the coarse morning sounds and smells of his roommates, he asked himself if it was he who was crazy, or the rest of the world. And *was* there still a world outside, or had it disappeared when he entered this one? As the days wore on, he stuffed his doubts down inside himself. He rested languidly in the rebbe's atmosphere; at times his mind was absolutely silent, clear.

On Shabbos, Shmuel Salomon's Hasids hardly slept. It would have been a sign of dullness or, worse, ingratitude to waste a moment more than necessary of that blessed share of heaven on something so humdrum as sleep. After prayers, the rebbe's Torah talks lasted far into the early hours of morning.

"Though you know in your hearts that you need God more than everything," Shmuel Salomon said, "do you not also know that God needs you? What would be the fulfillment of divine meaning, of destiny, without *you!*" He leaned forward on the last word. Yitzhak heard the "you" opening a yawning black cave in his head.

"Yes, there is 'you' and there is 'I,'" the rebbe continued. *I-I-I-I-I* undulated in waves of gold light. "And there is the 'I' that separates, and the 'I' that unites, for what did the Holy One, blessed be He, tell our father Moses but *'I AM THAT I AM.'*"

The Hasidim waited in absolute silence on Shmuel Salomon's word. The candles flickered; Yitzhak began his gentle descent to earth.

"When the Holy One, blessed be He, spoke first to our father Moses, Moses asked who He was, and how did He reply? He gave His Name to Moses, His true Name. *'I AM,'* He replied. We also say the same, but who is it who speaks when we say 'I AM'? A great secret is hidden here, and when we can answer this question truly, we can return from exile."

The smallest rustle of someone's cloak sounded to Yitzhak like a deafening roar. *Because my thoughts are silent,* he thought, and that thought itself rose like a bubble from a still pool of clarity. His body felt hollow, empty. The final word . . . *exile* . . . echoed in that emptiness as if the rebbe were speaking only to him. As if an angel had dipped a wing in his blood and written on his heart: *exile . . . return . . . I AM.*

The rebbe's voice dropped to a whisper. "You know this Name, the Name that cannot be spoken. Moses called Him by this Name, but it was taken from Israel by the priests, and *that* was the cause of exile. And also the cause of return. In exile, the Name cannot be used without being used falsely—for if 'I AM,' who are 'you'?"

Yitzhak heard each word, distinct and encapsulated; he climbed on them as if on a ladder, until at the point where he felt he would fall if he took the next step higher, something inside him turned, and he *did* fall, not *down*, but *up* into light.

All who came to Shmuel Salomon laid out their troubles and grief before the whole assembly. Nearly every day they came—the sick, the lame, the poor, the barren—a fragile, sad parade with their *kvittels*, little notes, for Eisik to bring forward to the rebbe.

Yitzhak watched a man with deep lines of pain and rage in his face drag his wagon-crushed leg behind him. Shmuel Salomon leaned over to touch him. "Don't think of anything but God," he said.

The cripple started to speak.

"*Sha!*" the rebbe said loudly, roughly. "Don't think about yourself so much! Be grateful that you have such a need, that you always need to turn to Him."

The man grunted and turned away, clumping out of the room. He was angry and disappointed, yes, but Yitzhak saw that his leg was not dragging so much as before; there was a vigor about him there had not been when he came in.

Shmuel Salomon sighed and coughed. "A man prays for his own pain to be lessened, but it may be that the Holy One, blessed be He, answers by lessening the pain of the whole world by some tiny, imperceptible amount. No prayer goes unanswered, but sometimes the answer is hidden from the eyes of the one who asks."

But sometimes the answer was not so hidden. A woman brought an infant in her arms, glowing with joy and gratitude for the miracle the rebbe had worked on her a year before, for she had been barren for twelve years.

Shmuel Salomon seemed uninterested in donations, embarrassed by gratitude. "Miracles are not so difficult," he liked to say. "But to be a real Jew, a Jew of the heart—that's more difficult." Then he laughed, a laugh that roared like the ocean.

One morning Eisik invited Yitzhak to go out into the city with him to buy candles. It was late winter, and the snow in the streets was brown and icy, worn hard by boots and carriage wheels. He trotted behind Eisik's confident stride, trying not to gawk at the city crowds.

"It was good of you to bring me," Yitzhak said shyly. His breath made a cloud before his face. "I've never seen such a place; I'd be lost. It's a miracle that I was ever able to find the rebbe."

"I'm happy to bring you," Eisik said easily. "It's not good to be alone, *nu?*" They were on the main street of the Jewish Quarter, passing a famous old synagogue.

"Sometimes you can feel alone even in the middle of people." Yitzhak nearly tripped over an emaciated beggar whose face was ragged with the marks of his gruesome disease. As the cripple tried to speak, a vile mess spewed from his mouth. Yitzhak, disgusted, was nonetheless riveted. Eisik hastily threw a few coins onto the sidewalk next to the beggar, who scrambled to gather them with a hand that looked more like a chicken's foot than a human hand. Yitzhak reached to help him, but Eisik took his arm and pulled him away.

"That poor man!" Yitzhak exclaimed.

Eisik's expression was serene, angelic. "Our rebbe could cure him," he said. "But he has to come himself, he has to ask."

A pale young man, his face chapped red by the cold, hurried by them. Yitzhak walked closer to Eisik, like a small boy. "So many people!"

Eisik had a tight smile on his face. "In the city, every day is a festival for the Other Side," he said grimly. "There are even Jews here who have lost the holy Torah. They dress and act like Gentiles, they study Gentile subjects. They are *apikorsim*, heretics." He shook his head angrily. *"Maskilim!"* He almost spat the word.

Yitzhak shivered.

A letter came, sealed officially with wax.

> *Dearest Brother*, Yitzhak read with surprise. *Blessed art Thou, Lord our God, King of the Universe, the True Judge. On the tenth day of Teveth, our father went to sleep with his ancestors. He collapsed while singing* hallel, *was carried to his bed, and died during the following night.*

The paper floated before Yitzhak's eyes; he put the letter down. He felt a physical shock, as if he had been knocked down; he was suddenly in another world. He stood up, stared into the air for a moment, involuntarily cried out. He took the cloth of his caftan between his hands and pulled until it ripped. He turned and started to walk from the room, then sat down again, picked up the letter, put it down. He had never expected to see his father again, and still, and still . . . he had never expected him to die, either. He read on:

> *I hope this letter finds you in good health. I am no longer in Przemysl, but in Ropshitz, where Asher and I are living. After you disappeared, our father declared you dead. He claimed he had a vision that you had converted; our poor mamma and sisters howled terribly, and even I, who knew better, had to shed a few tears. Our brother-in-law, Mordecai, spread wicked rumors about you, and also about my husband, accusing him of corresponding with his younger brother, who studies with* Maskilim. *He made other slanders, too, which I will not repeat. These were believed by everyone, and it was best that we leave Przemysl and try our luck here. We are as well as can be expected, praise be to God. Asher's boys are growing, and I am expecting a child in the spring, around the time of*

Shavuos. *Brother dear, are you still dreaming? I have dreams, too. I have dreamed of the place where you are, in Cracow. I hope it is God's will that we see each other again.*

Your loving sister,
Feigl

Yitzhak read the letter over and over. Even its rusty, quaint style—a scribe must have written it for her—filled him with sadness. He was unable, though he reviewed every childhood memory, to recall a single instance when his father had been anything but cutting and harsh to him, but the news of his death made him feel terribly, irrevocably cut off.

And yet the letter brought him a shameful joy. He imagined little Feigl dancing across the floor to him. He missed her madly, and missing her brought back the most tender nostalgia for his home and childhood. On one reading of the letter, he smelled his mother's kitchen, saw Bubbe sitting by the fire; the next time, he was again whispering with Feigl, listening to her sing her strange, secret language. He wondered why it had been his brother-in-law Mordecai, and not he himself, at his father's side when he died. *Yes, he hated me,* he thought, *but he was still my father.* Yitzhak felt baffled by destiny.

He would say Kaddish for his father. He would pray for those who remained: his sisters and their husbands, his mother, his grandmother, long may she live, the Hasidim of the court. They were all in the hands of the Holy One, the Creator and Preserver of the Universe, blessed be He. But now his family, his life, was here.

At Purim, a bright sun shone through the last chill of winter. The crust of old snow on the yard was beginning to melt. Inside, Shmuel Salomon's Hasidim had been drinking vodka and brandy all day, singing songs and preparing the

Purimspiel, the reenactment of Queen Esther's rescue of her people from the schemes of King Ahasueras' evil minister, Haman.

Yitzhak thought Yoel would have made the best Haman, but the Hasidim chose instead an old man who had been with the rebbe for many years. Casting him as Haman was someone's idea of a joke; every year that anyone could remember, he had played the honorable Mordecai, Queen Esther's relative and ally. The old man's quavering voice was too weak for the evil minister, and, drunk as he was, he could not remember his lines. So King Ahasueras, played by Yoel, whispered out Haman's lines, crudely mimicking the old man's stutter.

The crowd roared boisterously and, every time Haman's name was mentioned, banged on noisemakers. Yitzhak leaned against the wall, his eyes closed. Eisik, in a wig and a dress, was playing Queen Esther. He pleaded with Ahasueras for the Jewish people.

Ahasueras listened gravely. Haman stammered. The crowd erupted into noise again, augmenting the traditional raucous response to every appearance of the villain with special contempt for the aged actor.

Yitzhak could hardly stand upright. He leaned lower against the wall, wishing he could sneak off and go to bed. Ahasueras leered at Esther, throwing the audience into fresh howls. This is a stupid holiday, Yitzhak thought, but his numbed mind seemed to take hours to form this heresy. This was the day when good Jews were commanded to get so drunk that they would confuse the words to the prayer, "Blessed be Mordecai and cursed be Haman."

Finally, Mordecai and Esther succeeded, and King Ahasueras overruled wicked Haman's order to kill all the Jews in Persia. Two Hasidim not in costume, stagehands for this mummery, pushed out a crude gallows for Haman. The audience exploded in revelry as the old man was roughly pushed to the gallows. He struggled feebly and, in the drunken muddle, managed to escape his captors. Ahasueras made a wild grab for the fugitive and slipped, colliding violently into Yitzhak.

Yitzhak staggered, trying not to fall, but instead lunged toward the hot stove in the corner.

And lurched, crashed onto the fiery furnace. The sleeve of his thin caftan smoldered for a sickening second before bursting into flame. Yitzhak screamed, beating wildly at his burning arm.

Eisik, in his ridiculous wig and dress, was somehow beside Yitzhak, smothering the flames. Disoriented with shock and alcohol, Yitzhak imagined Eisik to be his mother and sobbed, clutching at the dress.

The rebbe's wife bound his blistered arm in a cloth soaked in sweet herbs. The rebbe touched him gently on his burned arm and on his forehead.

"There are no accidents in this world created and sustained by the Holy One, blessed be He," he said. "Everything that happens has to do with His will."

Yitzhak stifled a cry. His mind found no comfort in the rebbe's words, but comfort, nonetheless, was what he felt. The pain in his arm was terrible, but at the same time, like a current flowing into him through the rebbe's hand, his heart swelled in an immense wave.

"The world was created first with holy fire," the rebbe said softly. "The Fire-World, *Atziluth,* came first. This is an initiation for you, a *tikkun,* a healing for the mistakes of your life. Perhaps even a remedy for your dream."

He drew his fingertips lightly over Yitzhak's bandage, and Yitzhak felt a tingling itch that in its own way was as unbearable as the sharp searing of the burn. He began to weep again, but he was no longer crying with pain.

The Hasidim accepted as a matter of course Yitzhak's nearly instantaneous healing. If the Holy One, blessed be He, could create such a world as ours, with oceans, mountains, and animals, in only seven days, if His servant Moses could part the Red Sea by lifting his rod, why couldn't a man as holy as Shmuel Salomon, with God's help, restore a few square inches of flesh? Yitzhak could not explain, even to himself, how the rebbe had healed more than his burned arm. Even Yoel's gang treated him more agreeably, though he could not say the same for Yoel himself.

The week before *Pesach*, Yitzhak joined enthusiastically in cleaning every corner and crack of the house and courtyard, to remove every tiny crumb. The court filled quickly with visitors; they crowded around Eisik, each hoping to gain a special preference for his petition. Yoel was tense and sour.

On the night before the first seder, in the midst of the mounting excitement and joy of the holiday, the rebbe turned gray and slurred over the grace after the evening meal. The guests watched in horror as he passed his thin hand over his forehead and excused himself. Eisik helped him to his bed while Yoel finished the prayer.

The rebbe stayed in bed the whole next day. The court buzzed like a beehive hit with a stick. How was it possible for such a tzaddik to become ill? Yoel insisted that the rebbe was ailing only because he chose to be so, in order to deceive the demons, or to perform some important task in the invisible world. Eisik contended that years of healing others had taken their toll on the saint.

"Everything in creation is preserved," argued Eisik. "What do you think happens to the evil that the rebbe removes from others?"

"He destroys it!" shouted Yoel.

"No, no, brother," Eisik said sweetly. "Some of it is sent back to the Other Side, that is true, but each time some film remains. Our rebbe would rather feel pain himself than allow others to suffer; he has absorbed it, taken it in, and now it devours him."

Yoel appealed to the others at the table. "Listen to the

heretic! Listen to him dare to say that our rebbe is not all-powerful against evil!"

"You are the heretic!" Eisik responded sharply. "Only the Holy One, blessed be He, the Lord of Creation, has such power!"

The rebbe came to the first seder leaning on a heavy stick, nearly as pale as his white silk caftan. Only when he began to speak did he seem himself again. His voice showed no trace of weakness, and Yitzhak thought the rebbe's face was not pale with illness after all, but transparent, like a lantern-glass, to better allow the shining of his great light.

Reverently, Yitzhak sipped the wine, took the ritual mouthful of matzoh with grated horseradish. His eyes stung. He was at the rebbe's table, not by accident this time, but as one who lived at the court and imbibed the holy presence with every breath of daily life. As Yitzhak heard the words of the Haggadah, the rebbe's voice held within it all the Passovers of years past, and Yitzhak was transported through the centuries of Diaspora, back to the golden age in Spain, even to the bitter exile in Babylon, to the days of the Temple in King Solomon's time, and farther still, back to the earliest years in that ancient great desert. That desert vision enthralled him, though he had lived his whole life in the closeness of Jewish Poland. The vast open expanse of a golden brown land under an interminable sky, envisioned now as he swayed in prayer, was familiar to him; he could taste it, like a taste of home.

"I have done nothing my whole life except learn how to die. Now my work in this world is finished," Shmuel Salomon whispered hoarsely. "Don't cry for me—at last, I will see Him face to face." When he paused for breath, the only sound in the room was of muffled sniffles and an occasional escaping sob. The rebbe coughed, wheezed, continued: "I name no successor. You are all my heirs." His weak lungs produced a frail imitation of his famous laugh before he fell into a coughing fit. His wife wept beside him and held his glass of sweetened tea.

The Hasidim were crowded in a crescent in the rebbe's small bedroom. Eisik, tears streaming down his face, brought them one by one to the deathbed to receive the rebbe's last blessing and bequest. Yitzhak felt no grief, only a quiet curiosity. As Eisik beckoned to him, indicating his turn, Shmuel Salomon began a coughing fit that went on so long that Yitzhak wondered if the rebbe would expire before he could receive his last words. But even that concern was strangely devoid of urgency, as if he didn't care whether he heard or not. He reproached himself: Monster, have you no heart at all?

Eisik beckoned him forward. The rebbe's face was twisted in a grimace. He gasped and barked in a hoarse whisper, "Who is this 'I' who wishes to study?"

The memory of those words from their first meeting pierced Yitzhak's heart like a lance. Tears flooded his eyes, but the rebbe wheezed and panted in an attempt to laugh. His eyes glittered as they looked into Yitzhak's. "The worst liar is the one who lies to himself, Reb Yitzhak."

Yitzhak recoiled as if he had been slapped. But the rebbe caught his sleeve in his clawlike hand, his eyes mischievous. "I speak harshly to prepare you, because one day your fire will take you to a harsh place. A little like Moses, you are reluctant now, but you will lead your people over a vast desert. Do I say Moses?" he coughed violently. "No, no Moses. You are just looking for sparks in a far country where there may be Jews who have been a long time lost. There are sparks to be gathered yet. Go out and meet your destiny; perhaps you are the one to come home from exile. Take up a peddler's pack; the Holy One, blessed be He, has goods for you to carry. You have left your home, and you will not find another on this earth except in your heart. Don't worry, I will go with you. Only never forget that there is only one God, and that isn't you! Good-bye, little son."

Yitzhak watched the brutal coughing, transfixed. The rebbe whispered a few words that he could not make out. With his hand still tightly hooked on Yitzhak's sleeve, he pulled his bewildered face down and kissed him on the cheek. Yitzhak bent to embrace the tiny body, withered as a dry leaf, then ran from the room, sobbing.

In the grief and confusion that followed, Yitzhak tried to ignore the bitter schism between Eisik and Yoel, for despite the rebbe's express refusal to name a successor, someone had to lead the Hasidim who remained. Now that Shmuel Salomon was gone, there was as much malice here as Yitzhak had ever seen in Przemysl. How could a man of so much love and unity have left a legacy of such discord? Yitzhak withdrew, afraid that if he showed his friendship with Eisik, he would be mistaken for a partisan.

Yoel's open contempt for him was easier to bear than the look of betrayal in Eisik's eyes. Dreaming, he saw Eisik and Yoel locked in combat, their followers fighting even as the others, the evil ones, pushed them into the great boxes that moved ever closer to the flames.

He woke early one morning with the rebbe's last words in his head, though he was not even sure he remembered exactly, correctly. Perhaps the old man had been raving. Yitzhak knew only that he must leave, but he was afraid of the city with its carriages and heretics. He would go to the town where Feigl and Asher lived. He would find a merchant to advance him some goods to sell and make his way through the countryside.

When he had packed his few things, he stood with his satchel in the front room for the last time. The echoes and reflections of the songs and prayers that had changed him forever hung on the walls. Yitzhak turned around and left through the same door he had entered less than a year before.

5

CHANA

IT WAS LATE AFTERNOON, and even under the trees the heat of summer lay like a heavy blanket. Far down the road I saw the peddler coming, tall and skinny in a long cloak, walking slowly beside an old horse and cart—nothing special. I wouldn't have noticed him at all, except that no one new had come down our road for months. He looked like a Hasid, with his bright orange-red sidecurls sticking out from under his hat.

I didn't think Rivka would buy anything from him, but she came running out and bought a thimble and a pack of pins. She didn't need to; she got all she wanted from Malkuh's store, but she said it was good luck to be the first in town to buy from a peddler, even a funny-looking Hasid. She was pregnant again, praise be to the Holy One, and she needed the luck.

I pumped some water for the horse and gave the peddler a glass. He was looking down at the ground so he wouldn't have to see me. I stole a look at that funny hair, but I bowed my head too when he said the blessing for water before he drank. He let little Sorah pet his horse; I also wanted to, but I was too bashful to ask. It was almost time for the men to go to afternoon prayers, so I told him where the shul was, and the study house. Someone there would take him home for dinner and give him a place to sleep.

It was nearly time to get Moshe-Yoel from cheder. Everyone in the village marveled at how clever he was; he had learned the whole alphabet in a week, before he was four years old. At home, he chattered constantly about whatever Torah story they were reading in cheder, and he could recount the adventures of Father Abraham or Moses as if they were happening before our eyes. He was almost too brilliant; when Rivka or I went out with him, we were always having to spit to keep away witches and the evil eye.

One morning a few days later, Sorah didn't run to my bed to shake me awake as she usually did. When I went to her, her curly head was burning hot and her breathing slow and heavy. I called out to Rivka.

We gave her herb teas and wiped her with cool water, and four days later came the crisis, and she recovered. By that time, nearly half the village was sick, and quite a few had died. My mother was one of them. I didn't grieve much for her; she had already died to me many years ago, but her death was still fresh on my heart when the cheder teacher carried Moshe-Yoel home in the middle of the day.

Rivka and I stayed beside him for nearly a week. His little body shivered with fever, and twice he had convulsions. He couldn't drink more than a few sips of the teas we made. Rivka cried and tore her hair. Ephraim rode off to find a doctor, but we didn't have much hope; if so many here were ill, the cholera would be raging throughout the country, and what few doctors there were would have enough to do in their own towns.

Early in the morning, I sat beside Moshe-Yoel's bed. It smelled foul, though I tried to keep it clean. I wiped his face with a cloth soaked in herb tea, but he was hardly conscious.

He didn't even seem to know me. I tried to sing him a nursery song, but my tears caught in my throat, and my voice was trembling too badly to carry the tune.

I was so absorbed that I didn't hear anyone come into the room. I jumped when I heard him clear his throat, the skinny peddler standing in the doorway. I had forgotten all about him.

"There's no one here!" I said, standing up. "Can't you see, the child is dying?" Until I spoke the words, I didn't even know it; now I had shocked myself, and I began to cry.

The peddler's face turned as red as his hair. "I'm sorry," he said. "I'm leaving; I only came to thank you for your kindness when I arrived." Hesitantly, he came into the room. "Let me see the child," he said.

"Why?" I sniffled. "Are you a doctor?"

He blushed more deeply. "No," he shook his head. "But my rebbe . . ."

I stepped away from the bed. If he wanted to pray over the child, what harm could it do?

He sat down in my chair beside Moshe-Yoel. He looked about to cry himself; his full lips trembled as he laid his hand across the child's forehead. If he was praying, it was all in his head; he simply sat there staring. His face seemed to change, as if a pane of cloudy glass had passed over it. After a few minutes he stood up, muttered a blessing, and quickly left the room.

Moshe-Yoel remained in a deep hot sleep all that day, and Ephraim returned in the evening with no doctor. Rivka and I were making dinner and looking after the other children when we heard Moshe-Yoel's cry.

He was sitting up. "Mamma, Chana!" he said. "I want something to eat!"

Rivka and I clutched each other. *Praise be to Thee, Lord our God, Master of the Universe, King of All the Worlds!* Sorah was the first to run to her brother, but soon we were all on his bed, crying with relief and joy. In the commotion, I remembered the peddler's prayer, and Ephraim rode fast to catch him in the next town so that we could express our gratitude to him, as well as to the Lord on High.

Ephraim insisted that the peddler, whose name was Yitzhak, stay as our guest until at least after the next Shabbos. Even the skeptics, like our rabbi and Malkuh's Yossel, had to admit that something miraculous had taken place. But Yitzhak remained shy and modest, as if he had done nothing at all.

I was horrified when I realized what Ephraim and Rivka were planning. It was customary in our part of the country to arrange marriages for cripples and orphans after a plague had passed; it was a mitzvah to express gratitude to God by helping the unfortunate. They meant to fulfill this by marrying me off to this red-haired peddler, and Ephraim was negotiating to buy a small shop so that Yitzhak could have a business befitting a family man.

Now Rivka was always winking and poking at me. I had never seen her so happy, even as I became more morose. I didn't want things to change. I would be lonely without Moshe-Yoel and Sorah and little Zvi to play with. I didn't want to have my own house to keep. The thought of going to the market and bargaining with the peasants terrified me. I suspected a little of how married men and women were together with each other, and I couldn't bear to think of lying down with that lanky stranger with his hair like orange wool. Suppose it grew like that all over his body? And, however it happened, eventually it would bring children, and Rivka's screams in childbirth still echoed in my ears.

But what could I do? As much as the notion of marriage repelled me, I knew it was unavoidable. Everyone married, it was the way of the world since Adam and Eve, and the commandment to be fruitful and multiply bore as heavily on me as on any other woman.

I cried as bitterly as Malkuh had when my thin dull hair was cut. My knees were so weak that I nearly collapsed between Rivka and Ephraim as we walked to the *chuppah*. I didn't feel like a queen, only the same scrawny girl I had always been, wearing a scratchy new dress that hung on me like a shroud.

The wedding was simple, nothing like Malkuh's; for music we had only Chaim Loeb and his fiddle. Many people were still in mourning for those they had lost to the cholera. Life goes on, Rivka said, people shouldn't dwell on tragedy; but she was one who had something to rejoice about.

I sipped wine at a table surrounded by the village girls and women who had always ignored or made fun of me. Their wheedling, syrupy voices now didn't fool me; to all their chatter I only smiled with my lips closed as if I were a deaf mute.

Rivka pinched my cheek and winked at them. "See, now she's a married woman," she crowed as they smirked and sighed. Beyond them I could see Yitzhak dancing in a circle with the men; he stood out for being so tall, and his side-locks bounced up and down as he danced.

That night I burned with shame and fear as Yitzhak fumbled with me. I had seen horses mate, and cattle, but I had somehow imagined that God would have invented something different for us. A wild, nervous laugh escaped me, and Yitzhak leaped back as if I had struck him.

"Are you all right? Is something wrong?" his voice wobbled.

I shook my head. I couldn't look at him, much less speak. I couldn't explain what I found so funny; I didn't know myself.

"Forgive me," I whispered, and he began to caress me again. Then I knew he was trying not to hurt me, and so I stifled my cry when I felt the pain of tearing open. I closed my eyes tight and bore it as he entered me; I knew I was changed forever now. Now Rivka would be satisfied; I was a wife.

Marriage wasn't as bad as I'd thought. Yitzhak didn't care that I was such a poor cook, and, best of all, he shared my aversion for meat, and so our meat pot and plates gathered dust in the cupboard along with the *Pesach* dishes. He was happy with the kasha and vegetables I made, with a piece of herring or whitefish for Shabbos dinner.

Prayers were more important to him than food. He frightened me a little with his passion—not for me, but for God. But then, I had never known any Hasidim; perhaps they were all like that. Ephraim began to come on Friday evenings after supper to pray with him in our little front room, and Chaim Loeb the fiddler, and then Yaacov the woodcutter, the same one who had accidentally killed my brother. Sometimes one or two other men from the village joined them—just common people, nobody important.

Yaacov had lost his wife and two of his three children to the cholera, and he believed it was God's judgment for what had happened that awful afternoon so many years before. Yitzhak invited him and his child to join us for meals as well as for prayers. It was all right with me; I felt sorry for the little boy, Levi, and I had never had harsh feelings toward Yaacov.

Although the physical side of our marriage had begun so awkwardly, gradually Yitzhak and I grew familiar with each other, and came to know the joy that the Holy One, blessed be He, intended for all his creatures. My heart began to fill with wonder that there was another human being in the world who thought and felt as I did, who also preferred the company of trees to the loud talk and laughter of village social life.

He was kind and gentle and didn't tease me when I spoke to our horse as if she was my dearest friend. I assumed he was an orphan like myself. He never talked about his life before he had come to our village except when he mentioned the Cracower Rebbe, Shmuel Salomon, his teacher. And sometimes at night he woke sweating in terror from a nightmare that he told me had been with him since childhood.

Rivka took me with her on the first market day after the wedding. In the early fall morning, I pulled a small wagon as we walked under the bright leafy canopy of trees. I was more interested in the songs of the birds than in Rivka's instructions, so when we arrived at the marketplace, I had no idea what she had been telling me.

I hung behind her as she picked through bins of white and sweet potatoes. An old woman grinned at us out of a broad, wrinkled face. Rivka spoke a few words to her in halting, stunted Polish. The woman chattered back. Rivka's face reddened as she repeated her question. They argued. The sounds of the potato woman's speech fascinated me, and I listened as I did to the sound of the birds. I had never heard anyone speak anything but Yiddish; why would I, when I was always at home?

I watched the potato woman gesture and point as I listened to the strange sounds, and somehow I understood her meaning. "Rivka," I said timidly. "I think she says you should buy now, these are the last of the season, and soon there will be no more."

Rivka glared at me. "Chana, be quiet. Pay attention to me, don't make up stories."

So I was quiet, but still I listened, first to that potato woman, and then to the other sellers.

The next week when we went, it was like magic—I could understand them almost as if they were speaking Yiddish, and I even learned to speak a few words in return. Rivka didn't believe me at first, and then she was angry, but before long she was asking me to help her.

In my own way, I came to manage my household well enough, but unfortunately for our livelihood, the store that

Ephraim had started us in was a disaster. Yitzhak went out to nearby towns to pick up pots and things for mending, so I was left to mind the store alone, and it seemed I had absolutely no head for business. When poor people came in, I felt so sorry for them that I gave them what they wanted for whatever few coins they offered. And when the better-off women came, I was too bashful to speak. Even the rabbi's wife, who was careful to divide her trade fairly among all the shops, came to me even though her husband thought Yitzhak a fool and a fraud. She made me so nervous that when she asked for matches, I knocked the whole box onto the floor, and her impatient sighs as I stooped to pick them up only made me clumsier. Malkuh offered me advice at first, but she soon gave up. "If you sold candles, the sun would never go down," she sneered.

But Yitzhak's tinkering brought in a few coins, and Ephraim treated him like a real son-in-law and continued to help us. And after a time, Chaim Loeb, who had been living in a hut with a leaking roof, came to board with us, paying a small sum. Yaacov kept our firewood piled high all winter. So life went on, and the months passed.

Soon we had worse troubles than poverty. Many people began to come to our village from the east, from Russia. They were beggars, though many said they had once been prosperous, and they told horrible tales of cossacks, and of peasant neighbors become wild and murderous, destroying their shtetls. Sometimes soldiers had ordered them to leave their homes and towns immediately; some had been driven out with fire and sword in the middle of the night. Our village was so tiny and poor that these refugees didn't stay with us long. Being so tiny and poor, we couldn't imagine such things happening to us.

We were wrong. First it was only Yitzhak's sleep that was disturbed. His nightmares came night after night; he woke and trembled in my arms like a child. And one spring night,

57

during the week of *Pesach,* I thought it was his dream that woke him until I smelled the smoke and saw the red glow.

I jumped out of bed, grabbed our featherbed, and bolted through the back door. Smoke was everywhere; the whole town seemed in flames. I heard shouting, screaming, crying; the pounding of hooves. Huge horses galloped down our street, their riders swinging clubs and raising their whips high against horses and people alike, whooping and shouting. "Death to Jews! Death to Jews!"

Yitzhak staggered like a drunk. I thrust the featherbed at him and ran to help Rivka and Ephraim. I burst through their door; Rivka was bellowing like a calf. The children were clutching at her nightdress, crying.

Ephraim and I herded everyone outside, and we ran toward the river. Yitzhak still seemed to be dreaming; I carried the featherbed myself. When we got to the rushes by the river where we could hide, Ephraim soothed Rivka, and once she had calmed down, it was easier to quiet the children, too. We huddled under the featherbed, shivering and praying through the few hours that remained before dawn, and then we went back to see what was left of our village.

I cried to see that our horse Blinky was gone, stolen. Not only did we need her to make our living, but I had loved the creature like a friend. Even so, we were lucky. Neither our house nor Ephraim and Rivka's had been burned, though they were smashed up and looted of their poor treasures, and the feathers from Rivka's featherbeds were scattered everywhere like snowflakes. Half the village had been burned. The rioters had killed two men who had come out to defend their homes; they had beaten some of the families who stayed inside. They had dragged the Holy Torah scroll from the synagogue and urinated on it and then burned the synagogue to the ground. A family had burned to death in their house; a young girl of twelve had been raped by four men. Pitiful thing, she tried to throw herself into the river afterward.

And Shimon, Malkuh and Yossel's beautiful little boy, lay pale and unconscious. Trying to run away, he had somehow become separated from his parents and was kicked in the head by a charging horse.

They had managed to get a doctor, but he had only shaken his head and told them nothing could be done. Malkuh's face was drawn and red from weeping; she refused to eat and sat constantly by his side, sobbing, stroking his thin pale face. Yossel was busy directing the group of men who were rebuilding the synagogue; he only came home at nightfall to sleep for a few hours. Rivka and I came to sit with Malkuh, though Rivka expected her baby in only a few weeks.

The child was so close to death we could almost feel the brush of the Angel's wings. Rivka put her trembling hand on his head, while I tried to warm his little feet with my hands. He was still. Rivka stared at me. Moshe-Yoel's face flashed before my eyes. I knew what she was thinking.

"Malkuh," I croaked. My voice felt trapped in my throat. "Malkuh. Maybe Yitzhak can help."

Malkuh turned to me. "Him? What can he do?" Her voice was cold, grating.

Now Rivka spoke. "Malkuh, don't you remember how he saved my Moshe-Yoel from cholera? He is a healer, her Yitzhak, he studied miracles from a great tzaddik, the Cracower Rebbe."

"Yossel doesn't believe in those tzaddiks," Malkuh said proudly. "It's superstition, for ignorant people who don't know any better. Didn't you hear what the rabbi said?"

"Ignorant, what are you talking about? He saved my son, why not yours? Just because he doesn't go around bragging and making a big fuss about what he can do, that just proves how holy he is! Look at his eyes, how sweet and saintly! He could be one of the thirty-six just men who hold the world together, a *lamed-vov*!"

I felt embarrassed. I loved him, but he was just a man.

Rivka persisted. "What can it hurt, Malkuh?" she challenged her. "Let him come and pray over the boy. Maybe he sees into the inner world, how such a thing could happen to you. Maybe he can plead with the Angel of Death. Go, Chana, bring him!"

She could never get used to the fact that I was no longer her servant. But I didn't want to go for Yitzhak until Malkuh told me to. I stayed, rubbing Shimon's feet.

"Chana!" Rivka commanded. At that moment, it seemed the child moved or sighed. It was so slight, I could not be sure.

Rivka shook Malkuh's shoulders. "See! It's a sign! You saw him!"

Malkuh shrugged hopelessly. *"Nu,* all right." She spoke so softly that she might have been talking to her own hands.

I ran as if my feet were on fire. Yitzhak was with the rest of the men, rebuilding the village, using our wagon to haul lumber with Yaacov. Since we had no horse now, Yitzhak and Yaacov pushed and pulled the wagon themselves, sweating and straining.

I stood for a minute to catch my breath. My heart was pounding from the run and from the worry. I straightened my wig. Yitzhak looked too thin for such heavy labor.

"What is it, Chana?" Yitzhak's cap was soaked with sweat, his face so wet it looked like he had been weeping.

"Malkuh wants you for Shimon," I said. "To make him well, as you did Moshe-Yoel." Looking up at Yitzhak's clear eyes, my fears vanished. I felt proud of my husband, that even the wife of the great scholar Yossel Levy, who had studied in Vilna, was asking for him.

Together we walked back to Malkuh's. I glowed until I saw little Shimon lying so pale in his mother's bed. Yitzhak went to his side, moving his lips silently, twisting a sidecurl.

With a fingertip, he touched Shimon's forehead. Suddenly I saw a vision of my brother's sickbed long ago, my mother's tears, my father's prayers, and all the consequences of his return from the edge of the world-to-come. I stood still as a tree in the doorway as Rivka and Malkuh clutched each other, as Yitzhak prayed. Deep inside me, my heart silently roared: "No, God, don't do it! Don't save him! Let him die!"

The child seemed to move; Yitzhak bowed his head and quietly left the house. Malkuh collapsed on the bed in a fresh fit of weeping, while Rivka tried vainly to reassure her of Yitzhak's healing powers. I moved my leaden limbs into the kitchen to brew tea.

Little Shimon never woke. Malkuh grieved terribly, as only one who experiences misfortune for the first time in a favored life can grieve. The men prayed stoically in the brand new synagogue; Rivka shook her head at the mysterious ways of the Master of the Universe. Who knows why one lives and another dies? And I was ashamed before all of them, afraid they might suspect the awful thought I had had in that moment, my diabolical prayer.

Something in Yitzhak's eyes seemed to die, too. He went to the edge of the forest by the river and built a little shelter out of branches, as for Sukkos. He took a jug of water with him but no food. He touched my head lightly and sadly, and told me he would return by Shabbos, that if he did not, I should come for him, and in the meantime I should pray.

Those days that he was gone I felt as if I was underwater. Ephraim came looking for him, and then Yossel, his face hard and lined. I said he had gone out on business for a few days. What he had really done was unheard of, and I did not want to expose him.

When he walked in the back door, carrying the water jug and the one blanket I had thrust on him, his face was as unlined and clear as a child's. There was a light and softness about him that made him look fresh and clean, though his clothes were dirty and disheveled. It was Friday, early afternoon, and I had closed the store to come home and prepare for Shabbos. I ran to embrace him; he kissed me gently on the cheek without saying a word. He seemed so changed that I was afraid to talk to him. I handed him clean clothes so that he could go and bathe.

I finished the cooking and ran to the baker's oven to pick up my two braided loaves. I set the table for us, and for Yaacov and his son. I felt peaceful and happy for the first time in many weeks. When we were all together, I lit the candles, feeling their warm light in my own heart as I sang the blessing.

Yitzhak turned to me as he began the Shabbos blessing, "Who can find a woman of valor; her price is above rubies," and my face was surely the color of rubies for the emotion in his voice. But I remembered now how I had betrayed him, and knives cut me apart. If only he knew! My fragile happiness at having him home was extinguished like the sun's warmth behind a dark cloud. Yitzhak ate more heartily than usual of the whitefish, kasha cakes, and carrot stew, but the food I had cooked tasted like dust to me; I could hardly eat a bite.

Chaim Loeb and Yaacov joined in the grace after meals: "When the Lord brought back the exiles that returned to Zion, we were like dreamers. . . . Yes, the Lord did do great things for us all; therefore we are glad. Bring back our captives, O Lord, and our good fortune, like dry streams that flow again. . . . Though a man may weep as he carries seeds to the planting, he will some day return with joy, bearing the sheaves of grain."

Ephraim had come in. Yitzhak beckoned him to sit with us; I got up to leave, but he reached out and touched my arm.

"Stay, Chana," he said softly.

I had never stayed before for their chanting and singing, nor heard of any woman praying with men, but he was my husband, and I sat.

We waited, but instead of beginning with the usual song, Yitzhak began to tell a story.

"Once a boy dreamed of the end of the world. Maybe this happened long ago; maybe it has yet to happen. He dreamed, night after night, that first his town, then the country, and soon the entire world was covered in flames, and that the people he knew, his beloved family and friends, were pushed into great boxes, as if they were chickens, and there burned alive.

"As the boy grew older, the cries of those poor souls seemed to grow ever louder, and he began also to see in the outer world many signs that were in his dream. He had the blessing and counsel of a wise tzaddik, but still his terror remained. Knowing that he was protected in the inner world did not lessen his fearfulness of the outer one.

"The tzaddik knew the secret of bringing together the inner and the outer worlds, and when the young man himself was burned by fire, the tzaddik healed him and showed him how this could be done. But the young man misused this power, and in an instant he felt the Divine Presence leave him. He was alone. He had committed a terrible sin, to put himself in the place of the One God. In solitude he prayed for forgiveness and guidance, but he heard nothing. Then he knew that his dream was true."

Was this the end of the story? Yitzhak looked up expectantly, but the faces around the table looked confused. It wasn't only me who did not understand this bleak, unhappy tale.

Yaacov cleared his throat. "Well," he said. "What do you suppose it means?"

Ephraim gave him a withering look. Yaacov was a good man, but no scholar.

Yitzhak just shrugged a little. "He has a long way to go, that young man," he said softly. Everyone sat in silence. Shabbos was supposed to be joyful; the stories and songs meant to raise the spirit, even in the worst times. I stared at a spot on the tablecloth. After Shabbos, I would rub it with salt.

Yitzhak raised his palm. "Let us sing now, and welcome the Shekhinah, the Shabbos bride!"

Again I got up to leave, and again he stopped me. His face was still clear and childlike.

"Pray with us, Chana," Yitzhak spoke as if he were asking me to fix him a bite to eat, not to break a commandment. "We need you to pray with us, sing with us. I don't want you to be separate."

Chaim Loeb raised his eyebrows; Ephraim turned red. Yitzhak began to sing: *"L'shem yichud kudsha brichu, Ush'chintay, L'shem yichud kudsha brichu, Ush'chintay. . . ."* The men got to their feet and I followed, nearly stumbling. We swayed and sang. It was strange to me, but I forced myself to think only of Yitzhak at my side.

There was a long pause after the first song. Yitzhak looked at Chaim Loeb.

"Bring your violin," he said softly.

"Vos, Rebbe?" Chaim Loeb whispered, thunderstruck.

Yitzhak inclined his head lightly. About him there was that same look of great peace that I had seen when he first came in from the forest that afternoon. He spoke to Chaim Loeb, but it was for all of us.

"My rebbe, the Cracower Shmuel Salomon, may his soul sleep in peace, used to speak of how the harp and timbrel were played before the Lord in the temple in those golden days of Solomon. And in his court, even on Shabbos, there was a wonderful horn that prayed with us in a voice that called up those ancient times. So, *nu*, Chaim Loeb—why not pray with your violin?"

Ephraim's face was pale and tight. He opened his mouth to speak. Yitzhak was heaping the forbidden upon the forbidden. Yet that same subtle force of Yitzhak's which had compelled me to stand beside him to pray, and the others to accept that, now stilled Ephraim's protests. While I looked down at the floor, I felt the very currents of the air in the room shifting, unveiling a deep harmony among us.

Chaim Loeb bowed slightly and retrieved his violin from

the corner of the room where he kept his things. His eyes sparkled as he lifted the instrument to his chin.

On and on the songs went. Yaacov's little son fell asleep in a corner on the floor, covering himself with his father's cloak. Yitzhak clutched my hand in his; on my left, Ephraim swayed, his hands clasped together over his heart. Chaim Loeb's melody was a living thing; it flew around the room like a bird, soaring and dipping. I forgot the dirty dishes that still littered the table. I grew warm; my head itched unbearably under my wig. At first I only prayed for it to be over, but when I closed my eyes I began to feel I was dreaming, in another world. Not quite inside it; I only looked on it as if through a window, but in my fascination I lost track of time.

Finally I noticed that we had become silent again. Here we were, standing around my own table. Yitzhak looked around at us.

"We have seen terrible things, but more terrible things are yet to come before the Messiah will come to redeem us. And before that day when he will come, we may have to go to the very ends of the earth to collect all the holy sparks from the shells of evil where they now lie buried. There are deserts and mountains that none of us has imagined. The ten tribes have been lost for centuries, but they are not gone, and perhaps someday we will meet their descendants."

His voice no longer sounded like the voice I knew, and before my eyes his presence seemed to grow larger and his body to shrink. Just in the blink of an eye, I thought his familiar face dissolved in a shining mist. But when I looked again, it was only my Yitzhak.

Ephraim came the next afternoon. The bags under his eyes had deepened; the lines in his face were crevasses. I went into the kitchen while he talked to Yitzhak, but I heard every word.

In the shul that morning, we had heard our rabbi's sermon against Hasidim, so-called tzaddiks, wonder-workers. Yossel had privately spoken to Ephraim even more directly; he blamed Yitzhak for the death of his young son. It was as if he had forgotten all about the cruel cossack's horse whose hoof had struck that fragile head.

I had not known the village gossip, but Ephraim revealed that Yossel had been saying that it was remarkable—too remarkable—that the disastrous plague a few months ago had come only the day after this Hasidic charlatan had arrived, masquerading as a simple peddler. There was talk about me, too, that I was cursed with my mother's madness, that I had turned to witchcraft, that I spoke with wolves and demons. Malkuh had remarked on the ease with which I had learned to speak Polish with the peasants—such feats were a sign of possession by dybbuks. Thus, the most ignorant people of the village were set against us as well as scholars like the rabbi and Yossel, who had always been suspicious.

I was frightened. What could we do if the entire village turned against us? Ephraim said that even he had lost position by associating with us; he could no longer protect us.

I peeked through the door. Yitzhak sat with his eyes closed, as if he were meditating or praying. I couldn't understand the small smile that played around his face as Ephraim described our impossible situation.

"They are right to want me to leave," Yitzhak spoke. "They will have what they want. I was presumptuous to meddle. I have misused the faith of simple people, and I have no right to expect their forgiveness. In any case, it is God's will; I have not yet reached my destination. You have been kind, you have given me a most precious gift, a pearl beyond price, . . ." he nodded toward the kitchen. Meaning me? I blushed. "We will go to Ropshitz," he said.

Ropshitz? What was it? I was terrified all over again.

"Ropshitz?" Ephraim was mystified too. "Why Ropshitz?"

"I have a sister there," Yitzhak said. "My twin."

So I learned that he had a sister. Lucky that Rivka had not known he was a twin; it was considered a bad omen.

"You have been a son to me," Ephraim said heavily. "Only the Lord, *Ribono shel Olom,* knows why He took the boy. I am only a simple *shochet,* not a rabbi, but I don't think you did anything wrong. I will miss you and your prayers. Let me buy the store back from you at a good price, so you at least have enough for your journey."

When Yitzhak came back to the kitchen, I was weeping. Seeing him made me worse; I put my head down on the table and sobbed. He stroked my shabby wig, but I only cried harder. Ropshitz. I had never heard of such a place. And a sister, who would certainly look down on this poor relation, this savage, this witch.

6

CHANA

Yɪᴛᴢʜᴀᴋ ᴛᴏʟᴅ ᴍᴇ that life is a play where the same
actors play all the different parts. There are really only
three players: the Creator and Master of the Universe,
Ribono shel Olom; His child, Israel, who has left His home;
and the Shekhinah, the beautiful bride whom Israel must
seek, though it is she who finds him. What we see here on
earth is only a distorted shadow of the real world, the world-
inside-the-world, where the true story is always unfolding.

This was how he tried to console me as I gathered our belongings—with a fairy tale and a riddle. We were exiled, but
how could I be angry at him when it was really my fault?
Yitzhak believed we suffered for his presumption; I knew it
was for my own. I was the one who had prayed for Shimon
to die.

Yitzhak used some of the money Ephraim paid us for the
store to buy an old black gelding. I named him Midnight,
and when I watered and fed him and brushed the burrs out
of his patchy coat, I poured my tears and troubles out
against his strong, patient neck.

When our wagon was ready and our house stood empty, I
hugged each of Rivka's children close for the last time.
Moshe-Yoel was solemn, his jaw set, as he handed Yitzhak

his most prized possession, a picture book of Torah stories. The little soldier would not look at me; I saw his lips tremble, and, despite all my resolve, I began to cry.

Sorah sobbed, too, as she clutched my skirt and thrust a bunch of wilting wildflowers at me, and then two-year-old Zvi began to wail. Rivka, too, was crying now; if anyone had come along they would have thought there had been another pogrom, to hear us. Ephraim and Yitzhak embraced, and Ephraim gave Yitzhak his pocket watch and wished us well. Rivka and I could not speak for crying as we hugged each other, and she pressed a pair of pearl earrings into my hand. As we drove away, I looked backward, like Lot's unfortunate wife, until they were tiny dots in the distance.

I had never seen anyone like the apparition that greeted us when we arrived at Yitzhak's sister's house in Ropshitz. She was tiny as a child, round and dark like a walnut. She threw her arms around Yitzhak, all the time chattering and singing to him in a strange tongue. I wondered if all the people of Ropshitz spoke a different language.

I sat in the wagon like a log. My head itched madly, I was covered with a layer of dust and grime, and every bone in my body ached from the long, rough ride. Behind me on the wagon were our few sticks of furniture, our featherbed, a small box of Yitzhak's books, and another box that held all our household goods. Midnight was too tired even to whinny; he turned his head and looked at me sadly.

"Yitzhak," I said, afraid he had forgotten me. "Yitzhak, the horse needs water."

The nut-woman noticed me then and gave a shrill cry. She ran to the wagon and I shrunk back, looking wildly at Yitzhak behind her.

"Chana, come down," he laughed. "This is Feigl, your sister-in-law."

To my relief, she spoke to me in plain Yiddish, though very fast and in an odd rhythm.

"Welcome, welcome," she cried. "Welcome, Chana, sister-in-law. Come in and have tea, good tea, and a bite to eat, to eat!" She pulled at me.

"Yonah! Natan!" she shouted at the house. "Your Uncle Yitzhak is here, and Tanta Chana!"

Two boys, about ten and twelve years old, dark and long-faced, came running out. From the house, I heard a baby wail.

Feigl smiled crookedly at me. "Those great big boys are my stepsons; their mother died when they were tiny-teeny, tiny boys. That's my little Rachel you hear now."

I followed her inside while Yitzhak and the boys unloaded the wagon and took Midnight to the stable.

Feigl set out tea and black bread and pot cheese, all the time chattering. I was too overwhelmed to speak, but she talked enough for both of us. Her husband Asher was away; he was in the fur business and traveled almost constantly. When Yitzhak and the boys came in, Yonah and Natan gave me only a shy glance before sitting down at a table near the stove over their books.

"I felt your spirit near me as I said Kaddish for our father at Shmuel Salomon's," Yitzhak told Feigl. "The rebbe is also gone now, may his soul rest in peace. But what of our mother?"

Feigl sang sadly, "Oh Yitzy, Yitzy-pitzy. I think they are gone, all gone."

"I thought that might be so," Yitzhak said softly, "but I didn't dare. . . ."

A fire—perhaps accidental, perhaps deliberately set by those who hate the Jews—had swept through the fine court of the Rebbe of Przemysl only a few weeks after his death. The Hasidim had scattered, and Feigl did not even know if their mother and sisters had survived.

"So many Hamans and only one Purim," Feigl sighed. Yitzhak stared into the middle of the room, twisting his beard.

70

That old saying had been common in my village, too. Jew-haters were everywhere. In my mind I saw again the horses riding down the narrow streets of the old village, the whips and clubs. I heard again the drunken howls, the clattering hooves, the screams of that girl, the awful silence when they stopped. Pogroms, fires, plagues—Yitzhak and I would never have a home; we would always roll from place to place like the stones the boys kicked down the road.

Asher was nearly as tall as Yitzhak, though not so thin, and his hair and beard were streaked with gray. He had the same long, narrow face that his two sons wore. As soon as they heard his cart, they ran outside to greet him, while Feigl shrieked, "Praise God, praise the holy Name, to bring my husband safely home again!"

I never got used to the way Asher smelled from the fur pelts he traded in; I could not even look at them when he and Feigl spread them on the floor. They made me think too much of the wild creatures that had once lived innocently inside their warm coats; I could almost hear their cries.

Yitzhak was more practical. He still had a little money from Ephraim left to invest, and he joined Asher in the fur business. They bought pelts and hides from middlemen, who got them from Russian trappers, and then resold them to furriers from Warsaw and Cracow.

I was not happy about this business, since it meant that Yitzhak would be traveling with Asher most of the time, and I would be left with Feigl. She also had a little business, sewing clothes and trimming hats for rich ladies. I hoped she didn't expect me to join her. Where she was handy, I was all thumbs; it took me half an hour to sew on a single button.

Ropshitz was a big, dirty town. Dogs barked constantly; they roamed the streets, and no one seemed to care enough to drive them away. My old dreams of flying away like the birds now seemed like a joke. What I had wanted was to fly across the river over the tops of the trees and go to a land of magic. I didn't want to move here, to a village worse than the one I had left.

Feigl pretended not to notice how unhappy I was when Yitzhak was gone. She tried to cheer me up with silly songs: "The men are gone, gone, gone along; now we can get our work all done!" When she saw how poor my sewing was, she set me to cutting cloth scraps into pieces that she could sew into new clothes. I knew she meant to be kind, but I was always a little afraid of her.

"Gone are the men, the men, the men, . . ." she sang. "They will come back, again, again. . . ."

She didn't only sing to the baby, as anyone would have done; she sang that way to everyone, all the time. Well, Rivka would say it served me right: who was I to call anyone else a meshuggenah?

It was just before the first snow, and the sky was heavy and gray with clouds. I was pulling up a few stony carrots from Feigl's kitchen garden when I saw a tiny speck on the road in the distance. Asher and Yitzhak had come home the day before and were at the study house, so I knew it wasn't them. Gradually I made out a wagon with three figures, and while a thought leapt to my mind, I could not believe it until they stopped in front of me: Yaacov, little Levi perched beside him, and Chaim Loeb! I could hardly believe my eyes and my joy at seeing people from the old village. And they had come to Ropshitz, they were asking for Yitzhak!

I brought Levi inside to get warm by the stove and sent the men on to the study house. Feigl spluttered around the kitchen, worrying about having enough supper to feed unexpected guests. She found not only a little more barley and a head of cabbage but a few coins she sent me with to buy a chicken.

Yitzhak led prayers that night as if we had been given an extra Shabbos in the middle of the week. It was the first time since we had left the old village that Yitzhak had sung so. And again he asked me to stay after the family songs to pray with the men.

Asher protested. "It's forbidden!"

"No, brother, it is all right. It is a vision from my rebbe, the Cracower."

Asher frowned deeply but said no more.

"Come, Feigl," Yitzhak spoke almost playfully to her. "You, too, stay and pray with us. God created one world, not two."

Feigl shook her head and clucked. "Not for me, for me," she said as she scampered into the kitchen.

I was ashamed to stay, especially since I could see how Asher disapproved. I wanted to go with Feigl, but I would obey my husband. I was a part of him, like a bag he carried. I kept my mortified face turned down as I stood next to him. I didn't know where he had got such ideas. Surely the Cracower Rebbe had not prayed with women, nor gone off by himself into the woods for days, either!

"L'shem yichud kudsha brichu, Ush'chintay, L'shem yichud kudsha brichu, Ush'chintay. . . ." Over and over they sang, we sang, swaying together, and soon I forgot my embarrassment. Chaim Loeb's tune caressed my heart and lifted it out of my body until I felt I had finally found the way to fly above the forests. Then the melody stopped, and I rested in a peace as deep as that spot in the river where I had once gazed at a fish as long as my arm. We sang again: *"El Shaddai! El Chai v'Kayam!* O Almighty, Ever-Living God!" and now I dared to look around.

Yaacov's eyes were closed, and a tear lay on his broad cheek like a transparent pearl. Chaim Loeb's small face was so transported that I would not have been surprised to see two feathery wings coming from his shoulders. Even the lines on Asher's face had softened; his worried frown was smooth. His two sons stood on either side of him. Natan, younger and more delicate, looked pale and trembly, as if he might faint. Two spots of color rose high on Yonah's cheeks.

When we stopped, finally, Asher looked at Yitzhak with brimming eyes.

"Forgive me," he said softly. "You are more of a rebbe than your father, Mendel of Przemysl, was."

Yitzhak shook his head. "I am no rebbe," he said.

"You are *our* rebbe," Yaacov said. "Why else did we follow you here? Thanks be to the Holy One, blessed be He; until I prayed with you I hadn't thought my soul could ever find peace; I had murdered, shed blood . . ."

Yitzhak interrupted him, sharply. "You are no murderer, and I am no rebbe," he said.

My face burned. I had been a small child when I witnessed the act Yaacov spoke of, yet as I remembered it now, it seemed that that death, too, like that of Malkuh's boy, lay on my shoulders. Though I had not lifted a hand, I knew now that I had desired my own brother's death. I was the one who had felt he was not worthy to live as the idiot brute he had become. Yaacov had suffered all these years for a crime he had not really committed! It was I, not he, who should have been begging forgiveness, but I was mute.

I was afraid to raise my eyes to my husband's face. Perhaps he knew everything after all, like the tzaddiks of olden times; hadn't he just told Yaacov that he was no murderer? I didn't deserve such a saintly man; now I began to imagine that some terrible fate was certain to separate us. He would die, or go mad, or I would.

But when I did look at him, he was smiling softly at me, as he always did. Did he know nothing, then, or was he so good that he was able to forgive me? Tears started in my eyes; I turned away. I could never tell him what I had done; I would carry my guilt, like a big stone tied to my heart, alone.

Yitzhak and Asher were building an addition to the little house for us, but for now there were only the two rooms. It was crowded for those first few days after the arrival of our guests, who now called themselves Yitzhak's disciples. Yaacov soon found work with a lumber merchant, and left Levi with us while he moved to a small cabin in the forest where the loggers lived. Chaim Loeb had no difficulty either; everyone loves a fine musician, and he was given a tiny room at the local tavern, to play his fiddle for the peasants who came to drink there every night.

In the deep of winter, Yitzhak and Asher could not travel; there would be no fur business until spring. We lived on what Feigl had put by over the summer and fall, and from what she earned from her sewing and millinery, and from whatever Yitzhak and Asher could earn from tinkering and odd jobs. Feigl at last joined in our Shabbos prayers. Only I could see that Yitzhak was embarrassed when the others called him Rebbe.

In the long evenings, while the snow lay heavy outside, Yitzhak decided to teach me and Feigl to read. Feigl's mind was as quick as her speech; besides, she was a rabbi's daughter and had already learned to read Yiddish. Within a month she was reading Hebrew like a yeshivah boy, but for me it was another story.

Yitzhak was patient, but my head was thick as an ox's when it came to making sense of those black marks. The letters looked to me like the crushed bodies of insects, and as I strained over the pages of the boys' primer, my forehead creased with the effort, I imagined that the little bugs came alive, to leap off the paper to sting and bite me. As much as I loved Yitzhak, I began to dread those evenings, and at last, when I broke down and cried, he took pity on me.

"All right, Chanale, all right," he patted my shoulder. "Stop, please. The Holy One, blessed be He, marks every one of those poor tears that your miserable husband is the cause of. Please stop, I won't make you try to read anymore. Sarah, Rebecca, Rachel, Leah—none of them could read, and they were our Mothers, may they be praised forever. I only wanted for you to have some of the joy of learning. If it causes you such pain, never mind, never mind."

I sniffled.

"Chana," he pleaded. "Listen. You won't have to read; I will read to you."

I stopped crying and looked at him.

Encouraged, he went on. "Feigl has a Yiddish Torah, and Prophets, too. We can start with the beginning, Genesis, and you will learn how the world was created and the story of Noah and the flood!"

I remembered Moshe-Yoel's cheder stories that he had entertained me with in those distant afternoons. My tears nearly started again to remember Rivka's children, but I controlled myself. There were children here, too; there would always be children, and if it was God's will, someday Yitzhak and I would become parents ourselves.

While the boys studied, Feigl sewed, and Asher dozed by the fire, Yitzhak and I wept with Father Adam and Mother Eve as they were driven from Gan Eden, and rejoiced at the covenant of Father Abraham. I dug out Moshe-Yoel's old picture book that he had given Yitzhak when we left the village, to look at the illustrations as Yitzhak read.

My favorite was the story of Joseph, whose brothers threw him in a pit and sold him for a slave. He was falsely imprisoned because of the lies of Potiphar's wife, but he rose in Pharaoh's favor by his wisdom and his ability to interpret dreams. When he brought his father and brothers into Egypt and saved them from the famine, he said, "Be not grieved nor angry with yourselves that you sold me, because God sent me to preserve life." And then when their father Jacob died, and Joseph's brothers were afraid that Joseph would punish them for what they had done, he forgave them, saying, "As for you, you meant evil against me, but God meant it for good."

Those good words of Joseph that I heard from my husband's lips that evening, as a hard wind blew the snow against our walls, spread a wonderful warmth and lightness within me. I felt something that had bound my heart tightly inside my chest was finally loosened. Though I had promised myself never again to disturb Yitzhak with my tears, I could not stop them from flowing now. I had never wept like this; it was a flood, not of misery, but of relief.

I made him read those words over and over. I repeated them to myself. "You meant evil, but God meant it for good." Those words were my redemption and my forgiveness as much as they had been so for Joseph's brothers. At once I understood that it was the Holy One Himself, *Ribono shel Olom,* the Master of the Universe, Who had numbered my brother's days and those of little Shimon. It was God's will, and God's will also that had brought me into Ephraim and Rivka's home, just as it was God's design that had exiled Yitzhak from his father's court and sent him to Shmuel Salomon, and then to me. Our own wishes and plans for good or ill meant so little, then! When Yaacov had struck my brother, that was in God's plan whether I wished him to live or die. And even the tragedy of Malkuh's son—how could I know, or Yitzhak even, what God intended of that poor little life? Blessed art Thou, the True Judge—I had repeated the words a hundred times, but now I understood.

That Shabbos, I heard our prayers as if for the first time. *"Ain Kelohaynu, ain Kadonaynu,"* I sang. *"Ain K'Malkaynu, ain K'Moshi'aynu."* My heart, now unbound, flew with the music; my face was wet with tears of love, not just for my husband, but for the Holy One Himself, blessed be His Name forever. After the singing, Yitzhak told us how the creation emanated from the *En-sof,* the great Limitless Light, from step to step, from light to light, alternating male and female . . . from the source, *kether,* the crown, to the father, *chochma,* wisdom, to the mother, *binah,* understanding, to their son and daughter, the manifestation of the world. It was not from Yitzhak's words that I understood, but from the colors of his voice, the light in his face; and what I

understood was not explanations, but a feeling of the whole-
ness of all things, the world itself a blessing poured forth
from a loving Creator, from one container to another,
endlessly.

When Yitzhak took me in his arms later that night, or
perhaps it was already in the early hours of the next morning, he whispered to me of the union we made between our
bodies, that same union between the Holy One and His
Shekhinah that creates and brings harmony to the world.
We were joining our souls that had been once joined before
they descended to earth, and I felt the light and heat of
Yitzhak's soul enter me with his seed, as my own lost soul
rose to join him in that other world those souls had left so
long ago, the world that was only light, a pure, iridescent,
pale blue light. And now he was not disturbed by my tears,
but traced them gently with his fingertips, whispering,
whispering to me my own name, *Chana*, meaning "gift of
God."

It was still many weeks before *Pesach*, not even Purim yet,
and it seemed it had been winter forever. We had less to eat,
and I felt caged inside. Yonah and Natan had their studies to
keep them occupied, but Yaacov's Levi was restless and unhappy. The baby, Rachel, had a temperament as placid and
sweet as her mother's was noisy and erratic, but now she
had begun to walk around and had to be watched constantly
so that she would not fall into the fire or hurt herself some
other way.

Yitzhak began to read the story of the Exodus from
Egypt. I already knew of how Moses had been called by the
Lord to free our people from Pharaoh, but as Yitzhak read, I
was puzzled.

"Why did the Lord harden Pharaoh's heart?" I asked.

Yitzhak looked up from the book. Behind him, the fire
crackled in the stove. It was late, and quiet, and we could
hear a child's snoring from the kitchen. Asher, who had

been bent over his account books, looked up at Yitzhak expectantly, and even Feigl bit off her thread, ready to listen.

Yitzhak wound his fingers in his beard. "God made Pharaoh, too," he said. "Moses acted under God's direction, but so, too, did Pharaoh."

"Does God make pogroms, then, too?" I wondered.

"Not even God himself can understand the goyim," Asher grunted.

"It's easy to see that God sent the plagues to frighten Pharaoh, to show him His power," Yitzhak said. "Yet the children of Israel also needed to see God's power, so that they might rely on Him alone to fulfill their needs, and not on Pharaoh and his idols, as they did when they were slaves. We, too, are afraid to be free from our own darkness, just as the children of Israel were afraid to leave Egypt." Yitzhak pulled at the sidecurl that hung in front of his left ear and looked up at the ceiling. "We see light and dark in the world, but to God it is all light."

Asher stroked his thin beard and blinked his heavy eyes. I stared into the fire. Yitzhak had said that the Torah was written in fire, black fire on white fire. I didn't see how it could be the same kind of fire as we had here. In the stove it was warm, gave light, cooked our food. But I thought of the burning of our village and the fire that had destroyed Yitzhak's home, and I shuddered as I watched the coals snap and the flames lick the wood.

When the thaw began, Asher and Yitzhak went to Warsaw to get their contracts for the spring. But instead of new contracts, they brought only bad news, news of war. The Poles were rising up against the Russians.

I had never even known that the Russian czar ruled Poland. Back in my village I had always thought the *pan*, the Polish squire, was the ruler, and I had never even thought whether Ropshitz was in Poland. I couldn't see the difference, Poland or Russia, but Asher said this revolt was a disaster. The Poles would blame all their problems on the Jews. The Russians would make more laws, and he and Yitzhak would not be allowed to do business. Worst of all, the boys would be taken into the Russian army and be converted. Of one thing both Asher and Yitzhak were certain: whether the insurrection failed or succeeded, it would be the Jews who would suffer most, just as we always had.

It was a Saturday afternoon. We had all returned home after the service at the synagogue and sat with long faces. Suddenly Feigl laughed.

"Your dream-o-leem is coming true, Yitzy-pitzy," she said slyly. "And your story-ory-ory, too!"

Yitzhak looked at her sadly. "So what is there to laugh about?"

"Weren't you just reading to Chana, before you went to Warsaw, about Father Moses leading the children of Israel out from Egypt? A pharaoh, a czar; a czar, a pharaoh. Will God harden the heart of Czar Nicholas now? Will another Moses come to us and lead us across a desert? Chana and I will have to bake matzoh! Look out the windows now, Chana, see if there is yet a pillar of cloud to guide us!"

"Feigl, enough!" Asher frowned.

Yaacov cleared his throat. "Two of our woodcutters went off to fight," he said. "They say the only way for us Jews to help ourselves is to help the Poles throw off Ivan's chains."

"Since when have the Poles been such friends to us?" Asher said sourly. "Goyim are goyim."

Yitzhak twisted his curls. "In any case, a Jew should preserve life, not shed blood. We are to be a light to the nations, not a sword."

Feigl sang, "We better go away, away, if we want to live another day, o-day."

I felt frozen. The feeling I had had when we first came to Ropshitz, that we would forever be migrating, like the geese, came back to me now.

Asher's face was dark and set. He looked at Yonah and

Natan, those fine, strong boys. He sighed deeply. "Where would we go? To Germany, maybe, and become heretics? Or to Eretz Yisrael, the Holy Land, to perish in the wilderness with the Turks?"

Yitzhak smiled. *"Nu,* brother, we cannot go to Eretz Yisrael. There is no Messiah yet to lead us."

Asher wandered outside to watch the darkening sky for the three stars signaling the end of the Sabbath. In a few moments the last one appeared, and he came inside, nodding to Feigl. She brought the spice box and twisted candle for the Havdalah, the ceremony of separation. The boys put their books away; Asher sighed again and began the closing prayers: "Blessed art Thou, O Lord our God, King of All the Worlds, Creator of light and fire."

7

YITZHAK

CURIOUSLY, Yitzhak felt closer now to Shmuel Salomon than when he had lived at his court in Cracow. He didn't feel that he himself led the songs and prayers, but rather, that Shmuel Salomon led and he only sang along. This was his secret: there were times when he was not really Yitzhak.

Once, in the study house in Chana's village, he had wanted to explain this to Ephraim. It embarrassed him that Ephraim treated him the way people had treated his father. It wasn't right for the older man, his benefactor, to show him such deference. He wanted Ephraim to know that it was really the Cracower Rebbe who spoke and acted from the world-to-come through his unworthy disciple. But just as he had begun to speak, the rebbe's face loomed before him, eyes on fire, put a finger to his lips, and said, "Shh!" so loudly that Yitzhak was sure that Ephraim heard.

So he had come to blend his sense of himself with that vision inside, that great voice. If only he had remembered the difference! If only he had not forgotten he was only Yitzhak!

He hoped he had learned to keep still. Now he was like a horse who feels the pressure of the reins and goes first this way, then that, unable to see the driver sitting high in the wagon behind him.

Asher did not speak much, and on their long rides from town to town all that autumn season, Yitzhak had time for reflection. The rocking movement of the cart reminded him of swaying in prayer, and of his beloved rebbe, and then the love that swelled in his heart reminded him of Chana, the second great blessing of his life.

She had been like a wild mouse in the field, so frightened. He remembered her most, not from the first time he saw her, standing by the pump like Rebecca at the well, but from when he saw her thin, sad face bent over the bed of that little sick boy, Moshe-Yoel.

He had wanted nothing more than to bring the boy back to health, to relieve the pain of that young woman whom he thought to be the boy's sister. As he had sat beside the sickbed, the fingers of his left hand had unconsciously traced the scars on his right arm, and the face—the very fragrance!—of Shmuel Salomon appeared inside him. As he breathed and touched the boy, it was the rebbe breathing and touching through him; Yitzhak was not even there.

It had been God and God alone, praise be to His Name, who healed Moshe-Yoel. But it had been Yitzhak who was rewarded with a precious prize: Chana. Chana, who had none of the fleshy coarseness he had imagined in women; Chana, who was so unconscious of her own light. When he lay with her, he felt the very union of the Holy One with His creation, the union of God with the Shekhinah, and when he entered her, he sometimes whispered his rebbe's prayer to himself: *L'shem yichud kudsha brichu, Ush'chintay. . . . For the sake of the unity of the Holy One, blessed be He, and the Shekhinah. . . .*

Yes, he thought, I believed I was very holy indeed; I had become proud, and for that the Holy One, blessed be He, humbled me. Yitzhak remembered worse—every moment of the terrible afternoon a few days later. He remembered Chana's bright, trusting face turned to him as he stepped away from the heavy wagon. Yes, he had thought, I can heal this boy, too! And, now let the doubters see what wonders one of the truly pious can accomplish.

He had found out how truly pious he was. He had been well reminded Who it is that holds the power of life and death. Nothing in his life compared with his awful agony when he had learned that the second little boy he had so confidently and proudly prayed over had died.

A voice had roared in his head then: *Go out!* He felt like Adam expelled from Gan Eden, but betrayed by no woman, enticed by no serpent but his own pride. An Adam to be exiled alone, without his beloved Eve. He had gone into the forest to atone with fasting and prayer, as the Baal Shem Tov himself was said to have done.

How he had wept as he prayed in that rude shelter, undressed except for tallis and tefillin, Chana's blanket left unused on the ground. As he chanted psalms, he had felt that *he* was the enemy that David cursed; he had become the foe of God and of Israel. The bitter accusations of the prophets pierced his heart: they were true of *him*.

Every detail of his life, his whole history of wrong turns, stubbornness, pride came before his eyes. He felt afresh his father's disappointment in him, which now seemed completely justified. Why shouldn't his father despise him? He had failed in every duty. He had betrayed not only his family but God Himself, in that long-ago grass, drifting on the music from the monastery.

Yitzhak had sobbed himself to sleep. He did not dream but woke in torment at finding himself still alive. Only pride had led him to refuse the place his father had prepared for him; only vanity had led him to abandon his friend Eisik when he needed him most.

Shmuel Salomon had anointed no successor, but in a secret corner of Yitzhak's heart, where the snake of temptation always lay coiled and ready to strike, had he not nourished the delusion that he himself was the rebbe's true heir? Was that not why he had failed Eisik? Woe on him! Who was he to think that the blessed Shmuel Salomon spoke to him now? It was a hallucination, a temptation from the Other Side. Who was he? A *garnisht*, a nothing.

He had remained in that abject state for several days and nights. He had eaten nothing; if he stopped shivering for a moment, he dashed himself with cold water from the river so that he would suffer as he had caused others to suffer.

Yet gently, slowly came a new peace, a cold, clear, empty sensation. Yes, he had been an ungrateful son, an arrogant disciple, a betrayer of those who had loved him. He was guilty, yet here he was, alive in the world. From the forest canopy he heard the bird song outside, piercing and clear. He listened closely. The Word of God did not come to him, only bird song and then silence. The silence forgave him.

Praying with his friends—whom he could not call "disciples"—that evening when they rejoined him in Ropshitz, he again felt a transcendent presence. But this inner presence no longer bore the particular features and fragrance of Shmuel Salomon; it was more ethereal, more abstract. This presence was nothing less than the pure ideal of all the great teachers that had ever been since the beginning of time. As he swayed, clutching Chana's hand—Chana's hand!—he had felt for a tiny, evanescent moment that he saw the little group through the eyes of that Spirit-rebbe. He saw new faces among them, the lined, dark faces of men he had never met. When the songs were over and he spoke with that other voice, a spectre of understanding had glowed just beyond his sight, like something glimpsed through a fog.

Yitzhak shivered now in the wagon beside Asher. They were on their way home with a puny load of furs, their trade now

slowed to a thin trickle, disrupted first by the Polish rebel-
lion and then by its failure. Lately, the spirit of Shmuel
Salomon had come quietly back to speak in Yitzhak's heart.
Don't fool yourself, don't think you can settle down, the voice
murmured. *Are you a tree, to stand in the ground? No, wan-
derer, you have not even begun.* Yitzhak heard an odd roaring
sound behind his teacher's whisper.

Asher yawned. "*Nu,* Yitzhak," he said. "I'm thinking
about what Kalman said."

A trader in Warsaw had advised them to move to Poznan,
in the Austrian empire. Asher had been restless since the
suppression of the Poles' revolt; he was worried that his
sons would be conscripted into the czar's army.

Yitzhak scratched his beard for a long time before he
spoke. "I think we are going to the ocean," he said tenta-
tively. He surprised himself; why had he said such a thing?
The rebbe is playing tricks on me, he thought. Yitzhak had
never seen a body of water larger than the Vistula.

"The ocean?" Asher was astounded. "Where is it?"

Yitzhak shrugged, embarrassed. His inner voice was
silent. "I'm not sure," he confessed. "I think in Germany."

Asher snorted. "Germany, land of the heretics! Poznan
isn't bad enough? No, not for you; you have to go all the way
to Germany! First you pray with women and violins, next
you'll put on a short coat, shave your beard. . . ."

Yitzhak looked at him sideways and quoted a proverb:
"Better a Jew without a beard than a beard without a Jew."

"Hmmph." Asher sank back into silence.

Wryly, Yitzhak thought: So, Chana has already made a
heretic of me. Until he married her, he, too, had thought the
same of women as his father and all his ancestors had.
Woman is the light of the home, but Torah, religion, is for
men. Women were strange, their voices were too high, they
moved too quickly. Only his twin Feigl was a special case, because she was like a part of himself.

Chana had changed that. Though they still obeyed the
laws of purity, even there he had doubts. What purity could

man expect of a body that was, after all, only a piece of meat? It is as polluted as the world itself, yet we are taught that it is in the world—in the body?—that God Himself is most glorified. And Yitzhak's unity with Chana felt complete, more even than the one mind he and Feigl had shared in their mother's womb. It was like heaven and earth, which have no existence without each other; like the shimmering horizon of the late summer road, when land and sky vibrate together. It was in Chana's eyes that the precious kabbalah, the hidden wisdom, was revealed to him. When they joined together, they formed the two pillars of the Tree of Life: *chochma* and *binah,* wisdom and understanding; *chesed* and *gevurah,* mercy and severity. Praying without his wife now would be like standing on one leg—possible, but not a permanent arrangement.

He was not sure whether it had been his own voice or the spirit-voice of Shmuel Salomon that had first invited Chana to pray. With his mind and memory he knew that the Shmuel Salomon he had lived with in Cracow would never have imagined, much less incited, such a thing. But this new Spirit-rebbe in his heart, who both was and was not Shmuel Salomon, *this* rebbe urged him on: *Let the song be complete!* he said. *Let the sweet voice of woman join you in harmony.* And now it seemed so natural and pure that Yitzhak could not imagine why all the Jews of history had set women apart in a stuffy balcony, or behind a curtain.

It puzzled him that Chana would not learn to read, that she was so unwilling to push open the door into that rich world that had sustained Jews through the ages of captivity and dispersion. Yitzhak did not think her dull. Her wisdom was of another kind: she spoke with the horse and understood the trees when they told that rain was coming. And how entranced she was by the tales he read! She seemed to hear the stories of Noah and Moses as if they were grandmother-stories about people in the next village.

A few evenings ago, they had finished *Chumash,* the five

books of Moses, and he had begun to read how Joshua defeated the enemies of the Lord, conquering the land that the Holy One, blessed be He, had prepared for His children. "And the Lord said unto Joshua: 'Fear not, neither be thou dismayed; take all the people of war with thee, and arise, go up to Ai. . . .'"

He had come to the end of the conquest of Ai: "And all that fell that day, both of men and women, were twelve thousand. . . . he had utterly destroyed all the inhabitants of Ai. . . . So Joshua burnt Ai, and made it a heap forever, even a desolation, unto this day."

When he looked up at Chana, she was staring ahead gravely, not smiling and nodding with pleasure as she usually did.

"Go on," she had said. "What comes next?"

He had read on. After Ai came the conquest of Gibeon, where the sun stood still; then Makkedah, Libnah, Lachish, Hebron, Debir: "And smote with the edge of the sword . . . and utterly destroyed all the souls that were therein, and left none remaining . . . and there was none left that breathed; and he burnt Hazor with fire."

Chana had put her hand out, almost touching him. Her face was tight. "Why?"

"Why? The Lord commanded! Those were idolators; they did not worship the Lord. You see, next He will tell Joshua how to divide the lands among the tribes, the land He promised to Moses. It's the reward!"

Chana did not seem to be listening. She rose to her feet. "The horse needs looking after," she muttered to the floor as she walked out.

He had watched her, astounded. What was wrong with her? It was nighttime. The horse had been fed and watered hours ago, and surely he was asleep in his stall.

The road was badly rutted from spring rains, and they had stayed too late in the last town, hoping vainly for some piece of business to bring back, something to sell at home for a better price. But there was nothing, and they did not arrive home until well after dark.

Yonah and Natan woke up, rubbing their eyes and yawning, to greet their father. The little children, Levi and Rachel, woke too, excited. The women embraced their husbands, giving thanks to the Holy One, blessed be He, to have brought them safely home. Chana saw to the horse while Feigl made buckwheat porridge and a thin soup for the exhausted travelers. But even Feigl was subdued by their poor load of furs, the shabby pile of gewgaws they hoped to sell. They were poor—poor as a sack full of holes.

That night, Yitzhak dreamed of the ocean. Never having seen it, he nonetheless knew it for what it was: vast with promise. A huge wave lapped at the burning world of his ancient nightmare; clouds of hissing steam rose into the sky. He rode in a huge boat like the ark of Noah, Chana by his side.

The dream came back to him in pieces as he moved through his morning ritual. For the first time his dream hadn't ended with the fire. Chana had been there; that was the first she had appeared in his dream. And in the fire before the water, now he recalled the figure of Chaim Loeb, wrapped in a coat of flames, his blazing arms stretched up to the sky.

Over the morning meal of black bread and tea, Yitzhak watched Feigl wipe her daughter's laughing face with a rag.

"Washy, washy, goes the water, goes the water. . . . First a little, then a lot, washy, washy water!" Feigl winked at Yitzhak. "Water more than ever you've seen . . . water, water, all over your dreams. . . ."

"Feigele, are you reading my dreams again?"

"Some will go, and some will not, washy, washy water."

Feigl scooped Rachel up in her arms and took her shawl from a hook on the wall. "Stay with your man, your man, you can," she said over her shoulder to Chana. "I'm going to see if I can scrape a bit together for supper. You stay."

Chana perched tensely on the edge of the hard chair, like a bird on a branch, and mumbled something. Yitzhak leaned forward to hear her.

Chana looked at him and repeated, "Does she know what you dream, then?"

Yitzhak stared at the wall. "I did dream of water, of the ocean, in fact."

"I don't remember what I dreamed," Chana said. "I used to dream of the pogrom, like you, for a time after it happened."

Yitzhak thought she was sulking a little. He sighed, remembering the commandment to be tender to a wife. "Chana, dear, what is the trouble?"

He had a long wait before she spoke, and then it tumbled out roughly, like water over rocks. "Feigl told me this morning that Asher wants to leave Ropshitz," she said. "To go to another country even, so the czar doesn't take Yonah and Natan and even little Levi, and make Christians of them, Russian soldiers."

Yitzhak shrugged. "Things aren't so good here for us."

Chana bit her lip. "I know, but I don't want to go somewhere else, to another strange place. I don't remember what I dreamed, but I woke frightened. I woke thinking that we would always be traveling, that we would never have a home. That we are like those Israelites you read about, only at least we don't raise our swords everywhere we go, and burn cities, and kill everybody . . ."

"Chana!" He was as amazed that she had made such a long speech as by what she was saying.

"It's true." She looked at the floor. "I don't like these new stories of yours, always more killing."

"But Chana, our Fathers were commanded by the Holy One, blessed be He, to take the lands that He had given to them!"

90

He stopped. He wanted to comfort her, to soften himself. "I can't explain the ways of God to you, or the ways of the Fathers. But as for you and me, as long as we are together, what does it matter whether we live in this town or that one? If we cannot make a living here, we will have to go where we can."

"Yes, and are there trees in that other country, so Yaacov can make his living, too? He will not want to stay here without you, and he cannot care for Levi himself. And Chaim Loeb, what about him?" Chana began to weep; he watched her helplessly, irritated in spite of his good intentions.

"There are trees, yes, and taverns, and horses and men and women . . ."

"Oh yes, there are, there are, there are!" Feigl burst into the room like a gust of wind, little Rachel on her hip. She carried a tiny package of grain and a small jug of milk.

When Feigl's mouth opened, Chana's closed. Chana clapped her hands at Rachel, who giggled and hid in her mother's whirling skirts for a moment before climbing into Chana's lap. Chana buried her face in the baby's dark curls.

Feigl sang: "Taverns and horses and men and trees, cats and birds and dogs and bees. . . ."

Rachel laughed at her mother's antic dance. Chana watched her somberly.

Chana's mood didn't improve that evening. Feigl teased her about seasoning the soup with tears—"My mother did the same, the same!" she scolded. But Chana only shrugged her thin shoulders; she was through with talking.

Yaacov stayed in the woods all week with the foresters, but Chaim Loeb came every night for dinner. He could not eat the *traife* food of the tavern. But this evening he didn't arrive.

"Where is our fiddler tonight?" Asher asked.

"Perhaps there is a celebration at the tavern, and they've asked him to play," Yitzhak said.

"True," Asher sighed. "In the study house someone said *Pan* Wrocslaw's daughter was married today; they probably will carry on all night. What a life for a Jew!"

"God made music, too," Yitzhak said. "And a man must make a living where he can." He looked at Chana to see if she got his point, but she seemed far away. She is angry, he realized with surprise. It had never occurred to him before that she could be angry.

If anything, he was even more shocked by the rush of his own anger late that night, when they were awakened by a persistent scratching at the door and found a bleeding and dazed Chaim Loeb lying at the threshold. The women rushed over, shawls thrown over their nightdresses. Yitzhak's eyes fixed on the handful of splintered wood and dangling cords that Chaim Loeb still clutched in his battered hands: the violin. His rage boiled and erupted inside him, his belly felt filled with fire, with melted rocks. Wild, he ran outside in his nightshirt. He wanted to shout, but fear strangled his voice to a low growl, like a mad dog. He jumped and stamped the ground with his bare feet until he was sore and exhausted. When he limped back into the house, he was weeping.

Feigl and Chana were still binding the fiddler's wounds; they had poked up the fire and sat him in front of it. Feigl poured some of her precious raspberry syrup into the tea, which Chana spooned slowly into Chaim Loeb's swollen mouth. Asher paced, wringing his hands.

"Did they follow? Are they still coming?" he asked Chaim Loeb anxiously, leaning into his battered face.

Chaim Loeb could hardly move his bruised lips to speak; at first he only sobbed. He shook his head. Then moaned, "No, no . . . they threw me out on the road, like garbage." He sobbed again. "They broke my violin," he cried, hysterical. "They said there were Jewish notes in the mazurka. . . ."

Asher pulled at his hair. "How many of them?" he pressed. "Are you sure they are not coming here?"

"Leave him alone," Feigl chided. "Enough, enough." She shook her head, clucking to herself. "Ah, who would do such a thing to an innocent soul? What a world it is we live in! If God Himself lived on earth, someone would break His windows."

Yitzhak lay awake for hours. The inner rebbe he was accustomed to calling on seemed to have disappeared—frightened away, no doubt, by his anger. "Help me, Rebbe," Yitzhak whispered. Chana, beside him, reached for his hand and held it tightly.

"Yitzhak," she whispered at him.

"What is it?"

"Did you ever ask your rebbe why?"

"Why? What why? The goyim are crazy, and they hate us."

"No, Yitzhak, I don't only mean the goyim."

"What, then?"

"Life. Is life so hard because we are wicked, or is it because life itself is evil?"

Yitzhak was silent. Her question suggested heresy, yet he knew she was innocent. And he had no answer for her. That was his own heresy, which he sensed as a bad odor, like rotting onions, seeping out from his heart. Not the heresy of praying with women; this was something deeper and more malicious than the breaking of an explicit commandment. His faith itself, that had been a mountain like Sinai, was cracking open like an earthen pot dropped on the floor. He held Chana's hand and prayed silently, though his words seemed lifeless as sand: *Answer me speedily, O Lord, my spirit fails; hide not Thy face from me, lest I become like them that go down into the pit. . . .*

He will not suffer your foot to slip, he heard, yet he felt he was falling. And though he knew he was not asleep, he saw before him a huge wall of water, a high wave, and terror propelled him up, up on its back, and he was carried, with Chana, with the others; they were moving swiftly, swiftly across this great expanse of water under a gray, heavy sky. And then in the far distance he saw something from the visions he had seen at Shmuel Salomon's: that land of pure gold, endless and flat, stretched under a firmament so blue and vast that it must surely be heaven. Yitzhak watched, trembled, breathed. *Exile . . .* , he heard. *Return. . . .*

"Chana," he whispered deliriously. "We will not stay in Ropshitz, nor will we stay in Poznan. We are going to cross the ocean. God is leading us, as He led Moses, to some place so far that I do not even know whether it lies in this world or the next. I hope it is God that is leading us. Don't be afraid, Chana. I can't do it without you."

As he heard his own words, he was terrified she would protest. But she lay quietly beside him. He imagined she smiled.

"Chana, He is with us, and I am with you," Yitzhak said more to himself than to her.

Her fingers squeezed his gently. "Yitzhak," she whispered back. "Why do we have no child?"

Sinking, he thought she hadn't understood. He bobbed on the wave, gulping salt. He struggled. She didn't hear what I said, perhaps I only imagined I said it. Did she only feel her own shame at her barrenness? Ah! He floated again, buoyant as a cork. Now he understood why she had been so withdrawn, so angry. He took her in his arms. "Don't worry, Chana, darling. It's the will of God," he said softly. "I won't divorce you, don't worry. I promise you. No matter how many years." He closed his eyes, listening to her gentle breathing. "Have you heard me?"

"Yes," she repeated, like a little cheder child. "You will not divorce me. And we are going across the ocean."

Yitzhak sighed and wondered if he was mad.

94

8

CHANA

Even before Yitzhak told me about the ocean, I knew leaving Ropshitz meant forsaking any hope for an ordinary life. And what difference did it make? We had as much choice as a fish has once it has taken the worm that hides the hook. I saw that Yitzhak was not like other people, that all of us were outside the ordinary, common world. I understood now that that was why we still had no child, though I didn't tell Yitzhak that. So why should we remain in a country of human beings, Jews and Gentiles, rather than go to some fantastical land on the other side of the world, a land filled with monsters that ate human flesh? Where people—if there were people at all—walked on their hands instead of their feet; whose eyes were open while they slept and shut when they were awake; who slept during the day and worked during the night.

I was not the same girl who had arrived in Ropshitz confused and frightened as a baby fox whose mother has been captured in a hunter's trap. Slowly I had come to feel at home. I missed Rivka, who had been a mother to me, and her children, who had been like my own. But Feigl was good, the kitchen here was still a kitchen, there was water to fetch and firewood to chop, there were children to be fed and bathed and dressed. In Ropshitz, I had become a grown woman: Yitzhak's wife, Feigl's sister-in-law.

When Yitzhak first began reading to me, I felt as if I had really lived in those times and seen those marvelous things with my own eyes. It was as if Mother Rachel had been my own mother, as if Moses himself had been my father. Those stories had awakened something in me—like Yitzhak, I felt the Unseen Hand that moves behind the events of this world. And for a long time I believed that it was a loving hand, the hand of a kind Father who wants only good for His children.

But I didn't like the stories about Joshua; he seemed as cruel to me as the cossacks who had burned our village and tortured that poor little girl. "And smote with the edge of the sword . . . they utterly destroyed both man and woman, both young and old, and ox, and sheep, and ass. . . ." What had those poor people done to deserve such a fate? And their animals, too? It was like one pogrom after another, and yet it was our Fathers, the Israelites, who did those horrible things. What kind of God would command such horrors? If He was Creator of the Universe, why could He not find land for His children without demanding that they kill others? Had He created those people only to be slaughtered? Even Yitzhak, the wisest and kindest man I had ever known, had not shed the smallest tear over those stories, nor answered my questions. He was astonished that I would grieve over goyim. For that was what they were, idol-worshippers, and that was why God had commanded their destruction.

It was as if I had turned over a rotting log in the woods and let the myriad ugly creatures that lived underneath crawl out into the light. Had all the evil I had seen—insanity, desertion, plagues, pogroms—been commanded by God, too? It made me sick; the world made no sense. Yitzhak with his stories had replaced the God of my childhood, Who had comforted me under the trees and looked at me from the eyes of the animals, with a tyrant Who ordered His chosen nation to murder innocent women and children. And so I sank more deeply into despair.

That dreadful night when Chaim Loeb crawled home, beaten bloody, his precious violin broken to splinters, was only further proof to me of the maliciousness of God. No matter where Yitzhak and Feigl wanted to drag me, we would never escape that malevolence, for it was the nature of the world.

Something else happened that night: I saw that Yitzhak had begun to see things the way that I did. Even as I helped Feigl comfort and nurse the hurt fiddler, I saw the explosion within Yitzhak's heart as clearly as if the house across the street had burst into flames. I saw the horror pass over his face, not only at what those brutes had done to our companion, but beyond that, at the very heartlessness and cruelty of life itself.

When he told me his crazy story of the ocean and how we were to travel across it, I only laughed to myself. I saw that it was that ocean that would finally wash his faith away, as mine had been burned away. And now, without family or God, I saw that we would always blow across the surface of the earth like dead leaves in the wind.

We tried first to go to Poznan, where Asher believed we would have the best chance of making a living. But it seemed our ragged band had none of the things we needed in that empire. We had no permits, nor papers, nor even family names, so we were turned back at the border and wandered back through that flat country like gypsies. When the money that Feigl had received for selling the last of her jewelry was all gone, we were dependent on local Jewish assistance societies and on the kindness of people who hoped to earn a place in heaven by their good deeds.

The still heat of late summer beat down on us without mercy. The earth of the road beneath us baked into dust. At every stop Asher berated Yitzhak for taking us astray, demanding to know what his plans were and trying to make each of our way-stations into a final destination. But those towns were so poor that even Asher could see no possibility of settling there. We spent the High Holy Days in a village so tiny it did not even have a name; the day after Yom Kippur we set out once again along the road.

Yitzhak drove, humming one of his rebbe's melodies to himself, and Asher sat beside him on the box. Yaacov and I walked beside the wagon; Yonah and Natan ran ahead, while the others stayed inside, as we always walked and rode by turns. Suddenly, Asher buried his face in his hands.

"Yitzhak!" He cried out as if he were in awful pain. "Yitzhak, stop! In the name of God, I cannot live anymore like this! Where are you taking us?"

Yitzhak's mouth opened in surprise as Asher broke down and began to cry. We all stared as he threw himself on the ground, wailing. He pulled at his hair and beard and tore at his clothes, and pushed Feigl away as she tried to comfort him. Yaacov took him in his huge arms and held him in a bear hug until his cries gave way to sobs.

The boys ran in the field, waving sticks at each other like swords, Levi trailing after the older ones. I watched Yitzhak as he wandered away and stood by a large tree, facing the sun. Chaim Loeb played a game with Rachel, singing a nonsense song and beating time with two sticks. Yitzhak swayed in the sun; he raised his arms, he lowered them.

When Yitzhak came back to us, he was smiling. He went over to Asher, still sobbing in Yaacov's arms.

"Brother Asher, don't worry. Our troubles will soon be over."

Feigl laughed her wild laugh. "When are troubles over for Jews? When we are in our graves, our graves!"

Yitzhak's voice was gentle. "We will go to Cracow, where I lived with my blessed rebbe, may his soul rest in peace. Somewhere in that city someone must still be left of my fellow disciples; anyway, it is a big city with much business, and we can find there our way to the ocean."

"Your ocean!" Asher howled. "We will all be dead before then, if it even exists anywhere!"

But Feigl was watching Yitzhak. He kept speaking, calmly, the way the dairyman talks to his cows when he wants their best milk. "Shh, brother," he said. "In Cracow we will be able to earn enough to buy the papers we need. Chana and I will take the surname 'Salomon,' after my blessed rebbe, may he rest in peace. You may do the same, or choose what you will. Cracow is a free city; we can be citizens. Someone there will help us. I do not yet know who he is or where he is. But you once called me your rebbe, and now you must trust me."

Yaacov had tears in his eyes. "He has had a vision," he murmured reverently.

I turned away. It was more of his meshuggas, craziness, but what did I care?

When I first saw the great river of Cracow, I thought it was the ocean Yitzhak had dreamed of, until Feigl told me it was nothing but our own Vistula. We began the New Year in the shadows of that great dirty city, with the constant low roaring noise that surrounded us everywhere. I was frightened and would not leave our house, which was not even a real house but only two rooms in a courtyard, where all of us crowded together.

The children hated it as much as I did. The boys were in school all day, where the others mocked them and played tricks on them because they were from the country. The air was smoky and dirty outside, and inside there was always an old, sour stink. In the market, food was so costly we could not even afford as much as we had eaten in Ropshitz, and it was not as good. Now it was a lucky Shabbos indeed if we had a scrawny chicken to share among us, and often we had only thin soup of barley and carrots for supper, with a little black bread.

Feigl, it seemed, had been pregnant when we left Ropshitz, and the strain of the journey caused a miscarriage from which she did not easily recover. She was subdued, her songs and rhymes stilled. She seemed to fold up into herself, as if she was trying to take up less of the small space we had, even as Asher's two sons had suddenly grown nearly as big as men. The boys were always hungry, and Feigl always gave them food first; it was no wonder she was shrinking.

In this poor Jewish district, there were no trees or shrubs, nor any but the smallest, poorest weeds. There was nothing for Yaacov to do here in the way of woodcutting, but as he was large and strong, he hired himself out as a stevedore at the river docks, loading and unloading the boats.

Now I was calling them "the men," just as Feigl did. We had all been living together for over a year now, one family, but here we were so crowded and closed in that the intimacy was nearly unbearable. Day or night the noise and activity never stopped, until I could hardly remember the silence of the woods, the murmur of the river. Yitzhak had once seemed to me to be so uncommon; he had seemed aglow with light and a sweet warmth; now when I saw him with Asher and Yaacov, dressed in their hats and long Jewish coats, they looked like men one sees in any street, ordinary men hurrying to their business.

Poor Chaim Loeb had still not fully recovered. I did not think he would ever be well until he had a violin to play again. He could not work but lay in bed until afternoon and then sat drinking tea, looking sadly at the wall, smoking when he could find tobacco. He would sing to Rachel when she cried, and he sometimes hummed such beautiful melodies, tapping his fingers gently on the table, that I had to stop my work to listen.

I do not remember any light or sun in that city. The men bought and sold and hurried. For a short time they bought scraps of cloth and rags and brought them home in big sacks for Feigl and me to sort. We coughed and choked in the lint and dust; our eyes were red and irritated by the tiny particles that filled the stale air of our rooms. Soon we were keeping each other awake all night with our coughing, and the little children, Levi and Rachel, made pitiful sounds as they tried to catch their breath.

Thanks be to God, soon the men found another business. They took old Midnight out with a cart each day, bringing goods from the city to the villages on the outskirts, and then coming back with eggs and produce from the country. You would have thought we might have eaten better then, but they sold everything to scrape together every penny. Yitzhak had no time to read to me anymore. I hardly cared; I did not want to know what lay ahead in that book. Like our own life, it could only get worse.

That was a long winter. Shut up in our tiny, stinking rooms without enough to eat, we were like bears in a cave. The children seemed always to be sick, and shortly after Chanukah, Feigl also collapsed. She had become thinner than Yitzhak, her skin waxy and yellowish, and worst of all, she did not seem to care if she got better. She lost interest in everything, even her little daughter, and only lay in bed, coughing a terrible, deep cough. I did as well as I could to run our wretched household, making soups out of half-rotted vegetables and heating rocks on the stove to warm our beds.

So life passed. Feigl did not get better, but neither did she get worse. Chaim Loeb sang less and less frequently, Yaacov went stoically to and from his work on the docks, Asher became grayer and more downcast each day. Even Rachel was listless; she could hardly bring any expression to her little face.

Every Shabbos Eve I lit the candles and said the blessing. The men always tried to bring home something a little extra for this supper, even if it was just a small piece of herring.

Yitzhak led the songs and chants and prayers, but though the men's faces shone with the rebbe's old melodies, it was not the same anymore for me. I was like the old horse, putting one foot in front of the other, nothing more.

On a bitter afternoon, a few days before *Pesach,* I went out into the courtyard to get water from the pump. The wind blew a few drops of freezing rain that hit my face like needles; winter, like an inconsiderate guest, was taking its time departing. I was surprised to see Asher, alone in his fur hat and heavy, long cloak, leading Midnight and the cart into the stable; it was hours earlier than they usually returned, and where was my husband?

Asher carried the water pail up for me while I saw to Midnight. Poor thing, his ribs were sticking out. His eyes told me how, like me, he longed for the countryside. Tears came to my eyes as I stroked his nose. Then I left him, wrapping my worn shawl more tightly around me as I crossed the courtyard in the rain. Asher and I sat close to the little stove and spoke quietly, so as not to wake Feigl.

"He has met someone he knew years ago, from Shmuel Salomon," Asher told me. He looked at his hands as he spoke. He never looked at me; he was pious, and I was not his wife.

He sighed the deep, sad sigh that came so often from him that it was like his ordinary breathing. "Anyway, he thinks something will come of this. This man, name of Eisik, has become wealthy, though he still tries to live in the ways of his rebbe. He has taken Yitzhak home with him for tea, as they have their old times to talk about; I didn't stay."

I heard the clumping of feet outside as the boys came from school, all three of them. Natan and Yonah were tall, but they had grown thin and pale here, like plants growing without enough sun. Natan had never stopped coughing from the days of the lint. And little Levi, who had once been chubby, was now only the size of a thin child of four years, though he was nearly seven. It was hard to see them so: shivering, hungry, and tired.

As soon as Yaacov came home from the docks, I served barley soup and some of the black bread Asher had brought. It wasn't much, but it was what we had. I was ashamed of myself for being glad that Feigl still slept; though I tried to save her a portion, I couldn't bear to keep it from the children. As for me, all I needed was a little bread.

Asher, exhausted from the day's labor, questioned the boys halfheartedly about their lessons. Yonah had already been called to the Torah—he was bar mitzvah—and might have left school to help Asher and Yitzhak on the wagon, but Asher insisted he continue both in the government school and Hebrew school. He had a quick mind and proudly rattled off the answers, while his younger brother interrupted him. They were good boys and didn't quarrel, but each had to be the best, to know the most. At least they kept their voices low to spare their mother; it was funny to hear them striving and arguing in their hoarse whispers.

I rocked and softly sang Rachel to sleep; since Feigl had been sick, her daughter had become like my own. Asher and Yaacov fell asleep early, too; it wasn't easy trying to make a living in this bleak, rude city.

I was sitting alone by the last of the fire when Yitzhak burst in as if a gust from the sharp early spring wind outside had blown the door open before him.

"Chana! Look!" He frightened me; he was so flushed and excited.

"Shh!" I jumped up. "Are you crazy? Everyone's sleeping!"

"Well, wake them, wake them! Look!" As the others began to stir and groan in their beds, Yitzhak emptied the sack he was carrying onto the table. My eyes bulged: white bread, cakes, cheese, a big piece of smoked fish wrapped in oily paper, apples, little jars of pot cheese and sour cream. My cries woke the others; the children fell upon the food. Levi grunted happily, like a little animal, as he stuffed his mouth with a sweet cake. When Feigl woke, Yitzhak, beaming, reached into his coat pocket and held out to her a large white roll, studded with poppy seeds—and a miraculous orange!

Asher, his mouth stuffed with bread, finally asked, "Brother, what is this?"

Yitzhak was triumphant. "He Who provides life provides bread! Why do you think I wanted to come to Cracow?" he said. "Finally, today near the Ring-Platz, I saw the face in life of the man I had dreamed of when we were still on the road! He is Eisik, my friend, and he has forgiven me for deserting him, and he is going to help us! Praise be to God, Ruler of the Universe, Who has kept us alive and sustained us to this day, and Who makes all things possible!"

I could never have imagined such a palace as that house, nor conceived of a seder table set so magnificently with countless dishes, the glasses and cutlery gleaming like precious jewels. Even the candles seemed not to be made of ordinary wax, but of some heavenly stuff that shone and glowed like no earthly substance.

The serving-man who opened that grand door to us practically held his nose as he delicately took our ragged cloaks. Of course, we had no new clothes for *Pesach,* and what we had were in shreds. In honor of the occasion, Feigl and I had taken them down to the courtyard and washed them, but the strain had been too much for some of those poor rags. Thank God that Feigl was clever with needle and thread, and that the fine food Yitzhak had brought had revived her strength; she did her best to mend the disintegrating cloth. Even our patches had patches, even our holes had holes, as the saying goes.

But Reb Eisik and his wife were so kind that they treated us as if we were their long lost family. The wife was so gracious and beautiful and finely dressed that I thought she must be a princess, and their two golden-haired daughters were surely angels. Yitzhak was seated at Reb Eisik's right hand, and I beside him. I looked down the long table at our friends, and the radiance in the room seemed reflected in their faces, transforming us from a ragged bunch of beggars into a society as elegant as our surroundings deserved.

Reb Eisik held the matzoh high and chanted, "This is the bread of affliction. . . ." As I tasted the bitter horseradish, I could not help but think of the days only recently past when any of us would have been grateful for even bitter herbs to eat. And when little Levi raised his strong, clear voice to ask the four questions, I was proud of him, that his spirit had not been broken by our harsh life.

As the seder continued, Yitzhak, too, entered into the retelling of the story, the explanation of the symbols, the interpretations of the great rabbis. Their words, Yitzhak's and Eisik's, made a kind of music together, a fascinating play. And despite the doubts in my beaten-down soul, I felt the promise of the Passover festival: the hope of freedom, plenty, peace.

When the lavish meal was served, there was more food on the table than we had seen in months put together. Even I, who had not touched meat since childhood, found the roasted chicken so golden and tempting that I took a bite. Surely the manna that the Israelites had been fed on in the desert could not have been so sweet!

Something made me glance up at Chaim Loeb across the table, picking at his food as he stared at the wall behind me. I turned to see what he was so intent on, and saw on the wall, in a glass case, a pair of beautiful violins. I prayed with all my heart in that moment that one of them might find its way into Chaim Loeb's hands. I knew that without it, all the food of the earth could not satisfy his hunger.

As our voices rose in *hallel*, the psalms of praise, I thought I heard a moan escape the musician's lips. I looked at Yitzhak, my whole being absorbed in the strength of Chaim Loeb's desire for that instrument that hung idly in its case.

Through the back of my head, I could almost see it dance by itself through the air into Chaim Loeb's hands. Yitzhak, on fire with the bliss of his prayers, was oblivious to me; yet he turned his glance, just for a moment, to the fiddler, whose face was strained with longing. And then he looked over his shoulder and saw the case on the wall.

Yitzhak nodded and, at the end of the first psalm, gently put his hand on the sleeve of Eisik's silk caftan. I watched, unable to breathe.

"Brother Eisik, our hearts overflow with gratitude to you," he said.

Eisik smiled. "Brother, if the Holy One, blessed be He, has brought me such plenty, it would be incomplete if I could not share it with such an old and precious comrade, the friend of my youth. In memory of our blessed rebbe, Shmuel Salomon, may he rest in peace, ask for anything you want, and if it is in my power, I will gladly give it to you."

Yitzhak looked down. "Sitting across from me is a musician of such skill and devotion that the angels dance and clap their hands when he plays. But he has not played for many months, since his old violin was destroyed, and he nearly killed by our enemies. In memory of our beloved teacher, who so loved the horn that he allowed it even on the Sabbath, could our companion play on one of those fine instruments I see on the wall?"

Eisik beamed and clapped his hands for a servant, who at his direction opened the case and put one of the violins and the bow that lay next to it into Chaim Loeb's trembling hands. The instrument shone there as if it had dropped directly from heaven. Eisik smiled warmly at Chaim Loeb. "Try both, if you will; take the better and keep it for your own. They belonged to my father-in-law, may he rest in peace; they have not been played since he departed this earth three years ago, and his soul would rejoice to hear their music again."

As Chaim Loeb carefully tuned the old instrument, a tear

slowly rolled down his hollow cheek into his dark beard. He plucked a string with his forefinger, then lifted the instrument to his chin, closed his eyes, and raised the bow to the strings.

They began the psalm: "O praise the Lord, all ye nations; laud Him, all ye peoples," and the melody flew from Chaim Loeb's strings like the song of a lark that has been released from a trap. I closed my eyes and felt I was again in the midst of those beautiful trees by the river, the trees of my old village. And how we all sang and wept through the songs of thanksgiving!

"Next year in Jerusalem!" we chanted together as we raised the final glass. In all my happiness I shivered. This evening was like a dream, so far from ordinary life that I did not completely believe it, and I wondered where the next Passover would find us.

AMERICA, 1845

9

YITZHAK

YITZHAK LIFTED HIS HEAD from the railing and saw Shmuel Salomon, a tiny angel, wizened and sparkling, dancing across the waves. Bleary and sick, he stared. It might have been a fish or a hallucination. Chana, serene, stood a few yards away on the deck, her new wool cloak wrapped around her against the cutting breeze. Feigl's child Rachel, also tightly wrapped in new wool, held Chana's hand. The others remained below deck, sick from the ship's ceaseless rolling. Reb Eisik had bought them second-class passage on the *Bremen,* bound for New Orleans out of Hamburg with a load of fine cloth, farm tools, and German emigrants.

The white sails billowed above the deck. Yitzhak heard them hiss and snap. The figure of Shmuel Salomon waved a black-cloaked arm above his head. Yitzhak glanced at Chana, who seemed to see nothing more than the gray-green expanse of sky and sea. The little rebbe now appeared to be pointing ahead, in the same direction the ship was traveling, though God alone knew what direction that was. On this infinite, monotonous sea Yitzhak could determine neither course nor orientation.

The ship rolled; Chana slipped only slightly before

regaining her footing, laughing with the child. Yitzhak vomited over the side.

Their cabin was small and dark; it stank like a dirty stable. All but Chana and Rachel lay in their bunks in a state between waking and sleeping, terribly seasick, barely able to swallow the rancid-tasting water Chana brought them. To Yitzhak, Chana seemed the figure of an angel as she leaned over him with a dipper full of sour water, trying to hold it steady against the ship's motion.

"Drink, Yitzhak," she whispered. "Drink to stay alive." She looked frightened. If they were all to die, she would land in the New World alone. He mumbled a blessing, struggled to swallow a mouthful of water, nibbled from a hard ship's biscuit.

"Wake Asher," she said. "He has to drink, too. Feigl did, and the boys . . . you have to stay alive."

Asher groaned. From the other bunks, too, came the sounds of moaning, whimpering, retching.

For all their misery, they were more fortunate than they imagined; their crossing took only five weeks to port, and there were no major storms. The affliction that kept them confined to their fetid cabin was a blessing in disguise; they avoided the contagious ship's fever to which other passengers succumbed. Chana, who wandered restlessly at all hours, told Yitzhak of the canvas-shrouded bodies she had seen slipped over the side late at night. Yitzhak felt too sick to care; he was no longer sure of the difference between a blessing and a curse. He hardly cared anymore if the journey ended, or where.

He knew they had arrived by the difference in atmosphere, the change of routine. He tried to draw energy from the excited bustle around him as Chana mustered the others to gather their things. Everyone depended on him, but he was as lost as they were in the chaotic scene that greeted them on the New Orleans dock in the strange, humid air. Yitzhak was responsible and terrified. Taking Chana's arm, he boldly stepped down the gangway and the others followed, dizzy from illness and lack of food. Staggering under the weight of their luggage, they were held upright and moving only by the elation of arriving, at last, in America.

Incomprehensible shouts, colors, and noise engulfed them. Waves of powerful smells issued from bales of tobacco and loads of shellfish, mixed with the odor of coffee and sweat. Yitzhak's stomach cramped, he called on his rebbe, on the Master of the World, *Ribono shel Olom,* to keep him on his feet, to follow Eisik's instructions.

A line of half-naked men nearly as big as trees, with dark, shiny brown skin, passed crates up to the waiting hold of a ship in the next berth. The pier was crowded with people and baskets, boxes, trunks, bales, and variously shaped containers. Small boys, dirty and in rags, swarmed the debarking passengers, fighting to carry their bags. Wagons and coaches of all sizes and conditions lined the street, their drivers talking among themselves, chewing tobacco or gnawing on long loaves of bread, scanning the seething dock under the bright, hot sun. The air was heavy, overpoweringly moist.

Yitzhak stood in the maelstrom, soaked in sweat, praying silently. Asher was beside him.

"Yitzhak! What now? Do you know where we are?"

Yitzhak nodded firmly, desperately pretending a confidence he did not feel. "Brother," he said, steadying his trembling hand on Asher's shoulder. "God is with us. We have only to find the river and the boat to St. Louis. It's a big river, don't worry. We will find it." He had memorized the name of Eisik's relative-by-marriage, Reb Noah Cohn, the wealthy distiller and merchant to whose home they were going.

"God help us," Asher mumbled. He leaped back as a filthy urchin tugged at Yitzhak's cloak.

"Hey, Mister! Mister, gimme a penny!"

Yitzhak pulled away from the little creature in horror. God help us indeed! Rebbe, guide me!

A short, stocky young man pushed through the crowd toward them. He wore a greenish-colored coat and an oddly shaped cap. Yitzhak stared at his whiskers, which grew down the side of his face, leaving his chin and upper lip bare. The man, who could not possibly be Jewish, bowed slightly.

"Mr. Yitzhak Salomon?" he asked. "Fergis here, Mr. Noah Cohn's man, up from St. Loo—he sent me. You most likely not speaking English, you might use some help getting there."

Yitzhak recognized only his own name and that of his benefactor in the string of unfamiliar sounds. He stared in amazement: the Master of the Universe, the Holy One, has heard my cry! The stranger was clearly an angel, perhaps even the prophet Elijah in disguise! An angel—how else could he know me in this horde of people? He whispered a prayer of gratitude. But as he looked around, he realized that no one else was dressed as he and his friends were, in long, heavy black coats and broad-brimmed hats. *Payos* dangled in front of their ears, the long sidecurls that even the Jews of Germany no longer wore. He blushed.

Noah Cohn's servant led them briskly through the crowded street. A very fat woman, brightly dressed—perhaps a gypsy, Yitzhak thought—jostled against him. He stumbled, trying to avoid touching her, leaning into Asher, threatening to knock over the entire group like dominoes.

They were across from a public square, where a crowd watched what Yitzhak took to be a stage play. The servant roughly pulled him out of the path of a line of slightly clad, very dark skinned people with hair like black wool, led by a man on horseback. They had an odd, slow, shuffling gait; Yitzhak stared and saw with revulsion that they were chained together at the ankle—men and women and even a few young children. Chana clutched at his coat.

114

The green-coated servant shouted something in his ear, but Yitzhak didn't understand him. He surrendered, allowing himself to be led, and felt relief wash over him.

The river they traveled on was so wide it might have been another ocean; next to it, the mighty Vistula, even the Danube, were little streams. Smooth with power and majesty, this great sea of a river flowed past a wild, lush landscape. The immigrants were quiet, stunned, as if they themselves were newly born. Everything was larger, higher, wider than anything Yitzhak had seen before. He breathed deeply, filling his lungs as if he, too, would expand.

They were on the *Columbia,* a vessel that miraculously moved by noise instead of sail. Not so large as the ship that had brought them from Germany, she was much grander. She was painted a gleaming white trimmed in red and gilt; her black stacks rose from the deck, twin towers tall as Babel. Every inch gleamed and sparkled.

By the blessed loving-kindness of God, Noah Cohn's angel had freed Yitzhak from bearing alone his awful responsibility for the group. Yitzhak, delivered, inhaled the New World. The steamboat's paddlewheel churned the thick, brown water. Yitzhak became used to the noise, though he had gasped in fright when the mighty engine first started. What machines they had here! Yitzhak was thrilled with the wonders of God and man in this country. Even the sky seemed larger and more open, the way he had imagined the sky of heaven. Great soft puffs of clouds loomed and drifted in it like mountains, bigger than mountains!

He could hardly see the land beyond the river's banks, so far away as to seem yet another, even more mysterious country. Chana had told him that the people on the boat talked about wild Indians who lived in the forest; now he imagined them hiding in the distant trees. He had seen a party of tame Indians on the boat, three stolid men with long, black hair, dressed in ill-fitting American suits. They were usually at the gambling tables with Cohn's servant and the cheerful peasants who frequented the tavern on board.

The interior of the *Columbia* was like a grand duke's palace, hung with red velvet draperies and gilded mirrors. There was even a piano in the great hall, played every evening by a thin youth with whom Chaim Loeb struck a pantomime friendship, accompanying him on his violin late into the evenings.

In the dining room, a long serving table was spread with overflowing platters of food several times a day, an abundance even beyond the banquets they had eaten at Eisik's table in Cracow. The immigrants avoided the meats, certain that they were impurely prepared, and uncertain which might be pork. Many of the dishes they did not recognize; even the hungry children were repelled by the heaps of what appeared to be large pink insects served at every meal. But they devoured the breads, the vegetables, the sweet-fleshed fish, the rich cakes and pies.

The children could not be kept from swarming at the table, though Feigl and Asher struggled mightily to instill some decorum. But the boys had left their timidity back at the New Orleans dock. They gorged themselves freely and then roamed the boat from the hellish depths of the engine room to the heights of the glassed-in pilot house. Yitzhak surveyed his new dominion from the upper deck, Chana often at his side. Only Feigl still seemed ill and subdued.

They passed other steamboats on the river, with a fanfare of whistle-blowing and waving by the passengers of both vessels. Small rafts and barges were moved along by men pushing long poles against the river bottom, or pulled by teams of mules on the banks. Yitzhak saw Indians on the river, too: a long, narrow boat crowded with strangely dressed people and barking dogs.

In the evening, Yitzhak admired the pilot's skill in

carefully maneuvering the boat into a cove, to put in. The nighttime countryside appeared even more magical and unknown. He watched the men loading the firewood on board from enormous stacks on the bank. What kind of life lay beyond the river?

Just past the high bluffs above the river rose the low outline of the St. Louis waterfront. A luminous glow of promise emanated from the skyline. Yitzhak stood on the deck as the boat docked, lost in that radiance, ignoring the bustle around him as Fergis organized the others to debark.

They were met by a thin, coal black man—Albert, Noah Cohn's coachman. Yitzhak hardly noticed the anxious exhaustion of his companions; he was so exalted by the prospect of the fulfillment of his vision. This was where his rebbe had led him!

They turned from a shady road into a curving driveway and stopped before a tall two-story house. Beyond it, Yitzhak saw a large vegetable plot, an orchard, a stable, and two or three small cabins: an estate! He leapt from the coach and fell to his knees before the threshold. Albert, thinking he had fallen, rushed to help him to his feet.

"Baruch atah Adonoi Elohaynu Melech ha'Olom, she-hecheyaynu v'ki'manu v'higiyanu lazman hazeh. . . ." Yitzhak pushed off the coachman, deliriously chanting the blessing for festivals. "Blessed art Thou, Lord our God, Who has kept us alive until now so that we may find joy in what has just come to us. . . ." He stumbled to his feet. Chana took his arm. Asher stood protectively close to Feigl and Rachel, his sons on either side. Chaim Loeb and Yaacov, Levi clutching his father's coattails, still hung back near the wagon with the coachman. From behind Yaacov's broad body, Levi was staring at Albert's ebony figure.

A large, imposing man appeared on the porch, finely dressed in a German suit and a top hat. His features were

Jewish; he wore a full, dark, well-trimmed beard: Reb Noah Cohn. Yitzhak brushed feebly at the dust on his own long coat.

Reb Noah Cohn looked over the group of refugees, frowning. "So you are here. You have safely arrived."

Yitzhak bowed. *"Baruch Hashem,"* he said. "Blessed be the Holy One, *Ribono shel Olom."*

Noah Cohn's frown deepened. Behind him a small woman, whose large black bonnet seemed too heavy for her head, hurried out of the house. "My wife, Madame Estella. She will show you—" He waved toward the house, then brushed past them to the coach. Rachel began to cry; Feigl comforted her softly.

Yitzhak knew nothing about this New World, not even the language; Cohn provided for him, explained to him, supervised him. At dinner each night, he lectured in a broken Yiddish laced with German words that Yitzhak could not always understand.

"At last, here in America is the opportunity for the Jew to leave behind the medieval superstitions that have caused his persecution in Europe for so many centuries," Cohn expounded. "Here a Jew can live like every other modern man in the nineteenth century!" He repeated his words in English, partly as a pedagogic device, partly for the benefit of his wife, who spoke no Yiddish at all. Madame Estella was an aristocrat, from an old Sephardic family in Charleston. When she lit the Shabbos candles, she sang a melody as strange to Yitzhak as her accented Hebrew. Cohn explained that the dark-skinned woman who served them at table, her husband the coachman, and the cook in the kitchen were slaves, part of Madame Estella's dowry.

"Any man—even a Jew—may make what he wishes of himself in this country. But he must look forward, not backward."

Here there was no Jewish quarter; in America, Jews lived

among Gentiles. And Cohn was rich. His house was so big it had rooms Yitzhak never saw. Yaacov and Chaim Loeb shared a room over the stable, where Fergis also had his quarters, but Yitzhak and Chana had their own room on the second floor of the big house, next to another suite of two rooms for Asher and Feigl and the children. These three rooms were in the rear of the house, overlooking the vegetable plot; the Cohns had a larger suite, a bedroom and a sitting room each, in the front. Yitzhak had never imagined so much living space; the scale was exorbitant, like everything else in America.

Impressed and grateful as he was, there was something about Cohn that nettled Yitzhak. He felt again like that miserable youth who had suffered at his father's table. He became disgusted by the smell and sight of food; his stomach was constantly knotted, as when he was a child. His father's lectures had been on different subjects, a different philosophy, but something in Cohn's tone of voice was the same. With all the piety and devotion with which the late Rebbe Mendel of Przemysl had delivered his Torah sermons, Cohn propounded the American doctrine of secular redemption.

"In this country the only aristocrats are those who have risen by their own merit and hard work," Cohn said. "We have no crowns, no titles—any man may build a castle for himself." He might have been speaking of himself, for he had expanded a small distillery until he had become the largest distributor of locally produced and imported liquors in the entire West. Every fur company caravan to the summer rendezvous, every wagon train out to Taos on the Santa Fe Trail or to Fort Laramie and the Indian trading posts on the Missouri, went laden with Cohn's spirits, ales, lagers, and imported wines. He had been the chief outfitter for Frémont's expedition the previous year, and now that the little town of St. Louis was filling with German immigrants and settlers from the East, he had built and stocked the largest general merchandise store in the city.

It was in this emporium that the new immigrants were employed: Asher on the accounts and Yaacov in the blacksmith shop attached to the store. Chaim Loeb had never done any work but play music, but Cohn was pleased to inform him that in the New World every man must toil. So the fiddler worked with the boys, restocking and arranging the shelves. Feigl and Chana stayed at home with Madame Estella and the slaves.

For the first few months, Yitzhak worked on the account books with Asher, in a dusty office in the back of the store. Asher was comfortable with the work, but Yitzhak had never been good with figures, and the hot, close air of the room gave him a constant dull headache.

All summer, the numbers swam before his eyes, until one day he remembered their divinatory meanings, their inner symbolism. Fascinated, he stared into space contemplating *one*, the crown, the source of creation; *six*, beauty, the central sun. He combined figures into significant combinations and meditated on their meaning. He converted subtotals into Hebrew words according to their kabbalistic correspondences and shared their profound intimations with Asher.

"Asher," he beamed. "Look at this! Today is a day for divine mercy, greatness. Love and kindness! It is *chesed. Cheth, samech, daleth. . . .* You see, here is an eight, that is the letter *cheth*, plus sixty, that is *samech. . . .*"

Asher smiled thinly. "Ah, Yitzhak, we will surely need God's mercy if we are ever to survive this place."

Cohn was horrified when he overheard Yitzhak's ruminations. "I'm not paying you to be a philosopher!" he shouted.

Obviously, some other work would have to be found for him.

The entire family—Cohns and immigrants—went on Saturday mornings to the local synagogue. Madame Estella led Feigl and Chana to the women's section, separated from the sanctuary only by a waist-high curtain. Like Cohn, the community, perhaps two dozen Jews, was almost all from Germany. The liturgy and order of service were not what the Polish Jews were accustomed to; the service was shorter, more organized. These Jews were indistinguishable in dress, manner, and language from the Gentile burghers of St. Louis, and it took some months for the stir caused by Cohn's unusually clad guests to die down. At first, Yitzhak and his companions found everyone staring, and Cohn actually glowering, as they wailed and swayed in prayer. The German Jews prayed standing stiffly, hardly moving.

The Cohns did not pray at home, except for the Shabbos candle lighting and kiddush. Yitzhak could not find God in their house. Every morning and evening, he prayed outside in the garden, inhaling the sultry, fragrant air of the Missouri summer. He prayed as he always had, swaying and singing until that ladder of golden light hung before him, the ladder he scaled to the throne of heaven, entering into that state of communion which sustained his will. Though Asher prayed with him, he did not seem to share the ecstasy. Loyally, Chaim Loeb and Yaacov came down from their room over the stable to join with the rebbe they had followed so far, but Chana was too timid and only watched from a window. Cohn watched, too.

On their way from prayers one evening, Asher spoke to Yitzhak in the small orchard. Crickets sang, a mockingbird called. It was not yet dark.

"Yitzhak, where have you brought us to? These are Jews without Torah, they are lost, and we are lost with them."

Yitzhak stared at him. "What do you want? We cannot go back to Poland now!"

"God only knows where we can go, but we cannot stay here. Even the food is not properly kosher. With that black creature in the kitchen, how could it be?"

"Asher, on the boat already we ate . . ."

"That was not the same!" Asher's eyes were moist. "We had to eat that *traife* to live! *Pichuach neshoma,* to save a life, it is permitted! But this is a Jewish home! You are the rebbe, you must speak to him."

Yitzhak shuddered. He put his arm across his brother-in-law's shoulders. "We are Reb Cohn's guests," he reminded. "It is not a permanent situation. At least there are no pogroms and beatings here. This isn't Poland; with hard work we can do anything! Look at Reb Cohn himself! We will learn the language better, we will have our own business, you and Feigl will have your own house."

"Feigl is carrying another child," Asher said bluntly. "I am working all the time at the store, I have no time to learn languages. And it is not only Cohn. All of the so-called Jews in this country are the same, worse than Germany! There is not even a real shul, nor a proper house of study, there is no *mikvah*! There is no Torah! The Jews are not Jews, and how can a Jew live without other Jews? How am I to raise my sons here, and the one who is coming? My sons are going wild! Here there is no difference between Jews and Gentiles, and all are gone to the devil in their crazy pursuit of riches."

Yitzhak shook his head. "You must be patient. We can pray together, you and I. The entire Torah is in your heart, that is what my rebbe, may he rest in peace, told me, and that is what I'm telling you now. We will pray for Feigl's health and for the child that is coming. After the baby is born, by then we will know the language, we will know how to make a living—now we are like children ourselves! Wait a little, then we can go someplace else. We will build our own *Beth Midrash,* a house of study. We will build our own *mikvah.*"

"Someplace else! Someplace else! Always you want to go someplace else, and always it is someplace worse!" Asher walked away quickly, toward the house.

Yitzhak pulled his beard. A breeze rustled the trees. How could Asher be so unhappy? Yes, there were problems. This

122

was earth, not heaven, and the Messiah not yet come. Yet there was hope and beauty, and now Feigl would have a baby. An American baby.

It was Chana who reminded her husband that he once was a tinker, though it seemed eons ago that they had lived in the little village next to Ephraim and Rivka. Perhaps the people of St. Louis and the nearby farms also had pots that needed mending. He could take one of Reb Cohn's fine horses and a little wagon. Chana could already speak a little English, and now that the summer's canning and preserving were finished, she could go, too. Cohn was doubtful at first but agreed, provided they also bring some of the store's stock of new goods and convince the customers that some of their broken pots would be better replaced than repaired.

On this fall afternoon, the suburbs and farms were unaccountably deserted, and though they had taken the wagon farther from town than usual, they had done no business since early in the morning. The sun was low, and Chana stopped the horse for a moment to listen to the cry of that strange bird that sounded so much like a child.

They were not far from the river, and they started back toward town by a different route than the one they had come by. It was tranquil on the old dirt road through the lightly wooded hills. Chana drove, and Yitzhak nodded and dreamed. Gradually, Yitzhak heard something oddly familiar. It was the sound of people singing, singing in the woods.

But it was not the angel choir that had floated across the fields of his childhood; this music was not the singing of Christian monks. It was quick-tempoed and lively, like the music of the gypsies on the Polish plains, accompanied by shouts and hand-clapping. The noise grew louder, and beyond the bend in the road was a wondrous sight.

Tents and wagons were scattered across a large field like a crude town. Horses and mules were tied to trees or picketed at the edges of the clearing, peacefully nibbling grass.

At the far edge of the clearing stood one tent much larger than the others—the source of the sound that rose more fervent by the minute; a music punctuated by shouts, claps, and jangling tambourines. A few people stood gathered around the entrance under a large banner, while others milled through the clearing. A noisy crowd gathered under a spreading tree, attending to a black-coated man shouting from a stump, waving his arms.

What could it be? Perhaps this was an "election," an American event about which Yitzhak had heard much from Cohn, though its meaning still confounded him. Neither Yitzhak nor Chana could read the wide banner. Yitzhak knew the names of the English letters, but spelled them aloud to Chana from right to left, as if they were Hebrew: S–E–V–A–S–S–U–S–E–J.

"I don't know," Chana told him timidly. "I don't think it means anything."

They were still fifty feet away, but one of the men nearest the road waved his hat at them and yelled: "Welcome, brother! Praise God! Hallelujah! Come to the Lord!"

Chana frowned. "It's some goyische meshuggas, Yitzhak," she said. "Let's go home."

"Wait, Chanale." He put his hand over hers where she held the reins. "Let's just listen a minute. We don't have to go closer, we can hear from here."

The gold sun glinted through the trees. The shouting and clapping intensified; Yitzhak was fascinated, hypnotized, yet unable to move closer. He swayed in time to the music as if he were praying.

"Yitzhak, come. We will be late for supper, and we have not sold anything since morning, we have no excuse."

"Chana, only listen! They sound like angels!"

"Angels? If angels make such a noise, God must be deaf! Let's go now."

"Come with me, Chana," he pleaded. "It's something different, something American."

Chana shook her head. "You go, then, and be an American. I'll wait here with the horse."

Exasperated by her stubbornness, Yitzhak climbed down from the wagon and shook out his stiff legs. The sun dropped to the crest of the hills; crickets sang in the grass at his feet. At the side of the clearing, a few young men were laying down a large heap of wood for a fire. Children ran to them carrying sticks for kindling.

The atmosphere itself seemed to thicken as he approached the tent. People looked at him curiously as he cautiously stepped forward, but they greeted him with open, smiling faces such as he rarely saw on his tinkering and peddling rounds.

The knot at the entrance to the tent parted, allowing him to enter; he was plunged into a boiling mass of noise and energy. The air inside the tent was electric, hot. While a few white-haired elders sat on crude, woods-made chairs, most everyone else stood swaying or danced wildly.

Yitzhak distinguished a familiar word in the pandemonium: "Hallelujah! Hallelujah!" It dawned on him then that these people were another kind of American Jew. If, as Cohn said, Jews here were different from those in Poland, perhaps they were not all like the ones in the St. Louis synagogue.

Filling one side of the large tent was a swaying crowd of black slaves, bringing forth a glorious song. Amid the boisterous shouting, there was a sweetness in the blending of voices, harmonies he had never imagined. A large circle of people moved in a shuffling dance, singing "Glory, glory, Hallelujah!" as slave women shook tambourines. Standing nearby, a man played a large stringed instrument. Shouts of "Amen!" and "Hallelujah!" filled the air. Children threaded their way in and out of the circle and ran back and forth behind the dancers.

Sweating with the close heat and enthusiasm, Yitzhak swayed with the music. He closed his eyes, transported by the singing, the jangling, the singsong shouts. "Amen," he mouthed. "Hallelujah!" Behind his closed eyelids a familiar gold light appeared so suddenly that he could not remember that it had ever been absent. A smile curled his lips, opened his heart. With the light came a feeling of joy and peace such as he had not felt in months. Yes, God was everywhere, and he himself was a part of That. The blessed Shmuel Salomon of Cracow, may he rest in eternal peace, had indeed preceded him to this New World, had made this place for him here in the Missouri woods, here with this curious group of Americans: men, women, whites, Negroes, children—all praising the holy Name of God! Yitzhak stepped into the dancing circle.

He had not yet understood more than a few of the words sung, but now as he danced, he heard one high, clear voice above the others: "Je-sus, Lord of my soul, Jesus, Lord of my soul."

With a sudden, dreadful recognition of that name, Yitzhak plummeted into shame and confusion. Had he stumbled into a Christian rite? Only now did he see, just behind the ecstatic black choir, the large, telltale wooden cross! He gagged on the sob that rose from his chest. Had he so easily betrayed his God, the Holy One, the God of Moses and Abraham? As he turned to run, he was pushed back by a knot of shouting dancers, pressed against a large, corpulent white woman, her flesh shaking beneath her sweat-spotted dress as she writhed in religious delirium. She raised her arms high, calling, "Jesus, Lord! Jesus, Lord!" Yitzhak fought back a scream. The human odor in the tent was suddenly overpowering; he prayed, as he had prayed years ago at his father's table, not to vomit. The mass of hot bodies around him shifted with the rhythm of the crowd; he escaped the involuntary embrace and struggled through the door to freedom. The men gathered outside stared at his fleeing figure; dimly, he heard the laughter of children.

For a moment he stood in the clearing, panting, before he

126

recovered enough to run for the wagon. He leapt to the box beside Chana.

"Go! Go!" he shouted. Chana looked at him, bewildered, as he grabbed the reins from her hands and drove the horse down the road toward home.

10

CHANA

PRAISE BE TO THEE, Lord our God, Ruler of All the Worlds, who made the great sea. There was a blessing for seeing the ocean, so I knew it was real. But how could I have prepared myself for that voyage? Just above the close darkness of the ship's belly—our quarters for those five weeks—were the unlimited waves, rising and falling as far as I could see, green by day and by night the deepest black, under a wide, wide sky covered with countless stars.

Each day when I stumbled out under the white, billowing sails of the *Bremen,* my eyes were opened a little wider. Where I had come from there was always an edge: the end of the village, the edge of the forest, the wall around the city. Now there was nothing around me but space extending forever, dark green rolls of water that merged at the horizon into the gray canopy of sky.

As if the ship's motion had not already made my legs waver like weeds in the wind, the sight of all that unobstructed space made my head spin so that I could hardly stand. I had never dreamed I could feel so alone, for though I had always felt alone among people, I now felt alone in the universe. Yet in the midst of that awful loneliness I felt the pure joy of a bird, soaring high over those waves, bound for home.

So it was that in coming to America, the land without Torah, I regained my lost faith. My heart began to lift as soon as that marvelous and awful ship sailed, when I realized I was leaving my old country behind forever. Even as Yitzhak and the others lay suffering, I knew that whatever happened I would be held safely by the One Who called each of that multitude of stars by name, Who numbered every hair on my head. I did not know whether we might drown in a shipwreck or die of a plague; whether America was an actual, real place where we would find a new and happier life, or if we would be lost forever in a fancy of Yitzhak's imagination. Yet I was at peace; I no longer felt blown on the wind, but instead borne upward on the invisible, loving current that sustained all the worlds.

Though I had felt safe with God at sea, I almost fainted with fear when we first landed, weak as newborn lambs, in America. All around were madly moving people who could not speak without shouting. They even looked peculiar, like animals dressed in human clothes. They moved so fast and shouted so loud that they seemed larger than they were.

In spite of the sweet-smelling flowering trees that lined the streets, I thought that Yitzhak had brought us to hell. And while he took Fergis to be a rescuing angel, I thought him an imp, whose real master was not Reb Cohn but the Evil One. I even saw a few poor souls chained together in a line, driven by a devil on horseback!

Of course, it was not really hell, it was just another country. We came to a river as wide as ten Vistulas and the noisy boat that carried us to St. Louis. And on that boat, it seemed true what we had heard at home, that in America everyone lived like kings and queens. It truly seemed our days of hunger and misery were as far behind us as the country we had left.

St. Louis was a big, spread-out village, not as big or dirty as Cracow. I felt disoriented by the strange landscape, the river as slow and brown as the sticky molasses the people here liked to spread on bread. For that molasses alone, Levi and Rachel would have sworn eternal loyalty to America! I had never seen trees and plants such as grew here, though the animals were the same horses, cows, dogs, and cats we had in Poland.

Reb Noah Cohn was big and dressed like a nobleman in his fine coat and tall, black hat. Everything about him looked powerful; except for his features, I would not have believed he could be a Jew. His wife was much smaller, but she wore a big dress, made of black, hissing, silky stuff.

Every week in that magnificent, frightening house I discovered yet another room, each one filled with furniture, carpets, paintings. Fancy wood cabinets held strange and delicate objects made of carved wood and bone, painted ceramics, and skillfully worked metals—objects whose uses I could not imagine. When no one was watching, I ran my hands over the stair railing, the woodwork, even the windowsills. I caressed the walls, covered with figured paper: pictures of flowers, horses, people in strange costumes. Everything was polished and silent.

Yitzhak and I had a room alone for the first time since we had left the village where we were married. I found it difficult to sleep at first, without the sounds of others breathing, sighing, turning in their sleep. Feigl and Asher and the children were across the hall from us, but they seemed so far away that they might have been in another street.

Madame Estella's eyes were sharp and close together. Her black dress whispered loudly with every movement she made. I could not help staring at her hair. In my ignorance I thought they made fine wigs indeed here, but I was more amazed to realize it was her own chestnut hair twisted in such an elaborate pattern at the back of her head.

American Jewish women were different in other ways, too, besides wearing their own hair. I was too shy to speak to Madame Cohn directly, so I asked Yitzhak to find out where the *mikvah* was. To our consternation, there was no ritual bath at all. There was a sparkling creek on the other side of the orchard, and Yitzhak told me that would do. And so, without attendant, and saying my own prayers, I was able to purify myself each month. Feigl was pregnant and would have no need of a *mikvah* for many months.

One morning Madame Estella took me into the orchard. The trees were heavy with plums and peaches; the vines and shrubs of the vegetable garden were bowed and snarled with their bounty, ready to harvest. We had been in St. Louis several weeks, and I understood some English, but I was too timid to speak.

She pointed to the heavy boughs of a peach tree. "Fruit," she said slowly to me. "Pea-ches."

"Pea-chess," I repeated dutifully.

"In jars!" she said, shaping her hands into the shape of a container. "They must all be put up, in jars! Can you do that? Do you understand?" She peered into my face. I understood her words, but I couldn't make sense out of them. Did she want me to pick the fruit? I smiled at her as I reached up to one of the branches.

Madame Estella put her hand on my arm and shook her head. "No, no, Sally and Maizie will pick them. I need you in the kitchen, to help put them up." She made the shape of a jar with her hands again.

I nodded. She frightened me, and I didn't want to disappoint her. Whatever it was she wanted me to do, I supposed it would become clear eventually. She was exasperated now; she clucked at me over her shoulder and motioned impatiently for me to follow her back to the house.

Reb Cohn—Mister Cohn, he liked to be addressed, as he was an American—sat in the dining room with his newspaper. When Madame Estella spoke to him, he grunted and folded the paper, looking at me over his spectacles.

"I do not know what use she can be," she said to him. "She is small; she doesn't look very strong." She turned to me, her eyes black and shiny as the beads on her necklace. "You were starving in Europe, were you not? How fortunate you are to have come to our generous shores."

I blushed when I understood. What did she know of my life? "I can work hard, Madame," I said, my voice shaking a little. "I am strong." I spoke Yiddish even though I knew she did not understand. I thought I knew the English, but I was ashamed, afraid I would say it wrong and make her laugh. I let Mr. Cohn repeat my words in English.

She made a little sniffing sound; or perhaps it was her dress. "It's a pity that you speak no English," she said. This, Mr. Cohn did not translate, but I understood. She sighed and spoke to her husband again, who stuttered her words out in his stilted Yiddish.

"I want you to work in the kitchen with Maizie and Sally, after they bring in the fruit," she said. "And the vegetables, the cucumbers and beans, are ready to put up now. Do you know how to put things up? How to make pickles and preserves?"

With a sharp, sweet pain I remembered Rivka's sour berry jam; the kettle boiling in the house that had once seemed to me so grand and that, from my new perspective, I now saw as a hovel. Suddenly I longed for my village, the fields—to wander under the trees, to watch the animals. I shook myself. What a fool! When I had been there, I had only wanted to get away. I was like that dumb cow, always pushing at the fence with her nose, believing the grass on the other side was sweeter.

I spoke directly to Madame Estella, forming my new English words carefully: "I know," I said. "Yes. I work."

She was surprised by those, the first English words I had ever spoken. I felt proud to speak them, grateful to the Creator of the World Who had given me that ability. But her answer came too quickly, and I was embarrassed again, waiting for Mr. Cohn.

"Very well, then. There is certainly plenty to do. Jars to be

132

boiled, beans to be cut, fruit to be picked over and pitted. It's well for you that you are learning English so quickly. Perhaps you can also teach your sister-in-law. She is not in a condition to work; she ought to stay in her room. I will instruct the younger children myself. The school here in town will start in a few months, and they must be made ready."

"Both of them?" I was perplexed. "Rachel as well as Levi?"

Mr. Cohn answered. "Certainly," he said.

What a place is America, I thought, where girls go to school with the boys!

"Settled, then?" Mr. Cohn spoke to his wife. "She can work in the kitchen with Sally and Maizie. They are good girls, but they bear watching. Mrs. Salomon can keep an eye on our sugar for us." He laughed, but I heard no pleasure in it.

I understood Madame Estella's words better than I understood her heart; she was as cold as a stone. She insisted that Feigl stay in bed, but I saw that this was not so much to safeguard the mother and the coming child, but because she could not bear the sight of Feigl's pregnancy. She looked disgusted, even angry, when Feigl, bored and wanting company, made her way downstairs to the kitchen to sit with us as we worked. Estella had never forgiven God for her own childlessness.

How strange that though her own body could produce nothing, her vegetable garden and orchard were the most fertile in the neighborhood. From dawn every day until long after the sun set, we worked over those gigantic, fragrant, boiling kettles. There were mountains of cucumbers to be peeled and sliced, peas to shell, long green beans to cut, deep red tomatoes. And baskets and baskets of fruits to be pitted, peeled, cut, boiled. When I closed my eyes for a minute, the steam from the kettles became the mist over the sea, and I would see again that expanse, feel the rocking of the ship and the openness of the sky.

133

I liked Maizie, despite her fearsome appearance. Her skin was as black as if she had fallen into the fire, and her white woolly hair, when released from her tight red kerchief, stuck out in every direction. Her eyes were soft and kind, and she had a sunny smile. Sally, however, I remained afraid of. Her skin was not so dark as Maizie's; it was more the color of a tree, and she was nearly as big around as one. Her forearms looked especially fierce, as thick and strong as the clubs the cossacks had wielded in my village. She hardly spoke and never smiled, but went about her work as solidly and gruffly as a bear.

Sally cooked mountains of American food. We especially loved the puffs of bread called biscuits, which we spread with butter and sticky molasses or dipped in the juices from the meats and vegetables. The Cohns ate no pork; in that way if no other they still followed the kosher laws. But at the morning meal there was beef sausage, chicken, a dish of baked eggs and vegetables, grits, and piles of flat, light hotcakes. For the first time I tasted coffee, the bitter brew that the Cohns drank big cups of, but I could hardly swallow it. I made tea for myself and Yitzhak, and brought a glass to Feigl in her room every morning, as I had once done for Rivka. But Chaim Loeb loved the coffee; he drank as much of the stuff as Mr. Cohn.

When the morning meal was cleared away, Maizie and I poked up the stove and began peeling, cutting, and slicing while Sally washed the dishes and pots. Cohn and all the men came home from the store in the middle of the day to eat, but Maizie explained that because we were so busy making preserves, the midday meal was simpler than usual. There was soup, plates of fried fish and chicken, roasted meats, eggs, vegetable dishes, corn bread, and always biscuits. There were pies stuffed with sweet fruit and high, white cakes, as if every day was a holiday.

Sally and Maizie sometimes sang while they worked in

134

their sweet, full voices. They sang about the goyische God, Jesus; they sang about crossing the river Jordan and going home. And they also had songs about the same stories from our Torah that Yitzhak had read to me in Poland! And when they sang, "Tell old Pharaoh, let my people go," my own thin voice struggled to rise out of my throat to join in.

I didn't pray with Yitzhak in the garden, but from the house I could see him in tallis and tefillin, swaying and singing unashamed before his God. Asher, Chaim Loeb, and Yaacov bravely joined him, though the Cohns were mortified. Those meetings were hurried and furtive; we were not in our own place, and things were different between all of us. From my home village to Asher and Feigl's home in Ropshitz, and from there to Cracow, we had been like brothers and sisters, almost knowing what another would say before the words were out. But on this side of the ocean we were broken and disordered, the way the smooth brown surface of the river was splashed into pieces by the steamboat's wheel.

That summer, Yonah and Natan grew tall and strong, like men. Like the others, they worked all day, but unlike them, they learned English quickly and made friends with some of the other young men at the store—goyim. To Asher's dismay, they only reluctantly came to the synagogue and never joined the prayers that Yitzhak led. As soon as they could get away after Saturday services, they ran off with their friends from the store to race horses by the river or watch the steamboats at the dock.

It was hot, the air so close and humid that even breathing was difficult. Madame Estella had released Levi and Rachel early from their lessons so that she could rest in her room with a fan and a cool drink.

The kitchen was unbearable with the added heat from

the boiling kettles, and we had set up a table outside the back door where we could cut the long green beans we were putting up. Albert called to us from the yard as he came, the children following behind him. In his arms he held a huge, green fruit shaped like the egg of an enormous bird.

"See what he's brought!" Maizie crowed, clearing a space on the table for Albert to set the thing down. It was as large as a baby lying there. I drew in my breath as Maizie came up with her big knife. The children crowded close. Feigl had come out to escape the heat, too; she giggled and poked the fruit with her finger. Maizie laughed.

"You ain't never seen a watermelon before, has you?" she accused.

"Is it filled with water, then?" I poked it, too. It was hard, like a cucumber.

Maizie shook her head and laughed. "Well, you-all is in for a right treat!"

No, it was not filled with water, but with a bright pink grainy flesh studded with black seeds. Sweet and juicy it was, like biting into a summer garden: perfumed, fabulous, refreshing. Wiping the juice that dripped on my chin, I thought the watermelon alone was reason enough to come all the way here.

Levi grabbed a large slice and ran back into the yard. Maizie showed us how to spit the shiny black seeds, and Feigl and I began a contest to see who could spit them farther. Rachel tried, too, but she was no match for us. At least she was a cheerful loser; she romped and giggled and dribbled the sweet juice down her chin and the front of her dress.

"Child, you are somethin'! Look at yourself! You're runnin' wild as an Injun!" Maizie scolded her. "What's Miz Estella goin' to say about your dress, now?" She caught Rachel and swiped at the spots with a corner of her apron. "Miz Estella goin' to beat *me*, sure, if I don' beat you first!" she said, raising her arm.

136

Rachel wriggled away and ran to her mother. *"Sha!"* Feigl glared at Maizie.

"Oh, Feigl!" I said. "Maizie is only teasing."

But Feigl, muttering, led Rachel away.

Maizie looked at the floor. "You folks may have different ways where *you-all* come from, but Miz Estella say that chil' is like a wild animal, an' if I don't keep her clean an' nice, she's goin' to whup me."

I couldn't believe it, but I remembered seeing the whip hanging in the barn, and I felt, more than I understood in words, that there was something about Maizie and Sally and Albert that was more different than their dark skin and woolly hair. It was in the heaviness I sometimes saw in their faces or heard in their steps as they went about their work; more, it was in the Cohns' expressions as they spoke to them, contemptuous and yet somehow ashamed.

"She *whips* you?" I asked, but Maizie was silent. "Can you not leave, then, go somewhere else?" Mr. Cohn had been complaining just the night before that some of his men at the store were leaving, to go to the West.

"Go somewhere else?" Maizie laughed and shook until tears came to her eyes. "How in the name of Jesus would I be goin' to go somewhere else? If I run off, they goin' to set dogs on me an' catch me. The only way I be off this-here place'd be if Miz Estella *sole* me, an' I hope an' pray she don' do *that!*"

I didn't understand her. "'Sole' you? What is 'sole'?"

"Miz Honey, don' you know about how it is with us? Miz Estella own us. Her mama and daddy in Charleston, where we come from, that's Mister Ephraim and Miz Sarah. An' they be ownin' my mama an' my daddy. We's slaves in bondage, jus' like the Isreelites in Egypt. All our lives be in slavery, 'til the Lord Jesus take us home again. Don't you know, that's why Sally be always so low down. Miz Estella sole her child away from her, just the last year ago, an' he only about the size of this-here Missy Rachel. He up in Memphis, wit' the new master, all by hisself. Mister Noah, he didn't like it—the boy only fetch but fifty dollar. But he say we belong to Miz Estella an' she can do as she please."

I was suddenly cold to my bones. I had thought I knew something about America; Cohn called it the land of freedom. Was it possible that we, too, were slaves? Or was it only these dark-skinned people? How did it happen to them? I had a thousand questions that I did not dare ask. The fruit that only minutes ago had seemed the most wonderful food now tasted like dust in my mouth.

I had been afraid that Rachel and Levi would slip away from us, like Yonah and Natan were slipping away. There was less and less of "us" to hold them; each of us was being claimed by the Cohns, by America. And now I worried that our children could be sold, like Sally's child, and sent far away. Though my heart was heavy with dread, I resolved to keep my fears to myself until I knew more. I especially did not want Feigl, in her delicate condition, to become concerned.

Those long summer afternoons, when Madame Estella rested in her darkened room, I stole away from the kitchen to visit Feigl, bringing her a glass of tea or a dish of cooked fruit. Asher had brought wool and cotton yarn from the store, and Feigl spent her time knitting, sitting up in bed. Her flying fingers flicked the scraps into new shawls for all of us, and tiny coats and blankets for the baby that was coming.

She looked up at me from her knitting like a little owl. We had both happily discarded our itchy wigs, but while I covered my head with a kerchief like Maizie's, Feigl wore a peculiar round cap, an old one of Madame Estella's. Even though it was hot in that upstairs room, a light shawl lay over her shoulders. I could see her swollen belly make a hill under the covers, and I couldn't help but envy her.

"Chana-lana-wana," she sang, letting the words play around her mouth.

"That's not English," I said, smiling. It made me happy to

138

see her in a good mood; sometimes she was so melancholy. "We're supposed to speak English; I'm supposed to teach you."

Feigl rolled her eyes. "English-shminglish," she said. "Why do I need to learn to talk again? So I can talk to that one?" She made a sour face that was remarkably like Madame Estella looking down her nose.

Now I saw she was not in such a good mood after all. Her face was sallow, discolored by a shadow across her cheeks, and there were dark circles under her eyes. I set the dish of compote on the stand by her bed, but she didn't notice.

"Feigl, what is it?" I said. "By the time the baby comes, we can know enough English to start our own life here. Won't you like that better? Yitzhak says we can have our own business, our own house. Your child will be an American, and Rachel, too, and Levi. Yonah and Natan already—"

"If *she* doesn't poison me first, to steal my baby." Feigl spat the words out.

I was shocked. She didn't know what Maizie had said about Sally's child, and I hadn't even told her about the slaves; I didn't want her to have bad thoughts and hurt the baby.

"She takes children from their mothers, to eat them, eat them," Feigl muttered. She stabbed at the yarn with her needles. "Those black ones are hers, they are her devils, to do whatever she wishes. And see, see, how she already is stealing Rachel away, away, away! She teaches her to make spells against me. And Yaacov's boy, too, she trains to do her dirty business."

Yitzhak had told me how Feigl knew things, how she knew his dreams almost before he did. There was a strange look in her eyes now, as if she was looking at something I could not see.

She was in a delicate state, and I had to protect her. "Feigl, I do not love her either, but she only teaches the children to read and write, to make them ready for American school—"

"Are you betraying me, too? You too? You too?" Poor Feigl sang like an owl.

"Feigl, Feigl," I said, trying to avoid her knitting needles as I embraced her. "I will never betray you."

She sobbed. In spite of myself, I wondered if she might be speaking the truth. Perhaps my first impression of America had been right. I had a vivid memory of that poor parade of souls so mournfully chained together. What if this was the Other Side, the world of darkness, and Mr. Cohn and Fergis servants of the Evil One, and Madame Estella a witch?

Feigl stopped crying as quickly as she had started, wiping her face in the sleeve of her nightdress. The wild look in her eyes was gone; she had only the sad, resigned expression of a calf in the *shochet*'s yard.

"Ask Yitzhak about his dream," she said quietly. "Ask him if we have indeed come to the place of his dreams."

I knew now we had to escape as soon as Feigl and the baby were able to travel. We would take Maizie with us; she was familiar with the country. I thought about this, but I did not confide in anyone yet. I was afraid Yitzhak would do something reckless and ruin everything. Above all I did not want Madame Estella to discover my suspicions of her. It was safer to allow her to believe that I trusted her, and so as I became more proficient in her language, I even sought out her company.

Estella acquainted me with her frustrations and her loneliness; she was glad of a confidante. I listened humbly and eagerly, alert to any sign she might give of her real nature and intentions. Like her husband, she had always considered Polish Jews primitive and superstitious, persecuted and impoverished because of their failure to develop enough to mix unobtrusively with Gentiles. Yet she wheedled and hinted; she wanted to know if it was true that some of those old country rebbes could make miracles—make fruit to grow on a withered tree, make a child grow in a dry womb. She had heard that Yitzhak had studied with such a miracle worker. Was it perhaps true, then? And perhaps Yitzhak?

When she finally came out with it, I only looked dumbly at her. As if my own barrenness were not obvious! And she thought *me* a fool, illiterate village girl that I was. What could I say if I was not to burst out laughing? I told her that Yitzhak and I had been married for nearly ten years, and I had never yet been pregnant. Tears came to her eyes, but they were tears of disappointment for herself rather than sympathy for me.

I almost pitied her. She was a selfish and cruel woman, but I did not believe anymore that she was a witch. After all, my own mother, may her soul rest in peace, had been called a witch by ignorant people, and I had nearly been called one myself. How did I know whether witches and devils were real, or just grandmother-stories invented by ignorant, unhappy people? Feigl was disheartened, in an unfamiliar place, and she had always had a nervous temperament. She was like a tree, not so easily uprooted and transplanted in a distant land. It had affected her mind. In a little more than a month, her baby would be born—God willing, healthy—and she would recover her senses.

Yitzhak was miserable in the countinghouse; his face was strained, and he sighed when he woke in the morning. Like myself, he did not like to be closed up inside all day, and I at least had the relief of the odd errand in the orchard or garden. And Cohn was as dissatisfied with Yitzhak's work as Yitzhak was himself. One morning, after the others had gone to work, I overheard him talking to Estella in the library.

I was in the hall, struggling with a tray of freshly filled jars for the cellar. I heard his newspaper crackling, and then his voice. "Those kikes of Eisik's will be the ruin of me," he said. "Asher at least has some sense for business, but Yitzhak!"

I rested the edge of the tray against the wall and listened.

"He sits over my account books all day and gabbles about medieval philosophy!"

"Perhaps more suitable work could be found for him." I heard Estella's voice.

Cohn snorted. "We certainly don't need another rabbi in this town," he said. "Especially not one of these Polish wailers! Have you heard him in the yard? He howls like a Negro at a camp meeting!"

"They are backward," she agreed. "But they may yet learn to be Americans in time. I believe Chana is not as simple as she looks."

My face burned, and the jars shook on the tray. I went quickly, before I was discovered, but I could not forget what I had heard. What if we did not become Americans quickly enough?

That night I crept close to Yitzhak to feel his arms around me. He asked what was wrong, but I couldn't tell him. I lay next to him, holding back my tears. And I prayed, as I had prayed in my childhood, over and over, *Creator of the Universe, please deliver me.* And in the moments before I finally fell asleep, a bright picture came before my eyes. Yitzhak and I sat high on a wagon, on a country road such as the road into the countryside here, and I could almost see around the bend of it a plain where tall, white grass waved and rippled like the ocean we had crossed.

Even while Cohn made his objections and conditions, I could see the relief on his face at the idea that Yitzhak might become a tinker and peddler again. Many great merchant houses had begun in just this way, Cohn said, though I knew he never imagined such success for Yitzhak. And I was to go out with him, because my English was better. So I escaped the steamy kitchen and that suffocating house at last!

But the joy I felt when we went out in the wagon was spoiled by my guilt at leaving poor Feigl behind. Maizie or

Sally could bring her tea and fruit, but she would have no one to talk to. I told myself that she needed more rest this late in her pregnancy. And I was certain this was a good step for us, because it was a step—even though a small one—away from the Cohns.

Yitzhak always wanted to go a little farther, and that day he had taken us on a different road, one that went by the river. The light came softly down through the trees and dappled the road, and I caught the smell of the river and saw glimpses of its smooth, brown surface just beyond a row of trees. But I was worried; it was growing late, and I wondered if we were lost. Yitzhak pretended to know exactly where we were; that was his way.

When we came on the strange little town of tents in the woods, with the people all singing and shouting, I wanted to keep going, but Yitzhak leaped from the wagon before I could stop him. I had been uneasy and anxious all day, without knowing why, and now I was sure my premonition of misfortune would be realized. I was angry, too—it was so like Yitzhak not to think of me at all, but just to go wherever he pleased. Now he might be risking his life, and even if he came back safely, it was late. Did he think the sun would stand still for him? I was not sure how to find our way back in the daylight; how would it be when night fell?

And how he came running back, as if he were chased by demons! He drove the poor horse so fast that I forgot even to be surprised when, at the next crossing, we met the familiar road to town. He was too upset and too intent on driving to tell me what had happened in that place. And, of course, what met us on our return drove all other thoughts from my mind.

The sun had just set when we reached home. Albert ran out to take care of the exhausted horse.

"Miz Honey," he said to me excitedly, "Miz Fay is sho' goin' to be happy to see you."

As soon as he spoke, I knew, and this time it was I who leaped from the wagon running.

In the dining room, Mr. Cohn sat alone at the long table, eating supper. I ran past him up the stairs to Feigl's room.

Her skin was waxy, beaded with sweat. She was not crying out, but her breath was heavy; her huge belly heaved under the covers.

Maizie tried to wipe Feigl's face with a cool cloth, but Feigl pushed her away. She was staring at Madame Estella, who stood at the foot of the bed, her lips tightly pressed together, wringing her hands.

Feigl's eyes were so filled with pain I could not meet them.

"Chana," she whispered hoarsely. "Get her out."

Estella did not know Yiddish, but she understood. She flushed a deep red.

"They must be finished with supper now; I'll send Albert for the midwife." Her words seemed to push her out of the room.

I stroked Feigl's forehead and took the cloth from Maizie.

"She won' let me touch her, Miz Honey," Maizie complained.

I bent down to hear. Feigl was still muttering quietly. "Something is wrong, she has done something to me. I have been a mother before; this is worse, worse pain. Something is wrong, she has made a spell."

I tried to comfort her. "Cry, Feigele, scream. Let it come out. It will be all right. Rachel is already seven years old, you have forgotten." I remembered something then, from Poland. "Maizie, bring me a piece chalk."

Maizie fled the room. Feigl moaned now. "Keep them away, keep them away," she said, in a strange low voice that was like both a whisper and a scream.

I held her hands tightly in mine. "It will come soon, Feigl, don't worry. In a minute I'll go for Yitzhak and ask him to pray."

144

"They have already gone to the shul, all the men, and the boys, too. Oh, if only I could have gone to my poor parents' graves before we came to this place!" Feigl wailed, then caught her breath as her belly tightened with another pang.

Maizie hurried in with a piece of soft limestone. I made a circle on the floor around Feigl's bed, and drew signs on the wall like the ones the midwife in my old village had drawn for Rivka. I wished then I knew how to write, for special words would help, too, but what could I do?

"Feigl, listen." What a fool I was to think I could reason with a woman in labor! "Maizie is good, let her stay with you for a minute while I speak to Yitzhak. He knows special prayers from his rebbe, he can. . . ."

She clutched at my hand, her eyes pleading. I was helpless, I did not even know if the prayers of Yitzhak's rebbe would still be effective in America. As I tried to ease her, Madame Estella returned with the midwife, a stout, stern-faced German woman of middle age, dressed in black, with a white apron like a butcher's.

Feigl screamed out loud then, and her terror chilled me. "God help me, another one!"

Estella spoke tersely. "Chana, go and eat something now," she said. "She will be fine, you can come back and see her in a minute. Mrs. Weiner is the best midwife in the county."

I leaned close to kiss Feigl's wet cheek. "I'm coming back, don't worry," I said.

I could not eat. Yitzhak met my eyes. His face was awful, but I could not speak to him in front of Cohn. In the hallway, we whispered together.

He closed his eyes, struggling with his tears. "I must speak with her," he said.

I led him upstairs. Estella and the midwife tried to keep him out, but just as he was about to give in to them, Feigl screamed, and he pushed them aside, and I followed.

Yitzhak knelt by her bed and took her hand.

Feigl looked at her brother. In that moment, her mind seemed completely clear.

"No, Yitzhak," she said firmly. "Let me go. I do not want to live here anymore."

"But Feigl!" Yitzhak sobbed. "Feigl! Think of the child!"

"It is too late," Feigl said. "The she-devil has already taken my soul, now she will have my child. Even God can do nothing for me."

Yitzhak, crying, moved his lips as he held her hand. He reached to stroke her head.

"You must leave her!" Estella shouted. "Leave this room at once, you are straining her! It is not a thing for a man!"

"Please, Madame Estella, they are twins!" I ran to block her path toward Feigl's bed.

In the middle of Yitzhak's prayer: "You who are the Master of All the Worlds, the Creator, Master of life and of death. . . . *L'shem yichud kudsha brichu, Ush—*" Feigl spoke, faint but firm:

"Good-bye, brother. You and your God cannot help me now."

Estella and the midwife together, shoving past me, pushed Yitzhak from the room, and weeping, I followed him.

He sobbed as he spoke to me in our room. "Ah, don't you see? It is all up to Him, to Him! If she refuses me, I can do nothing; I am no magician!"

Feigl screamed all night and the next day. The following night she was too hoarse to make a sound, and the midwife left, shaking her head, to fetch the doctor.

How can I bear to recall my own despair and horror! Feigl's labor was too hard, it lasted too long. She was lost, lost! Yitzhak suffered in his own hell; my pleas to him to call on his rebbe were useless. Estella made Maizie scrub the chalk marks from the wall and floor; Yitzhak prayed in the shul with the others, but they were only the ordinary prayers that had failed to help so many poor Jews, in the old world or the new. The doctor came in a fine coach with a big leather bag.

And Feigl found voice again for screams that made my hair stand on end. In my desperation I called on the God I had known on the ocean, as if that Power were not too vast and impersonal to attend to one poor Jewish woman.

At first it seemed that both mother and child survived the awful delivery. The baby boy was well, though it would be months before his head would heal from the scars and misshaping gouged by the doctor's instruments. But by the end of the following day, Feigl was delirious with a high fever, which the doctor's leeches and calomel did not relieve. My fragile faith collapsed and broke apart over the grim days that followed as Feigl suffered and declined. Estella sent to her parents in Charleston for a wet nurse, a slave girl whose baby had died, and a *mohel* came to make the boy's *bris* on the eighth day, but there was no joy in it, for already Feigl was dead.

11

CHANA

MAIZIE COMPLAINED that it was one of the coldest winters ever, though I did not think it nearly as bitter as our winters in Poland. Yet a bleak feeling enveloped me like the shroud Feigl had been buried in. Through her agony I had clung to a vain hope that she would recover, and I had not completely felt my hope fail until I saw her laid out, white and still as a wax figure, with candles at her head and feet. Then a sob had wrenched its way out of me, until I groaned and screamed and could not stop, like a wolf with its leg caught in a trap. That cry of mine set all the children to howling, even Yonah and Natan, who thought they had outgrown their mother, yet cried out loud like babies as they looked upon her empty shell.

We wailed and tore our clothes; I thought Asher would rip his beard out by the roots. I heard Mr. Cohn clear his throat, and saw Estella's tense, uncomfortable face. I howled even louder, perversely wanting to deepen their shame. It was their fault; with their German ways, their American ways, they had frightened poor Feigl to death. Now Estella's arms tightened around Feigl's baby. Asher had named him Mendel, after Feigl and Yitzhak's father, the Rebbe of Przemysl.

That winter their house was for me as cold and dark as a grave. Feigl's worst fear, that Estella would take her baby, now seemed realized. Estella did not want me to care for Mendel; she played with him herself and gave him to the wet nurse or Maizie when she tired of him.

Maizie took Rachel and Levi to the schoolhouse every morning and called for them in the afternoon. Though I knew Rachel badly suffered from the loss of her mother, I hardly had a chance to comfort her. Asher was like a dead man himself, yet one cruelly prevented by fate from joining his beloved in heaven; he wandered between earth and hell. And as for his new baby son, once he had named him, Asher acted as though he did not exist; he could not bring himself even to look at him.

What was Yitzhak thinking of all that winter? He hardly spoke to me; he was lost in his own world, a stranger. Perhaps he was ashamed that he had failed to save Feigl; in my own heart, I thought perhaps he should be. Perhaps he told the truth when he said he could not heal her against her own will, but I could not believe he had done all he could to save her. When I watched him sleep, I could see how his dreams tortured him, but he did not confide in me, nor I in him.

And I dreamed, too. Night after night I saw us riding high on a wagon, crossing an ocean that was not an ocean, but a flat land that stretched as far as we could see. Above us, white wisps of cloud played in a sky so clear and blue that I knew we were in heaven, and then I knew that I was dreaming. And how cruel it seemed, to wake every morning from that bright heaven into the dark hell of the Cohns' house.

There was no house of study in St. Louis, and Asher and Yitzhak spent the winter evenings reading and discussing over a table in the corner of the parlor. Yitzhak always began with a simple lesson for Levi, and Rachel insisted on joining them. It was the American way; she went to American school with Levi, why should she not learn Hebrew as well? Asher tried to make Yonah and Natan study, too, but they were Americans now who had no use for their father's foreign ways; he had no authority in this house. So Yitzhak and Asher pored over the moldy books they had carried all the way from Poland. How I resented that those old books had survived our journey, when dear Feigl had not! And it seemed that only in study did Yitzhak and Asher come to life. They twisted their hair and tugged at their beards and waved their hands around as they argued, for all the world as if they had never left Ropshitz.

With my clumsy fingers I began the tedious work of completing the blanket Feigl had been knitting. The difference between her work and mine was night and day, Poland and America. Her stitches made tight, even rows; she had woven the many colors into beautiful designs, bright as a field of flowers. My work was knobbly and uneven, the colors muddled. Yet I continued stubbornly, sitting by the fire that gave no warmth to my soul.

There were not many winter days when the road was clear enough for the wagon, so with his meager English, Yitzhak began to clerk in the store. I had not much to do; Estella seemed to have forgotten about me. I sometimes slipped out to the barn to talk with Nell and the other horses; as in Poland, I felt the animals were my only friends. In my melancholy and loneliness, I scarcely thought anymore about our escape.

The weather had been clear and cold for several days, and a messenger from the store came to the house to say that a very large shipment of goods had come in on the river. Mr. Cohn and the others were staying at the store for dinner to save time in unpacking and checking the bills. I helped pack the food—meats, breads, soup, dishes of preserved vegetables, three pies—and went with Albert to bring the meal to the men at the store.

I was warm in the coach, with the steaming pails and packages of food around me. I had hardly been out-of-doors for weeks. I stared out at our street, quiet and white, as we turned onto the wider boulevard that led into the center of town. There were other coaches, wagons, people walking and riding. Though I had been in the city before with Yitzhak when we were peddling, I had never really looked around. Now, as I watched the busy street and the people who crowded the sidewalks, I remembered Cracow, where we had been only a year before. Only a year—yet it might as well have been a hundred. Cracow had been dark and closed; crowded with old, stone buildings carved with figures, a city sighing and weeping in the sounds of Polish and Yiddish. While we had suffered awfully there, our suffering had not seemed to be ours alone, but ingrained in the very stones of the city; it was in the normal order of things to suffer there. In America it seemed almost unnatural to be unhappy.

The warm, spicy smells of the dinner I carried filled my head. There was more food riding in this little coach with me now than ten of us had shared that whole winter in Cracow, until God took pity on us and led Yitzhak to Reb Eisik! It was God Who had led us here, across that marvelous ocean. And if He could do that, what could He not do?

Yitzhak was only His servant. However he might have fallen short, if it were not for him I would still be starving in Poland, or dead from a pogrom or cholera. I was ashamed that I had been bitter against him over Feigl's death, as if I blamed him. I had thought he hardly spoke to me now, but it was I who had not let him approach my sorrow. I felt a flood of remorse and love for him. He had tried his best. He was a man straddling a chasm, one foot in the world above, where God ruled, and one in the everyday world, where he struggled to bring the will of that One to earth.

The streets around me came to life. The snowy surfaces gleamed in the sun; the icicles hanging from the eaves of the buildings glittered like diamonds. I wondered about the different people crowding the sidewalks and streets. Who were these three rough men, with red faces and bushy beards, wearing battered clothes and hats made of animal fur with the tails hanging down behind them? Were they hunters, come in from the forest for the winter while their quarry slept in caves? And that one must be an Indian: the tall, lean man with his deeply lined face, his long, black hair tied at the nape of his neck, a bright red and black blanket over his shoulders. Was he, too, a visitor from the forest? Had he a wife somewhere? Two gaily dressed girls, furs thrown over their richly colored skirts, laughed as they picked their way over the icy sidewalk like two cats. I thought I recognized them; they were Jewish girls, sisters I had seen in the synagogue. I envied them painfully, not for their pretty hats and fine furs, but for their freedom and liveliness.

The buildings of St. Louis were wood and brick, newer and seemingly more temporary than the heavy stones of Cracow. They rose from wide, straight avenues as different as could be from the narrow, crooked streets of Polish cities. And the people were somehow green, like trees. The Jews here were not like the Jews of Poland—Cohn was right—because here they were Americans, too. They did not dwell on the misery of the past, but looked with hope to whatever might lie ahead in the future.

In the huge front room of the store, an enormous profusion of goods was stacked on open shelves and spread over the counters, even hung on the walls. A dozen men sat by the stove in the corner, waving their pipes and arguing. A long counter was lined with big glass jars, filled with colored candy. Clusters of children pointed and chattered as they made their choices. I recognized the clerk, one of Yonah and Natan's friends; with his round, self-satisfied face and shiny black hair and mustache, I could see why the boys admired him.

Yitzhak was working with the other men and boys,

opening crates of blankets, pots and kettles, men's clothing, and long guns. Mr. Cohn looked on, dictating figures to Asher, who checked them on a paper. The room was warm; sweat beaded on Yitzhak's brow. I couldn't remember when I had been so happy to see him.

"It's for the army," he explained. "Big business."

"What army?" I looked at the guns. So many! Rifles, they were called; I knew Mr. Cohn had given such guns to Yonah and Natan to hunt rabbits and squirrels.

Yitzhak shrugged. "To go to Mexico," he said. "With General Taylor."

But we weren't thinking of Mexico or of General Taylor, or of any war at all. My husband and I were looking into each other's eyes for the first time in many weeks. I wanted to take his hand, to touch him, but we couldn't even talk here.

"Chana . . ." Yitzhak said my name, very softly.

Mr. Cohn looked up from his pile of papers and saw me.

"Boys!" he said, raising his hand in the air. "Boys! Dinner is here!" He took his large gold watch from his vest pocket. "Thirty minutes!"

After supper that evening, we sat in the parlor together. Mr. Cohn crackled his newspapers and talked about the war. "The knock of a great opportunity," he called it. Yonah and Natan, who understood him best, nodded attentively. Yitzhak frowned, perplexed.

I was always curious about the sounds and meanings of new words, trying to connect them to things I knew. But these new words were a mystery: John Bull, Oregon, 54–40, Texas. I understood they were places in the West, a wilderness that reached even to another ocean; God had meant them to be part of America. Cohn believed that countries had destinies just as men did, that it was the will of our God that the United States reach from one ocean to another. "The promised land," Cohn called it, and that made me shiver; it made me think of those terrible stories about Joshua and the Israelites. . . . *And smote with the edge of the sword*. That was what the guns were for.

"I'd like to shoot a few redskins myself," said Natan brightly. He raised his hands as if holding a rifle, and made noises: "Or Mexicans! Pew! Pew!"

"Vos?" Asher, alarmed, looked at his son.

Cohn looked at Natan approvingly. "Well, my boy, you may get your chance yet. Perhaps you and your brother can make your fortunes out West; others have. The fur trade may be nearly gone, but who knows what other riches lie there!"

Natan, encouraged, went on. "Silas at the store says in Oregon they've got land for everyone, big spreads, and no snow in the winter, but spring all year 'round. Why, he says his pa says you can get three crops a year."

"And what makes you think you could grow anything?" responded Yonah. "You're no farmer."

"Could so!" said Natan.

"You never could!" Yonah could not leave his younger brother alone; he always knew more. "Besides, Silas and his pa don't know nothing. Everyone says California's better."

Levi made popping noises and pointed his finger at Rachel. "Injun!" he said. "Yer dead!"

Estella cleared her throat. Mr. Cohn glared. Asher looked at his sons, bewildered. But it was Yitzhak who spoke to Natan.

"Natan, *vos ist,* Oregon?"

Both boys tried to speak at once, but Cohn hushed them. "Oregon is a vast and verdant territory in the West, beyond the desert, Salomon," he said. "There are only a few white settlements there now, but the Indians are friendly and the land is good. I expect soon the territory will be under the full protection of the United States, if John Bull knows what's good for him and leaves gracefully without our having to boot him out." He winked at the boys. "Certainly,

there are great opportunities for farmers—and traders—
who have the courage to cross the wilderness."

Yitzhak nodded uncertainly; I didn't think he had understood. I spoke to him softly in Yiddish.

"Yitzhak, it is another country to the west. It's far away,
over a desert, and there are Indians, and a great bull."

Yonah heard me and snorted. "Not a real bull, Tanta
Chana, it's England. They call England 'John Bull.' Oregon
belongs both to England and the United States now, but
President Polk will soon have it all for us, won't he, Mr.
Cohn?"

"Certainly," he beamed. "And no doubt we'll take Texas
and California as well!"

Yitzhak half-smiled, as if he knew a secret. "Across the
desert," he said quietly. "Yes."

Mr. Cohn gave him an odd, sideways look and turned
back to his paper.

"I see those damnable Mormons have been run out of
Illinois now," he grunted. "Peculiar, clannish folk. Fanatics. We had enough of them in Missouri. Latter-Day Saints
indeed!"

None of us knew who he was talking about, but I did not
like to think of anyone driven from their homes. After all, it
had happened to us. Chaim Loeb yawned. Asher and Yaacov,
too, had grown tired of trying to follow the conversation. It
was growing late. One by one we excused ourselves. Yaacov
passed by Levi's chair as he left and kissed the top of his
son's head. He said good night to him, speaking gently in
Yiddish. "Better you study, little one, than be so eager for
shooting. We have all seen enough of death."

I lay down beside Yitzhak with a strange feeling in my heart.
For the first time since Feigl's death, he seemed to be aware
of what was going on around him. His mouth formed the
word *Oregon* the way I had once before seen it form the
word *ocean*.

He reached for my hand. "Chanale, even in this dark place are the holy sparks of light. Can you not see them dancing?"

I said nothing. If he could see such light in this dark room, in this dark house, I still could not. But I reminded myself that his ability to see what I could not had saved me from dying in Poland. "You want to go to this Oregon," I said.

"I want us to go across the desert," he said.

What could I say? My eyes were closed. Like an after-image on the inside of my eyelids, I saw the high wagon, Yitzhak and myself seated on the box. All around us were other wagons, horses, mules, oxen. Tall grass was around us, rustling.

"So why not?" I smiled to myself. "Do you remember when we lived in Ropshitz, how Feigl teased you?" It was the first time since her death that I had spoken her name aloud. "When she said you would be like Moses and lead us through the desert?"

"Ah, Feigl," he sighed. "I still am no Moses."

"So?" I asked him. Something broke loose inside me, like a spring of fresh water gushing forth from a rock. I wanted to laugh! "Do you think that Cohn is a pharaoh?"

I did laugh then, and Yitzhak with me. We held each other, laughing like idiots, too stupid to have any fear of the future.

"I doubt very much you have what it takes to be a pioneer, Salomon," Mr. Cohn said. "To begin with, there's the expense."

Yes, I thought sadly. We had nothing of our own, and no prospects except to continue working for Mr. Cohn and his store.

"Could we not do business for you there, Mr. Cohn? Take a wagon with goods to sell and send you the money? Or even make a store there in Oregon?" I blushed as I said this, remembering our dismal failure with the store we had kept for Ephraim in my village.

Mr. Cohn shook his head. "Mrs. Salomon, it's not only the money. It's no place for a woman, and your husband hardly speaks English! It's one thing to mend a few pots and pans around here. But out West, there's a rough game. Why, those old trappers around the stove at the store could certainly tell you!" He took another sip of coffee. "I sent a train of wagons out to Mexico a few years ago on the Santa Fe and lost everything! Six good men, three wagons, and a fair-sized herd of horses and oxen, and the Comanches took it all. Murdered those poor souls and left their bones to rot on the trail. No, no, I shouldn't think that life is for you."

Yitzhak pulled his beard. "We have Yonah and Natan," he said. "They are good shooters, no?"

Cohn shook his head impatiently. He called the boys by the American names they used with their friends and at the store. "Johnny and Nate are good boys, Salomon, they're quick learners. But they're still pretty green. Sure, they can bring in a squirrel or a rabbit, but how would they do against a war party of wild savages?" He laughed. "Give them another year or two."

"*Vos ist,* 'green'?" Yitzhak asked me, under his breath.

"I think he means they are still too young," I whispered. "They don't really know enough American, either."

Cohn was looking out the window, drumming his fingers. I watched his jaw working under his beard. Behind him through the window was a veil of low, gray clouds; soon it would rain. A flash of sunlight suddenly penetrated the lead-colored sky. Yes, I saw, the sun is always there, though often we cannot see it through the clouds. How little we see, really, of all that is! For a moment, I saw the room fill with light, but I could have imagined it. In that light I saw the image I had seen so often in my dreams: the wagon, the ocean of grass, Yitzhak, myself. As the light moved, I saw that ocean of grass give way to a stark, white plain—just for an

instant—and then I was back in the room. Yitzhak was looking at Cohn with the deepest concentration; it almost
seemed the light came from my husband's intent face
rather than from the window.

Cohn spoke again, more to himself than to us. I held my
breath.

"Hmm, well, after all, I suppose something must be
found for you. They say the new trail to Oregon's a bit
rougher than the Santa Fe, but the Sioux are less ferocious
than the Comanches, and there's the advantage to going out
early. The early bird gets the worm. Why should the other
fellows have all that profit, hmm?" He turned to Yitzhak.
"Salomon, I know you are a religious man. I admire your
faith; you are obviously quite devout. Quite devout," he repeated, staring at Yitzhak. "You've come this far on your
faith, why not a little farther? Perhaps we can find a party
for you to go out with. Perhaps you can set up a store somewhere on the trail or even in Oregon territory. I believe
Lieber at our synagogue here knows someone out at Fort
Bridger. You need to practice your English. I suppose you
had better learn to shoot, too. I'll talk to Lieber."

He stood. The interview was over.

That year Passover came early, in a season of cold rain and
wind when the snow was hardly off the ground. The hole
that Feigl's death had torn in our lives was slowly beginning
to close over. I finished the blanket, and though my handi-
work was awkward, I felt that in completing what Feigl had
started, I had put a seal on our friendship, our sisterhood.
Estella thought the blanket ridiculous—half worked in
Feigl's careful, exquisite style and half thrown together in an
untidy hodgepodge—but I put it away for Rachel.

Baby Mendel was growing strong, and Asher had begun
to take an interest in him. Yaacov was teaching Levi and
Rachel to ride. She rode astride, like a boy, to Estella's dismay and Levi's delight. Though we had no more discussion

with Mr. Cohn about going West, I knew the strength of Yitzhak's intention, and I was confident that we would leave St. Louis in the spring. Like the blanket that Feigl and I had made together, that knowledge was something to put away for the future.

But for three weeks I had not time to consider anything; I labored with Sally and Maizie under Estella's direction to make every inch of the big house spotless for *Pesach*. Every corner must be aired, every surface polished, every crumb removed. When the sun came out, we hung all the linens of the house on lines outside, bleached white as fresh snow. When it rained, we grunted and pushed the heavy pieces of furniture aside to clean behind and under them. Finally we were done, and though Estella frowned and sneered as she made her final inspection, I could see she was secretly pleased. And then, grumbling but good-natured, as if he were humoring children for a party, Mr. Cohn performed the traditional ritual with feather and brush, to look for the last crumb in the house and burn it.

Sally worked as hard as three ordinary people, roasting several chickens and an entire lamb. Vegetable dishes, kugels, and puddings were prepared with all the care and attention to kashruth that the *rebbetzin,* the rabbi's wife, of my old village would have taken. Estella and I picked snowdrops, crocuses, and sweetly fragrant white narcis-suses for the table. There would be guests; among them the shammes at the synagogue and his new wife, and a whole family of Liebers. Mr. Cohn had sent for kosher wine from Germany; the matzoh had been shipped down the river from Cleveland.

This was the "bread of affliction" that Mr. Cohn raised high above the table to begin the seder. Levi asked the four questions, and Cohn began the story: "Once, we were slaves in Egypt. . . ." Maizie's kerchiefed head dipped as she brought and removed dishes. "Once we were slaves in Egypt. . . ." Now in America also there were slaves. I was dizzy from the wine, served in glasses the size of small pitchers. I heard the familiar story of the Exodus and thought of our own exile, and imagined crossing an ocean or a desert, going toward our real home, where we were meant to be.

The door was opened for Elijah, the last glass of wine poured, and the last prayers said. Estella sat at her piano and asked Chaim Loeb to play with her. I saw in his face that he, too, was remembering the long way we had come. But none of us could have imagined the journey we were yet to undertake.

12

YITZHAK

Feigl's death cast Yitzhak into a dark vortex that he had no will to struggle out of. Chana's silent accusations, the way she shrank from him in their bed, did not encourage him to speak of his grief and his guilt. He felt knocked off balance by the loss of an invisible leg; he had not realized how much he needed his twin. Now she was gone, and he was answerable.

His moment of ecstasy and treachery in the Christian tent had deeply shamed him. Among those worshippers of the goyische God, he had seen the Divine Light as clearly as he ever had in the court of Shmuel Salomon. His vision—and mortification—had still been with him as he entered the house. He knew with excruciating clarity what was to be, even as Chana pushed past him and ran up the stairs. Feigl would not live; she would leave this world even as she brought her child into it. And whatever of Shmuel Salomon's power might still remain with him after his heresy, he would be helpless to save her.

Feigl had already left her spirit behind in the old country: she had never really come to America at all. And that was why she had not allowed him to call on his rebbe to save her; she did not care anymore to live.

He remembered their childhood, how she had plucked the telltale strands of hay from his coat when he came in from wandering in the fields. "Is there hay now in the house of study?" she would ask playfully. "For all the donkey-donk-donkeys there?" For all her foolishness, she had always known that this world is only a vestibule for the world-to-come; that we are meant only to prepare ourselves here to enter into the banquet room beyond. She had led a pure and simple life, free from the spiritual pride he was cursed with. Not that she was punished for his sins—her lucky soul would live in paradise. No, her death was punishment for him: he was severed forever from his twin. "Of course I know what you think-think-think," she had said when they were children. "We shared the same breath before we were born." He had not wanted to acknowledge their deep connection, and now self-reproach chafed his heart to a raw sore.

Out of the fire that consumed the world in his dream, from the cloud of smoke above the huge wheeled boxes, appeared Shmuel Salomon, his guide and teacher. He appeared in Yitzhak's tortured dream, not as the kind, cryptic teacher of his youth in the court at Cracow, nor as that sprite who danced over the waves of the Atlantic. This rebbe rode high on a fearsome black horse, foaming with sweat. His countenance was terrifying as he bore down on Yitzhak. *Still here?* he thundered. *Have you not yet gone forth to your destiny?* The rebbe's fierce, wizened face burst into flame and glowed white, like burning ice. The echo of his voice hung in the dream sky like the northern lights.

Yitzhak woke with his throat parched and dry, as if he had been screaming or crossing a desert. He lay trembling, desperately penitent. In the months he had been in America he had prayed, but he had forgotten the essence, the wine, of devotion. Had he become as dry and empty a shell for the Lord as his father had been? Asher, Yaacov, Chaim Loeb—they had entrusted not only their lives, but even their souls

162

to him, and he, his head in a cloud of fantasy, had stumbled into a pit and dragged them with him.

Shmuel Salomon had said that oblivion is the root of exile and remembrance the root of redemption. Yitzhak had not only forgotten, but forgotten that he had forgotten. His mind raced as if he had a fever. Aware of Chana beside him, he was sure that she, too, had the secret that Feigl had known, the secret of remembering so well that you no longer knew you were remembering, because it was part of you, in your veins, your bones. He longed to immerse himself in her, to remember it there.

But Chana had set a wall between them; she would not meet his eyes or touch him. She would not even place an object in his hand, but pointed when he asked for something, as if it was a certain time of the month. Except that now it was he who was unclean.

What have you forgotten? roared the ferocious rebbe of his dreams. Tears sprang to Yitzhak's eyes. He had not only lost his sister, but his soul; he had lost the Torah, more precious than life itself. "Turn it and turn it for all is in it and look in it and grow gray and old in it, and turn not away from it, for there is no better rule for thee than it." Eisik had used to quote that ancient scholar—who was it? Yitzhak had forgotten that, too.

He vowed to turn back to Torah, back to his books, the books of law and wisdom, the sayings of the Fathers. He would retrace his steps until he found again his own heart. Study was not the only thing he had forgotten in this country, but at least it was a place to begin. He read with Asher; they repeated the ancient arguments. Asher was a good adversary; he had once studied at the court of Yitzhak's father. At times Yaacov and Chaim Loeb joined them, and the little children, Levi and Rachel.

One evening, as he and Asher argued through the explications of commentaries, and commentaries on explications, Yitzhak stopped in confusion.

"What is it?" Asher asked. "Are you all right?" It was very late, they were alone, a low fire still burned.

Yitzhak blushed. "I forgot. I forgot where I was."

Asher looked at him sharply. "Then go back to the beginning!" he said. "But tomorrow, please. It is late now."

"Yes," Yitzhak sighed. The beginning. Upstairs, as he removed his clothes for bed and lay down to say his last prayers of the day, he saw: the beginning. The beginning was not in books or in the observance of medieval rules. The beginning was Moses. Moses, who talked with the *I AM*. Moses, who knew and spoke the Secret Name. Who crossed the desert.

For every Moses there is a pharaoh. Yitzhak now cursed himself for not responding to Asher's complaints about Cohn and the German-American Jews. They rode in coaches to the shul and even worked on Shabbos, the holiest gift of the Holy One to His people. They were idolators, worshipping the images graven on their golden coins. Asher had warned him; he had been speaking also for Feigl, even for that lost part of himself. Feigl had not been able to truly leave Poland, but Yitzhak had not been able to carry anything with him; his crossing was so complete that it had left him bereft.

But his failure to observe the Law, the *Shulchan Arukh*, was not so serious an affront to the Holy One as the absence of passion in his worship. He had become so accustomed to the indifferent practices of the so-called American Jews that he had come not only to tolerate the American ways, but to feel inferior. Gradually his own worship had become as formal and anemic as theirs.

Their dependence on Cohn's charity for every crumb had forced him to acquiesce, had made him powerless even to pray in his own way, his rebbe's way. His tiny band was spinning apart. How could he be their guide when he had always to look to Cohn for his bread, his shelter? He heard the thundering voice of his rebbe: *You should have been looking to God.*

His suppressed passion enflamed him; the full force of his feeling turned against his keeper. The bloodless, materialistic mold Cohn forced them into was choking the breath from their souls. Yitzhak seethed. Cohn's features appeared to coarsen, his voice sounded like the braying of a donkey.

Through the mysterious current that flowed between them, Chana sensed that he had changed and began to soften. She embraced him again; the wall that had been between them vanished. Her tenderness made a refuge for him from his excruciating fury. His renewed sense of responsibility now made him clever. If they were to survive and escape, he must become more fluent in the American language, the American ways. He prevailed on Chana to tutor him. As he struggled with words and phrases, gradually his awareness widened, he took more notice of the world outside.

Though he could not speak more than a few words, he listened to conversations around him, the talk of people whose existence he had hardly acknowledged before. He worked at the store now, checking shipments as they were brought in or sent out. He counted: so many boxes of cotton cloth, so many blankets, so many ladies' hat forms. The men were young and rough and loud; what Yonah and Natan admired so much, Yitzhak found a little fearsome. He was amazed at how large people grew in this country. They had a confident swagger about them, so different from the sly subservience of Polish peasants. They laughed and talked while they worked. A tall boy with a yellow beard wanted to join the army; the others laughed and called him a fool.

"Say what you will," he laughed back. "They say ev'ry man what volunteers to Mexico will have a piece of free land out there—sixty fine acres!"

"You won't catch me marchin' for anythin', but I'd go for Oregon," said Silas, a young man wielding a crowbar.

Yitzhak knew him a little; he was a friend of Yonah and Natan's. "My pa an' my uncles'r talkin' about sellin' the farm to a couple Irishmen, an' outfittin' ourselves for Oregon, come spring."

Yitzhak heard the word: *Oregon.* The sound swung wide, like a gate. He would ask the boys what it was. His mind wandered. With a start, he realized the men had moved on to another crate before he had finished checking the contents of the last one.

"Wait!" Yitzhak held up his hand. "Wait! What was?"

Wrapped in a wool coat, a fur cap on his head, Yitzhak walked in the icy fields beyond the house. This was his evening ritual now, his nightly effort to let the winter air cool his fire. Fueled by the heat inside him, he felt he could walk forever. He strode along the road and then struck out over the partly frozen field behind the barn, passing near the slave cabins. The slave cabins! How had he lived here without noticing this added evidence of Cohn's perfidy? Even the men at the store argued about it, the wrongness of keeping slaves.

In the soft silence of winter dusk, his ear was caught by the sound of voices from the barn. He slowed his step. Was it voices he heard or only the wind? At first he did not think of stopping, but something drew him closer.

It was Mrs. Cohn's voice—Estella's—rising and falling. What was she doing in the barn? "You took it," he heard her say angrily. "Thief!" There was the low voice of the slave cook, Sally. He heard the sharp sound of a slap, and Mrs. Cohn's shrill voice again. Then another voice—Fergis's. Sally again, pleading. Yitzhak, spellbound, heard the unmistakable sound of a riding crop whistling, landing—on flesh? Yitzhak stood, appalled, unaware of the growing cold. Sally's soft pleading, the whip again, Fergis's grunts, more cries, and—worst of all—Mrs. Cohn's utter silence now. The horrid scene was unmistakably clear. Maddened with revulsion, Yitzhak clenched his fists at the barn door. He would kill them! He imagined bursting in, seizing the whip from Fergis's hand, breaking it into pieces. And then? An inner voice mocked him. You have such courage? The realization of his position fell on him like a weight. *Oh, Master of the World,* he prayed. *See how I am helpless here even to stand for what is right. I am hardly more than a slave myself.* He ran toward the house.

A few evenings later, as they studied together, Yitzhak noticed that Asher's attention was not on the tractate. Their argument, about whether a good heart or good associations were of more benefit, faded into a long silence. With increasing agitation, Yitzhak's mind drifted to his obsession with Cohn.

Asher pulled at his beard, now grown all gray. He coughed, cleared his throat. "Yitzhak, I must tell you something. I want to go home. This country has brought me nothing but *tsuris.* I should have stayed at home."

"Home? What is home?" Yitzhak tried to hold his temper, but his sense of betrayal flashed up like a blaze of dry straw. He stood and paced the room, trying to diffuse some of his outrage in motion. "You mean the home where they beat Chaim Loeb nearly to death? Or the home where we starved?"

Asher shook his head and looked at the floor. "I don't care. At least there, the Jews speak like Jews and look like Jews and pray like Jews."

"Yes, and suffer like Jews!" Yitzhak waved his arms, desperately trying not to shout in the late, silent house.

Asher shrugged. "So, the world is the world, whether it is the old world or the New World. Look, now comes a war, just like Poland! Already Fergis will go to it. Mizz-oo-ree Wol-un-teers." Asher's mouth rolled around the unfamiliar English words.

Yitzhak wanted to shake him. "Asher, you are being a

fool. The war they are talking about is not here but far away, in a place called Mexico! And see, it makes Cohn richer, not poorer. If he loses one man, he can buy ten more."

"War is war. How can you forget so soon? If it is good for Cohn, what has that to do with us?" Asher put his hand on Yitzhak's arm, stopping him, looking at him. "Who else does well in an evil world but a devil?"

Yitzhak sat down, suddenly deflated. He had no argument with Asher's judgment of Cohn; he was only ashamed that Asher had seen Cohn's character before he did. "Well, that is why I want us to go to Oregon. There will be no Cohn there, no heretics. We will build our own synagogue."

Asher laughed a bitter laugh. "A shul for whom? There are no Jews there, either! No, for me, even Poland is better."

Yitzhak heard a buzzing in his ears. He closed his eyes, feeling the hazy aura of a vision he could not quite see, like trying to remember a dream. He blinked. "We can be Jews there, ourselves. And perhaps we will find other Jews there who have forgotten they were Jews."

"You may talk nonsense to yourself all night if you like." Asher stood up. "I am going to bed. And in the spring, God willing, I will borrow money for passage from the welfare fund of this synagogue of unbelievers, and I will go back to Poland with my children. Perhaps there is a widow there who will not find me such a poor match, and I will marry again. And find a Jewish husband for my little Rachele and proper wives for my sons, that they might know the taste of kosher food and live in a decent Jewish home."

"Now you are the one talking nonsense! In Poland your sons will be taken for the czar's armies!"

"And here?" Asher's eyebrows rose nearly to the line of the skullcap that he, like Yitzhak, still wore in defiance of Cohn's jibes. "What difference does it make if they die in the army of the Russian czar or in the army of the American czar?"

"There is no czar in America," Yitzhak said triumphantly.

168

"Here is President Polk!" He couldn't help but be proud of his American facts.

Asher was unimpressed. *"Machs nicht.* Just as I said, it makes no difference. Good night to you."

Yitzhak stared into the dying fire for a long time. His rage, too, had burned down to embers. Asher's defection was a blow; Yitzhak had counted on him—his learning, his steadiness—to help found the new community. He buried his face in his hands. How could Asher be such a blockhead as to want to return to Poland? Perhaps grief had unhinged him.

Yitzhak poked the coals, releasing a tiny spray of sparks. Let him go and be damned, then, he thought. Immediately, he reproached himself. No, no, it is my fault, I am accountable. It is I who brought him here, I must not abandon him, even if he abandons me. Shmuel Salomon used to say that he would follow a disciple even into hell. I cannot let Asher go. How can I convince him that our real religion waits for us in the desert, and beyond? That Poland is the land of the dead, that we cannot return, that we will only redeem ourselves as Jews in that western wilderness of the future? That religion is not a matter of food or candles, but the Living Light itself that permeates everywhere—it is our connection with the One God.

By the end of Cohn's Passover seder, Yitzhak could hardly even listen to the sad sweet airs from Chaim Loeb's violin and Estella's piano; he was so exhausted with the strain of pretense and hypocrisy. In bed at last, he pressed Chana's thin body close to him. He buried his face in her hair, now grown to her shoulders. He could not live without her.

"You think about Oregon, *nu?"* She spoke tenderly to him, as if he were a child.

Beneath his weariness, he was taut with restless energy, almost trembling. "Chana, if you knew the truth, I can hardly bear to spend another night in this house."

"Well, we cannot go tomorrow! You must find a way to live with Cohn a little longer; we cannot possibly go without his help. We need wagons, horses, oxen. Everything must be ready. The dangers don't frighten you a little?"

"Danger? Here is a far worse danger; our souls are in danger! If we die out there, at least we will die saying our own prayers, we can die as Jews! Like those martyrs who chose death rather than conversion."

Chana put her hand over his lips. "*Sha!* Don't talk about such things! I don't want to go there to die, I want to go there to live! And for the children, Feigl's children, and Levi."

Yitzhak's breath was almost a sob. Her mention of the children brought a new anxiety. He had not spoken to Chana of Asher's crazy plan; he had not wanted to think of it. "We won't have the children. Asher doesn't want to go. He wants to go back to Poland."

Chana tensed against him. "No! Yonah and Natan will never go back, and he cannot take Rachel and the baby, either. They will starve there or be beaten to death. Doesn't he remember?"

Yitzhak shrugged. "You remind him. He does not want to listen to me." Had he given up, then? "Yaacov and Chaim Loeb have come all this way, they are such fools that they love me still, even here where I am hardly a rebbe to them."

"Yaacov and Chaim Loeb are not fools," Chana said gently. "Someone else loves you still. But Asher is part of us; he must not go back. You must talk with him again. Feigl cannot be brought back from the other world, and the Poland Asher thinks he remembers cannot be brought back either, or gone back to."

Moonlight flooded the room through the thin, lacy curtains. Yitzhak wondered why he had never noticed them before. And how had he not noticed before how intelligent Chana was? That she knew so well what they must do.

Chana had only paused for breath. "And his sons are Americans now—look at them! They ride and shoot like

170

American boys, they have American names. They want to go to the West, they will never go back to Poland. They are young and foolish; they could go to the army, like Fergis. Natan says—"

Yitzhak interrupted her. "That is why Asher is so angry with America, that the boys could do such things. They don't study Torah. They are hardly Jews anymore. And he is angry with me."

Unspoken feelings moved between them on little currents of air. Chana spoke hesitantly. "Do you remember those nights in Poland when we prayed together after supper? When you made me pray, too, with the men? Feigl was afraid—remember? And Chaim Loeb played; he still had his old violin. That is what Asher wants to go back to."

Yitzhak contracted again with yearning and remorse. "Remember? Chana, I . . ." he stopped. "I tried to pray here with them, in the garden."

She squeezed his hand, pressed her lips together. "No, not that. It was too close to the house, still in Cohn's shadow." She looked into his eyes. "Yitzhak, you must go tomorrow night with Asher, and bring Yaacov and Chaim Loeb too, and tell Chaim Loeb to bring his violin. You must go by the woods, past the barn, by the little stream where we make the *mikvah*. No one comes there, not the Cohns, or Maizie or Sally or Albert. Pray there together, all of you. When Asher hears your rebbe's songs again, feels them in his heart, he will know he belongs with us."

Yitzhak's consternation was not that he thought her plan foolish, but that he had not thought of it himself. Silently, he thanked the Holy One for blessing him with such a marvelous wife. Her conviction reassured him; Asher must go with them, otherwise all of their suffering would be for nothing.

"Yes, Chana. We will pray here, and we will pray in Oregon. The desert will purify us; we will bring my rebbe's songs to the very ends of the earth and find there the last of the holy sparks that fell when the world was created. We will redeem them and ourselves."

Chana laughed. "Will we bring the Messiah, then?"

He didn't answer. Clouds passed over the moon. For a moment, the beauty of the night sky through the window, his wife beside him, stopped his thought.

The sweet fragrance of dogwood and forsythia filled the evening air. A crescent moon hung in the purple sky above the line of trees along the creek. A narrow path was worn through the grass here. An evening bird called out over the shrill rhythm of the crickets.

Yitzhak felt light with excitement and a teasing sensation of danger. He wished Chana had not stayed at the house. As for Yonah and Natan, God alone knew where they went these early spring evenings.

The four men reached the low spot of sand at the edge of the creek, which they had used for a ritual bath. The patch was barely wide enough for them to stand facing each other in a kind of huddle. Chaim Loeb stepped back to raise his violin.

Yitzhak began the *sh'ma*, the salutation with which he had begun every day of his life since he was able to speak. Asher's voice was barely a whisper; Yaacov's only a little stronger. Yitzhak began again, taking strength, trying to find the place that had not been corrupted, that place that could not be touched. *"Sh'ma Yisroel, Adonoi Elohaynu, Adonoi Echod!"* Now there was a touch of defiance in his voice. *"L'shem yichud kudsha brichu, Ush'chintay. . . .* In the name of the unity of the Holy One and the Shekhinah, blessed be He." He sang his rebbe's old melody without realizing he had altered it slightly over the years he had sung it alone. The men stood shoulder to shoulder and sang; shining notes poured from Chaim Loeb's instrument; they swayed together, first gently, then forcefully.

They didn't feel the chill of night now; they were catching

fire. The song swelled to encompass them, raising an invisible temple around them. The inhibition that had made them pray so discreetly before melted away in this heat; their voices rose until they shouted: *"El Shaddai! El Chai v'Kayam! El Shaddai! El Chai v'Kayam!* O Almighty, Ever-Living God!"

Yitzhak saw the air shimmer, heard the mild gurgle of the spring-full creek as if it were the wellspring of the waters of life. He grew larger with their combined voice; no longer merely swaying, they were dancing and stamping. Their faces gleamed with tears and sweat. Yitzhak felt the tiny circle expand. He was certain—for a moment—that Chana swayed beside him. He heard the voice of his old friend Eisik joining the song. He smelled the fragrance, felt the breath of Shmuel Salomon. . . . Suddenly Asher staggered, nearly falling; Yitzhak caught him in an embrace. The violin faded, the song died. Yitzhak and Asher held each other, sobbing.

13

CHANA

ALL AT ONCE, in one morning, it was spring. The trees burst forth, first in the most delicate leaves, then in a profusion of fragrant pink and white flowers. Flocks of little birds suddenly appeared, chattering and singing in the fresh sunshine. It was a lush, green world in that country, and everything was bright and new to me. Walking back along the river one evening from the improvised *mikvah,* I saw a fox with two kits sitting just in front of a grove of thick mulberry bushes. I stopped still as a rock to look at them. Her black eyes glittered in her red face; I felt she was trying to tell me something, that mother fox, but I could not guess her secret and only stared helplessly until she turned away, her kits following her back into the bushes.

Albert turned over the soil in the vegetable plot, and I helped Maizie and Sally plant the seeds we had saved from the fall harvest. Albert had started some small plants—peas, tomatoes, and corn—under a large piece of glass propped up in the yard, and we planted those seedlings, too. I did not find it harsh to stoop and bend all day; indeed, it was wonderful to feel the warm sun on my back again, breathe the moist green air of spring, and rub the soil between my fingers. And while I knew I would be gone when the time came to harvest these crops, I did not care.

Now Cohn was delighted by our plan to go to Oregon. He would be rid of us at a profit, for he had calculated the price his goods would bring in the Far West to be ten times what he could sell them for in St. Louis. We were bringing cases of whiskey, guns, cotton cloth, kitchenware, knives, and small tools. Cohn had a book, a guide for emigrants, that described the whole journey and advised about everything that was needed, and he had talked with other businessmen and traders about what goods would be best to sell.

In the blacksmith shop behind Cohn's store, Yaacov and Yonah were building wagons, following the instructions and plans in Cohn's book. We would have four of these, two just for the trade goods. We had several horses and eight teams of oxen. Cohn had heard that Oregon was a fine country for sheep ranching, and that the wool and meat would bring good prices, so we would drive a small flock of them with us, too. They could provide us with some food along the journey—though Cohn's book said there were giant bison on the prairie, easily hunted, and meat from only one of them could feed us all for a month.

Cohn was so absorbed in planning our journey that I feared he wanted to come himself. Every evening he read to us from his book, repeating passages he thought particularly important. Such a book! I wondered how we had ever made our way from Poland to America without a book like that.

But neither Cohn, nor even Yitzhak, was as excited as our two young men, Yonah and Natan. They swept Levi along, too—Levi would have leapt off the bluffs into the river if they said it was a good idea! They read books, too, and talked to their friends at the store and argued incessantly with each other over every detail. Their enthusiasm began to infect even Asher, who at last had agreed to make the journey west with us. Even he could see that taking his sons back to Poland was no more possible than pushing back the wind.

Estella did not know anything about how to care for a baby, that was clear. Mendel grew quickly; he was a robust, active boy. When he was barely six months old he already stood and tried to take a few steps; now, a month later, he could almost walk. He bawled and wriggled when Estella forced him to sit in her lap; he wanted to be free, pulling himself up on the furniture. He was a loud, noisy baby, always babbling and crowing.

But Estella dressed him in starched, lacy dresses, thick leather shoes, elaborate bonnets. The slightest stain or streak of dust on his white dress brought her to a rage; she would shout for Sally to bring fresh clothes and wash the soiled ones. When ladies came to tea, she liked to show him, stuffed so tightly into his fancy clothes that he could hardly move. He shouted angry syllables, his little face reddened, he struggled with his plump arms and legs and then began to howl. In her frustration, Estella sometimes even slapped him, which only made him cry harder. And he learned quickly that if he kept crying, she would call Maizie or the wet nurse, Annie, to take him away.

Annie was very young, tall as a man, slender except for her huge breasts. Her skin was even darker than Maizie's, but where Maizie's face was coarse and misshapen, Annie's features were like carved wood, and her eyes were great, dark pools. She was a homesick, melancholy soul, grieving for her own baby who had died, and I feared at first that little Mendel might take in her sorrow with her plentiful milk. I hoped that by befriending her I could stay closer to the baby than Estella would ever allow me. But Annie was so afraid of me that she barely spoke to me—fortunately, not even to object when I wanted to hold Mendel and play with him. I was careful only to approach her when Estella was not at home, for if the girl was frightened of me, she was a thousand times more so of Estella. And although Mr. Cohn seemed not even to be aware of her presence, Annie trembled violently whenever he came into the room; she would not look at him.

I waited for Estella to leave the house, holding my breath as I watched her climb into the coach, out to the dressmaker's or to meet with other ladies to knit and sew for the soldiers going to Mexico. I hurried to the baby and loosened his stiff clothes while Annie looked on apprehensively. He was happy to see me; he had a beautiful smile and already many teeth. When I pointed them out to Annie, she almost smiled, but sadly. "He do chew me," she said softly. As if he understood, he imperiously turned to her, pulling at her loose dress. I watched, fascinated, as she gave him her breast. For a moment I had the fancy that perhaps in heaven Feigl suckled Annie's dead baby, and that both were comforted in the mercy and justice of the Holy One, blessed be He.

In a minute Mendel had pushed Annie away and reached out his arms to me. I took him greedily; he threw his head back and forth and laughed. I made my shawl into a wide loop and drew him inside it; he made me laugh, too, and I swung him around me in circles. Something of his mother played around his eyes; there was a light about him. He would bring us luck on our journey, our American baby. Perhaps Annie could travel with us for a few months, so he would not need to be weaned.

We make plans, but God rules the world. I woke in the night feeling that something terrible had happened. Yitzhak slept deeply. There was no moon; all was quiet and still. I thought I heard footsteps somewhere in the house, a creaking floorboard. I might have imagined it, or been awakened by a dream I could not remember. I slept again.

The next day, something was not right with Estella; her face was more pinched than usual and very pale. Kindness had never been her virtue, but this day she scolded with every word. At dinner she did not look at or speak to her husband.

"Would you ask Mr. Cohn to pass down the biscuits?" she asked Natan, who sat beside her, though the table was not so large nor Mr. Cohn so hard of hearing that she could not have asked him herself. And neither did he reply directly to her.

Estella hardly touched her food. When Maizie had taken away the plates, Cohn cleared his throat and began to speak as usual. Two red spots rose on Estella's pale cheeks. She nearly stumbled leaving the table, but Mr. Cohn went on speaking without pausing to look after her.

"Boys, one of you must stand guard over the sheep every night. I recommend you take watches, as soldiers do."

I went upstairs while the men were deep in discussion; I was tired of hearing about it. From behind Estella's door I heard a strange, rasping sound. Slowly I realized she was crying.

In the kitchen the next morning, Maizie was feeding Mendel a gruel of cow's milk and mashed-up bread.

"Is Annie ill?" I asked her.

"Miz' Estella sent Annie back home to Charleston, Miz' Honey."

"But why? The baby isn't weaned yet." I did not think Estella had suddenly been moved by pity for Annie's home-sickness.

Mendel, taking advantage of Maizie's distraction, pushed his bowl away with such force that it overturned on the floor.

"Now jus' look at that!" Maizie bent to clean up the mess while Mendel crowed and rubbed the sticky gruel on his head.

He made me laugh. I wet my handkerchief and began wiping his face and hands as he howled. If Maizie was answering my question, I could not hear her above the din the baby was making.

"Hesh that baby!" Sally came in the back door with a load of wood. She was scowling, but her eyes were soft. Everyone loved Mendel. "Is he pinin' for Annie's titties?"

Maizie giggled and muttered something I didn't understand, but I thought she said, "If he is, he ain't the only one."

"Why did Mrs. Cohn send her away?" I asked again.

"Hmmph," Sally snorted.

"Lord only knows," Maizie said piously, now holding the struggling baby on her hip. "This chil' be growin' strong enough with this mush, I suppose. An' Miz Estella don't want no young girls around."

Sally snorted again. She might have been laughing, but for her stern face I wasn't sure.

A few days later, Maizie brought Mendel into the kitchen, where I was helping Sally. I held his hands and walked him around the room; he wobbled along in his high shoes, singing "Ba! Ba! Ba!" Sally had polished the floor so slick that the baby's shoes could not get a purchase, and his song soon turned to grunts of frustration. I picked him up and took the high shoes off and pulled off his fine stockings. Now he was sure-footed enough that I let go his fingers, and, crowing, he made his first brave unaided steps. I cheered and clapped; even Sally smiled to see him. And Estella must have heard, for she rushed in.

Mendel sat down on the floor with a thump and began to cry. As I picked him up, Estella pointed at his bare feet.

"What are you doing? Dress him at once! Do you want him to catch a chill? Give him to Maizie."

I held tight to Mendel.

"He can't walk with those shoes, Madame."

"He is much too young to walk! His limbs are too small; you will damage his bones!" Sally and Maizie were so silent that they seemed to have melted into the walls.

I felt I held not only Mendel in my arms, but Feigl herself; I had to protect them. My anger made me fearless, and I met Estella's eyes.

"He is big for his age, and walking will make him stronger, and he needs to be strong for Oregon!"

Estella's eyes burned like coals. "You are a foolish, ignorant peasant! You cannot possibly take the baby to Oregon. It is much too perilous. There are savages and fevers and diseases of all kinds. And you people cannot possibly give the boy the advantages I can. He is my child, and I will rear him."

I set wiggling Mendel down; he still clung to my skirt. Feigl's spirit called to me to defend him; it was as though the baby had let me partake of his will and his strength.

"Madame Estella, he is not your child. He is no relation to you at all. He is Asher's son, he is my nephew, and he will go with us."

She glared at me furiously and stalked out of the room. Her dress hissed like a snake as she left. My strength seemed to have gone with her; I dropped to my knees and hugged Mendel. I was afraid she would speak to her husband, that I had ruined everything, that now we would never be able to leave.

I could not bear this burden alone; I cried out all my anxiety to Yitzhak as I told him what Estella had said.

"I'm a fool," I wept. "I'm nothing, I can't even read."

Yitzhak held me. "Chana, Chana," he whispered. "You do read. You are like the Berditcher Rebbe, may he rest in peace. You don't read the black letters on the white parchment, no; but you read the white parchment *behind* the black letters. You are a brilliant star, Chanale, you have saved me many times."

"But don't you see?" He was dreaming again, he had not heard me. "She will talk to Cohn, and he will not let us go unless we leave Mendel behind, and we cannot do that. He is Feigl's baby, and she is watching from the other world."

I practically shouted her name. I knew Yitzhak would be moved, but I did not expect him to crumple so completely. His eyes filled with pain. Remorse stabbed me; I took his hand.

"Yitzhak, Asher will never stand up to Cohn, even for his son."

Yitzhak's eyes closed. "Chana, the baby stays with us. Don't worry. I will talk to Cohn. This journey is a business for him; he doesn't care about babies and women and wet nurses—you are worrying too much. But don't talk to me any more about Feigl. I know very well where she is. She is gone."

I felt her in the room with us then, but I didn't say it. Yitzhak took my face in his hands.

"Chana, next week we will leave for Independence. Do you know this American word? I do, Natan has told me. *Independence*—it means no one can tell us what to do. Don't worry. We will sell Cohn's goods and repay him for all he has done for us, and we will be free. Americans. In Oregon."

While our wagons were still being loaded at the store, Estella began to carry on. Cohn looked at her coldly as she insisted that Mendel must stay.

She stamped her foot. Her face twisted. "He is mine!" she cried. "He is my son!"

Cohn raised his eyebrows and turned to Asher.

I concentrated with all my might, praying to Feigl's spirit and to God Himself to speak through Asher and save our baby.

Asher spoke in slow, formal Yiddish: "The boy is my son, and I cannot leave him behind." He lowered his eyes. "He and Rachel are all that I have of their poor mother, may she rest in peace."

Ah, only the Holy One, blessed be He, could have given Asher's simple words such power! I turned away so Estella would not see the joy that spread uncontrolled across my face.

Estella shouted and cried, but in the end, Yitzhak had been right. Her husband fixed her with a look so forbidding, it was like a cold wind sweeping through the room. She ran upstairs and remained in her bedroom. Maizie brought her meals to her on a tray. And so we never said good-bye, but I thought it no loss.

"Eh! Eh monsieur! You are the friend of Monsieur Cohn to go to the West?" It was a peculiar man who approached us, with a dark, creased face nested in a tangle of gray hair and beard. He wore ordinary work clothes, except for his animal-skin hat. It was hard to imagine how Cohn knew such a creature.

He was bowlegged and limped, though he was quick; his walk was like a little dance as he clambered up the stairs of the Independence Hotel. Yitzhak rose from his chair, and the man extended his hand in the American way. Yitzhak extended his own hand, gingerly, and winced as the man grasped it tightly and pumped it vigorously up and down.

"I am Rougeau! And mighty goddamn pleased," he said brightly. He tipped his hat to me.

"Likewise," Yitzhak muttered. "Fine, thank you." I stood close by, ready to help him, as his only English words were some social pleasantries and a few simple phrases from the store.

Rougeau looked us up and down. "Goddamn Isreelites," he snickered. "I don't got nothin' against them; I rode with one by Fort Hall. And Monsieur Cohn, *certainement.*" He spoke Cohn's name with deference. It reminded me to be grateful, for only through Cohn's influence had we been able to find a room in Independence, let alone pay the price. The little town was filled with emigrants, wagons, tents, and animals, all trying to make their way through the muddy streets to form up trains for the westward journey.

"I expect you go out to peddle his liquor, goddamn. And it ain' so bad, neither!" He smirked. "Isreelites, well goddamn, at least you are not the Mormons!" He fairly spit this last word and laughed, a high, dry, cackle.

Yitzhak, baffled, looked at me for a translation. I was missing some important words. I shook my head.

"All right-ee, then. Who-all are the folks in your party?"

Yitzhak understood only that this was a question. He gave me a desperate look. "Fine, thank you," he said cheerfully.

Rougeau spit, aiming carefully but missing the large brass spittoon on the hotel porch. "Goddamn, I say," he spoke more slowly. "How many are you, to travel west?"

I understood now and stepped forward. "Seven, mister."

Rougeau rubbed his face with his hands. "Women?" he looked at me.

"Only me," I said. "Six strong men."

He looked at Yitzhak doubtfully. "Any children?"

"Two childrens," I said. "And baby."

"Goddamn," he said thoughtfully. "You have wagons, oxen, horses. An' the sheep. Maybe they stay alive, maybe *non.* If the oxen die and the Injuns steal all the horses, maybe you can hitch up the sheep!" He laughed and wheezed to a stop. "Goddamn! You mus' take fifty pound of flour for each of you." He counted on his calloused fingers. "Sugar, and the *gras,* lard. Bacon, a couple barrel is enough."

Bacon, lard, I knew what that was. *Traife,* even the Cohns didn't eat that. "No. No bacon. No lard."

He chewed slowly, like a cow. "Goddamn. Suit yourself then. How about salt? You folks take the salt?"

I nodded.

"All-rightee, then. Salt. Coffee be goddamn nice—the 'black medicine.' Maybe we find the buffalo, the antelope, we eat them. Injuns like the calico, vermilion, the little gew-gaws. Monsieur Cohn has load you up with all that?"

"We have good wagons," I said, thinking of the work of Yaacov and Yonah and Silas in the shop behind the store.

Rougeau spat again. "Well, goddamn, you are in the safe hands, Monsieur *et* Madame. I was many years in the West, in the Rocky *Montagnes,* I trap the beaver, goddamn." He spat. "Isreelite! Better 'n goddamn Mormons!" He laughed and slapped himself until he fell into a coughing fit.

We spent our first night out from Independence at Indian Creek, beyond the woods. Only two or three trees marked the place by the little stream where we were to camp. And there were many wagons gathered, with all kinds of animals and people as far as I could see. I thought of the stories the people in my village had told, about the emperor and his great army, who made war on the czar and tried to march all the way to Moscow. Yaacov had been a very little boy; he remembered it. And perhaps the Exodus from Egypt had looked the same, like an entire town moving.

I held Mendel in my arms; my triumph and Asher's. Rachel made faces at her little brother and played with his bare toes. On the boat to Independence I had thrown the baby's stiff shoes into the Missouri.

Now Chaim Loeb and I and the younger children stayed with our wagons and animals. The others had gone to a meeting, an election, to choose leaders and make rules for the train. Chaim Loeb said he didn't know enough American to go—he would let Yitzhak cast his vote for him. The rain had stopped, and we sat on a log under a tree with the baby. Rachel and Levi went running to find some other children to play with.

I had heard other women in the camp complain of being away from their houses, but I was happy. The animals made wonderful music as they baaed and lowed and mooed, looking for grass. As I watched them, I vowed not to cook any meat on this journey. We would eat as we had in Poland—grains and vegetables.

I asked Chaim Loeb to get his violin, and he played some of the American tunes he had learned from Estella's piano; two women from another group came over and listened, too. A girl with curling hair and a sweet face began to sing:

> Oh, the sun shines bright in the old Kentucky home
> 'Tis summer, the old folks are gay . . .

Others came, bringing some little cakes, which soon lured the children back; I had a large store of tea and made up a pot, and so we had a little party. The men came back with the word that our captain had been elected; it was Mr. Owl Russell, the tall man with the big hat who spoke with so many long words.

Our guests went back to their own wagons and tents and I heated more water to wash the mud-spotted children. All around us the fires glowed. We cooked and ate a simple supper as the moon, just past full, rose in the eastern sky.

14

YITZHAK

YITZHAK WALKED beside the slowly moving wagon. As far as he could see, wagons fanned out across the nearly milewide trail. It was beautiful country, green and fresh, sprinkled with bright wildflowers. The slightly curving waves of grass around them looked like an ocean. Overhead, the sky was a vast bowl of bright blue, holding only a few puffs of curly white clouds. To the right was the line of trees that marked the bank of the river. A miracle, thought Yitzhak, that the voice of his rebbe—the voice of God, really—had brought them so far.

Rougeau and the other guides were far ahead of this vast, moving city, a combination of several large trains with emigrants from New England, Illinois, Kentucky, and Missouri, bound for Oregon and California. Asher and Yitzhak each drove a wagon, and Yaacov had charge of the two that held their supplies and trade goods. Chaim Loeb and the boys took care of the spare oxen and the sheep, who, with the various herds of cattle and horses, ran behind the wagons. The sheep were already difficult to manage, tempted by the green pasture beyond the trail and complaining loudly at the distance they were expected to travel each day.

Yitzhak hummed a vaguely remembered melody of his

rebbe, or perhaps it was one of his father's. The countryside reminded him of the fields beyond Przemysl: the tall grass, the sweet song of the larks. He let his recollection lead him to the border of that dangerous land of childhood reminiscence, where Feigl's ghost waited behind every door. Yitzhak held his melody in his heart as a charm against the pain that Feigl's memory always brought. He was sweating in the late spring heat. In his head, Feigl's voice sang words to his melody:

> *Away, away, away across the sea,*
> *Yitzy-pitzy, Chana-lanna and the others and me . . .*
> *Poor little bird, she flew so high*
> *Watching her little ones from the sky, from the sky . . .*

The sky was so wide here, surely there was room enough for Feigl's joy beside his grief. . . . He softly joined his own voice to her spectral one:

> Yitzy-litzy, went to pray, away, away . . .
> Across the sea to be free, free . . .

The prairie grass hissed and rustled. Yitzhak could almost hear in it the voices of the monastery choir of Przemysl. His thoughts flew on the breeze. He felt again the weight in his hand of Feigl's wedding jewels, the pearls wrapped in a kerchief. The prickly terror at leaving home. His flight to Shmuel Salomon, guided only by a whisper in the grass. *A whisper in the grass.* Yitzhak listened now, but heard only a wordless rustle.

The thin curls of clouds were gathering together. Yitzhak smelled electricity in the air. Mendel began to cry, and Chana comforted him.

Yitzhak looked at the sky. On the horizon, clouds were massing in great gray heaps. The animals murmured, then moaned and bellowed and neighed at the first faraway sound of thunder. Ahead, other wagons were stopping to make camp before the heaviest rain. Yitzhak felt a few scattered drops, saw a white flash in the distance, braced himself for the roar and crack. He murmured the blessings for seeing thunder and lightning. He heard Feigl's giggle, from a place he could not see or name.

Asher kept track of the days, and on Friday, as the huge, slow train began to move after the noon stop, he strode purposefully up to Yitzhak.

"Yitzhak, tomorrow we must not travel, it is Shabbos."

Exasperated, Yitzhak wondered if Asher would ever become what his rebbe had called a Jew of the heart, instead of a Jew of words. He waved at the sky. "Look how the Holy One, Master of the Universe, is here with us! Do you only find Him in the performance of ritual?"

Asher was stunned. "But Yitzhak, we are free of Cohn now. You promised—it is the Law!"

"The Law? The Law? The Law is to preserve life," Yitzhak declared. "Do you think the whole train will stop for us? If we fall behind, there will not be enough grass left for our animals. And if we fall too far behind, we are alone in this wilderness. We have to stay with the train, with Rougeau."

Yitzhak pointed at the horizon, a long, unbroken line. They were in the middle of emptiness. "Do you know where we are? Where we are going? Where to cross the river? If we are lost, we will die, and that is forbidden. And if we die, we will not get to Oregon, and the Holy One, blessed be He, has commanded us to be a light to all the nations, even every nation of the world. We must go to the Jews of the West."

"There are no Jews there! There are only savages and a few crazy goyim!" Asher seized on this.

He should be grateful for what we have, Yitzhak thought. On the trail, with Chana cooking, they followed the dietary laws better than they had since leaving Poland. It was

Asher's temperament; he always had to find something wrong.

Yitzhak tried to mollify him. "Tonight we will pray together," he said. "Chana will make a Shabbos dinner and we will sing and dance. No Cohn is here to stop us. The goyim themselves sing and dance every night by their camp fires; they will never even hear us above their own noise." Yitzhak laughed. "Already we are free!"

Asher frowned. "Yes, in America, 'free' is very important. But who is free from what the Creator of the World commands?"

Yitzhak sighed. "Asher, when we came on the ship, we did not ask the captain to stop for Shabbos. This train of wagons and animals is like a ship, *nu?* Just like a ship, Captain Russell is the captain, Rougeau is called 'pilot.' And we are traveling to fulfill a greater commandment."

Asher looked at him. "Yitzhak, I have followed you for thousands of leagues, as a man should only follow God. I hope in His holy Name that you know what you are doing."

Yitzhak looked at the sky. Shmuel Salomon, may he rest in peace, would have had a saying, a story. But Yitzhak had nothing but his urge to move forward, always forward, to the West.

In the evening, the wagons and remudas stopped; the animals were set to graze. The dust settled a little after they made camp. Rougeau went away with his friends and, Yitzhak suspected, a bottle of Cohn's whiskey. The wagons spread wide along the banks of the Blue River, still far from the country of dangerous Indians. In the twilight, Chana stooped in the front of their wagon, sheltered from the breeze. Yaacov and the boys had not yet returned from helping another emigrant chase down a runaway horse, but the others watched Chana carefully light two candles with a brand from the cooking fire. Her head was covered with a white kerchief that she had somehow kept from the dust. Tears came to Yitzhak's eyes as she sang: *"Baruch atah Adonoi Elohaynu Melech ha'Olom, asher kid'shanu b'mitzvotov, v'tzivaynu l'hadlik nayr shel Shabbos . . . omen."*

More precious than rubies, he whispered to himself. Moses rejoiced in the gift of the Sabbath, as a man rejoices in his bride. . . . Chana poured a cup of wine for him to bless. Like the ancestors fleeing Egypt, they were moving too quickly to allow time for bread to rise, but Chana had cooked a braided pancake over the fire and set it on a plate.

As he was about to make the blessing, he heard something behind him. A grizzled, wiry man with a heavy gray beard stood a few yards away, stopped in his tracks, his mouth gaping. He dropped to his knees in the soft ground, buried his face in his hands, and sobbed.

Yitzhak rushed to comfort him. Lifting his head, gasping for breath, the man put his hand to his nose and blew with a resounding, melancholy honk. He wiped his hand on his filthy shirt and pulled a large, soiled rag from somewhere in his greasy buckskins and wiped his face. He shook his head violently back and forth.

"Oh, my, oh, mercy, oh my, oh mercy," he repeated, muttering. "Forgive me, folks, do forgive me. But that song! That song!" He looked up at Chana with the face of a small boy incongruously set in the mass of whiskers and pockmarked wrinkles.

Chana's face was lit in the glow of the candles. Yitzhak beckoned her down from the wagon to interpret.

As Chana approached, the man burst into fresh sobs. "My mamma, my mamma!"

Levi and Rachel, holding Mendel's hand, stepped up now, curious.

"I know him!" Levi said importantly. "It's Old Moe—he rides with the Illinois folks!"

"Moe?" Yitzhak leaned closer. "I am Yitzhak here," he said. "You are guide?"

"Naw, I ain't no guide," Old Moe sniffed. "Just an ol' mountain trapper goin' home. Just an ol' trapper what came back East t'sell a skimpy last load of skins and to see—to see—" He stopped, as if he could not remember what he had wanted to see. He looked up at Yitzhak. "Where'd your woman learn that song, that's what I'm askin'. It were my mamma's song, I ain't heard nary of it for forty-fifty year." He choked on a sob.

Yitzhak stared at him.

"Bist du yiddische?" Yitzhak asked, incredulous.

"Aw, I'm sorry," Moe shook his head. "No parlee-voo."

Yitzhak looked at Chana in frustration.

"My husband asks you, are you a Jew?"

"Aw, no ma'am." He pulled off his trapper's hat—like Rougeau's, it was fur, with hanging tails—in a belated gesture of respect. "Just an ol' trapper. An orphee-yon. All I can remember is Gus an' me, he was my grown brother. We was from the old country, Gus use to tell me it was a place called Pozen, or somethin', an mamma died. I never knew my pa, an' we was bound over to a man in Tennessee, Mr. Fitch, what bought our passage to cut timber." He pointed at Levi. "I wasn't but his size, neither. But a tree fell on Gus, an' kilt him, an' then I ran off, an' by 'n by I took up trappin'. Then the fur run out, an' I had a good squaw what died, too, an' I come back East, but. . . ." He threw up his hands. "Anyways, I'm goin' back, squaw or no squaw. I got a little cabin in one of the purties' spots in the whole—but you ain't told me yet, ma'am, how you learned my mamma's song, when I didn't recollect it myself!"

Chana looked at Yitzhak, then to Moe. "It's a *brucha,* a prayer. For candles. For Shabbos. Jews say it. If your mother sang it, perhaps she was a Jew?"

Moe shook his head. "Ma'am, she was a fine woman,

what I hardly remember of her. From your ways I guess you are a foreigner, like she was. I thought I was seein' her again for a moment. My mamma was an angel." Tears welled in his eyes.

"Perhaps you know this *brucha,* too?" Yitzhak asked hopefully, turning to the bread and wine. Holding the glass, he sang the Cracower melody: *"Baruch atah Adonoi Elohaynu Melech ha'Olom boray pri ha'gofen . . . omen."* He took a sip from the glass and handed it to Chana, who sipped and handed it to Moe.

Moe, his hand trembling, drained the glass. "Naw," he said. "I ain't never heard that one, but I'm still dry, if'n you got any more of that p'izen." He smiled ingratiatingly, displaying a mouth half full of blackened teeth.

"Will you eat with us, then?" Chana asked him gently. "We have plenty food. We sing more later."

"Reb Yitzhak! Reb Yitzhak!" Yaacov rode up on his gray horse, with Levi close behind him on his roan. He looked like a different man out here on the prairie. His face was happy and open, brown from the sun. The train had been stopped for two days for a series of long meetings. One of the men who had been defeated by Mr. Russell in the election for captain had demanded that all the officers resign and new ones be elected. Yitzhak had been napping in the wagon; he ignored the deliberations. Except for Mr. Russell, who was so tall, Yitzhak was not sure he could distinguish the candidates. At the sound of Yaacov's voice, he came out of the wagon, blinking in the bright sunlight.

Rachel crawled out, too, from the back of the wagon where she had been sulking. She had wanted to ride with Levi and Yaacov, but Chana had needed her to watch the baby.

"We saw a wolf, Rachel!" Levi shouted.

"You never did! You saw a mangy dog!" Rachel screamed back.

"Rachel!" Chana called from behind the wagon.

192

"Rachele, don't talk that way. Go see if you can find some wood."

Rachel stuck her tongue out and jumped down. "And why should I, when Levi gets to ride!" The hem of her dress caught on the wagon tongue; she ripped it away angrily.

"Rachel, look! Be careful!" Yitzhak scolded her. "You should be helping Tanta Chana, not making more work for her."

"It was a wolf, it was!" Levi called after her.

Yaacov laughed. "Yes, it was, Levi, but don't argue with Rachel!" He turned to Yitzhak. "Reb Yitzhak, Levi is right about the wolf. I think they are killing the sheep. Every night when we bring them in, one or two more are missing, and we have not enough time to look."

"Papa, I could shoot the wolf! Why don't we shoot him?"

"Hush!" Yaacov snapped. "Captain Russell says no shooting without he orders. Do you want Indians to come? Or those fanatics that Rougeau talks about? Mormons?"

Yitzhak looked at the sky. So vast! This was a place for the contemplation of dreams, the mystery of the universe. And Yaacov—who had come to him hungry for redemption, for ecstasy—he worried about sheep? He looked at his disciple.

"So maybe they will come back, the sheep."

Yaacov's mouth opened. "Come back? Rebbe, they are eaten!"

Yitzhak shrugged. "Rougeau said already the sheep are a mistake here. He knows more about this than we do. In any case, if we can do nothing, then there is nothing we can do." He smiled benevolently. "The wolf is God's creature too, *nu?*" He surprised himself; it was something Chana would say.

Much to Rougeau's disgust, Moe had attached himself and his mule to their group and stuck to Yitzhak like glue. Yitzhak did not understand most of the old trapper's incessant monologue. He didn't mind; he allowed himself to drift, nodding and grunting at what seemed the proper times, while Moe droned in a low, confidential tone. If God had sent him this new American disciple, surely the Master of the Universe had His reasons. Perhaps the Holy One Himself, blessed be He, was silently giving guidance to this old Jew who did not know he was a Jew, a guidance that somehow emanated from Yitzhak's body like a fragrance that he himself could not detect. He felt the light breeze of the prairie morning and remembered another presence, the Spirit-rebbe, the spirit without a face. He felt that presence now, as if someone were walking behind him.

At a long nooning stop a few days later, Yitzhak escaped from Moe to lie under a tree and listen to the hum of the insects, the call of a bird. The grass shivered with the movement of a small animal that he didn't see. Half asleep, Yitzhak heard a familiar voice.

"Hey, Itchy! Doc Itchy! Can I have a word with you?"

Yitzhak turned over. A word, he thought? Moe had spoken ten thousand already this morning—what were a few more?

"Doc, can you take a look at somethin'?"

Moe stood on one leg, holding his other boot, his bare foot raised high. He stumbled to the ground and thrust the bare foot, black and swollen, toward Yitzhak. Yitzhak reeled, choking. He pointed to the stream.

"Wash! Wash! Put in water!"

Moe's mouth opened in surprise. "You mean get *wet?*"

"Put in water," Yitzhak repeated. "Then we look." What did this poor lost Jew with a sore foot expect from him?

Yitzhak lay back and closed his eyes. In the near distance he heard Chana and the children. Was that a human foot that Moe had thrust at him, or a lump of mud? In his strange state of mind, nothing was as it appeared. The waving grass was water; a distant tree was an old friend. How could he know? He imagined a man's foot: a high arch, slender toes, curving nails. . . .

He woke, without knowing he had been asleep. Rachel

held out a bowl to him. For a moment he thought it was Feigl, bringing him tea with raspberry. . . . No, he shook his head, that was years ago, he is grown, this is Feigl's daughter, and Feigl is dead. "Uncle Yitzhak, wake up! Tanta Chana made soup!"

He drank most of the thin soup. He could not have slept for more than a few minutes; the sun was still high. And here was Moe, hopping and stumbling from the direction of the river.

The old trapper sat on the ground. "Can you look here now, Doc?"

The foot looked more like a foot. It was pinkish gray, creased with dirt that would probably be there forever. Yitzhak saw a swollen, red knot at the joint of the big toe.

"I am not doctor . . ."

"Aw, don't say that, Doc Itchy! Don't say that! Why, I seen all them books you got in your wagon! An' you're about the only one on this whole train that's had a kind word for Ol' Moe." He smiled hopefully. "Maybe a little whiskey'd help."

Yitzhak gingerly touched the bunion. What would this foot look like without it? In his mind he saw it clearly.

"Don't walk," he said. "Ride in the wagon. Today, two days. Don't walk. Don't take whiskey. Is for sale, in the West. *Fershtet?*"

Moe looked at him with eyes like a calf. "You ain't gonna give me no medicine?"

Yitzhak sighed. "Medicine? God is medicine." In the distance, he thought he saw the parade of invalids and supplicants that had approached Shmuel Salomon every afternoon, the crowds of the lame and sick at his father's court. It was not Moe's fault; it was the human condition, to suffer and to seek solace. He looked at Moe more kindly. On an impulse, he took the bowl with a splash of soup in the bottom and poured it on Moe's foot.

"Hoo-ee! Hoo-ee, Doc! Now I know for certain I'm a-cured!"

Yitzhak felt an icy gust of warning, of humility. In Moe he had the disciple he deserved. What on earth was he doing? Acting out the old proverb: Moe was the perfect *shlemazel*, the one on whom the *shlemiel* spills the soup. Yitzhak prayed, swiftly, that he had done the man no harm. "Save him from me, Master of the Universe," he whispered. "Save me, too."

God is indeed all powerful and hears all prayers. After only a little more than a day riding in the wagon, during which Chana nearly stopped speaking to Yitzhak, and Yitzhak himself was faint from the man's smell, Moe declared his foot had healed completely.

"Look how I got my boot on agin! Glory be!"

"Thank the Holy One, *Ribono shel Olom,*" Yitzhak cautioned him.

But Moe went off to his cronies, singing not the praises of God, but of Doc Itchy.

Rougeau, red-faced, dragged a weeping Moe to the morning camp fire. He gripped the old man's ear firmly, his other hand holding a pistol, a Colt revolver, Yitzhak noted, knowledgeable from taking inventory at Cohn's Emporium. As Moe whined, Rougeau pushed him forward with the barrel of the gun.

"Goddamn! Here is the varmint who steals the sheep!" he shouted triumphantly.

"Please, Doc Itchy, I never done it." Moe sobbed.

Chana turned from the fire, saw the gun, gasped. "No!"

Rougeau didn't acknowledge her but spoke to Yitzhak. "Goddamn if I don't kill him right now, this rummy goddamn scallywag!" He brandished the gun.

"Don't shoot," Yitzhak said, temperately. "Wait. Say slowly."

Rougeau, furious, spat each word. "This-dirty-dog-is-stealin'-sheep! He sell to Indians, to ever'body! He's been leechin' and stealin' you blind! I know this type! He's nothin' but a goddamn thievin', low-down, cussed goddamn yellow dog!"

Yitzhak looked at Moe, who now knelt on the ground. "Moe."

"Naw, naw, I never, I never done it!"

"You steal sheep?"

"Naw, naw, I never! Injuns done it, Injuns'll steal the horse out from under you if they get up close. Injuns stole your sheep, I never did."

But he did, Yitzhak saw. He saw it in Moe's face. He turned to Rougeau.

"Don't shoot," he said, firmly. "Sheep is less than man. Moe is human being, not dog." Yitzhak smiled. "He is a Jew. Not a good Jew, no. But a Jew."

Rougeau spat on the ground. "Don't matter what he is or ain't. If we don' have law here, we're goners, goddamn." He waved his arm angrily at the train. "Look here, all these god-damn folks. They come from everywhere, other countries—they are no kin, not even friends. What happens, everybody do as they please? Goddamn stealin', fights, everything!"

Yitzhak understood enough. He glared at Rougeau. "Like stealing whiskey?"

Rougeau looked down. "Goddamn, now!"

Yitzhak, encouraged by righteousness, tried to spit as Rougeau did, but only dribbled feebly. He wiped his beard with his sleeve.

"Jews have law," he said sternly. "We are Jews, we have law. Don't shoot Moe. Is not Jewish law."

Rougeau glared. "You keep t'yourselves, then, goddamn, if you're so stuck in your own ways." He flung a kick at Moe as he stalked off.

In his sleep Yitzhak heard the wild, deep laugh of Shmuel Salomon. It seemed to come from behind a wall of crack-ling flames and thick smoke. But the crushing-boxes of his childhood nights were no longer to be seen, and he did not feel the terror of nightmare. He watched with detachment, almost peace. He woke and slipped out of the wagon to walk in the moonlight.

From beyond the whispering grass came the coyotes' eerie song. "*Yaaa*," he heard. "*Yaaaah-hoooo.*" Yitzhak felt penetrated by a stillness, a stillness filled with life. Thoughts, words in his mind, danced around the stillness. His inner voice spoke to him: Is it so strange that you feel a part of this, that this peace is a part of you? It is no small thing to bring these people such a distance. You have followed the path your rebbe saw for you on his deathbed. It is that light that Moe sees, you have rescued him, yes, you, Yitzhak—why should you not heal a man's sore foot when that man's soul has been returned to Israel?

15

YITZHAK

TRAVELING THROUGH THE WILDERNESS, Yitzhak remained serene, certain in his destiny. They had left Independence a little more than a month ago, and they had not seen anything like a human settlement since Fort Kearney. Almost every day they encountered the crudely marked grave of an earlier emigrant who had gone no further. Yitzhak could not read the words on the simple plank Chana showed him on a little mound of earth torn by animal tracks, but the dates told him that it was an infant's grave.

Now they had reached the Platte, a river that was less a river than a thin layer of mud spread across the plain.

"Too thick to drink an' too thin to plow," Moe smirked. He repeated this all day long, on the day they actually forded the river. He warned them away from one crossing place, where quicksand had claimed several other wagons and animals. Yitzhak rode ahead to look for Rougeau to ask his advice and found him already engaged, helping the quicksand victims, cursing and sweating as they grappled with ropes and borrowed wagons and oxen. Yitzhak stared at the scene with horror: the shouting, cursing men, the struggling animals. *Lord of the Universe*, Yitzhak prayed, *don't let that happen to me.*

He rode back to where Yaacov and the boys had enthusiastically entered into the challenge of the crossing, while Asher shook his head and Chaim Loeb watched nervously. The spare oxen and horses crossed easily enough, but Yaacov had to build a raft for the sheep and ferry them over. Other groups had similar difficulties, or worse, and it took several days for the entire train to reach the other side of the river.

Though it was not yet midday, the prairie air was hot and still. Yitzhak was already sweating in his long, black coat. Yaacov and Chaim Loeb, like young Yonah and Natan, had begun wearing American clothes during the last months in St. Louis, but Yitzhak and Asher persisted in their Polish cloaks and broad-brimmed black hats. Yitzhak would have discarded his, but he was the rebbe and preserved this little bit of form and tradition to satisfy Asher. And as for Asher himself, Yitzhak could not imagine him in an American shirt, any more than he could imagine the ox wearing overalls. He would not be Asher.

Asher grew more anxious every slow mile; he worried over every report or rumor of danger, sickness, a broken wheel or axle. The rough trail, the poor food and water, the hot days and chill nights had weakened him; he rode in the wagon more than the children did.

As Yitzhak walked beside the wagon, the sky slowly darkened. Puzzled, he looked up. A dense, dark cloud lay on the horizon, yet it didn't feel like a storm; it was too hot and dry. All the sky turned a peculiar color; birds sang wildly. An eclipse of the sun, Yitzhak thought, another sign from the Almighty, blessed be He. He mumbled a prayer.

Chana, walking slightly ahead of him on the other side of the wagon, called out.

"Yitzhak! Look over there! The grass is on fire!"

Yitzhak peered into the distance where she pointed. Yes, a fire! He trembled a little. The Day was approaching; the signs of his dreams were becoming fulfilled.

200

Slowly, the immense, unwieldy wagon train was coming to a stop. Up and down the trail, the sound rose: men shouting, women calling to their children, oxen trumpeting, horses neighing. But in the vastness of the prairie, even this great noise sounded puny. To the north, billows of dark smoke rose on the horizon.

Yitzhak saw now how the emigrants' wooden wagons resembled the crushing-boxes of his nightmare. With horror he wondered if it was nightmare or prophecy. The faces of the goyische emigrants could indeed be the faces of those who . . . he looked wildly around for his party: Chana, with Chaim Loeb's help, was gathering the children. Asher, who had been resting in one of the wagons, was now looking around in consternation. Moe was nowhere to be seen. In the distance, Yitzhak recognized the mounted figure of Yaacov, riding with someone else—Natan? Yonah? Then where was the other boy? The train was in confusion: some wagons pulled up, trying to form circles, while others drove on, raising clouds of dust that with the distant smoke obscured any view of the trail.

Suddenly Yitzhak coughed in the dust of Rougeau's horse. Without dismounting, the guide called to him: "Monsieur! Keep on, goddamn! You don't need to stop and watch it!" He waved his arm at the disordered train. "Look, all goddamn fools! The wind, she blow the other way! The fire is not come this way!"

Yitzhak stared at him, still not sure if he was on the prairie or in his dream. *"Vos?"*

"Sacre! Grass fire, goddamn!" Rougeau shouted to be heard above the general din, making it even harder for Yitzhak to understand him. "See how the smoke blow! It ain't come nigh here. . . . An' goddamn, look, the buffalo out over yonder!" He waved his rifle toward the southeastern hills. Yitzhak squinted at the dark splotch moving down the side of the hill. Rougeau grinned. "Monsieur Russell say, go out an' get some meat, boys! There be good fat cows, too,

goddamn! I take your boys out to shoot. Even if you Isreelites is such almighty damn fool, you must no be so goddamn fool as to miss a feast of hump ribs!" He looked down at Yitzhak doubtfully. "I don' think *you* be to buffalo huntin' yourself," he spat. "It take hard ridin'. The horse, he not broke to it—if he step in the prairie-dog hole, *sacre,* he bust his goddamn leg!" Rougeau spat again, for emphasis.

Bewildered, Yitzhak scratched his head. Chana had come to hear what Rougeau was yelling about. She listened, lifted her face to the breeze, took Yitzhak's arm.

"Yitzhak, the wind blows the fire away from us, not to-ward us. I don't know the rest—they are hunting cows?"

Rougeau still shouted. "The one boy, I see him out there with your herd, but I don' see the older one nowhere. Johnny. Where he gone to?"

Yitzhak and Chana looked at him dumbly.

"Goddamn, he miss the big chance of his life if he don' catch up to the buffalo hunt! An' he will be one damn fool if he try to ride there by himself. You see him, you send him out to me." He wheeled his horse and rode on.

The train ponderously re-formed itself; Rougeau and a group of thirty or forty men rode toward the cloud of smoke, carrying their rifles. Yaacov sent Chaim Loeb to tend the herds, then grabbed a rifle and rode off with them. As they drove their wagon slowly on in the dust, Yitzhak heard the shouting in the distance: "Ya-hoo! Ya-hoo!" The buffalo herd was a dark mass moving down the low range of hills. Yitzhak wondered where Yonah was.

Moe's face, beard, and hair were covered with grease; he waved a dripping slab of half-cooked meat in his hand. Yaacov, his eyes shining, stood before Yitzhak.

"Rebbe, it's kosher, isn't it? The buffalo? It's like a cow. . . ."

Yitzhak didn't know. Like a cow? He had ridden out to where the huge, shaggy beasts were being butchered and carried back in pieces to the camp fire. He had never dreamed God could make such a beast; He is wondrous indeed, the Almighty. The men called it a "cow," but it was like no cow he had ever seen. Was it kosher to eat? Of course not, there was no *shochet.* But the God he saw here on the prairie was more interested in life than in rules; here the great Law beyond laws ruled supreme. There was no czar in America, and where they were now was hardly even America anymore; Mr. Russell and the council made the laws for the wagon train. Yitzhak's head felt clear as the prairie air, filled with gold light. Here was no need for a God who was like a czar, here God was a bountiful creator. He would keep his stupid, heavy black coat if Asher needed that, it was a kindness to him, but Yaacov could eat what he liked. He was a big, strong man, riding hard every day, not a yeshivah scholar to survive on vegetables.

Chana refused to have anything to do with the slaughter or the banquet, and Asher would have nothing to do with the other emigrants, nor with meat that was not ritually slaughtered. Yitzhak remained with them; the sight of the beasts bleeding to death on the prairie had not whetted his appetite. Everyone else went to the huge fire. Rougeau, Moe, and the few other men in the train with prairie experience led the feast, which lasted late into the night as the moon rose in the still-hazy sky. The sounds of fiddle music, singing, dancing, and the occasional—if officially forbidden—gunshot punctuated the night. Only Yitzhak, Chana, Baby Mendel, and Asher remained in their wagons—even the children joined the crowds around the fire, gorging themselves on chunks of the fat, roasted buffalo meat.

The combined depredations of wolves, Indians, and Moe had reduced the number of sheep in their flock to seven, but there were still the oxen and horses. In this dry country, there was less grass for the animals, and they ranged farther and farther, falling further behind the train each day. Whoever had charge of them for the day—Yonah, Natan, or Chaim Loeb—had farther to ride up to the camp fire when the train stopped for the night.

A few days after the buffalo hunt and feast, Yonah did not appear at all for the evening meal. Asher was already asleep in the wagon; too tired to come to the camp fire, he had taken only a small bowl of soup for his supper. Yitzhak didn't dare disturb him with the news that Yonah was missing. Natan, who knew his brother best, seemed more evasive than worried.

"So where is Yonah?" Yitzhak asked. "Wasn't he also watching the animals today?"

Natan shrugged. "I dunno."

"Shouldn't we look for him? You and Yaacov, go! What if something is wrong?"

Natan looked down. "We don't need Yaacov. We don't need to . . . nothin's wrong, Uncle. Johnny—Yonah—ain't lost."

"Then why is he not here? Where is he, if he isn't lost?"

Natan mumbled. "He goes with the Illinois folks."

"*Vos?*"

Natan looked away. "He's courtin'." He barely pronounced the English word; Yiddish failed him.

"*Vos? Vos ist,* 'curtain'?"

"He likes a girl, Uncle Yitzhak. He's courtin' Eliza Reed."

Yitzhak was dumbfounded. Natan could not possibly mean what he thought. A sinking sense of horror grew in him. Yonah should have been married, he realized. A young man of eighteen years . . . a wife should have been found for him years ago, but how? They were always traveling, and now? Where would Asher find a Jewish wife for him? Sympathy pierced Yitzhak's heart; now he saw why Asher so desperately wanted to return to Poland. Asher must—must what? He must not know. He, Yitzhak, was the leader here; he was responsible for his little group as Mr. Owl Russell and Rougeau were for the whole train. He must pull Yonah back from the edge of this . . . this mistake. And what of the American girl's parents? He shuddered. Would they not shoot or hang a Jew who tried to steal their daughter? And Natan was only two years younger than his brother.

Yitzhak looked at Natan, and his hands kneaded themselves into fists. He could feel his face reddening. His voice surprised him—low, like a growl.

"Bring him here. Bring him here now. Bring your brother before . . . before . . ."

Before we are all destroyed, he thought, but Natan had already ridden off.

Yonah—Johnny—pretended that he no longer knew Yiddish. Finally, stubbornly, he spoke.

"I don't care. Go tell my pa if you want. I'll tell him myself. It's nothing to me what he wants or what you want. I love Eliza, and we're going to be married. I'm not going to Oregon with you, anyway; I'm going to California with her and her folks, and the Donners and them. Her pa's got plenty—you should see their wagons. They got one that's like a house on wheels, it's so fine. You go up to it on steps, and they got a stove in there and a story built over the floor for the beds."

"But Yonah, you are a Jew! How can you marry this girl? Her parents . . ."

Yonah looked directly into Yitzhak's eyes. "I ain't!" he said. "I ain't a Jew! I was a Jew when I was a little kid, and when my mother was still alive, but I ain't a Jew no more! I don't have to be. I don't have to be nothin' I don't want to be. What else are we goin' west for?"

"Master of the Universe, *Ribono shel Olom,*" Yitzhak murmured to himself. His apostasy will break Asher's heart. Yitzhak was a tall man, but Yonah was taller, younger, and stronger.

"This girl's parents . . . ," he stammered. "Surely they

already have chosen a husband for her. Someone of their own religion. This is not right. Surely it is against their laws, American laws, too. I will speak to them. You must bring me."

"I ain't gonna! And they don't—they don't *pick* husbands and wives! And it ain't nothin' wrong!"

Yitzhak couldn't believe the boy's defiance. Was he possessed? Yonah was shaking his head back and forth. He is so sure, Yitzhak saw. He is right, then, perhaps. There are no laws here. But what of the Law, that greater Law of God: Be fruitful and multiply, meaning, our people. . . . Yonah's sons would be goyim.

"You ain't gonna talk to them, and my pa ain't! I can talk to Eliza's pa myself. He's a fair man, he'll give me a chance. I've been helpin' out their hired men with their herds. He knows I'm a hard worker. And Eliza loves me, too."

That he wanted to marry, Yitzhak could understand. His heart stirred for the boy. But to convert! Yet, where was there a Jewish wife for him? How could the Lord of the Universe not have foreseen this? Yitzhak heard an inner voice. *He knows all.* Then, perhaps this, too, was somehow His will. . . . Yitzhak was helpless before circumstance and the boy's passion.

While the others were busy with the day's ending tasks, picketing the horses and mules, gathering wood and water, checking the supplies, Asher sat on an overturned box on the ground, weeping. He had torn his coat in mourning; he wept silently and continuously.

Chana found it unbearable, but she dared not speak to him. She sent Rachel to him with a bowl of wild berries they had gathered, but he would not even look at it.

While Natan and Yaacov cared for the animals, Yitzhak left the fire to squat beside Asher. He put his hand on Asher's arm.

"A man buys a knife to cut meat; he slips and it cuts his finger. He buys a candle for light; he drops it and it burns his coat. He did not buy the knife to cut his finger, and he bought the candle to give light, not to burn his coat. And a man has children to respect him and follow in his ways, and give him joy, not to betray him."

Asher sobbed. "He is dead, he is gone, my first born son."

In the distance Yitzhak saw the other wagons, other parties in the train preparing for the evening meal and camp fires. He had thought this traveling city to be an Exodus like that of Moses, but the truth was that only he and his small group—now smaller by one—were really followers of Moses. They were not only in a strange country and an alien landscape, but traveling among aliens; they were outsiders among outsiders. A breeze rustled the grass. Yes, were they not all impermanent as the grass? Were we not all, Jews or goyim, in some way aliens on the earth? *Man is like unto a breath; his days are as a shadow that passeth away. . . .*

He felt that Asher accused him for the loss of his son. But was it his fault? It was the voice of his rebbe, the will of God, that had brought them here. Their evening prayers and songs in this open land, beneath the wide sky, had a luminosity and brilliance he had not felt before. Their journey would be a *tikkun olam,* a remedy for the world. . . . Yes, it was Asher who had made the greatest sacrifices, but perhaps that was a sign of favor. After all, was not the patriarch Abraham called on to make such a sacrifice? It was Asher's unyielding stiffness that caused him so much suffering, not the will of God or Yitzhak's clumsiness in serving Him . . . but still, he felt responsible.

Yes, Yonah is dead, he thought; and Johnny—who was this "Johnny"? No son of Asher's. Yitzhak thought of the little graves they had seen along the trail; he wondered if there was a burial place anywhere for such a loss as this, a young man who betrayed his father and all his forefathers and became someone else.

Asher shook Yitzhak's hand off his shoulder, wiped his face on a handkerchief. He rose from his seat, almost stumbling, and paced back and forth in the dry, stubbly grass behind the wagons. Yitzhak followed, hesitantly. In this vast space, Yitzhak thought, the poor man can only walk a few steps back and forth. He carries his own limited world with him, even here, even to the West.

Chaim Loeb had changed, too; his melodies had opened. He might begin with the old tunes he had played as a young man in Chana's village, but now he brought in a thread of the American popular songs of Estella Cohn's piano and the folk tunes that the other emigrants played around their camp fires. When Yitzhak heard Chaim Loeb's music now, he heard not only the Polish woods, the smoke rising from the chimneys of the shtetl huts. Mixed in now were the boisterous notes of the American frontier, and a sweet, melancholy taste he could not identify—of a faraway country, a tone he associated with the voice of Fergis, Cohn's servant.

And on this night of the new moon, after the strains of the violin died down, when they were all silent around their camp fire, Yitzhak told a story. It was a story of Shmuel Salomon's, one that he did not even know he remembered, one that he had perhaps never really even heard himself until he told it.

"In a little town near Cracow lived a man who was very pious. He had become wealthy and built a new study house and given much to charity. He paid the school fees of all the orphans and gave dowries to poor girls, and on his birthday one year even ordered from Vilna a gorgeous new Torah cover of ornately carved silver, such as no one in this little village had ever imagined.

"There also lived in the same village, as there always is, a man of no account whatsoever. He had a large family, which he could never support; every venture he began ended in disaster, and one trouble after another fell on his household. He had quarreled with the rabbi years before and would not go to services except on the holiest of days. He was often heard in the streets of the town raising his fist to the sky and loudly cursing God, berating the Holy One for causing whatever fresh misfortune had fallen on his head.

"Well, time passed; a cholera swept through the town one summer and both the rich, pious man and the poor heretic were carried away. The pious man stood before the gates of heaven.

"'What are you doing here?' asked the Messiah.

"'What is *he* doing here?' countered the pious man, pointing his finger at the ragged poor man, whom he could see inside, seated on a throne discoursing with the Patriarchs.

"'He spoke with me every day!' thundered the voice of the Lord, the Holy One, blessed be He. 'Every day! And you, only when you wanted to be admired!'"

Yitzhak looked into the fire. "And so," he said softly. "So it is that fortune can be a misfortune, and what seems a misfortune, the greatest blessing of all. The prayer of our father Moses was, 'Lord, I am in need of Thee.' The way of Moses is the way of hopelessness and need, the only way to God."

Just above the line of trees in the distance beyond the camp fire, the new moon rose. Yitzhak sang the ancient prayers of welcome. Chana, Asher, Yaacov, Chaim Loeb, Natan, and Moe stood in a tiny crescent behind him. He rose on his tiptoes three times, as his forefathers had done, as his rebbe had done, and then began to dance.

16

CHANA

THE COUNTRY BEYOND THE PLATTE was dry, almost a desert; the waving grass had given way to wide, sandy plains. The sun's glare burned my eyes and cracked my lips. Dry dust choked my throat. I tied a rag around my face and tried to do the same for Mendel, but he fussed and pulled it away. Even inside the wagon, the fine, gritty dust lay in a thick layer over everything.

Here were no more stands of ash or elm trees, only gnarled cottonwoods by the banks of the wide, slow river. But in a curious way I found this brown, open country more beautiful than the green fields of grass and brightly colored wildflowers we had passed through. The strange, pungent smell of sage was somehow sweeter to me than all the flowers of St. Louis. It was mysterious, thrilling, the scent of promise. Though Yitzhak woke every morning with a prayer for strength and guidance on his lips, and Asher groaned even before he opened his eyes, I awakened like the children: curious and filled with wonder.

Early morning before the fiery sun rose to bake us was the best time of day for me. I changed Mendel's clothes and gave him a piece of dry bread to chew while Rachel and I gathered what we could for the morning fire. Sometimes we could not find wood and instead burned flat cakes of buffalo dung. While the men tended the animals, we built up the cook fire and made the morning meal. A family traveling near us had two milk cows, and the woman gave us fresh milk every day in exchange for our coffee. Our bread was like the unleavened bread of the Exodus, cakes of flour and cornmeal fried over the open fire.

The wagon train was like a moving village; when we stopped, smoke rose from little fires all over the camp just as smoke had risen from the chimneys of my village in Poland. But here were no houses, only wagons and tents; the cattle spread out to graze, the horses and mules picketed nearby. There were no boundaries here, no roads or fences. I looked up into the unbroken sky to see great birds of prey circle and swoop, hunting the small whistling creatures that came out of their tunnels in the ground to sniff the morning air.

"Your baby is sure big!" The woman who traded me milk for coffee was called Sarah, a Jewish name like so many goyim here had. She was tall, with large, red-knuckled hands. She was from Missouri like we were; her family traveled sometimes just behind us, sometimes just ahead. We had eaten each other's dust for hundreds of miles. She had two girls that Rachel played with, though they were older, nearly grown, and we had all picked berries and wild fruits together.

Mendel *was* big, the size of a child of three, though he had not yet had his first birthday. He was active and restless and would climb all over the wagon if I did not take him out and let him toddle and lunge in the grass. Amazingly, he had not once been sick on this journey, though other emigrant families were not so lucky. America was different from Poland in many ways, but here, too, was cholera. And though a doctor traveled with Mr. Russell, here in the wilderness a mishap on a horse or a fall from a wagon could easily mean death.

"You're such a bitty thing yourself," Sarah said, shaking her head as she filled my jug with fresh milk. "It is a wonder. It must have been hard on you, birthin' him."

I blushed. It was not just the curls of smoky fires that made for a resemblance between the wagon train and a Polish shtetl. Women were the same everywhere.

"He and Rachel are my sister-in-law's children," I explained. "You are right, though, it was a hard birth. His mother did not survive it."

"Poor thing," Sarah lamented. "It is good of you to raise him. I've got one of my dead sister's girls myself." She straightened up from her careful pouring and squinted into the morning sun. "Ain't you got none of your own, then?"

I shook my head. Used to it as I was, my barrenness was still a shame for me.

"Well, maybe it is the better thing. The Lord giveth, and He taketh away. My mamma was a kind of granny-woman, when we lived in the cabin my daddy built in Kentucky, an' she had a charm for barren women. She would pick a bunch of mugwort out under the full moon, on account of it grows by water, an' she would hold it right over the woman's belly and say, 'Mary, Jesus, meek and mild; help me please to get with child.' An' you know, there was four women she worked that charm on, and three of them had fine babies the followin' year, and one of them, by an' by, had a family of five, though she was past thirty year old when she begun."

I thanked Sarah for her good wishes. No one in this country seemed to know what a Jew was, even the Jews themselves. If the Holy One, blessed be He, wanted me to have a child, I did not think it would not be by the charms of the goyische God.

We spoke nearly every day about one thing or another, and it was Sarah who told me first, with a sly smile, about Yonah, and so I was the first of us besides Natan to know. Yes, the train of wagons was indeed like a village, with the same gossip. What a disaster to lose Yonah this way! I knew, perhaps better than Yitzhak, that Asher was already in a precarious state. But what could I do? If it was already gossip, it was already done. Yonah was a man and had become a stranger to us even in St. Louis.

So he would leave us now and join those rich Illinois people with their fancy wagons and fine horses and large herds. I could hardly conceive that someone of us, a little Jew from Poland, could associate with such grand people, goyim, and yet in this country so full of empty space, anything could happen. I wondered if Natan would leave us too, to join the goyim, but I saw that he pitied his father. Though Asher was about forty years old, he looked like a withered man of sixty as he sat on his box and cried.

I was angry at Yonah for leaving us without even one backward look. How much could Asher bear to lose? I cuddled and fussed over Mendel to protect him, praying he would grow to make Asher proud. But I had other secret feelings in my heart. I was ashamed of it, but somehow I admired Yonah—or Johnny—that he had dared to become a new person, someone else.

The trade goods we carried in the two extra wagons were to be taken all the way to Fort Hall, beyond South Pass. Cohn had determined that there he would get the best price. Trying to carry them further would be risky, and in Oregon there were goods already, brought by ship. Yaacov and Asher were chiefly responsible for guarding the wagons, but Asher was not really able to do more than worry. Yitzhak had only half an eye out for Cohn's goods; for him, Cohn and St. Louis had ceased to exist the hour we left Independence. He had never had much interest in material affairs in any case; now he seemed to be completely concentrated on something only he could see.

So when Sarah wanted coffee or a piece of cloth in exchange for the fresh milk of her cows, what was it to me? I knew those goods were meant for Cohn's profit, but he had so much money already. All through time people had struggled for money, earned it, and spent it, but where was it all now? Gone. Whereas here was milk for Mendel and Rachel and the rest of us, and what difference did it make if we brought two hundred pounds of coffee to Fort Hall or one hundred and fifty? Sarah told other women, and soon it was as if I was keeping a store again. Asher didn't know, and Yitzhak didn't care. Yaacov told me only to be careful of the whiskey and guns, but the women weren't interested in those; they only wanted some of our extra food or household things. And no one of us complained about the milk or the cheese or the delicious sour pickled cabbage that a Dutchwoman scooped from a barrel in her wagon to trade me for a shirt to replace one her husband had lost when we crossed the muddy Platte.

Moe stuck to Yitzhak like one of those thorny burrs that tangled in the horses' tails. Sometimes I listened at the fire late at night, after the children were asleep, as Moe droned on in his high, whiny voice about his trapping days. Yitzhak saw him as a lost Jewish soul, but I knew him as a coarse, rough man who had led a hard life and done much harm to others. He told such horrid stories that I was glad neither Yitzhak nor Asher understood English well enough to know what he was saying. But Natan's eyes grew wide and my stomach turned as Moe described his battles with Indians— scalpings, festering wounds, and what a man's head looked like, exploded by a pistol shot at close range. And what he called "good times" were more appalling yet. Moe shrieked with laughter as he told of pouring whiskey on an unfortunate comrade and setting him afire; he glowed with pride at the recollection of gouging a man's eye out with his thumb in a brawl over the Indian woman who became his wife.

Except for that wife, Moe had not many good words for Indians, so I was surprised when he came with two of them to the trade wagon late one afternoon. It was just after the Green River crossing, where we had spent a day heating pitch to caulk the wagons tight to float them across. I had found a frying pan and some extra clothing for someone Sarah had brought around. This poor soul from Ohio had buried her husband on the trail a little way beyond Fort Kearney; he had somehow fallen beneath the wheels of their wagon and been crushed before she could stop it. Now she was a widow with three little ones and no one to protect her. Her wagon had not been well enough caulked for the crossing, and half her goods had floated away down the river. Besides the things she asked for, I gave her a small sack of flour and some potatoes.

I was rearranging the wagon when Moe brought the Indians. They were tall men, half-dressed, with dark, shiny skin; I blushed to see their bare, hairless chests. Their black hair hung in long braids, decorated with beads and feathers. I stared.

I had seen such Indians for the first time soon after we crossed the Platte, when there was still grass on the trail. The Oglala were staying by the river that summer, and we passed a camp of theirs. Though I had heard frightening stories about them, I was curious. The Indians in St. Louis seemed just another strange variety of American, but in their camps along the river, these folk reminded me of the gypsies who had sometimes traveled through my shtetl in Poland.

We passed close to their village of round, peaked houses made of animal skins. A group of young men on horseback were playing a game, riding back and forth and trying to touch each other with long sticks. Women, many carrying babies on their backs, were hard at work carrying wood and water and stretching and drying animal skins in the sun. Like gypsies, the Indians seemed to have at least as many dogs as children.

As these two approached the wagon with Moe, their bodies suddenly blocked the afternoon sun. Grisly images from Moe's horrible stories filled my head. With my heart pounding, I crawled out of the wagon very slowly, looking vainly for Yaacov or Natan. I did not trust Moe, despite the fact that my prayers still made him weep. To me he was as mysterious and wild as an Indian himself. At the very least he was crazy, meshuggenah.

"Missy Honey"—he called me so, though Sarah and the other women on the train called me 'Hannah'—"Missy Honey, these Injun boys got some fish to sell ye!"

One of the Indians took a large, tightly woven basket from his back and lifted the lid.

I caught my breath. I had not seen such beautiful fish since Poland! Here were four fat ones, their scales shimmering. What a wonderful supper they would make, two of them, and the others I could smoke over the fire. . . . I could not believe they had come from the thin, sour stream beside the trail.

I asked Moe, "Where do such fish come from?"

"Injuns go way up the river, Missy Honey. They get to places no white man knows."

I nodded. Well, then, to trade. Indians liked whiskey, I had heard.

Moe spat on the ground. He spoke out of the side of his mouth.

"Don't give 'em no whiskey, Missy Honey, nor no guns neither. Just some tobaccy, an' one of them red shirts, maybe."

Quickly I scrambled to the back of the wagon to pull a shirt from the crate. But there were two Indians . . . poor as I was at business, I knew the two shirts were worth more than a few fish. And tobacco, too! But fresh fish, for Shabbos dinner, and perhaps these Indians would be our friends if I gave them the shirts. I held them out, with a small package of tobacco. Both Indians smiled broadly as they fingered the bright red cloth.

Rachel came around the corner of the wagon, leading Mendel by the hand. She stopped when she saw the Indians, but Mendel, crowing, lurched toward them. He was fearless; perhaps he was attracted by the red color of the shirts they held. Mendel smiled up widely at those two strange men, raising up his arms.

Like a flash, I ran forward and scooped him up in my arms. The Indians laughed loudly.

They came nearly every day after that. They brought fish and once an antelope, which I sent them to Sarah with. And when we had to cross a deep, swift-moving stream whose name I did not know, it was the Indians who helped us get the wagons and animals across, in exchange for coffee and tobacco and some tin pans. Mendel became excited whenever he saw them, and they were always amiable to him. So my own fear lessened, and I allowed the baby to approach them.

One day the older of the two men squatted down in front of Mendel and around his neck placed a tiny bag of painted leather tied to a thin leather thong. He straightened up and smiled at me with a look of such kindness that the last of my fear melted away. Mendel laughed and pulled at the bag, but the thong was strong, and it held.

"Wait," I said to the Indian, hoping he could understand me. "Wait." I pronounced the word carefully in English, then repeated it in Yiddish and Polish. I crawled back into the big wagon and found a string of red glass beads for him.

The mountains we were climbing into were gigantic, an immense wall that ended somewhere in the clouds. The ground was hard, dry, rocky. There were no more buffalo or antelope here; there was no grass for them, nor much for our animals. The oxen grew tired and thin as they climbed, though the wagons were lighter than when we had begun. One of the poor creatures, half-blind with fatigue and hunger, stepped into a deep hole, breaking a foreleg. I cried with the ox as it bellowed; there was nothing to do but for Yaacov to shoot it. Asher stared at the lifeless body, which

217

had once been so strong, such a faithful servant. He muttered that it was not fit to eat, but Moe and Sarah's Jim butchered it. Sarah and her girls cooked and smoked the meat; of our family only Natan and Yaacov would eat it.

In the mountains, rain fell every afternoon, in sheets that turned the ground to yellow, thick mud. Our teeth chattered; we could not keep dry. When it did not rain, the sun beat so fiercely that we were drenched in sweat, while the nights were so cold we spent them all together in one wagon. On the prairie I had sometimes taken my blankets outside and slept under the canopy of stars; but here I huddled close to Yitzhak and kept Mendel and Rachel tucked in beside me.

And as we climbed higher, not only Asher but Chaim Loeb lay in the wagon, weak and nauseated. Yitzhak began to get terrible headaches that forced him to lie in our wagon with his head covered for much of the day. Even his sleep was disturbed, and he cried out at night as he had with his terrible dreams. The trail was very rough, the wagons swayed and bumped, and Yitzhak moaned.

One sunrise as I breathed in the scent of the sagebrush, I looked down and it seemed to speak to me; I plucked some leaves and boiled them, and made a poultice to lay on Yitzhak's head. He slept better, but he was still too ill to work. He lay pale and shaking in the wagon, with the fragrant herbs tied around his head, muttering and praying. Asher was worse; though he had not so much pain, he was listless, his eyes were empty, and though I pushed the thought away, I began to wonder if he would ever reach Oregon with us.

We fared better than many other travelers, but my optimism and joy were fading. As the first wispy clouds appeared in a clear sky and slowly built into thunderheads, fear and doubt came again to my heart. Yet somehow I kept my strength, and with the help of God, those of us who stayed well were able to care for the others. And now we got word from Rougeau that our train would stop for a day or two; here was a large spring and a pool of clear water, and all the women had prevailed on the pilots and Mr. Russell to stop for a day to wash our filthy clothes and rest the animals.

I washed clothes in the river with Sarah and her girls, the way I had beside Rivka and Malkuh so many years ago and so far away. With a feeling so sudden it was as if I had slipped into the chilly water myself, I realized that I would never again see that shtetl, or any place in Poland! It was not that I had any longing to return—rather, such a feeling of *otherness* came over me, that for a few minutes I was not sure *where* I was, as if I had somehow slipped off the edge of the world. I kneeled on the spongy ground and felt it with my hands. *Ribono shel Olom,* Master of the Universe. Yes, I was still on His earth. I leaned forward to put my hand in the icy water. The sun beat on my back.

And then I felt a hand there. It was Sarah. "You're all right, ain't you?" Her voice was gentle. "It looked like you might be havin' a dizzy spell. D'you need my smelly salts?"

I shook my head. "I'm all right."

She and her girls began undoing their own bundles, shaking the dirty clothes out into the stream. "You said you were for Ory-gon, didn't ye?" Sarah pushed a strand of stringy hair back from her face.

I wrung out a shirt. "Yes, Oregon. You too, no?"

"Well, that was what I thought, too, because that is where my brother went out for two years ago and wrote us about how fine a place it was. But now my Jim wants to go to Californy instead, and I am mighty vexed about it! I purely don't care to be driven from pillar to post. It seems nigh as hard as those poor Mormons have got!" She pounded the overalls she held with a small rock. "The place up beyond the South Pass, by the Sody Springs, they call it the Partin' of the Ways, an' that's where the folks goin' to Ory-gon go one way, up to the Dalles, and the folks that are goin' to Californy take the other way, down into Californy, where as far as I know, there is nothin' a-tall."

I was impressed by Sarah's knowledge of places and roads. I was like one of the animals, I thought, putting one foot in front of the other and looking for grass.

"Californy isn't good, too?" I asked timidly. That was where Yonah's new people were going.

Sarah sniffed. She was close to tears. "Well, it's good enough for fancy folks, the likes of them your big boy hitched up with. But it ain't where my brother is, nor where my neighbor's man took her off to last year, an' I won't know nary a soul in that Californy, and I can't see why he has to go an' change, anyways!"

"I think my husband is still for Oregon . . ."

I thought Rachel was watching Mendel, but I heard him cry out, sharp and loud. I jumped to my feet.

The baby sat on the ground, howling and holding his arm. I saw the brown flash of a snake slip into the high grass behind him. I screamed.

"He's snake-bit!" Sarah yelled out, rushing to him with me. She grabbed his arm, where two tiny marks showed where the snake's fangs had pierced the skin. She covered the wound with her mouth.

I stared at her in shock.

She turned her head and spit on the ground. "I'm a-suckin' the p'izen out!" she gasped, turning her mouth back to the baby's arm. Mendel howled and struggled away. His arm was swelling. I could not help it; I began to cry.

Mendel lay in my arms by the fire in a dull sleep. Natan had ridden up for the doctor with Mr. Russell's party; he had not come but only sent word back that if the poison had been sucked out, there was nothing more to do. Sarah brought an herb tea for him, but she was doubtful. She had seen the snake, and it was a kind she did not recognize, and she did not know if the snakebite remedies she knew from home would work. But she fed Rachel and Levi while I sat with Mendel, unable to do any more than cry. I had forgotten how to pray. I had tried so hard to protect him, and now I had failed, failed, failed! If he died, I did not want to live, either. Then Rachel came and stroked her brother's head, bending so that her curly hair fell against my cheek. How dare I think of death? Instantly I felt more remorse.

Yitzhak woke and came from the wagon, groaning and clutching his head. He struggled to recover himself when he saw my tear-streaked face. Through sobs I told him what had happened. The pain and concern on his face made me cry harder; he was not strong enough now to help. He went to wash himself at the river and prayed over the baby, but his voice was just a whisper.

"You pray, Chana," he said softly to me.

"I cannot," I sobbed.

"Only try," he said. "Somehow, God will help you, will help the baby."

But I had no confidence in Yitzhak and his prayers now. He had not been able to help his own sister. How did he think He would heal her orphan?

Late in the night while Yitzhak slept again, I lay in the wagon with Mendel. I stared at the leather charm the Indian had placed around his neck. Outside the wagon, Moe and Yaacov had built up the fire. Chaim Loeb must be feeling better, I thought, as I heard his violin in the chilly night air. I felt as though I was dreaming as I reached forward to touch the strange leather thing on Mendel's chest. I picked it up and carefully untied the little bag from its cord. I held it in my hands over the baby's arm, now grotesquely swollen. I heard words in my head I had never before heard: *O Spirit,* I prayed. *O Spirit, help this baby to live and grow strong in the land of the West.* I closed my eyes and saw a huge bird, sharp-beaked like the big golden bird of prey Moe told me was an eagle. I drew in my breath.

With trembling fingers I unwrapped the leather. Inside

was an odd collection of tiny objects: a piece of bone, dried leaves, little feathers, a large bright bead. Quickly I wrapped it again and tied it to the thong around Mendel's neck.

He sighed deeply in his sleep. Once, twice. His eyelids flickered. The trace of a smile crossed his face. I thought I heard the rustle of a bird's wings; I sighed, too, and slept.

17

YITZHAK

Yɪᴛᴢʜᴀᴋ gradually began to make sense of Moe's witless rambling. He did not understand most of the English words, but pictures formed in his mind as Moe spoke. He understood: men in the West drank whiskey and fought, just like the Poles with their vodka. Here, men drank whiskey and killed Indians—perhaps as the Poles drank vodka and killed Jews. But here Indians also drank whiskey and also killed. Even Moe's former livelihood was killing; he was a kind of hunter, but now the animal he had hunted— the beaver—was all gone. All killed. Yitzhak remembered when he and Asher had been in the fur trade in Ropshitz— the awful, rank smell of the pelts, the strange, fine dust they gave off. There was something else about it, too, a feeling he could only vaguely remember. . . . Chana did not like it at all. Here he was awestruck by the beauty of this wilderness, the mightiness of the Creator who had made such a world. He wondered why such men as Moe could find nothing better to do in it than kill.

"Just as soon as I get back to that place I left out there, I might try my hand at farmin'. I surely have tried about everythin' else. And this-ee place I got me is so pretty an' green, with a sweet-water creek on it."

"Farm, yes," Yitzhak nodded approvingly. "We go to farm, too. You know it, farming?"

Moe looked embarrassed. "Well, actually, I never did try it. But I can pick it up all right-ee, you bet!"

"Why you don't come to Oregon wit' us? We farm together."

"Aw, Doc Itchy, I couldn't do that. No. Too many people in Ory-gon for me. Just look-ee at all these folks here on this train, most of 'em for Ory-gon, exceptin' the few's for Californy. An' I hear those darned Mormons are all comin' to Ory-gon, too! Ol' Rougeau told me they got scouts out there now, and Brother Brigham himself! An' Mormons, why, they breed like mice, an' before you know it, Ory-gon's gonna look jus' like St. Louis! People all over the place!"

"People is good," Yitzhak protested. "What's wrong wit' people? Is not good, live by self alone."

"Well, ain't nothin' wrong with 'em, they jus' makes me mad. They is always after my money or my woman or some-thin'. They always want to fight me, an' then I fight back—"

"Fighting is not for Jews," Yitzhak said sternly. "King David said, '*Hinay matov uma nayim, shevas achim gam ya-chod.*'"

"Well, I never met no King, David or nobody else. An' you know already I don't parlee-voo."

"Wait. Means something like, 'is good for people to live like brothers, all one.'" Yitzhak beamed. God was surely helping him; he knew words he did not know he knew. "King David was a great king of Jews."

"Well, maybe that was all right for *his* folks. But it ain't like that nowhere I've ever been." Moe spat. "Everywhere I ever been, it's jus' one yellow dog eatin' the other." He spat again.

"You come wit' us, Moe. We live like Jews. Help each other, don't fight each other. In Oregon. I teach you Jewish ways, the ways of our people."

Moe laughed. "Well, you can teach, Doc, but I ain' gonna

learn. I never had no schoolin' a-tall, and I know I'm too
bullheaded now. No, you go on an' take your folks to Ory-gon.
I'll be in that little valley, not so far from Taos, puttin' down
meat for winter an' lookin' out for Injuns!" he cackled.

Yitzhak found the Indians fascinating, though a little frightening; he had seen their skin-house villages, with the strips
of buffalo meat drying on sticks. He had watched the Indian
men riding without saddles, nearly naked, seen the women
in their long, beaded dresses, the brown children. He
wished that Feigl could have lived to see such curious
sights—the way they piled their goods on sleds, though
there was no snow, and how even their dogs pulled little
loads. He wondered if the ancient Hebrew tribes had also
lived in such villages, in tents made of skins. . . . Could these
be the lost Jews of the West he had dreamed of? Were they
some remnant of exile, descendants of the lost tribes?

Moe sweated and strained with Yitzhak, Yaacov, and
Natan—even little, wiry Chaim Loeb helped in the crossing
of the North Platte, where they again heated pitch to caulk
the wagons and pulled them across the river with ropes.
The country they climbed through now, with huge mountains rising ahead of them, was desolate, barren: a desert.
What water there was, was so sour the animals could not
drink.

Yitzhak thought of that other desert, centuries ago, and
at night, as the moon rose, he drew his people together into
a magic circle of prayer and song. Even Chana joined them
again in the ancient celebration of unity under the stars:
"*L'shem yichud kudsha brichu, Ush'chintay; L'shem yichud
kudsha brichu, Ush'chintay.* . . ." Yitzhak danced. The sparks,
the holy sparks, crackled from his heels as they hit the
ground. Sparks flew from his red hair, he was a fire rabbi,
the king of sparks! "*Ha! Hi! Hi!*" he shouted, as the sparks of
ecstasy flew from his eyes. And Moe sang, too, leaping and

stamping as Yitzhak did to the *"El Shaddai! El Chai v'Kayam! El Shaddai! El Chai v'Kayam! El Shaddai! El Chai v'Kayam!* O Almighty, Ever-Living God!"

Afterward, they stood in sweet, golden silence by the fire. Moe seemed to glow, not with the passion of whiskey and blood that Yitzhak had seen in his face before, but something else, something brighter, more clear. Yitzhak watched him. This Jew was still so far from being a Jew, but he might yet be a *mensch.*

And now the great mountains were upon them; the trail climbed steeply, high above the rushing Sweetwater River. Two more oxen faltered, too weak from the lack of grass and water to pull their heavy loads. In this dangerous, untamed world, Yitzhak saw that it was Moe who was the teacher, the leader, and he who was as ignorant as a child. But surely all of them were led by God, and God had brought them Moe, this barbaric creature, and surely the Holy One had something in mind.

The sickness that overcame him as they ascended into the massive, terrifying mountains left him weak and trembling. He struggled against it, but he could not walk; after even a few steps he was breathless, and within a few days the terrible headache came, the pain that felt as if his head was being split on an anvil of this mountain rock. Moe called it "mountain fever" and prescribed whiskey, but the drink burned him; it was like drinking fire, and his headache only became more violent.

One day Moe called out that they had reached another landmark, Independence Rock. Chana, like the others who were unable to write, scratched her mark on the soft stone and begged him to rouse himself to write their names. Yitzhak stumbled into the bright sun—a sun he only wanted to shrink from—to the foot of the huge, round monument scrawled with the names and marks of those who had passed.

"Put your name up there, Doc!" Moe, grinning, handed him his hunting knife. Yitzhak blinked, struggling with the pain in his head. A knife, a rock . . . what was so familiar? Shaking, he formed his initial, a tiny *yod*, in the rock. It swam before his eyes, like a little fish. *Yod. He. Vav.* . . . Was he writing the holy Name, then, the Ineffable, the forbidden?

Finally he crumbled and, like Asher, lay in the lurching, rocking wagon, gritting his teeth to keep from screaming as it rolled from side to side. At night he fell into a fitful, dream-troubled sleep.

In Yitzhak's dream, the fire raged across the prairie and scorched the desert. Rocks melted; he heard the bellowing and roaring of animals: sheep, horses, oxen, buffalo. He watched, helpless, as the world burned. And here were the crushing-boxes! Yes, now covered with canvas like the wagons on the train, and it was the emigrants, their faces demonically twisted, who rode down the people to press them into . . . but wait! It was not the Jews of Przemysl being pushed into the wagons, to be sent into the fire—it was those tall, naked, sun-browned men with their black hair braided with beads and feathers, it was their women in buckskin dresses, covered in beads, it was their babies. In his dream, Yitzhak screamed out to God: *"Adonoi! Adonoi!"* And heard the muttering voices of his father and the old Talmud teacher: *And smote them with the edge of the sword . . . and burned it with fire . . . and did not leave any living thing.*

Yitzhak tried to scream. He heard another voice, a deeper voice, the Voice behind voices, the Word behind words. And knows: *It is wrong.*

He heard the Indians singing, dancing to the drum and rattle: *"Ya-ho, ya-he-wah-he, ya-ho, ya-he-wah-he, ya-ho, ya-he-wah-he. . . ."* Written in flames in the smoky, swirling dream sky Yitzhak saw the four letters, the letters that spelled the Name: *Yod. He. Vav. He.* . . .

"No!" Yitzhak screamed now. "No! It is wrong! *Yah—!* It cannot be said!"

He woke up, feeling the chill mountain air on his face. His mouth was dry, his lips swollen and cracked. He had been sleeping too much again, he must rouse himself. Through the opening of the canvas cover, he saw the just-risen sun glowing red and gold in a space between the clouded peaks of the mountains. It seemed so very near. He was only half awake, still he raised his hands and whispered, "*Sh'ma Yisroel, Yah—* . . ."

Suddenly he was wide awake. He tried to repeat the morning prayer, as he had been taught to repeat it, as Jews had repeated it for centuries, but his heretical tongue betrayed him again, forcing from his throat the forbidden Name, the Secret Name, the Name he had only whispered, the name he cried aloud in his dream: **"*Ya-Hu-Ve-H.*"**

He was only dimly aware that they still climbed. He did not know how long he slept; the sun was already high. He dreamed again, wildly, vividly, bright red and gold dreams of chanting, dancing Indians, of Feigl, of a serpent in the beak of a great bird, of Shmuel Salomon walking with Chana, arm in arm, rhythmically whispering the word *echod, echod, echod, one, one, one,* like a heart beating. He whispered his prayers and listened to the morning noise of the camp. There was Chana's gay voice, the sound of children—of children! He heard the baby's audacious laugh and sat upright.

In his dream he had seen Feigl lying in pain, he went to her and took her thin hand, he prayed with that forbidden Name and saw her grow strong again, healed, laughing, her new son beside her. And then it was her son he saw . . . hurt in some way . . . and had he prayed?

That was no dream, that was real, that the child had been bitten by a snake, and though he had tried with all his might to summon the strength and concentration to pray, he was drifting in and out of consciousness; he had not the power in his own body to call down the light of the Holy One into the body of the child. He had prayed only in his dream. But here was the child alive!

"Chana! Chana!" he called, struggling to rise, staggering a little, but he was better, the pain in his head subsided to a dull ache. He blinked his sore eyes.

Chana came to him, Mendel on her hip, her face joyful.

"Yitzhak, he is well! He is well!"

"Baruch Hashem," Yitzhak whispered. Praise God.

Chana set the baby down beside Yitzhak. She fingered the leather charm. "Yitzhak, I think this charm from the Indian—when I held it I could pray again, and now he is well! All well!"

She is still so beautiful, Yitzhak thought. And her simple faith. "But you prayed, then!"

Chana blushed. "I am not sure. Yes, I prayed. I looked at the charm of the Indians and heard a prayer, and then came to me the picture of a big bird, an eagle!"

"Well then," Yitzhak said. He tickled Mendel's cheeks to make him laugh. "If the Holy One, blessed be He, could send a raven to feed Elijah in the desert, could He not be also the god of the Indians, and come as an eagle to save Feigl's boy? *Adonoi Echod,* the Lord is One; perhaps the Indians were once our brothers from ancient days. And they have helped now to heal Feigl's American baby." He took Chana in his arms. "I am better now, too, dearest one. Have you made tea this morning?"

And as she went to the fire, and as Yitzhak whispered praise and thanksgiving, the Name came to him unbidden; he heard a whisper: *Yah—* Startled, he jumped. But Chana was not there. Did he whisper it himself, speak the unspeakable?

Chaim Loeb smiled as he raised his violin; Yitzhak was well enough to lead prayers for the first time in many days. Yaacov and Moe helped Asher from the wagon to sit beside the fire on a pile of blankets. Yitzhak sang in gratitude for the healing of Mendel, for his own restoration to health: "Who can express the mighty acts of the Lord, or make all His praise to be heard. . . ." They sang together, as Chaim Loeb's violin rose to the stars: *"Ain Kelohaynu, ain Kadonaynu, ain K'Malkaynu, ain K'Moshi'aynu. . . .* One is our Lord, One is our God, One is our King, One is our Saviour . . ." and in the distance they heard the yips and howls of coyotes in the spaces when they paused for breath.

Yitzhak looked into the camp fire. He felt himself expanding inside his skin; a swelling, flowering sensation inside his chest; he heard the great Voice, as if it was coming not from a bush burning outside of himself, as the camp fire burned, but from something that burned *within* him. He raised his arms, then lowered them, taking hands with Chana on his left and Yaacov on his right, Yaacov taking Moe's hand on his right, clasping them tightly, bending their elbows so that they stood shoulder to shoulder in a crescent, with Asher and Chaim Loeb held partly inside it. Yitzhak hummed a note and swayed and dipped; this song was new, he had never heard it until it burst from him, until he pronounced the unpronounceable name: ***"Ya-Hu-Ve-H Echod. . . . God is One!"***

Only Moe joined him; the others froze. Asher raised himself on an elbow to stare in horror. He lifted a shaking forefinger to Yitzhak but spoke to Chaim Loeb.

"He is in a delirium, he has gone mad!"

Yitzhak could not stop: ***"YaHuVeH** Echod!* ***YaHuVeH** Echod!"*

Asher shouted at him. "Stop! Stop! Madman! *Apikoris!* Heretic! Be quiet!"

Yitzhak blinked and came back into himself. He looked around. "Forgive me, Asher," he said. "I was dreaming."

He knew he was lying. His mind spun and rolled like a tumbleweed in the wind. It was the Master of the Universe Himself Who put that Word in his mouth, yet he had not the courage to insist with Asher. Which one of them was mad? No, Shmuel Salomon, his beloved teacher and master, never would *he* utter that Name. But: *Remember the secret,* he had whispered. Was that not the secret he had meant, the secret of the burning bush, the true Name, taken from an undeserving Israel? Yitzhak strained to recall his teacher's words. *In exile, the Name cannot be used without being used falsely . . . for if* I AM, *who are you?* A riddle. But perhaps this was no longer exile, here in the wilderness? Was it not an exile that had completed itself, come a full circle and become a return, a return to this place that must be like the desert that Moses knew? Perhaps they were already home, or near.

Moe had spoken of the place somewhere nearby where the waters divided. On one side the rivers flowed east, into the ocean between America and Poland; on the other the rivers flowed west, into the ocean he did not know. Was this division, then, the center of the created world? The true home of Israel?

Asher trembled with shock and rage. Yitzhak would not have believed the man had enough force in him to shout like that. And in Asher's face now Yitzhak saw the face of his own father, fierce with righteousness, and that of his boyhood Talmud teacher, the old man, surely dead many years by now and thousands of miles away. But he had not escaped them. Nor had he escaped the spirit of Shmuel Salomon, whose echoing laugh mocked him. *So now you see,* whispered the voice of his rebbe. See what? Yitzhak wondered.

There was no marker at South Pass to indicate that they were crossing the summit. Only a broad, flat saddle between the peaks, a wide plain of sand and sagebrush. As they began to descend the western slope of the Rockies, Yitzhak's headache faded, his vitality returned. He felt clean, purified, as he had when he had emerged from the riverside hut long ago where he had tried to do penance for his pride. Had he succeeded? It seemed to him now that pride rose and fell like the wind. *And every mountain shall be laid low,* he heard. *And every plain exalted.*

Where had he been? While his body had crossed ocean, prairie, and mountains, it seemed his soul had been on another journey, a journey of dreams and visions. A journey where he was guided by the Name he still scarcely dared say aloud, the Name that was given by God to Moses, the *I AM, Ya-Hu-Ve-H.* And why did God give this Name to Moses? Because it was what he needed to bring his people out from slavery, to cross the wilderness, to come home. Because only the power of that sound was sufficient. Now Yitzhak heard this Name echoing everywhere: in the sound of the wagon wheels over the rocky trail, in the bellowing of the animals, the shouts of the men. At night, trembling, he embraced Chana and, for a moment, heard the Name in the quickening of her breath beneath him, and he bit his lip to keep from crying out. Behind his closed eyelids the holy letters rose in towers of flame: *Yod. He. Vav. He.*

Yitzhak almost laughed aloud. With this Name he could do anything—no wonder the rabbis had forbidden it! He could fulfill the will of God, he could bring his people across the desert and the mountains, he could fill Chana's womb.

They had crossed twenty more miles of dry wasteland, and at the crossing of the Green River—a deep, rushing stream— Rougeau announced that the wagons he led would detour south to Fort Bridger. Some of the California-bound emigrants—the people that Yonah had gone with—would leave at the Big Sandy, taking a new road, while others headed for California—led by Captain Boggs—would not break from the Oregon Trail until Soda Springs, at the Parting of the Ways. The decision to detour was angrily disputed, and about twenty impatient Oregon-bound families chose to continue due west on the cutoff by Slate Creek and Emigrant Springs. Moe grumbled, too.

"Whatever it is they need, they surely won't find it at Old Gabe's place," he said. "It is the puniest excuse for a fort I ever hope to see. If you ask me, Rougeau's goin' off with those Californy folks. Prob'ly paid him better."

The dispute, and the Green River crossing itself, took two days, and Yitzhak took advantage of the stop to inspect the two wagons of trade goods. He felt pressed, less by a specific guiding voice than by a guiding *feeling*, a sense that he *must* do this. He took a rough inventory as he once had done in Cohn's storehouse.

In the first wagon the stores of food had been diminished by Chana's trading; some of the crates of ready-made clothing and kitchenware had been opened, too. In the second wagon he found what he was looking for. He had guessed right about Rougeau—and probably Moe as well. Still there was a great deal of whiskey left. Too much, he thought. He found the four crates of guns, mostly rifles—Hawkens, a few of the new Springfields—and a dozen Colt revolvers. He whistled a melody of his rebbe's.

"You mean to sell all that whiskey at Fort Hall?"

Yitzhak turned, saw Moe behind him. He grunted agreement.

Moe spat. "Well, you can do as you like with it, I guess, it bein' your'n."

"It is the whiskey of Mister Cohn," Yitzhak said stiffly.

"Oh, I know," Moe answered, slyly, "but you'd make a lot more on it, way I see."

"I know what to do wit' the whiskey."

"Well, but iff'n you trade some to the Injuns what are camped around Fort Bridger this time of year, you can trade for more in skins an' buffalo robes an' such; an' then carry those off to Ory-gon, y'see?"

"No," Yitzhak shook his head.

"Why them folks out in Ory-gon'll pay good money for buffalo robes, better'n you'll ever see from those Fort Hall traders for your whiskey! Buckskins, too, an' fine beadwork, an' it's been a good buffalo year. I bet Injuns'd have jerky to trade, too."

"No," Yitzhak repeated. "Whiskey no good for Indians. Maybe whiskey no good for you, neither."

Moe laughed wildly. "Maybe, but it don't make no difference! Them traders'll scalp you, . . ." he laughed again. "Meanin', that is, they won't pay ye but as little as they can, an' they'll turn around an' trade your whiskey to Injuns themselves anyway, so why let them have a profit off you? Someone's gonna drink it."

Yitzhak held up his hand. "Moe, thank you for advice. I know you want to help. But enough now. I do what I must do."

He felt light inside; light yet powerful, like a brisk wind, a rushing mountain creek. Inexorable, his movement could not be stopped. Shmuel Salomon urged him on. *Get Yaacov,* the voice whispered. *You are the rebbe now. Send Moe to get Yaacov.*

Moe still argued; Yitzhak fixed him with a stare. A rebbe's look.

"I am the rebbe here, now you go. Send me Yaacov here, I need to talk wit' him."

Moe backed away. "All right-ee, Doc Itchy! You bet! But you think about what I'm a-tellin' you!"

Yitzhak stooped in the wagon, breathing hard. He turned to the first crate of rifles. . . .

"Are you all right, Rebbe?" Yaacov asked.

Yitzhak nodded. The voice in his head spoke: *You will know what you need. The Holy One, blessed be He, provides for His creatures.*

Yaacov came closer. "Rebbe, you know now we have trouble with the oxen that are pulling the front wagon. I don't think those two will make it. And one of the ones on the third wagon is bloated. We have no more, we will not have enough animals to pull all the wagons. We must see at Fort Bridger if we can buy another ox; two would be better."

Yitzhak smiled. "God is good," he muttered. He turned to

Yaacov. "I know. That is why I sent for you now, I need your help." He held a rifle in each hand.

"I think just—" Yitzhak closed his eyes. *Chesed,* mercy. "Four rifles. Take these and put them in the other wagon, hide them. You still have your gun, no? And Natan has?"

Yaacov nodded. Puzzled, he did as Yitzhak asked, carrying two of the long guns carefully under each arm. When he came back, Yitzhak had separated the three other crates of kitchen goods, a few boxes of bullets and powder, six bolts of calico, and two of flannel.

"These, too," he said. "Make room in the other wagons." In the distance they heard the call to start up. Yitzhak and Yaacov quickly emptied the wagon of everything except the barrels of whiskey, the four crates of guns, and about half of the ammunition.

Moe came up with his mule. "Ridin' out now, Doc Itchy!"

Yitzhak nodded. "Yah. We ready. We go slower now, and for this wagon here we put one ox only. I stay here and drive him."

They fell back to the end of the train, with the emigrants' thinning herds of oxen and tired remudas of horses and mules. The going was very rough, the narrow trail winding steeply down the jagged, rocky mountains toward Fort Bridger. Moe told Yitzhak with a smile of satisfaction that the "fancy folk" of Yonah's had had to abandon their piano and several crates of furnishings. Yitzhak sent him away. He wanted to be alone.

The single, tired ox pulling the last wagon looked gratefully at Yitzhak as he unhitched it. The trail curved sharply down past a steep, rocky slope. Panting but filled with a strength he did not imagine he had, Yitzhak put his shoulder to the rear end of the wagon and pushed it to the edge of the trail.

"*L'shem yichud kudsha brichu, Ush'chintay, . . .*" Yitzhak

breathed. "In the name of the unity of the Holy One and the Shekhinah." He leaned his shoulder to the wagon again. With all his strength he shoved, and the wagon rolled down over the mountainside in an enormous, splintering crash, spilling its contents wildly, bouncing on the rocks. Yitzhak whispered, hoarsely, the magic unpronounceable Name of God.

Chana, Asher, Yaacov, Chaim Loeb, and Natan came running at the sound and stared over the edge of the road into the gully below.

Asher rocked back and forth on his feet and pulled at his hair. "*Oy! Oy!* What more! What more can befall us!"

"The ox!" Chana screamed. "The ox fell down the mountain!"

"Hush, Chana," Yitzhak went to her. He pointed to the ox, who had wandered to the other side of the trail and was nosing at the gravelly dirt in a vain search for grass. "See, the ox is all right."

Yaacov scratched his head. "Rebbe, if the ox did not slip, how did the wagon? . . ."

Yitzhak shrugged. "An accident. Who knows how it happened? I heard noise, I looked around, I saw—but it was too late to stop it."

"Look, look, the goods!" Asher wailed, pointing to the whiskey barrels split open on the sharp rocks, the broken crates of guns. "We are responsible! What will we say to Cohn now? How will we pay him?" He looked bitterly at Yitzhak. "We are cursed, cursed with your blasphemy."

"Asher!" Yitzhak protested. "Of course this journey has been filled with dangers. Only the loving-kindness of God Himself has brought us this far with so little loss. Look, we are all alive. So we have lost a little merchandise." He took Asher by the shoulders. "Besides, we will never see Cohn again. We will send a message back with Rougeau. By the time Cohn gets it, we will be in Oregon, making a good living on the fine land that waits for us." He smiled. "A promised land, *nu?* Don't worry, Asher. We will repay him, don't worry."

Moe came up now and leaned over the edge. His jaw was clenched; he worked it back and forth. When he spoke, his voice was tight, as if he were trying to hold back tears. He sniffed the air, catching the fumes of spilled whiskey that rose up to the trail.

"What happened here, Doc Itchy? Ox slip an' go down?"

"*Vos?*" Yitzhak stared at him. "Ox is there." He pointed.

Moe stared back, incredulous. "Aw, Doc, how'd the wagon go down then, without the ox pullin' it went lame and fell over?" He walked again to the edge, looked down, paced back and forth. He crossed to where the ox still nuzzled the dirt and carefully lifted each of the animal's feet. He shook his head. "No-ee, no-ee, I jus' don't see how!"

"Listen to me, Moe," Yitzhak said gently. "I am your rebbe. The Holy One, blessed be He, works wonders. We don't understand His ways. Who can describe them? Perhaps now, you see such a wonder. *Baruch Hashem.*"

Just before Fort Bridger, at the Big Sandy, the "fancy folk"—the Donners, Reeds, Breens, and Murphys, with Yonah and his Reed sweetheart—set out on the new, shorter route to California. Yitzhak watched with a silent, secret blessing for Yonah; a wild hope that he was not really gone.

And though Asher had behaved as if Yonah were already truly dead, this departure set off a new grief for him, as if the fresh wound were now sealed with boiling oil, as the Jewish martyrs had once been tortured in Spain. Yitzhak sat with Asher by the fire and recited psalms with him far into the night.

Moe's assessment of the supplies available at Fort Bridger was correct; there were no oxen for sale, nor even mules. They did not stay there long. The train was shorter now as they came up to the Bear River, where there was grass and good water, easier going. They heard the hiss of springs for some distance before they reached the bubbling pools of Soda Springs; a little further on, more miraculous still, was a geyser that spouted steaming water at regular intervals of a minute or so, like a heartbeat from deep within the mountains.

"You see how well the Holy One plans," Yitzhak nudged Moe. "Better leave to Him the planning, and we carry out."

Moe shook his head. "What are we gonna do if we lose another ox?" he grumbled. "We got hardly nothin' to sell or trade now, neither, since we lost that wagon."

Yitzhak noticed that Moe said "we," and smiled.

Indians were camped by the river on the outskirts of the fort. But Rougeau and the other pilots decided that this was where the emigrant train should camp, and raised up a party to encourage the Indians to move on. Though it was a large camp of Indians, it was not a war party; women and children were with them. They were there to trade. Yitzhak watched how hurriedly the Indian women broke camp, shouting at the children and dogs as they packed their skin houses onto their sleds.

Moe watched, too. He had not gone with the party of riflemen, led by Rougeau, that went to parley with the Indians. He had told Yitzhak that he would leave them at Fort Hall, taking his mule south, traveling for awhile with the emigrants headed for California and then riding over the mountains to his cabin. But he would return a different man, Yitzhak thought. Now he knows a little of what a Jew is. Not I, but the Lord God has changed him; the Lord, the *I AM*. And have I also changed?

18

CHANA

CHAIM LOEB began to recover from the mountain sickness almost as soon as we crossed the pass. Now that there were no sheep for him to watch, he spent time with the children, telling them nonsense stories about Chelm, the town of the fools. He had been a grown man when I was a child; now he was growing old. I remembered how he had played for every festival and wedding in our village. I felt I had known him forever. Now, seated by the fire in this beautiful mountain valley, he held a crude top he had carved from a scrap of wood for Mendel, trying to make it spin on the uneven, rocky ground.

The men at Fort Hall warned us that the trail ahead would be very rough. The mountains we would have to cross were steep and the canyons narrow, and it would be impossible to get large, heavily loaded wagons through. Moe said it wasn't so bad as that, they were only trying to persuade people to dump their supplies at the fort for a low price. We did sell almost all of the cloth and kitchen goods, and most of what was left of the coffee, salt, and sugar. On Moe's advice we bought four mules, and had a small sum left to send back to Cohn, though it was certainly less than he must have expected. Yitzhak sent a letter, explaining about the animals that had died and the wagon that had fallen into the gully, and promising to repay him from the money we would make on our farm in Oregon. Yaacov and Moe repaired our remaining three wagons, and we packed everything securely for our journey.

Though our rest seemed to have helped Asher to recover physically, he had fallen into a mood of angry fearfulness. He jumped at every sound and spoke harshly even to Rachel, sending her off in tears when she only wanted to ask him something. And he was suspicious of Yitzhak, unable to forgive him for that night when he had called God by His Secret Name. Though Yitzhak was careful now not to pray that way again in Asher's hearing, I knew that in private it was still the name he used.

Just beyond Fort Hall, as Sarah had told me, the last of the California-bound people who had not left us before now bade us farewell. Sarah's Jim had made up his mind for California; I was sad because she had become my friend. Rachel and I cried as we embraced Sarah and her girls for the last time, and Sarah gave me a beautifully embroidered handkerchief. We had sold most of our trade goods at Fort Hall, but I gave her a length of calico that I had held back; she was clever at sewing, like Feigl had been, and I thought she might make a sunbonnet or an apron from it.

As Rachel and I stood in the trail, crying and waving at their wagon, Moe rode up through the dust, leading his mule. I thought he, too, had come to say good-bye; he was to travel just a little distance with the California people before turning south on his own. He slipped down from his horse.

Yitzhak extended his hand. "Well, Moe," he smiled.

"Doc Itchy, I been thinkin'. About your young 'un's an' all, an' your wife here." He nodded his head at me. "I mean, do you think you could maybe use another hand? I reckon I could go out with you to Ory-gon, just for my keep, y' know? An' then, you see, I could go back home in the spring."

Yitzhak was beaming now. "You stay wit' us, Moe. You stay wit' Jewish people."

Moe was grinning, too. "Naw, naw, Doc; I told you, I ain't *stayin'* in Ory-gon, but if'n you could let a wagon go over without even the ox goin' down lame, you surely do need my help."

And so Moe stayed with us, and we watched the California wagons roll away on their southwestern trail. I whispered a prayer for them.

It was hard going on this stretch, high above the Snake River. The rocks were so sharp that the oxen's feet bled; they slipped in their blood, and the mules and horses did only a little better. We were moving very slowly; not us only, but all the wagons. It was a long, hard day of struggle to travel only two or three miles. In one spot we stopped for hours waiting for a wagon ahead of us to be repaired, and I let Rachel go out to look for wildflowers.

A brisk, icy breeze blew down off the mountain, and in the distance thunderheads piled high. The river was far below us. Now the stopped wagon in front of us began to move out, and Rougeau came to tell us we must press on still a little farther to where there was water and wood for camp. I left Mendel in Chaim Loeb's care and went to look for Rachel.

It was late in the day, really too late to travel, but Rougeau had given the word. I wandered for quite awhile before I saw her with Levi; I shouted at them that we were moving on again. When I came back, it was by a different way, and I found myself just ahead of our wagons, at the end of the train.

Yitzhak and Asher faced each other in the trail. They didn't see me; I stood as still as a deer. I could hear every angry word they shouted at each other.

"Yes, in *Polania* we had troubles, life is troubles, but there were people there, Jewish people, there was life there."

"Asher, there was *death* there! You are a fool!"

Asher's face was grim. "Yes, I am a fool! I was a fool ever to listen to you, to follow you to this, this . . . this *nowhere!* Now I have gone far enough with you, madman. I stop right here, I will leave myself here to die without even a wall to turn my face to. I can follow you no more. I followed you believing that you were the son of your father."

"That hypocrite! Never! May he rest in peace; he was a bigger fool even than you!"

"But not than you! He was a great man, a true rebbe. He was not swayed by the spells of women."

"What are you saying?"

"Your wife has bewitched you, that is obvious."

"Chana?"

"Who else? Who else has used sorcery to make you speak the forbidden Name?"

Tears filled my eyes. Asher still shouted.

"Don't you think there is a reason that our people do not pray with women? They are impure, and your heresy has made *you* impure. Under her spell you have gone from one blasphemy to another. And do you know, heretic, what tomorrow is? Have you not counted the moon? Do you not even know that this is *Erev Yom Kippur,* the eve of the holiest day, and yet your sorceress wife prepares food as if it were a day like any other? You are cursed now, and now we run headlong toward darkness, to disaster!"

Yitzhak stepped back. "Asher, for that I ask forgiveness, not from you, but from the Holy One, the Lord God Who goes before us. We will fast, we will pray. There will be no disaster."

Asher laughed bitterly. "No, it is too late. We are already cursed. Do you think you are the only one who dreams? I, too, have dreamed such dreams. I have seen the wild savages raising their bloody arrows and shooting us with guns, the guns of Cohn that you let roll down the mountain!"

"Asher, I beg you—"

242

Asher's face twisted into a sneer; he spat at Yitzhak's face. "Hah! Better I should go no further. Better I should sit down here and die on this cursed Oregon Trail."

Yitzhak wiped his face slowly. He did not shout now but spoke softly. "Please, Asher, you cannot. Despair is forbidden. It is forbidden to take your own life, and that is what it means if we do not remain together. It is wilderness here, but God will lead us. Have a little faith."

Asher raised his hand to strike Yitzhak. I could hardly hold myself back from rushing forward. But Yitzhak was quick, strong; he caught Asher's hand and held it.

A wave of cold fear washed over me; I felt catastrophe very near. God, Spirit, I prayed. Have we not had enough?

Yitzhak threw Asher's arm aside. I could see how angry he was; I could almost smell it in the air. "I cannot allow this, Asher!" He turned, his face as red as his hair, and bellowed: "Yaacov! Natan! Help me!"

I knew what Yitzhak wanted: for them to take Asher forcibly and put him in the wagon, tie him inside there. But how would Natan lay hands on his own father? There were shouts, a struggle. Asher began to run. Then, just ahead, on the trail, he stopped and turned, looking like a madman, spittle gleaming on his gray beard. He bent to the ground for a handful of small stones and hurled them wildly toward Yitzhak.

A stone must have struck one of the oxen hitched to the front wagon; the creature, with its mate, bolted frantically down the trail toward Asher, dragging the wagon. Asher leapt out of the way of the oxen but did not quite clear the wagon. It rolled so fast I hardly saw what happened, but I heard Asher scream and saw him lying in the rocky trail, moaning in pain, his face paler and grayer than the granite of the mountains. I did not see at first what was wrong, but then I did see; it was his leg, crushed and bent away from his body. The oxen and wagon had stopped only a few feet ahead from where the heavy wheels had rolled over Asher's leg.

Yaacov gently lifted Asher onto a plank and laid him inside the wagon, and Moe took our fastest horse to ride ahead to catch the wagons that had gone for California, where that doctor of Mr. Russell's had gone.

And this time the doctor did come, though it was not until late the next day. We had camped there where we were, hoping vainly that we could catch up with the rest later. Natan and Levi climbed down the steep, rocky slope to the river for water. Yitzhak did not leave Asher's side; he cried and prayed over him, but Asher kept his gray face turned away.

The doctor only had to look briefly at Asher's leg, crushed below the knee. He spoke somberly to Yitzhak.

"He will die of gangrene if I don't take the damned thing off now. And I have no laudanum left. Have you whiskey?" He looked at Yaacov and Natan, their pale, horrified faces. "You two are the strongest—I'll need you to hold him down."

Asher lived, but more than his leg was lost. We did not move forward for over a week, so that he might regain a little strength; Yitzhak would not allow us to risk him any further. Asher would scarcely speak a word to anyone. I was dispirited too—the accident would not have happened if Asher and Yitzhak had not quarreled, and I felt their quarrel was at least partly my fault. Had I not heard my name? Had not Asher as much as accused me of witchcraft? I thought of my poor, insane mother and the bad luck that had dogged us, and I wondered if it was possible to be a witch without knowing it.

And if we had not been cursed before, surely we were now; we had fallen hopelessly behind the other wagons. We were alone in the wilderness. Rougeau was long gone now. He was responsible for others on the train as well as us, and his obligation to Cohn had ended now that almost nothing of his goods remained. Following behind a large train in such desolate country, we would not find grass left for our animals, or wood, and our small party would be vulnerable to Indian attack. We had only Moe to guide us, and Moe did not know the way to Oregon.

Moe said our best hope was to go over the Wasatch Mountains and continue south to his cabin in New Mexico. He calculated that if we hurried, we could get there in time to build another cabin or two and lay up food and wood before winter. And he could get help from his friends in Taos. Yitzhak looked dully at him and agreed.

There was hardly a trail at all where we were going, and certainly no road, so we would have to leave our large wagons behind. Yaacov, with Natan's help and Moe's direction, made a smaller, narrower wagon from the parts of the large ones we were abandoning; Asher would ride here, and we would all crowd in to sleep, as we had nothing to make tents with. We packed our food and supplies onto our animals, and I made from blankets a padded seat on the back of an ox to carry Mendel. We had to leave most of our belongings behind, and though Asher was already suffering greatly, it made it worse for him that among the things we had to leave were most of the books he and Yitzhak had carried all the way from Poland. I took only a few pots and dishes. Moe said we would need all the blankets and trade goods, too— cloth, beads, vermilion, and coffee—in case we met with Indians who would expect presents to guarantee our safety. Each of the men now took one of the rifles, though I did not see how Asher could use his. The provisions we had left to us would need to last until next spring. Moe said we would have to eat meat now and be glad of it.

In those long, difficult weeks, we concentrated only on surviving. Moe told me which plants and roots were good to eat, and Rachel and I gathered them. He and Natan and Yaacov hunted game and taught Levi as well, and when they brought an antelope or deer, Moe showed us how to dry the meat in thin strips over a slow fire as the Indians did.

We crossed steep, beautiful mountains, walls of gray granite dappled with dark green pine and cedar trees. It was now already autumn, and the nights were very cold; the days searing hot until the late afternoon, when thunderstorms cracked open the sky and we were pelted with rain and hail. Moe exhorted us always to go faster, but it was not possible. We went on foot much of the time, to spare the animals. It was misery; Asher moaned in his rough cart though Natan did his best to comfort him, and even cheerful Mendel cried. Rachel was stoic, trudging silently along the trail, whether soaked with rain or beaten by the sun, but I pitied her so; I only wished that I was strong enough to carry her on my back. We were all exhausted, even Natan, even Moe. Sometimes Asher had so much pain or the children were so tired that we had to waste a precious day resting. Moe watched the sun rise later and set earlier each day, and I began to feel the north wind that would bring winter with it. I knew without Moe saying it that he doubted we could reach his cabin in time.

As we descended from the mountains, we came again to land that was nearly desert, dry and brown, broken only by short trees like pines, and sagebrush. The days had become gray and short—not much time before winter, and hardly any strength. In the distance I saw that the river below us flowed into what I thought must be the ocean. We came closer; waves of water extended to the horizon, and the shore was crusted with white crystals that indeed tasted salty. There were large birds in such numbers that their wings made a great noise, frightening even brave Mendel when they rose up in flight from the rushes. Moe laughed at our astonishment; he knew this for what it was: a vast salty lake, dead and undrinkable, with not a single fish. Still, we found it a good resting spot; there was cottonwood for a fire and bunch grass for the animals, and groves of small cedar trees and aspens farther up the small stream.

Natan shot a big rabbit, and Moe made it into stew, while I made a little barley gruel for myself, Mendel, and Asher. I thought to bring a bowl of it to Yitzhak; he had wandered off somewhere. I found him sitting beside a large boulder, just sitting. I set the bowl on the ground next to him. He turned to me slowly, without speaking. When I saw his face, I sat beside him on the ground. I looked into his pale eyes, burning in his face, now brown and creased from the weeks of sun and dirt.

Behind Yitzhak's eyes I saw our life together: that strange, skinny young boy who had led his lame horse into a shtetl so small it did not even have a name, to a girl so ignorant she did not even know it was in Poland; the home and the store we had struggled to make together; how we had made one exodus after another, never secure in anything but each other and God.

He spoke to me, but he seemed hardly to be in this world. He was tired and weak, yet I saw his strength, like a lantern with a dirty glass. It was his will that had brought us here, not for nothing, no, but in service of that greater Will. Moe squatted by the fire. I thought of the terrible sins he had committed, before he had known he was a Jew, the people he had murdered. Yet he had saved our lives.

"You have given his soul a home," I whispered to Yitzhak, nodding in Moe's direction. I murmured to him, as if I was putting a child to sleep. "And Yaacov, whose heart was so heavy with guilt though he had done nothing wrong, he had nothing to atone for, but you have made him feel he has atoned. And you, too, have nothing to atone for."

Yitzhak shook his head. "There is no atonement," he said, and his voice was low and terrible. "God is mercy, yes, but man—the mind of man will never allow him to forget." There were tears in his eyes. "Asher has lost his leg, and I have lost the inner voice of guidance. In the moment he fell beneath the wagon, I realized that I had listened too blindly, that I had taken our fate on my own weak shoulders, a burden that I cannot carry. Chana, I do not know if we will live or die, any of us." His voice trailed into a whisper. I held his hand, tightly. I wanted to cry, but I was dry.

Cold rain fell that night, and in the morning we could see that the hills we had meant to travel over were dusted with snow. Moe cursed violently. We were still several weeks' travel from his cabin, he thought, perhaps longer, as not only ourselves but our animals were completely weary, used up. This was only a light snowfall, but it was a foreboding; there would soon come greater storms. The way ahead of us would quickly become snowbound, and we would never be able to accomplish our journey. There was really nothing to do but stop where we were, where at least there was wood and water, and where the grass and reeds nearest the shore could feed the animals. We would have to build a cabin quickly and settle in until spring, and pray that there were no hostile Indians nearby.

Once again, I thanked God for Yaacov's skill and strength as a woodsman. He took Yitzhak and Natan with him to fell the small trees that Levi, Moe, and even Chaim Loeb and I used to build the cabin. We worked even in the rain and—as it soon came—the snow, and before the worst of it we had a crude but snug shelter. It was one large room with a packed dirt floor and a fireplace and chimney made from large stones rolled down from the stream. We laid poles across the top, placed animal hides over them, and covered the whole with pine boughs to make a roof. It was funny, but it reminded me of nothing so much as the hut I had shared with my mother as a child. I had come such a long way to end in a place so much the same.

Game was not scarce here; Moe or Natan brought meat nearly every day, and what the men did not immediately eat, Rachel and I dried for jerky. Yes, it was repulsive to me, but I looked at the children and saw how hard the men worked, and I knew we must have it to survive. One day Moe shot two deer. I ate some, for I was so weak, but it made me gag. Natan even persuaded his father to take a little; the boy had hardly left Asher's side since that ghastly accident. Natan changed Asher's bandages and wrapped the stump in a poultice of leaves that Moe said his Indian wife had used for wounds. Whenever the boy was not needed for hunting or woodcutting, he was with his father, trying to ease him. Gradually through his influence Asher began to speak again, even with Yitzhak, and to recite psalms with him. Though he could not stand, much less dance, he joined in the songs and prayers that we continued in defiance of our hardships. Chaim Loeb carved a crude wooden leg for him, and Natan patiently helped him to learn to walk with it. He hobbled around the yard in front of the cabin, but most of the time he preferred to sit or lie on a pallet.

We had left by now a half-dozen each of mules and horses and one poor ox. We were not high in the mountains; Moe said the snow here would not be so heavy on the ground for the animals to push it aside to graze, but I feared for them if the snow deepened. When Moe said we would probably finish by killing at least some of them for meat, I cried bitterly for them, even though I knew he was right.

Moe showed me where there were wild roots to dig and boil into mush as the Indians did. Rachel and I gathered as many of these as we could before the ground froze. Moe warned us against going too far from the cabin, unless he or Natan or Yaacov accompanied us with a rifle. Though we never saw them, he said there were Indians about, watching us. These were not the Indians we had met on the plains but a fiercer tribe that Moe did not know well, and he and Yaacov and Natan took turns every night guarding our stock.

I had thought the hardships of the trail and the lack of food were the reason I felt so weak and ill, but as the winter lengthened, I began to realize that there was something else, something so strange and miraculous I could hardly believe it. But soon I was certain: after these many barren years, I was carrying a child.

That night as we lay in the cabin, snug in our bed, a broad smile spread across Yitzhak's face when I whispered my fabulous secret, the first time I had seen him smile in many weeks. He was tender and careful with me and did not want me to do any heavy work, but I did not want Rachel to be burdened, and so I continued to do as much as I could.

By God's mercy we had enough food, though some days we had only a thin soup of boiled animal hides, with one of the roots carefully hoarded in the cellar. For a week the snow blew and the men could not hunt; even afterwards, they could find no game. I sobbed as Moe slaughtered first poor Billy, the weakest of the mules that had served us so faith-fully, and, two weeks later, the broken-down brown horse, Mazel, who had come all the way from St. Louis with us.

My condition meant the completion of our journey to Oregon would be further delayed. Moe had planned to lead us out in the very early spring, still many weeks before my baby would be born. Though babies had been born even on the wagons we had crossed the prairie with, and their moth-ers on the trail the next day, Yitzhak would not hear of it. He insisted we must stay here until after the birth and go on only when both the baby and I had grown strong enough for the last leg of our journey west.

I should have been frightened of that winter, and of bear-ing my child alone, with no other woman to help me. The wind blew drifts of snow against the cabin and howled as if it carried all the demons of a frozen hell with it. Between storms, when I went outside the cabin for a blessed breath of fresh air, we seemed so isolated that we might have been at the very ends of the earth. But the child inside me re-stored both me and Yitzhak to faith, and I felt the force of his prayers nourishing that child more surely than the poor food I ate.

Inside the cabin every night we huddled beside a small fire, using as little wood as possible to make it last longer. Our songs and prayers helped to warm us, and at times we even felt that we were no longer in our pitiful cabin in a desolate wilderness, but at the throne of heaven itself. And as great a miracle as my pregnancy was, it was not so great as the miracle of Asher, learning to stand unsteadily on his wooden leg, supported by his son Natan on one side and by Yaacov, our rock, on the other, singing with Yitzhak as tears streamed down his face: "*El Shaddai! El Chai v'Kayam! El Shaddai! El Chai v'Kayam!* O Almighty, Ever-Living God!" For somehow, Natan's tender care, the love of his companions, and Yitzhak's prayers had restored something of life and hope to Asher despite his terrible affliction. He was like the man in Yitzhak's story, the poor man whom God loved because his wretched condition demanded that he continually turn to Him.

Yitzhak watched the sky, and at the first full moon of spring, we had a humble Passover—bitter herbs we had plenty, though the last of our wine was long gone. I had saved out a little flour and asked Yitzhak to bless it for matzoh. Already the snow was melting, the stream was running high. Moe said we should soon be on our way; every morning he asked me if I thought the baby was coming that day, though he could scarcely have been more impatient than I. He watched anxiously for the new grass to grow so that the animals could fatten on it. He did not think we should stay here long. Indian hunters were already in the country, and he feared for our safety. Still, my baby was not ready to be born, and Yitzhak would not hear of our traveling. My legs swelled, and soon I could not stand for long without pain. Yes, I was more eager even than Moe for the birth, though my eagerness was well tempered with dread. I had seen enough childbirth to have an idea of what lay in store for me.

Finally it was really spring, bright and warm. The baby inside me moved and thumped, and I felt it would not be long now. The animals were growing sleek on the fresh grass; the children were happy to run outside again. And never in my life, in all the places I had been, had I seen and heard such a number and variety of birds! I strained to fill my lungs with that wonderful air, though I was now grown so large I hardly had room for a deep breath.

I had just gone outside with Rachel to look for fresh roots when I saw two riders in the distance. My heart nearly stopped; surely they were Indian scouts, and what if our puny trade goods were not enough for them?

I could not move, nor stop staring; outside of our little group, I had not seen any human being in months. They came up at a gallop, their horses kicking dust at me as they wheeled to a stop. I gaped in astonishment. They were white men, lightly bearded. One stayed on his horse, a rifle cradled in his hands, while the other dismounted, a tall, rangy-looking man with a hard face. Asher was sitting in front of the cabin on his pallet to get some of the spring sun; Chaim Loeb played with Mendel nearby. Yitzhak and the others were working at making a new wagon from old parts, one that would be small and light enough to travel through the mountains, yet large enough so that not only Asher but Mendel and the new baby and I could ride.

The stranger stood in front of them, blocking the sun.

"This your place?" he spoke sharply.

Moe stepped forward. "Sure it is, Mister. We're here, ain't we? What'r you doin' here on it?"

"This land is for the Lord and His people," the stranger said.

"Yes, certainly," Yitzhak said, stepping between him and Moe. "The earth is the Lord's, and the fullness thereof—"

The stranger spat at Yitzhak's feet. "Don't you dare quote scripture to me, you damned Gentile," he said harshly.

"Gentile?" Yitzhak protested. "No, not Gentile—we are Jews!"

"Jews?" said the stranger scornfully. "Israelites? Then you have rejected the last covenant, and by my lights you are Gentiles yet. And just as the Indians have told me, you are trespassers on this blessed land of Deseret, land that the Lord has ordained for us."

Now Moe stepped forward. "What 'us'? This-here land don't belong to nobody but varmints an' Injuns. Just which one of the two are *you?*"

"President Brigham Young has sent us here, a godly battalion to prepare the way for the people of the Lord in this land that is given unto us, that we may make it into a paradise on earth."

Yitzhak stared, speechless, his fingers twirling his long sidelocks.

"Well, we don't stay here long—my wife . . ."

But Moe stepped in front of him, his face red and angry. "The devil, you say!" he shouted at the stranger. "Get off! Get away before I shoot ye!"

I was frightened. Moe's gun was a few feet away. The stranger's pistol hung at his side, and his silent companion still sat, watching us, cradling his rifle. But the tall man only frowned and mounted his horse again.

"You have been fairly warned," he shouted as they rode away.

It was like a bad dream, those men coming to us out of nowhere. And perhaps that was why I was struck with such a headache the next day I hardly wanted to rise, but rested inside the cabin though the day was bright and warm. Rachel stayed with me, and Chaim Loeb was there to help care for Mendel, and of course Asher was there, gray and silent, for our visitors had worried him. Moe and Natan had gone to hunt. Yaacov was in the yard, cutting wood. Levi had stayed with him for awhile but then wandered off; he was sulking because he had wanted to go with the hunting party. Yitzhak had gone up to the stream, now swollen with melted snow, to look for some fresh greens to cook for supper. I almost sent Rachel to go with him; she was usually so eager to go out, but instead she stayed—I no longer remember why.

Sweet child, she had taken Mendel outside to play. The baby inside me thumped and kicked. Suddenly I heard the sound of hoofbeats and sat up in alarm. Rachel, struggling to keep Mendel in her arms, rushed through the door.

"Papa! Tanta Chana! Papa! Chaim Loeb! Indians are coming! Indians are coming!"

Yaacov came right behind her, rifle in hand. Quickly he loaded two more rifles and gave one each to Chaim Loeb and Asher.

"Chana, take the children and hide. Go to the root cellar!"

Oh, what a nightmare memory this brought back to me! It was a pogrom, a pogrom!

Asher wailed. "How can I fight, a cripple with one leg! We are lost, all lost!"

Yaacov fixed on him. "You will fight, you will shoot! Stay inside, here, and shoot out from the door when they come close. Chaim Loeb and I will each take one side; we will shoot as they come. We must make noise, let them think we are many. Run, Chana!"

Rachel and Mendel and I ran outside behind them. The root cellar was behind the cabin, but it was a small, dank space. I could not bear the thought of it; my stomach came up into my mouth, and instead I ran, bulky as I was, to the stream, Rachel right beside me, holding Mendel in her arms. I prayed to find Yitzhak so we could hide together.

But we did not find Yitzhak by the river, and as we scrambled, looking both for him and for a hiding place, I realized with alarm that we had not seen Levi, either.

I thought again of Yaacov, his strength. Surely he would be able to fend off the attack. I had caught just a glimpse of the attacking Indians as we ran; they did not seem to be many. I prayed with all my heart that Moe and Natan would return from hunting in time, and that Yitzhak—who would carry no gun—and Levi—who, brave as he was, was still only a boy—would not.

I remembered a place at the stream bank that would be good to hide in, a low ledge beneath the side of a large boulder, where the rushes and grass grew high. The Holy One, praise Him from everlasting to everlasting, did not suffer my foot to slip as I clambered, breathless, over those slippery rocks. I shuddered as I heard the rifle fire in the distance, over the rushing sound of the stream.

This cave had not much more room inside than the root cellar, but at least here we had a little fresh air and light. And we would not have to hide for long, I was sure of that.

I was sure, but I was wrong. We were there all that day and night and the next day as well. A short while after the awful gunfire had stopped, I thought I heard someone nearby and wondered if it was Yitzhak come to look for us, to tell us it was safe. Rachel crept out to see, staying low to the ground, but came back trembling. She had seen a strange sight indeed, three riders stripped to the waist and painted like Indians, carrying both rifles and bows. But they were not Indians, she was sure of that. They were bearded, and one had yellow hair, and they spoke English words to each other, though she could not make out what they said. We huddled together in that cave, praying, cold, and sick with fear. I had never heard so many coyotes yelp and howl, nor heard them so near.

Rachel stayed close to me all that night; she put Mendel to sleep and then comforted me as my labor began. At first it was not so bad, and I wondered what all the fuss was about. But as the night deepened, so did the pains, until sweat poured off my face and I began to doubt that I could survive. I had not imagined it possible to bear such agony; it was incomprehensible to me that a merciful Creator had so arranged His world that people came into it this way! The pain was like a sword of fire in my belly and my lower parts, yet I was still afraid to scream aloud. Rachel gave me the Indian's charm from Mendel's neck and I held it tight. I bit my lip almost through to keep from crying out and giving away our hiding place, for I feared that the men Rachel had seen were still about, that it was not safe to come out. And I could not believe my baby thought it safe enough, my little girl, but with all my might I pushed her forth into the world, bloody and slippery, as the sun lightened the sky outside our tiny cave.

19

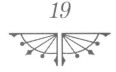

YITZHAK

A SHER LAY IN THE WAGON nearly unconscious from pain and shock. Yitzhak sat, morose, on the ground at the edge of the high trail and picked up a small stone. It was like the stone that Asher had thrown the day before, the stone that hit the ox; perhaps it was even the same stone. Yitzhak worried it in his hand and tossed it at a nearby tree. They were camped here, waiting—waiting to see if God would favor Asher with recovery or with death.

Stranded in failure, Yitzhak dreamed: first the fire, the fire that burned the world, but then suddenly there was a new world, a golden city rising on the desert beside a vast sea. And instead of the screams of people being crushed into wagons, he heard strange prayers and shaking rattles and drums. . . . He saw herds of buffalo, a river of shaggy beasts that turned the prairie into a moving brown sea; he saw them running, running before long caravans of wagons, six abreast; hordes of people who were coming to the city, to the new world that rose from the ashes of the fire, the burning of the world. Now the dream was confused—was it he leading the people to the city, or was it he who had set fire to the world?

Always the dream of the burning world. As much a part

of him as his hand or foot, with him for as long as he could remember. Awake by the morning fire, Yitzhak stared at his hand and wondered if he was also dreaming this crazy journey. Had he always been dreaming? Had he dreamed the lost Name, the Name that led Moses? *The Name of **Ya-Hu-Ve-H** is a strong tower; the righteous runneth into it and is safe.* Like the Patriarch, with this Name Yitzhak had brought his people through, out of slavery. But they were no longer whole. He saw their wound: piercing, exquisite. Yitzhak clenched his teeth against the familiar, bilious cloud of remorse, self-loathing, disgust.

As he had seen the futility of attempting to catch up with the rest of the wagon train, Yitzhak saw the hopelessness of their situation. Something had gone terribly wrong; with inexorable logic he knew it could not be God, and therefore it was he alone who bore the blame. His disillusionment with himself was beyond any that his previous defeats had induced; his disgrace was deeper. His sister was dead, her husband now a helpless cripple, not likely to live long in this primitive world that he, Yitzhak, had brought him to. His two steadfast disciples, Yaacov and Chaim Loeb, were growing old in this desolate country, soon too old to reap any happiness from the community he had imagined they would found.

And his wife? He watched her bustling about the camp fire, holding Mendel on her hip, sending Rachel to bring an herb brew to Asher. Her hair was already graying. The journey had exaggerated her thinness; she looked years older. How would any of them survive? Now he had further betrayed them. Because he could not control his anger, he had driven Asher to his disastrous misstep, and now their exodus had foundered; they were doomed to wander, perhaps forever, in these nearly impassable mountains. *The righteous runneth into it and is safe. . . .* So, then, if he was not safe, it was because he was not righteous.

There was something worse than the anger that had

clouded his reason, the anger that had goaded him on to keep arguing with Asher, continuing to provoke him instead of making peace. Behind that sin was a greater one: He had forgotten that vision must be guarded with a little humility, that God does not love the man who coerces another with his revelation beyond the boundaries of that one's faith. God is infinite, yes, but man's mind is finite; each must take hold of what part of God he can, use what name he can use. *He* was the one with the vision of the Name, the Name that had not been used by Jews for so many centuries. . . . It had been nothing but arrogance to press this on Asher.

So Yitzhak was passive and helpless before Moe's exasperated directions, and when the relentless cycle of God's seasons dictated that they must stop, why should he not surrender? So here they would stay, perhaps for the winter, perhaps forever.

Yitzhak felt the heavy satisfaction of the axe in his hands, the salvation of simple, physical work. He gave himself up to the rhythm of working as he and Yaacov alternately struck the young tree from opposite sides. At Yaacov's call: "Stand back, Rebbe!" he leapt away, awestruck at the swooshing sound of the heavy branches slicing the air.

"Good work, Rebbe," said Yaacov cheerfully.

Yes, Yitzhak thought gratefully. It is good to work. No wonder Yaacov always seemed to keep his equanimity, his peace. How much better would his own life have been had he been a simple woodcutter like Yaacov, a fiddler like Chaim Loeb, a coachman, a cobbler, anything but a rebbe. Worse yet, a rebbe who must be a savior.

Paling November light dappled the trees. Yitzhak heard the call of a bird above him. They were getting ready for winter, too, the wild creatures. Once again, he thought wryly, his heart had been restored by prayer, by work, by the love of his wife and his friends. But for what? It seemed to him that each time he stood up, he fell again, and that each time he fell, it was deeper into a pit, and his companions fell with him, and he could not rescue them.

He watched a squirrel scurry into its hole in a tree. I hope we will be as safe in our cabin, he thought. Chana and Rachel had gathered roots and stored them in a cellar dug behind the nearly finished cabin. Moe and Natan were good shots; if there was game to be found this winter, they would eat. Moe had lived through hard winters before; he knew how to use every part of the animal, how to boil the hide. He had more than once even eaten his shoes, he told them! Yet Moe was worried about Indians, too. Yitzhak sighed. The Holy One, blessed be He, had brought them so far—although at what a price!

The cabin was finished; the log sides made snug with pitch, the dirt floor packed hard. There was even a window covered by a flap of deerskin at night and in foul weather. In this one large room, Chana had made a home; she nursed Asher, cared for Mendel, prepared their meals. Tonight would be the first Shabbos here; Chana cut the candles they had in half, to have twice as many, and now she carefully lit two of the stubs and sang the *brucha*.

The warm candlelight filled the room, bearing with it an aura of peace and well-being to the travelers, weary and anxious though they were. Chana made a soup of wild greens and roots and added a little barley from their store. On an outdoor fire, Moe roasted some venison. And somewhere, miraculously, Chana found a last bottle of wine in the boxes and sacks of food that she was arranging. Yaacov had even made some furniture; they sat on stools made from stumps around a crude table. The little supper was quickly gone, and Yitzhak closed his eyes to sing the grace after meals. For a moment he was almost lost: the rituals, the words. They had been given so that exiles like themselves might make for themselves the security of a temple, a home, in the midst of wilderness or captivity.

Yitzhak rose to his feet and sang, *"L'shem yichud kudsha brichu, Ush'chintay...."* Yaacov beamed and lifted his voice, putting an arm around Asher's waist to support him in a half-standing position, Natan holding him up from the other side. Chana, holding Mendel against her body, yawned deeply, then swayed and sang too, her eyes reflecting the light from the candles.

Much later, as they lay in the dark, Yitzhak saw a smile cross Chana's face. He touched her cheek with his finger.

"Dearest, what do you find to smile about?"

"I was thinking of how this cabin resembles the huts we lived in in the shtetl, don't you remember? And how my heart ached when I was a child, to be someplace else, though I did not really know that any place else existed. And now, look—I am farther away from that place than I ever could have dreamed. I never had any idea how large the world is; I would have thought Przemysl was on the other side of it. And now we are much, much farther away, but doesn't it make you laugh, too, to see how everything is the same? We still have to get wood and water to make soup."

Yitzhak took her in his arms. "I only hope I have not brought you so far for nothing," he said softly.

"No, no, it is different here. There are almost no people! It is empty, an empty world. A world waiting to be filled." She hesitated. "And, Yitzhak, soon there will be in it one more. One more soul."

Yitzhak drew back, trembling. He held her face between his palms. Could it be? "Chana..." he whispered. "Do you mean...? Is it true? Are you sure?"

She smiled broadly at him. "Yes, yes, it is true. First Mother Sarah, then me. Do you remember the Shabbos night at Fort Bridger? We will have a child in the spring, after Passover, I think, but yet before *Shavuos.*"

Joy filled him like a spring, overflowing, pouring over. Yitzhak hugged her closely. He could hardly keep from shouting; he wanted to waken everyone in the room to tell them of this miracle of God's mercy and forgiveness. Chana pregnant—it was a sign, and more than a sign. He would continue, his line would continue, he was meant to go on.

God's loving-kindness made yet another miracle: the return of Asher's heart. Yitzhak was especially grateful because he knew he had no part in this; it was a mercy of the Holy One expressed through Natan. In that frightful moment of pain and loss, when the boy and Yaacov had held Asher under the doctor's saw, Yitzhak had seen the birth of true compassion in the tears that poured down Natan's face. *Baruch Hashem.*

Yitzhak did not neglect, many times each day, to praise God. He Who made man's stomach will make bread to fill it. But when the wind shrieked, when he woke in the night— he was suddenly aware of their utter solitude, their meager resources. As Chana slept, he shuddered with an icy fear that she would not survive childbirth. He could not live without her! And how would his child survive? He breathed deeply, repeating the Secret Name. *O Thou my God, save Thy servant that trusteth in Thee. Be gracious unto me, O Lord; for unto Thee do I cry all the day. Give ear, O Lord, unto my prayer; and attend unto the voice of my supplications. . . .*

The fire had burned to coals, and only Yitzhak, Asher, and Chaim Loeb were still awake in the cabin. Natan was outside guarding the stock, with a stone heated in the fire to keep near his feet. Chaim Loeb hummed quietly to himself as he carved a whistle in the shape of a bird.

"*Nu,* Yitzhak," Asher spoke quietly. "Sometimes I think there is something about this wild land that makes a man a little wild, too, drives him out of his head. Surely that must have been what happened when you spoke that forbidden name."

"Perhaps so," Yitzhak replied. Though he knew the truth himself, he knew something else now—that God nourishes every man with only so much truth as he can swallow.

Asher spoke again. "And perhaps I, too, have been a little mad. It tests a man, to be so alone in a land, to be among strangers, always hearing a foreign language. I felt like those who had been carried in captivity to Babylon."

Yitzhak nodded. "I had a guide to direct my steps— Shmuel Salomon, may he rest in eternal peace. But what did you have but my feeble words? I have not been such a good rebbe to you."

"I have not been such a good disciple, either, Rebbe." Asher said softly.

"Without your nagging, how long would I have looked the other way at Cohn's wickedness? You have no reason for remorse."

Asher's thin face was lowered. He pulled at a gray side-lock. "Oh, I have envied you, brother. I could not stand it that you still had your wife, while mine . . . *oy*, I miss her still, that little bird."

"And I, too." In the long silence Yitzhak almost heard Feigl's singsong voice: *Woe, woe, such a long way to go . . . such a long way, whittled down every day.* He sighed deeply. "It is said that if the Holy One, blessed be He, loves a man, He crushes him with painful sufferings. I wish it had been my fate and not yours."

Asher's hands moved to his stump and massaged it. "Ah, it is He Who does everything, what do we know of it? It was my fate, not yours, and I embrace His will with joy. I was angry, I thought you a heretic. But I, too, was disloyal. It was not only you I mistrusted, but God Himself. Until I saw Him looking at me from Natan's eyes—and in all our terror and loneliness, have you not heard my little Mendel laugh out loud? And now you, too, will have a son. In the midst of all this—this desolation," Asher waved his hand at the dim interior of the cabin, "still there is life."

Across the room, Chana made a noise in her sleep, as if assenting.

In the glow of the last coals, Yitzhak fingered an old scar on his arm. "Yes, we have come a great distance," he smiled. "But do you think we have come any nearer yet to Him that made the world?"

One day, all at once, the world was gentle and green again. After the cold and confinement of winter it was good to be out in the open air. Yitzhak wandered farther up the stream, stopping to sit and gaze at the fish—so many, so fat, he could almost grasp one with his hands for Chana's supper. Chana was nervous now, she must be close to her time, and those men had frightened her. He himself was not very troubled about the visitors of the day before, men who did not know a Jew from a Gentile! Surely there was plenty of land here, and in any case they were not staying more than a few weeks longer, two months at the most. They would go forward—yes, with his new son! They would go forward, they would cross the last barrier, perhaps they would even cross the river Jordan, on their way to the promised land.

He knew which wild greens were good to eat as well as Chana did now, and as he placed them carefully in his sack, he gave thanks to the Provider, the Holy One, blessed be He, Who made green things grow from the earth.

The birds made such a noise here! Some melodic, some raucous, but all joined in chorus to their creator. Yitzhak listened blissfully; he did not hear the distant sound of shouts, gunfire, screams. He was sitting on a log by the stream in a wooded glade, a precious spot of green. He felt his breath one with the air around him; he felt the world breathing in the soft spring breeze. Behind his closed eyelids a glow of yellow light absorbed him completely. As if from a great distance, he felt his body shiver. He saw the word *danger* before him and opened his eyes, startled.

A flock of birds suddenly circled out from one of the trees above him. A crow cawed, four times. It seemed as if the sun had gone behind a cloud, but there were no clouds. He got to his feet.

He heard a shot, quite close, and shouted: "Hey!" And waited, in the silence. He heard steps, the swishing sound of brush being moved aside. And then Levi stood before him, a grin on his broad face, a solid-looking boy of eleven, wearing the trapper's hat that Moe had helped him make, with the raccoon tail hanging down his back. He held a rifle in one hand; the other held up a dead badger by the feet.

"What're you doing here, Reb Yitzhak? Look what I got!"

"Levi!" Yitzhak was startled. "You have a gun!"

Levi frowned. "My poppa said I could."

Yitzhak shook his head. "*Sha*, Levi, no. Don't tell me a lie. You don't hunt alone."

Spots of red rose on the boy's high cheekbones; he protested. "But look what I got! One shot, Reb Yitzhak. It'll make dinner—I know how to skin and cook it, Moe showed me!"

Yitzhak sighed. Let Yaacov discipline his own son; he had no heart for it. "Go ahead to the cabin, then," he said, picking up his sack. "I am following you."

Yitzhak, still dreamy, followed slowly along the stream, and so he did not know what to make of it when just before he reached the cabin, a breathless and agitated Levi, his face wet and streaked with tears, collided with him. Yitzhak caught the boy in his arms. Levi flailed and struggled; he was a big boy, built like his father.

"Reb Yitzhak, they are dead, all dead! My poppa doesn't move; he is dead, they are all dead!"

Yitzhak, finally hearing, shook the crying boy by his shoulders.

"Chana! Where is Chana!"

The boy sobbed; words poured from his mouth now as the tears and snot flowed down his face. "I don't know, Reb Yitzhak, I didn't see her, it is horrible, horrible. The Injuns, see what the Injuns have done! They have taken her away, and Rachel, too, and the baby! They have killed everyone, and took them! And the horses, all gone too! And my poppa doesn't move!"

Yitzhak ran now with Levi toward the cabin. He saw Yaacov first, covered in blood, one arrow protruding from his shoulder; a gaping bullet wound high on his chest, near the collarbone. But as he approached, he thought there was a small movement; he bent close and found Yaacov still breathing, weakly, but surely he was near the end. Yitzhak stared, horrified, then knelt beside him. Gently he touched him, held his pale face between his palms. "Yaacov, try to stay alive," he whispered hoarsely. Blood softly seeped from the hole just below the collarbone. Without thinking, Yitzhak covered the wound with his hands and pressed down with all his might, praying to press life into the body of this man who had been so faithful and so strong. He cried aloud: "He doesn't deserve this, God, not him, but me! And have You also taken my wife from me, and my unborn child?" He sobbed, "Take me, too! Take me, instead!" As he rose to his feet, Levi fell, sobbing, onto his father's chest.

Staggering with shock, Yitzhak looked further. A few feet away lay the body of the little fiddler, Chaim Loeb, several arrows protruding from his side and back. He lay gray and cold, a pool of blood beside his lifeless mouth. And there in the doorway was Asher's corpse, now gone to his fathers at last. Asher. An arrow pierced his neck, and his body was riddled with bullets.

Over Levi's howls, Yitzhak raged uncontrolled at the clear sky. "*Ya-Hu-Ve-H!* Listen now, I am calling You by Your real Name! Why have You allowed this, and what have You

266

done with my wife? *Ya-Hu-Ve-H!* What kind of God are You, Who permits this? Listen, I am talking to You!"

Chana and the children were nowhere to be seen. Levi still bawled over his father's inert form. Yitzhak went to Yaacov's side to comfort his dying disciple, but he could find no words of consolation. Yaacov! Who his whole life had done nothing but serve, never faltering. . . . Yitzhak felt his heart crushed like a bug, an empty shell.

He stumbled into the yard. Chana. He must go to where these devils had taken Chana. There were no horses; the Indians had taken them, too. One of the mules from Fort Hall grazed calmly behind the cabin, the one Yitzhak had named Yoel, after his old enemy at Shmuel Salomon's court. As he approached it, the mule shied away. Stupid beast! Yitzhak thought. In a fury, he grabbed the rope hanging from the creature's neck, threw a saddle across its back and cinched it tightly, barely dodging a kick. He must find Chana. He looked around wildly. With a rush of wings, three large black birds, crows, rose from a tree on the west side of the cabin. Was it from there, from the west that the Indians came?

He rode away from the stream, west, into the afternoon sun, cursing the impassive, intractable mule. He could not shake from his head the grisly scene he had left at the cabin, the boy crying over his dying father. Perhaps he should not have left them, but there was nothing he could do there. . . . The dead ought to be buried before sundown, but Moe and Natan would return soon, unless they had also been ambushed. It was too horrible a thought. Yes, he should have stayed to console Levi, to comfort Yaacov, to bury Asher and Chaim Loeb. But Chana! Chana! He was in torment, feeling an inner certainty that she was alive somewhere, but in what condition, and where?

He pressed on, imagining the Indian camp to be somewhere in the direction he was traveling, toward the sun.

They had come to steal horses, he imagined, and perhaps food, or perhaps they were looking for whiskey. Yaacov would have fought them bravely, but there were too many. Indians did not kill women and children, unlike the Poles; it was against their religion. Somehow he felt sure of this, sure that Chana was alive. She could not die. He agonized; should he have waited for Moe and Natan to return? But he did not know how far they had gone, and he could not wait, Chana needed him. . . .

And so he urged the mule on, without stopping, as the sun before him sank lower, lighting the sky with tongues of flame, crimson and orange streaked by thin violet streams of clouds. Night fell; Yitzhak heard the coyotes in the distance. The country became very dry; the white, alkali plain gleamed in the moonlight. The mule stopped then, thirsty or hungry, but Yitzhak had no mercy; he leaped from it, beat it with his hands. He found a dry stick on the ground and beat the mule with that until it broke, and the startled creature lumbered off. Yitzhak tried to chase after it, but he was exhausted, and the ground was soft with sand; his feet sank and he stopped, panting, crying, cursing, until he sank to his knees.

The thirst he had not allowed himself to feel during the previous afternoon and night now woke him before dawn, searing his throat. He was hungry, too, as if a great hot wind was roaring inside him. Fine, dry sand filled his eyes and nostrils. Fool, he thought to himself savagely. Fool, you did not even bring a jug of water. Perhaps the mule had found some; he looked around for it. But the mule was nowhere to be seen; in fact, Yitzhak saw nothing anywhere. Too dry even to whisper, he mentally recited his morning prayers.

When he opened his eyes, he saw before him, seated on a bench, his old teacher. Shmuel Salomon tugged at his wispy beard; he pulled Yitzhak into the deep pools of his eyes. He cleared his throat with a little cough.

"So, my boy, here you are."

Yitzhak, on his knees in the sand, forced a rasping breath. "Where?"

Shmuel Salomon laughed, laughed and wept. "You are in the world, Reb Yitzhak! The world! The world that is always burning, always on fire, and the world that remains always at peace. Look!" He extended his hand, palm up.

The old man's hand was soft and clear. Yitzhak stared into the smooth palm. Suddenly he saw a green world, like a garden. A brook ran under draping, leafy green trees. Birds sang. Yitzhak lunged for it, lost it. But now he could swallow; there was a trace of moisture in his mouth.

Shmuel Salomon continued. "You have not failed, Yitzhak. The world you sought still exists, as it always has, though the world you fled exists also. In fact, they are the same: one God, one world. You see what you are looking for; you have come now to the place beyond your dreams. A thought, a form, a name: this is how creation proceeds. Yes, a name. A name like the one you use so fearlessly. *That* Name, the Ineffable, taken from Israel by the priests when she had become so corrupt that she could no longer see the truth, and so the true Name was taken away." Shmuel Salomon's face opened in a radiant, twinkling smile. "But the *real* God, the one true God—that One has no name at all! To name anything is to shrink it; how could that One be named?"

The old rebbe held Yitzhak close with his eyes. "You, Yitzhak. Always so—so *ambitious,*" he said softly. "But God doesn't mind that. It is a feat, a marvel, that He has helped you to accomplish. America! The West! But still, it is the world. If you had gone to China, still it would be the world. Even California, or Oregon."

Yitzhak shook his head back and forth. He began to weep, dry tears, a dry cough. "Not there," he managed, not with his mouth, but with his mind. "Not yet there."

"You are where you are supposed to be," the old man said

gently. "You are coming to me, *nu?* And no, it was never for you, Oregon. You have done well to press on. But would you have gone forward without a destination? You have faith, yes, but no man has that much faith, to go deliberately into the unknown. So you believed instead you were going to Oregon. Now you, Yitzhak, you have nearly reached the end of your journey. Chana—and your daughter—they will go on. The children, and their children's children. Look again!" He pointed to his eye.

Yitzhak blinked sand from his eyes and looked closely into that deep well. Chana smiled out at him, her face clear and bright. He saw sadness in her eyes, but something else, a deep fire, almost jubilation, as she held the baby at her breast. He sobbed, "Chana!"

The old rebbe blinked, and she was gone.

"A little longer," Shmuel Salomon whispered. "Go in peace."

The red morning sun, behind him now, burned halfway between horizon and meridian; Yitzhak stumbled to his feet, turned, and looked toward it, toward the east. The white plain that surrounded him shimmered and moved in the wavy light. Yitzhak tried to blink the dust from his reddened eyes, stopped, covered his face with his hands, tried to squeeze out tears. When he looked up again, he thought he saw something in the dim distance, in the rippling light. A city seemed to rise there, a city, white and golden . . . Jerusalem? His heart rose and burst into that light. *Ya-ru-sha-lim. . . .* The word shouted itself, resonating in Yitzhak's head; the only name he had for a city so strange, so beautiful, so holy.

Yitzhak's throat opened, he cried out to Chana, to the others. But when he looked again, he saw only the bare, white, dry horizon. He turned around. A hot wind picked up from the west, blowing a fine, sandy dust into his burning face. He walked into the wind, slowly lifting his feet.

He no longer knew how many days and nights it had been. Even that hideous scene of pain and death he had left at the cabin had faded and blurred; he could no longer distinguish between memory, dream, vision. The sun's fire turned the ground into an inferno. He saw, or imagined he saw, water: cool, blue water, the water of the river Jordan, perhaps only a few steps further on . . . but everywhere was only the white, blazing plain of sand that turned and spun before his eyes. He could no longer separate the white ground from the white sky from the white sun. Collapsing to his knees, he struggled up again and moved . . . forward? He no longer knew even what direction he was moving in, he no longer knew where he was going, he no longer remembered why he was here.

Great black letters rose before him in the air. Through his burning eyes he watched them, traced them with his trembling finger. He was on fire, and these black letters were on fire. *Yod. He. Vav. He.* The sight took his breath away in an ecstasy; they were the letters of the Name itself, the holy unspeakable Name that his mind, his mouth had insisted on speaking aloud. The signature of God. Shivering with rapture, he tried to shout it now, that Name, but his throat was burned and parched. He only wheezed. The letters, he must go to the letters; but like the great city, they shimmered away as he approached them. He closed his eyes, gritty with sand, but his legs somehow kept moving.

Now he could not move. It was not exhaustion, nor the deep sand that held him; he had met an obstacle. He could not open his sand-crusted eyes, but he felt with his hands, he had stumbled on an abandoned, ruined wagon. He tripped over something lying at his feet—a half-buried bone. He shuddered, then began to shake violently, falling to the ground. The wagon! The wagon was on fire! He struggled to his feet again. The world was on fire! Without breath to sob, he fell again and rolled madly, the sand now filling his eyes, his mouth. He was on fire! The world was on fire! Desperation pressed him mercilessly; he surrendered, slipped through a tiny opening, where the razor edge of his pain pivoted him into an ecstasy far, far beyond anything he had ever felt. And now the letters, the huge letters written in flames against the flaming sky, were the last thing he saw.

20

CHANA

A ND SO MY HUSBAND, may his soul rest in peace, never found the river Jordan; it was another river he crossed over, and like our father Moses, he was not permitted to enter the promised land. He had gone as far as he could; it was for God to judge if he had gone too far.

And what happened to me? Still another day we waited in our cave for someone to come. Toward evening, brave Rachel went back to the cabin; we had no food, and Mendel was very hungry. And so we were rescued, for she soon returned to tell us that, in a manner of speaking, it was safe to come out.

Moe and Natan had returned from hunting at sundown, with enough meat to feed those already dead. Moe knew how to push the arrow through Yaacov's flesh to remove it, and he bound up his wounds and gave him a root to chew to keep off fever. He and Natan quickly dug two graves, and as the moon rose, Natan sang Kaddish for his father and wept.

Moe rode out to find Yitzhak, tracking him into the desert until the trail disappeared. Even then Moe went on— he told me later how strange it was, that long after his eyes could no longer distinguish any trace of the path Yitzhak had taken, he had felt drawn to the spot as a moth is drawn to a light. He was only a little too late. Yitzhak had not been dead long when Moe found him.

But for my baby I would surely have died of grief myself at the sight of Moe riding up to the cabin with Yitzhak's body draped over the saddle behind him. I watched, unable to believe, as we buried him beside his followers, Asher and Chaim Loeb. For Yaacov lived, a miracle my heartache would not immediately let me appreciate. Levi told me how Yitzhak had placed his hand on his wounded disciple before he rode out to his own death in the burning desert, and I understood that it was that same touch that he had given to Rivka's little boy so long ago, the touch that Feigl would not allow. Yitzhak had poured into Yaacov the same healing power that he had wanted to rescue me with, but God knew best who it was who needed rescue. Though I was old to become a mother, and though my heart was broken in half, I was well and strong very quickly after the birth. I named my daughter Chaya, meaning "life."

I fed Chaya on my tears along with my milk. Natan and Moe finished building the light wagon that Yaacov and Yitzhak had begun. We had an ox and two mules and the two horses. We were all thin, even stocky Levi, but we were not starved. Moe's grave eyes looked at me from the tangled gray mess of his long beard and hair. I was too empty to make a sound.

"Well now, Missus Honey," he began. He swallowed. "What do you think you would like to do now?"

I looked at him dumbly.

"I mean, where would you like to go to? I don't reckon you want to stay here, I mean. D'you want to go back to the states?"

I stared at the ground. "Oregon," I said. "My husband wanted us to go to Oregon."

"Tanta Chana," Natan spoke gently to me. "Tanta Chana, why don't we go instead to California, where Yonah went? Everyone says it is better. We might find Yonah there, and I must tell him . . ." his voice broke off.

I looked around. There was no one else to decide, no one to discuss it with. Natan had nearly grown into a man, but under his wispy beard I still saw a boy's mouth. Yaacov was barely sensible. And everyone else was dead.

"I don't care," I said. Nothing could have been more true.

"Well, I think Californy might be the better place," Moe said. "I could take you there. We would go up to Fort Hall anyways; there'll likely be folks goin' out from there that we could join up with."

"All right, then." I said. "Californy." And I burst into fresh tears.

For most of that journey I felt as if a heavy curtain had been drawn around me. Everything was overshadowed by two pictures in my mind: Moe riding in with Yitzhak's poor body behind him, and the grave under the small pine tree, next to the fresh graves of Asher and Chaim Loeb. Though the mountains we climbed through were beautiful in spring, with patches of wildflowers everywhere beneath the fresh green of the trees, I pulled into myself, like an animal going into its den for the winter.

I held Chaya close to my body day and night. Though I could have laid her in the wagon to sleep, or given her to Rachel to carry, I could not bear to be separated from my baby. What a mockery it was, after so many years of longing to hold my own child at my breast, that my joy should be darkened so by my loss. It was beyond comprehending that I would never again see Yitzhak, that he would never see our child. Through my tears I saw how beautiful she was, with delicate, pale skin and a soft fuzz of hair, the same bright red shade as her father's. For months, as she grew, smiled, reached out her tiny hands, I turned my head as if Yitzhak was there beside me, only to find an empty space, a hole where he should have been.

At Fort Hall, Moe traded one of the mules and what was left of our gewgaws for food—flour, beans, and salt—to sustain us across the desert and mountains. We attached ourselves to a small wagon train that had left Illinois when the ground was barely thawed and made a rapid journey across the plains. They were bound for California. I whispered my apology to Yitzhak for abandoning his dream of Oregon, but Natan held a desperate hope of being reunited with his brother, and Moe had the practical view that we should join the first train we could.

Yaacov was strong, a lion, and though he lay almost senseless for many weeks, slowly he healed. Even as he recuperated from his awful wounds, it was clear that his right arm would remain forever useless, and he would never cut wood or forge a horseshoe again. Far worse than the physical pain he suffered was his shame at being a burden to us, unable to work—he, who had always been our rock.

Between my despondency and the strain of caring for Chaya and Mendel, I had no strength left to nurse Yaacov, too. Levi cared for him, and so changed overnight from a brash, active boy to a serious young man. No longer did he wander off far from the trail, exploring the woods. He walked alongside our wagon, always attentive to his father, and when we stopped for the night, he did as Natan had for Asher, and sat with Yaacov beside the fire. In his halting Hebrew he read psalms from the old book, brought from Poland, now frayed and mildewed from our journey, even as threadbare as we felt ourselves.

Poor orphaned Rachel, too, gave Yaacov the care she might have given her own father; Moe showed her how to make poultices and teas for him. Yaacov liked to have her and Levi around him; he told them stories about our village in Poland, grandmother-stories that I remembered hearing myself as a child. Sometimes it seemed to me that it was only for the children's sake that Yaacov even bothered to stay alive, but then, perhaps, I was thinking of myself.

Natan was not around camp much; he had a man's work to do now, and he might well have had enough of caring for cripples; besides, he had his own grief to suffer. I had lost my husband, yes, but Natan and Rachel and Mendel were

now fatherless, like my baby, and Levi's father was as helpless as a child himself. We were all in mourning, and though
we traveled in a train with a dozen other families, we did
not know them at all.

One evening, as we camped along the trail, Moe shyly
brought me two pieces of candle he had stuck into holders,
and I realized it was Shabbos—how many weeks had I forgotten? But though the warm glow of the Shekhinah's light
brought us a little quiet peace, and we were grateful for our
meal of soup and fry-bread, there was no one to lead the
prayers and songs that had once raised us all to that joyous
mountaintop, from which all our sorrows and difficulties
had seemed unimportant and faraway. And so after we sang
a few feeble psalms and prayers in half-forgotten melodies,
we went to sleep early so as not to spoil the holiness of the
Sabbath with the pall of sorrow that lay over us without our
rebbe, my husband. It was a sad thing; I would never again
enjoy the rapture of those songs, those wild dances. We
would never again hear the sweet sound of Chaim Loeb's
violin, though the violin itself I still kept, packed away
among what remained of our things. And that sadness, too,
I kept packed away.

The Holy One must have decided that at last we had suffered enough, and so made a way before us and put a wind
at our backs, and we made good time. We were on the old
road to California; we heard rumors that the people who
had taken the new cutoff last year had been too late getting
to the California mountains and met a terrible fate, and we
would not risk it.

We came down the mountains well enough in our light
cart, though the heavier wagons in the train had to double-
team, and even the little children had to walk or be carried.
We came down to a great desert, and began our crossing
when the sun went down so as to save ourselves from the
merciless heat.

Below our feet was a fine sand that glowed white under

the light of an almost full moon. That moonlit journey across the sand was terrifying and wonderful. It was empty here, and silent, without even the sound of coyotes. I felt the cool moonlight suffuse my body, encircling me and the baby at my breast, and holding us in love the way Yitzhak—I could not think of his name without tears rushing from my sore eyes—the way Yitzhak had once held me in his arms. With the moonlight and the motion of the wagon I began to dream, though I was still awake. Chaya tugged at my breast, I stroked the fuzz on her head. I closed my eyes and felt Yitzhak, as if he were lying beside me. I heard him whispering the words of one of his rebbe's prayers: *L'shem yichud kudsha brichu, Ush'chintay. . . . In the name of the unity of the Holy One and His Shekhinah.* His spirit enfolded me as if he still had a body and arms; he was speaking to me, urging me on, to bring our daughter to the place he would never see with his own eyes. Yitzhak would never lead us in prayer again, but his prayer was a living thing; it accompanied me yet, it protected our daughter. It was as real and as eternal as the Holy One Himself, as the Secret Name that had passed Yitzhak's lips, the Name I now whispered myself.

As we followed the river to the foot of the high mountains that were next to cross, a little peace returned to my heart, like a cat creeping up to warm itself by a fire. Yitzhak was no longer with me, but he had left me something, something more precious than any gold treasure or jewels. There was Chaya, of course, but I myself had grown larger; something inside me was rising to join my husband even as a part of his spirit had descended to earth, to me. Yitzhak had rescued me after all; I was no longer mired in the suffering earth.

Above us the sky was an endless, enormous blue. I had never seen such a sky!

We climbed steeply through sweet-smelling forests of pine and cedar. I was strong now and able to walk much of the time, though the air grew thinner as we ascended the California mountains. We met a small party of men on their way back East, who told us the war was nearly over, and California would be a territory of the United States. Moe and Natan and Levi threw their hats in the air and cheered; I could not see why. The land was so wild here, there were no towns or houses. Even the trees grew thinner as we approached Kit Carson's Pass, and though it was now early summer, we could see the peaks still covered with snow when the clouds that veiled them parted. This was the home of those golden birds that I had seen in my dreams many months ago, the eagles; they circled and dipped above us.

Just over the pass, in the midst of the pines, was a large lake, a beautiful blue, like a jewel. We rested by a running stream, and I watched Rachel, the breeze lifting her dark curls, take Mendel to the edge to touch the water. From a piece of wire Moe fashioned fishing hooks, and he and Natan and Levi quickly caught enough of the large, irides-cent fish that swam there to make a good supper. I said the blessings and gave thanks from my heart as we ate that meal in the mountains. The children were healthy; Natan and Levi were growing into men, and behind Rachel's child-ish face I could see the woman's strength she had already earned. Mendel was too little to understand that he had lost his father; he was still a gay child, who only did not under-stand why now I always had another baby in my arms. He had begun to point at things and ask their names; Moe thought him clever and teased him by teaching him words in the Indian language he knew.

Down from the mountain we came, along the river, into rolling grassy hills that rippled in stunning shades of gold. My heart lifted at the sight; it was a promised land, the hills the color of honey and the air sweet and mild. A herd of graceful antelope grazed only a short distance from the trail; some of the little ones, on their spindly legs, gazed at us as we passed. Fields of bright orange and blue flowers spread before us, and trees with wide-spreading branches and small, spiked leaves of glossy dark green. In the valley were herds of deer and elk, too. This landscape was a marvel, like nothing I had ever seen. Seeing and smelling it, I nearly wept under a wave of relief and comfort. Inexplicably and unmistakably, I felt that I had finally come home.

At Sutter's Fort we were sheltered and fed, and at last Rachel and I had a chance to wash our filthy clothes. There were not many men about here, only a few Indians to keep the farms going. The others had gone to fight the last battles of the war. And here it was that Moe, the Jew who had not known he was a Jew, left us at last. He stayed up all night that first night, talking to those few men who were left at the fort, and decided that he too must fight for America. He was given a good horse and would ride to Monterey to join with Captain Frémont's volunteers near there. For, after all, we had been safely delivered to a kind of civilization, and thus he had completed his obligation to us. Watching him ride away, I was a little surprised that I felt such a pang of loss. Unruly as a Polish cossack, Moe had come from nowhere and bound himself to us. He was a coarse and ruthless man, and I had not trusted him at first, but he had proved himself more than loyal; indeed, he had saved our lives.

What were we to do now? Yitzhak had wanted us to become farmers, but we knew nothing of farming. Natan wanted us to go to Monterey or Yerba Buena, port cities where there would be trade, and perhaps we could begin a store, but what did we have to sell? We had nothing; yet we had to find a living.

Captain Sutter offered us work at his colony; Natan went up the river to where Mr. Marshall was building a sawmill, and Yaacov was able to work a little in the bean fields and vegetable gardens. When I was not busy with Chaya and Mendel, I helped the Indian women who worked in the kitchen and laundry. There was even a school for Rachel and Levi, though when the hot, dry summer began to wane and the harvest was upon us, they also worked in the fields. Captain Sutter planned a great town here, and he was eager for new citizens, and so we joined other emigrants who had found their resources gone and their plans overturned by the time they reached the end here of their long journey.

It seemed a good enough life to me, but it was not to last. We had only a few months of peace at Sutter's Fort before our lives were once again upended by events we could never have envisioned. Natan was one of the men building the mill on the river when the first pieces of gold were found, and though hardly anyone believed it at first, it was not long before the whole world knew. I believe it broke Captain Sutter's heart; he tried to keep the gold a secret, at least until the sawmill was finished, not because he wanted it for himself, but because he knew that a horde of fortune seekers would mean the end of his dream—and mine—of a peaceful life.

But to Natan it was wonderful news. He quickly staked a good claim and sent word that we should all come to help, so we went up into the hills to the little village of shacks and tents that was growing in that place on the river that the miners called "Dog Leg." Levi helped wash the fine gold powder and occasional little nuggets out from the river gravel and even Yaacov could do a little panning, one-handed. The miners paid me well for suppers of soup and bread, and with Rachel's help I washed and mended their clothes, too. I was almost the only woman, surrounded by so many men from every place in the world. There were Mexicans and Kanakas, English and French, and a pair of Chinamen with long pigtails. Even a Jew from Russia came, a man named Levinsky; he came as a peddler but soon opened up a real store and sent for his three brothers. With the constant hard work and the wild, feverish atmosphere of Dog Leg, days sometimes passed when I was too busy to remember my grief.

We did well enough before our claim played out, and Natan felt we ought to move down into the city. We were lucky to find a made house in San Francisco at the western end of Happy Valley, while so many newcomers still lived in tents and shanties around Yerba Buena cove or on the hills that overlooked the bay. There had been a great fire the year before, and the city was in a mad frenzy of rebuilding. It looked as if a forest had grown there in the bay, with ships' masts for trees; it was so crowded with abandoned vessels whose crews had gone to the gold fields. Instead of a store, we began a boardinghouse; there were still so many coming to California, and almost all were men without families, who were grateful and willing to pay well for a bed and a hot dinner.

Natan invested our earnings from the gold fields and soon became a successful businessman. He was sober and did not like gambling, and certainly he had learned hard work, and so he was able to survive the "busts" and ride the "booms." He obtained a good position for Levi, too, in a shipping firm. Now they both wore fine American suits, and Natan even had a top hat made of silk. It was a wonder that I wished his parents might have lived to see, that he was more finely dressed now than the noblemen in Poland. And a wonder, too, that there were other Jews here in San Francisco, and not one, but two, synagogues!

Yaacov did not remain long with us. Though his body had healed, without his rebbe and his work a light had gone from him. It was as if, as he saw Levi grow so quickly into manhood—in this land where everything grew with such haste—he felt his last work was done. One morning at breakfast, a few weeks after the service when Levi had proudly been called up to read from the Torah, Yaacov told us he did not feel well, perhaps it was indigestion. He lay down, and

two hours later he was dead. With him, I felt the last of my
old Polish life had gone forever.

Natan became a rich man, and so we soon gave up the
boardinghouse in Happy Valley and moved to a finer house
on Mason Street, on a hill overlooking the bay. We began attending the German synagogue instead of the Polish one,
because Natan's new friends and business associates were
mostly *Baiern*—German Jews—and the father of the girl he
was courting had been among the founders of Temple
Emanu-El. To be truthful, I did not care so much what shul I
went to, or even if I went at all. I had always felt closer to
God in the outdoors, in the woods and fields, or gazing at
the sky or the sea. German service or Polish, it did not matter to me. I believed Yitzhak's teaching—that it was the
heart's intention that pleased God more than any rules and
forms of worship.

Little Chaya was petted and spoiled by her older cousins;
Natan always had an expensive toy or bauble in his pocket
for her, and Levi took her on buggy rides and carried her on
his shoulders to the fishing docks to watch the Portuguese
and Italians bring in their catch. And Rachel was like another mother to her; she sewed for her, beautiful little
dresses and matching hats.

But Chaya kept a sweet disposition. She had Yitzhak's
grave, pale eyes as well as his bright red hair; and even as a
very little girl, though she could be lively enough, I often
found her sitting quietly looking out the window, lost in
thought. Of all the children I had cared for and raised, she
asked the most amazing questions, demanding to know if it
was the trees moving that caused the wind to blow; she
wanted to know if the birds could understand each other's
different songs, and whether there was a place on the other
side of the world where the sea and sky mixed together, and
how did they come apart again? One day, when she was only
seven, watching me unpack an old trunk, her eye fell on

Chaim Loeb's old violin, and she begged to play it until Natan found her a music teacher.

One evening, Natan burst in the door, his face glowing; behind him came a vision I hardly recognized: Yonah and his wife Eliza, whom Natan had met, miraculously, at the theater. Yonah, whom I had first known as a skinny boy, was now a large man with a thick beard and a ruddy face. He and Eliza had been living quietly on their ranch in the north, in the Napa Valley; Yonah had come to San Francisco for a few days to do some business, and Eliza, who was lonely in the country, had accompanied him.

We all sat, rapt, as Yonah recounted the harrowing story of the ordeal they had suffered on their way to California. They had been trapped at the summit of the California mountains in a great snowstorm and been starved and frozen. It was a miracle that these two had come through; half of their party had died. Eliza nearly wept, and Yonah's voice trembled as he told of how they had fashioned snow-shoes and set off with a small group of brave souls to find help.

Yonah reached over to take my hand. "And Tanta Chana, you will never imagine what came to me then. We were lost, deep in the snowy mountains; we had eaten even our snow-shoes, and we were too weak to speak. I felt sure that at any moment I would sink into that sleep from which there is no waking. Though I struggled with every ounce of human strength to keep my eyes open, my lids closed, and a pale, golden light seemed to fill my head, and I began to feel a deep peace that I was sure was the entryway into the next world. And then, at first ever so faintly, I heard all of you singing: yes, Rebbe Yitzhak, and you, and my father, and Yaacov. *El Shaddai! El Chai v'Kayam! El Shaddai! El Chai v'Kayam! O Almighty, Ever-Living God!* Louder and louder it came, and I felt that Life course through my veins and fill me with the will to go on. Liza was stronger; when I opened my eyes I saw her dear face above me, and I knew that we would survive."

The room was silent except for the tick of the big clock. I was glad Chaya had already been put to bed, so as not to have heard such a frightening tale; Mendel's eyes were as big as saucers. The company was stunned; yet it was no surprise to me that Yitzhak had come to Yonah in his extremity, as he had so often come to me. After all, who else but Yitzhak, acting alone on his vision of God's will, had brought all of us through? For how many centuries had Jews been driven from place to place, starved, suffered, massacred even as Asher and Chaim Loeb had been in that little cabin? My husband had died in the desert, alone with his God, but his God lived to protect us.

Natan and Rosalie's wedding was a grand affair. After the ceremony, the guests were driven in coaches from the synagogue on Sacramento Street to the Palace Hotel, where the reception was held in the grand ballroom. I was shy at first to find myself among such a crowd of elegant people, but there I sat, the wolf-girl from the shtetl, surrounded by my family at the head table, wearing a new silk dress with a skirt that hissed like Madame Estella's. I raised my glass with the others and shouted *L'Chaim*, and though the men here did not dance and stamp in a circle as they had in Poland, I knew Yitzhak danced in heaven to see this, our latest blessing.

Rachel became a young woman; she had inherited her mother's skill at needlework and made the most beautiful clothes. Especially splendid was the blue velvet cloak she often wore and her fine hats trimmed with feathers and silk flowers. Her shiny black curls, her red cheeks, and lively spirit made her very popular with the young people from the synagogue. After a time she accepted the proposal of Morris Stern, a first cousin of Natan's Rosalie, who owned warehouses and a block of buildings near Portsmouth Square. And in one of the rooms in Rachel's beautiful new home hung a peculiar knitted blanket. Yes, the same one that Feigl had started and I had finished.

And then Levi, too, was married. He was soon offered a better position, at a bank in the Santa Clara valley, and he and Minnie moved to a farmhouse with a fruit orchard. And there the children and I went every summer for a week or two, to enjoy the warm sunshine and the fresh fruits and vegetables of the country.

The years passed quickly, and though we always had Friday dinner all together at Natan and Rosalie's, only Mendel and Chaya still lived with me. San Francisco was growing into a large city, and our neighborhood on the hill soon became so crowded that I felt closed in and longed for the countryside. Mendel argued; he was fond of city life, and both he and Chaya went to high school now. And so we compromised, and Natan bought a piece of land and had a small house built for us at the very edge of the city, in the sand dunes near Point Lobos.

It was the middle of nowhere, but for me it was the closest thing to paradise, this cottage in the mist and fog, with the cries of the sea birds and the sound of the wind and the ocean. For Mendel's sixteenth birthday Natan gave him a buggy of his own and a fine horse, so that he could drive himself and Chaya to high school and bring me into town as well.

Though I had never been very friendly with the ladies of our synagogue, Rosalie urged me to join the Hebrew Ladies' Benevolent Society, and I spent many hours at the Orphans and Foundlings Home. The little ones there loved me and crawled in my lap, and asked over and over again to hear my silly stories of a she-wolf from the Polish forest who crossed the ocean on a big ship and had such adventures crossing the prairie and going over the mountains. And in this way were my hardships turned to fancy.

Mendel showed such great aptitude in his studies that Natan wanted to send him East for a proper education, but I did not want him to go so far from home. He read me the newspaper every evening and loved to explain everything; my world had become much larger, and I knew all sorts of things now. I knew that Mr. Lincoln—who was named Abraham, like our patriarch—was the president of the United States, and that a great war was being fought to preserve the Union and to free all the slaves. I thought of Maizie and Sally and Albert in St. Louis, and I was glad for them, for freedom was a treasure that they had longed for and well deserved. And though Mendel chafed at being too young to volunteer for the Union, I was very relieved that he would not be a soldier, even for such a good cause.

Chaya was a pure joy to watch as she grew in body and spirit. She was a good student, if not diligent; she loved best to take long, long walks in the dunes, listening to the birds, sometimes walking all the way out to the cliffs overlooking the ocean, gathering shells at the shore. Though she was quick and intelligent, she was the despair of her teachers because she would not chain her mind to the subject at hand, but spun out wild ideas and dreams, as if Yitzhak had been beside her all along, whispering in her ear. The only thing she would concentrate on was her music; she was devoted in her violin lessons, and her teacher thought her particularly talented at improvisation. If I hummed to her a melody I remembered from the old days, she would pick it up in an instant and play it so truly that if I closed my eyes, it was almost as if Chaim Loeb himself was playing again.

Rosh Hashanah came in the middle of a spell of the hottest weather we had had in all our years in San Francisco. We were to have a big family reunion at Natan and Rosalie's house; Yonah and Eliza and their children were down from the Napa Valley, and Levi and Minnie had come up from San Jose with their little one. Natan had promised us all a carriage ride that afternoon, before the evening synagogue service. Mendel put on long pants, and Chaya looked lovely in a green dress trimmed with lace and a matching hat that Rachel had made.

The carriage came, and we rode out through the dunes on the Point Lobos toll road, all the way to the Cliff House. Though the sun still shone, it now seemed farther away, and we could see a high wall of fog rising on the distant horizon behind the ocean waves. As we walked on the sand, a stiff wind carried little droplets of mist and made us shiver. The heat wave was breaking; the cool fog was coming in. The long dune grass bent before the wind; the big waves roared as they rolled in from the other side of the world. I breathed deeply with wonder and admiration, grateful that God had made such a world and brought me to it, and given me family.

We drove back to the city and the synagogue as the fog blew in behind us. As I looked up at the imposing brick building, a last ray of sun shone through the fog and reflected from the round window in front, bright as the very eye of God. Already they were raising money for a newer, grander synagogue, though this one seemed a palace to me. Only a few weeks ago the new rabbi had announced that we would all sit together, men and women. I wondered if I should live so long as to see any of Yitzhak's other unconventional ways taken up by this congregation.

In the front row I could see the peculiar figure of a man dressed in military uniform, elaborately decorated but so old and worn that the color, which must have once been scarlet, was now faded to a rusty shade of brown. The gold braid that trimmed his coat was torn, and his sleeves were frayed. Though he held himself with a noble bearing and seemed quite distinguished, when he turned around in his seat, I could see that there was something not quite right about him. There was something of Yitzhak in his eyes, so that I could hardly stop staring at him.

"That's Emperor Norton, Tanta Chana, don't you know him?" whispered Mendel, sitting next to me.

"An emperor? In America?" For I was no longer so ignorant as I had once been.

Mendel laughed. "No, not a real emperor. It's a joke— he calls himself 'Emperor of the United States and Protector of Mexico.' He hasn't any money, though, he's a beggar. He writes proclamations and has them published in the newspaper."

I hushed him then as the choir began. Gradually I had come to like this kind of American service, with the singing, and prayers in English and Hebrew both. I sighed deeply as the rabbi raised the shofar to his lips and blew a blast. The New Year had begun; the cantor sang: "The Lord is my light and my salvation; whom shall I fear?" I listened as I had once listened to Yitzhak and the others singing with Chaim Loeb's violin, and now I heard Yitzhak's voice joining with the cantor: *If I had not believed to look upon the goodness of the Lord in the land of the living!* The land of the living! My eye fell again on Emperor Norton's shabby uniform, and the words of the prayer reminded me of my girlhood in that Polish shtetl that did not even have a name, where the same psalm had been recited every New Year, and where Yaacov had been a small boy when, as he had liked to tell us, the emperor of France—a *real* emperor!—had marched his army only a few miles from our very village on his way to Moscow.

We had a grand Rosh Hashanah dinner in the beautiful home on Rincon Hill that Natan's father-in-law had given to him and Rosalie. The little children ran through the house on their way to the table, led by Natan and Rosalie's oldest, seven-year-old Isaac. For as Natan had explained to me, "Yitzhak" was too old-fashioned and Polish-sounding a name for an American boy.

I sat beside Natan at the head of the table. I had not yet lit the holiday candles; the men were still discussing the new telegraph line that went across the whole American country. I hesitated, suddenly overcome by the memories—how indeed, as in the story of Joseph and his brothers, God had meant it all for good.

Across the table from me I saw Mendel, the orphan I had raised. I remembered him as a chubby baby, stuffed into starched dresses, on the polished floor of the Cohns' St. Louis home. Somewhere among his keepsakes I knew he kept an odd leather charm. Now a few soft hairs were sprouting on his cheeks. Perhaps he would go away to study—who could know what he might become? I looked at Chaya's red hair—she was like a piece of Yitzhak, alive on the earth, yet she was completely herself, new.

Now everyone was looking at me; even the littlest children were quiet. I felt terribly bashful before that huge table. I tried to clear my throat, knowing they all expected me to speak, but my tongue stuck in my mouth. Then, suddenly, I felt Yitzhak standing behind me, a feeling so strong that I almost turned in my seat. *See, Chana,* I heard him whisper. *See, God is everywhere . . . a unity; there is no unity in any way like His . . . One God, everywhere.* I felt a smile rise out from my heart as I looked around the table, holding the unlit match in my hand.

"God is everywhere," I said, but not very loud. And then I lit the candles and sang the *brucha.*

RUHAMA VELTFORT was born in Cambridge, Massachusetts, in 1944 and reared in Palo Alto, California. She graduated from Barnard College and later attended graduate school at San Francisco State University. She has been writing fiction and poetry for over thirty years and has published two chapbooks of poems, *Whispers of a Dreamer* and *Miles on the Bridge*. *The Promised Land* is her first novel. She lives in San Francisco.

Interior design by Will Powers
Typeset in URW Antiqua
by Stanton Publication Services, Inc.
Printed on acid-free 55# Booktext Natural paper
by BookCrafters

MORE FICTION FROM MILKWEED EDITIONS

Larabi's Ox
Tony Ardizzone

Agassiz
Sandra Birdsell

What We Save for Last
Corinne Demas Bliss

Backbone
Carol Bly

The Tree of Red Stars
Tessa Bridal

The Clay That Breathes
Catherine Browder

Street Games
Rosellen Brown

A Keeper of Sheep
William Carpenter

Winter Roads, Summer Fields
Marjorie Dorner

Blue Taxis
Eileen Drew

Kingfishers Catch Fire
Rumer Godden

Trip Sheets
Ellen Hawley

All American Dream Dolls
David Haynes

Live at Five
David Haynes

Somebody Else's Mama
David Haynes

The Children Bob Moses Led
William Heath

The Importance of High Places
Joanna Higgins

Thirst
Ken Kalfus

Circe's Mountain
Marie Luise Kaschnitz

Persistent Rumours
Lee Langley

Ganado Red
Susan Lowell

Swimming in the Congo
Margaret Meyers

Tokens of Grace
Sheila O'Connor

Tivolem
Victor Rangel-Ribeiro

The Boy Without a Flag
Abraham Rodriguez Jr.

Confidence of the Heart
David Schweidel

An American Brat
Bapsi Sidhwa

Cracking India
Bapsi Sidhwa

The Crow Eaters
Bapsi Sidhwa

The Country I Come From
Maura Stanton

Traveling Light
Jim Stowell

Aquaboogie
Susan Straight

The Empress of One
Faith Sullivan

Justice
Larry Watson

Montana 1948
Larry Watson